G000098149

JILLIAN BONDARCHUK

THE SHIELD AND THE THISTLE

THE GREY TOWER
CHRONICLES

Hardcover ISBN: 978-0-578-94342-8
Print ISBN: 978-0-578-94343-5

Edited by:
Jennilynn Wyer
Anna Neilson
Janet Klatt

Cover art by:
Franzi Haase
www.coverdungeonrabbit.com
@coverdungeonrabbit

Formatting by:
Qamar Saleem
@creative_bookish

For my husband, Josh, because without his loving support I never would have started this journey.

And for Castle, who was a better person than most people, even though he was a dog.

TABLE OF CONTENTS

One of the cruelest things one person can do to another is give away the ending of a book.

CHAPTER 1

Meggie

The condensation from my ice water picked up speed as it slid down the glass and soaked into the paper that protected the white tablecloth. The busy Italian restaurant, filled with the buzz of boisterous conversation when we arrived, was just a faint murmur to me now.

"Meggie, will you not talk to me?" my boyfriend of two years asked while he tapped his manicured fingers against his empty beer bottle. My cheeks reddened with humiliation and anger and I dragged my mismatched eyes up to glare at him.

Our conversation had drawn the attention of the other diners, and I pulled my dark brown hair over my shoulder in embarrassment, silently wishing I was anywhere else.

"I'm not sure I need to say anything at all, Steven. You made yourself quite clear when you said you wanted me out of our apartment. Did you expect me to beg to stay? I won't, even though you know full well that I have *nowhere* to go."

Steven leaned back in his chair and ran his fingers casually over the point of his chin. "You won't be on the streets. I'll pay for you to stay in a hotel for a few nights."

I shook my head in disbelief. What a snake!

"A few nights? You know how hard it is to find a decent roommate in this city! Why the rush?" Words flew out of my mouth in a hiss, and I fisted my hands tightly in my lap. "We had sex *last night,* and today you break up with me? I don't understand you."

Do I even know him anymore? I asked myself. From the guarded expression on his face, I'm thinking the answer is a big fat NO.

Jaw set, his dark brows pulled down low, hardening his features into a mask I did not recognize. Into the face of a stranger; cool and detached. I felt the first stirrings of unease and watched regret, followed by resolve, pass over his face when he broke my stare.

"I wasn't going to tell you this… but I met someone a few months ago." He worried the peeling label on his beer bottle with his thumb, unwilling to look at me again. "She's in the same field as I am, driven with the same aspirations I have… not a muffin maker destined to work in a little bakery the rest of her life. I've outgrown you, Meggie. We're done."

Mortified and grappling with the betrayal I felt low in my gut, I slowly stood up from the table and blinked away the hot tears that blurred my vision. I refused to allow them to fall and give him the satisfaction of seeing *this* little 'muffin maker' cry. He wasn't worth it.

"You're an asshole. I'll pack up and be out by next week." I turned to leave, but what he said next stopped me in my tracks.

"I already had your things boxed and delivered to this storage facility in Brooklyn." He slid a bulky orange-handled key and a business card across the table. "It's paid up for the next month," he added with a small smile, as though he did me a favor.

"You packed up my things in eight hours?" Gripping the sides of the table, I wanted to smack that little grin right off his face.

"Not exactly. I hired professionals. It's easier this way. A clean break," he declared with a small sigh. Standing, he tossed some money on the table. "Take care of yourself, Meggie." And without a backward glance, he strode past me and out of my life forever.

I looked numbly at the money thrown next to my water glass; its ice nearly melted to nothing. My fingernails dug half-moons into the meat of my palm as I squeezed my hands into tight fists at my sides.

The douche bag kicked me out of my home and only left our server a two-dollar tip on a thirty-eight-dollar tab. Muttering to myself and cursing all men, I pocketed the key and business card and fished out the few singles I had to add to his meager tip. It was still a pathetic gratuity, and I felt the pang of guilt merge with my anger. Confused and mortified, I turned on the heels of my navy-blue flats, avoided the pitying stares around me, and marched out the door with my head held high.

The heat of May immediately wrapped around me when I exited into the busy clamor of Manhattan during rush hour. Standing on the curb, I realized Steven had not only walked all over my pride, but he walked out before paying for my hotel room. That figures. He's always been the one to look generous on the outside, only to vanish when it came time to honor his commitments. In fact, I had found him to be increasingly forgetful lately. Canceled date nights, a few missed mid-week lunches together. His forgetfulness happened a lot in the last couple of months, and he blamed the forgetfulness on the extra late hours.

Now that I knew the real reason, the deception was hard to swallow. I'll admit, we felt more like roommates that were occasionally intimate, but I still felt committed, and I assumed he was too. It was hard not to feel betrayed.

Pursing my lips, I gazed down the busy avenue towards what used to be my home: a quaint fourth-floor apartment on a quiet street off East Houston. It had taken us three months to find that perfect spot, and I'd be a liar if I said I wasn't sad to never see it again. Sure, the bathroom was elbow-knocking small, but the kitchen was extraordinarily large and suited me perfectly. Its ample counter space was the perfect platform to make my culinary creations.

Delicious creations that have never included *muffins*.

Fat, silent tears broke free to roll down my cheeks and land with a plop on my grey cotton T-shirt while I dug out the business card for the storage unit and sneered at the location. Brooklyn. The jerk didn't even want me on the same landmass he inhabited.

My insides were roiling with resentment at Steven and annoyance at myself that I failed to see the end of our relationship coming. Because of that ignorance, I was now technically homeless.

With the insanity of Friday evening rush hour foot-traffic surrounding me, I turned in the opposite direction of what used to be my home and headed for the subway that would take me to the borough of Brooklyn and my belongings.

~

There's something about New York City, or maybe it's just the immense population of self-important people that allows one to disappear in the crowds. I let my tears fall freely, knowing that no one cared and certainly wouldn't ask me what was wrong. People here mind their own business: like ostriches shoving their heads in the sand, they rarely came out of their own little bubble, let alone focus on someone else sharing their oxygen.

When I first arrived in the big city with Steven last year, he had just graduated with his MBA and me from culinary school. It was never my dream to live in New York, but when he landed a job at Bank of America, it took little to convince me to join him. In hindsight, that was a stupid idea. But you live, and you learn, right?

Finding a job for myself was easy, and I made a quiet entrance into my field at a French bakery around the corner from our apartment, making fluffy chocolate croissants and pear-almond tarts. I once dreamed of owning a bakery while taking my classes, but the desire became slowly whittled away by the cost of living in Manhattan and the island's demanding people. I missed the slower-moving Raleigh, North Carolina, and the locally owned bakery I worked at while in culinary school. I missed having regular customers that shared bits of their lives with each visit. It fulfilled a part of my life that was missing. I missed the old ladies that gave my hand a little pat when I handed them their pastry and the motherly advice from the women that came in with their children. I don't have that here. In the city's bustle, the bakery is a revolving door of suits and nameless faces that blur from one to the next throughout the day. People rushed from place to place with rarely anything more than a quick smile and a generic thank you when they plunk some change in the tip jar and are quickly replaced with the next tap of a credit card. It depressed me, and my daily tasks of doing what I loved soon made me feel isolated, bleak, and dispirited. In a city full of so many, it surprised me at how quickly I became to feel so alone. And now, my one consistent source of company and communication effectively severed me from his life like he would a threadbare shirt.

Weaving through the intricate, busy subway station, I dried my tears and resolved to shed the worry from the break-up starting tonight. Feeling slightly lighter in spirit, I tried to ignore the smell of hot metal, old cigarette smoke, and body odor. Doing my best to carve out a little personal space in the sea of bodies staring either straight ahead or at their phones, I waited for the L train that would take me to Brooklyn and my new life packed in boxes.

Luckily for me, a man was playing his violin in the packed car I stepped into. With no seating available, I squeezed between two businessmen close to the rear of the car and held onto the bar hanging from the ceiling. Swaying with the ever-present motion of the train, I closed my eyes, tipped my head back, and lost myself in the cheery notes the musician played for his audience. He was no Lindsey Stirling, but he was good enough that most of his audience kept respectfully silent. I wished I had more than the loose change left in my wallet after compensating for Steven's crappy tip, but I happily tossed it all in his jar when he walked through the car collecting before my stop. When the doors released the flood of passengers, the opening notes to *The Devil Went Down to Georgia* chased after me as I stepped onto the platform in Brooklyn.

Unsure where the storage building was, I flagged down a cabbie and gave him the address. Staring out the open window, I enjoyed the wind in my face after the subway's stuffiness and let my long hair blow wild. While I watched children play on the sidewalk and adults hurrying to their homes after a long day of work, I wondered where I was going to stay tonight. My savings wouldn't last me long in this city, and I didn't relish the idea of using any of my inheritance on temporary housing.

With my thoughts packed full of slim opportunities, the cab driver pulled alongside the curb and looked at me impatiently through the rearview mirror. After sliding my credit card through the reader, I bade him good night, and he sped off to either a warm dinner or his next fare without a backward glance.

The storage building was small, its red brick walls blackened where it met the sidewalk and near crumbling with age. I scowled at the sight.

Steven certainly spared no expense here, I thought sarcastically.

Inside, the walls were yellowed from decades of cigarette smoke staining the once-white paint. A young woman behind a glass partition put aside her gossip magazine to look at my key and ID before directing me down one of two hallways behind her little office.

"Hey, you have cool eyes. But I bet you hear that all the time." She smacked on her gum obnoxiously and gave me a nod, like she was correct in her assumption.

She was right, though; people have complimented my eye color my entire life. Having one blue eye and one green is something that people notice right away and feel compelled to comment on. I cannot recall a person I have met that has not noticed and eventually made one remark or another. Or, at the very least, stared at me longer than necessary.

"Thank you. My mother gave them to me," I chirped when she buzzed me through to the door to the left of her desk. The sparse fluorescent lighting blinked and hummed, guiding me to unit 22 at the end of the hallway.

Fitting the key into the padlock at the bottom of the roll-up door, I thought of my mother. Both of my parents died in a car wreck when I was eighteen. I miss them terribly, especially on days like today. There's nothing I wouldn't give to call my mom right now and pour my heart out to her. To hear her guidance and loving support. Now the only family member I have left is my Nan. She would have to do. I needed someone to talk to desperately.

Scrolling to her number, I hoped she wasn't already in bed. With the five-hour time difference, it would be almost midnight in Scotland. Taking a deep breath, I tapped the call button and hoped she picked up when I lifted the rollaway door with a loud clatter. Nan was an early riser on her farm, known to go to bed early unless she had company. Relief washed over me, and my bottom lip trembled when I heard her voice, sleepy but strong.

"Meggie," she breathed.

"Yes, Nan, how did you know?" My voice broke.

"Och, lass, no one calls yer auld Nan at this hour. What has ye callin' me so late? And cryin' to boot?"

I could hear her moving around at the end of the line, followed by the telltale sound of the tap running in the background. She must be making tea in preparation for a long talk.

"Steven moved my things out today. He told me he met someone else—months ago! Cheating bastard. I just got to the storage facility where he dropped all my shit, and I don't know what I'm going to do. I just wanted to hear your voice. It's the next best thing to Mom's. I just—I need to figure things out," I rambled as I pushed into the small room and flipped the light switch. A single, naked bulb flickered to life angrily.

Lifting the tops off a few of the boxes, I peered inside, surprised to find my things in relatively moral order, if not thrown inside. At least someone categorized everything correctly. My clothing, toiletries, books, and cookware were all in their own respective boxes and totes.

"That daft diddy. Ye're better off without that scoundrel, I say. Where're ye gaunnae go, lass?"

My lips turned up in a soft smile at her thick brogue and Scots' speech. Leave it to Nan to say what needs saying.

"There are plenty of hotels in New York, Nan. I won't be sleeping on the streets, but it's going to take me a while to find a roommate that's not a total weirdo." Moving past a chair, I found my suitcase in the back corner and hauled it on top of an end table to fill with clothes for the next week while Nan muttered to herself.

"What was that, Nan?" I asked.

"I'm just right upset, is all. Last time we spoke, ye said ye didnae so much like the city life. Do ye plan to stay?"

I thought about that for a moment. What was keeping me here? There was a job I didn't plan to work at forever and a few girls I hung out with every few weeks—no close friends, and now, no boyfriend.

"I didn't think about that until just now. No, I suppose I won't, but I can't just pack up and move back to Raleigh. At least not quickly since I sold my car and mom and dad's house last year. I'd be returning to nothing." I pouted, regretting ever coming here.

Standing in the dim room surrounded by my things, I promised myself never to make another life decision based on what someone else wanted. I would decide my paths based on what *I* wanted and what *I* wanted only.

"So, come here, sweeting. It's been an age since I've seen ye, and ye have yer dual citizenship. Ye can work while ye figure it out," she suggested. "The lowland weather is beautiful in May, and I widnae mind the company."

It had been four years since I'd been to Scotland to bury my parents on my grandmother's land, and I'd been longing to visit. Today's circumstances presented the perfect opportunity. I may not hear my mother's voice, but I could still talk to her. She waited for me at Nan's farm.

I wiped viciously at the salty tracks of dried tears on my cheeks and drew in a deep breath. Letting it out, I felt my anxiety disperse.

"I'll be on the next flight, Nan."

CHAPTER 2

Meggie

A light tapping on my shoulder woke me from a dreamless sleep, and I found my face plastered into the pillow pressed against the window of the plane. I smiled a sleepy thank you to the woman next to me and secured my wild, unbrushed hair in a braid.

I had spent most of the night in the dingy storage room, sifting through clothing to bring with me to Scotland. Late May weather was still cool during the day and straight-up cold at night. A welcome change from the heat of New York; it was one foot into the rainy season. Layers were essential in the Scottish Lowlands.

The first flight out to Glasgow was early and fully booked. If I had any hope of securing a seat, I needed to arrive on time with all my fingers and toes crossed for a last-minute cancellation. While I stuffed my suitcase, the woman on the phone took my payment and told me I would be on standby. It was a risk I was happy to take, and I was rewarded with a window seat in the very back at six a.m.

I was more than ready to watch the city disappear behind me.

Once the plane taxied and docked, I made a quick call to Nan while I waited for my turn to depart, telling her I landed safely and that I would meet her in baggage claim. After pulling an all-nighter in the storage facility, followed by a seven-hour flight, I desperately needed caffeine. Preferably mainlined into my veins. Checking the local time,

I saw that it was just after six o'clock, and cringed. I hated the feeling of losing time. Just seven hours ago it was six a.m. in New York. It left me feeling odd.

After grabbing a double shot grande Caramel Macchiato at the biggest Starbucks I'd ever set foot in, I hustled to baggage claim and burned my tongue on the delicious brew along the way. Searching for the familiar cap of white hair, I spied Nan before she set her eyes on me.

She hadn't aged a day since I saw her last. Dressed in simple jeans and a lightweight grey sweater, she stood tall with her slim shoulders back and her capable hands on her hips. She scanned the crowd for what I assumed was a teenager and not the twenty-two-year-old I was because her eyes passed right over me before swinging back. Her eyebrows shot up in genuine surprise when I set my bags down at her feet.

"What a beauty ye've become, Meggie," she cooed and ran her hands up and down my arms before pulling me into a fierce hug. "I ken yer mum would be so proud if she could see the grown woman ye are now."

"She sees." I melted into her embrace and breathed in the clean, soapy scent of her. "Thank you for suggesting the visit. It's exactly what I needed."

She took my largest carry-on and led me to the carousel to wait for the rest of my baggage. Unsure of when I would return to the States, I had packed enough for an extended stay.

"Well, ye may no' be sayin' so when ye help me clean the chicken coop tomorrow."

I shook my head at her mischievous grin and wagging eyebrows. Nan never turned down an opportunity at free labor. She'd been running her small farm alone since my grandfather died when I was a toddler. I don't remember ever meeting him, but my mother told me enough stories of her life growing up on the farm to know that he was a good man who loved his family. During the summer months, the neighbor's sons do the hard labor she can't, but boys grow up and move away, and I wasn't sure how much longer she would have the help.

"You know I don't mind getting dirt under my nails, Nan." Waiting for my two red rolling suitcases to spit out from the chute, I stretched my arms high above my head and talked through my yawn. "Some sunshine and fresh air in your garden is a welcome relief from the stink of the city this time of year. I swear every other street has me blocking my nose."

Spotting my bags, I easily pulled them off the line, grateful for the last year spent unloading heavy sacks of flour, sugar, and other baking goods off the delivery trucks every other day. That, paired with the four flights of stairs I needed to climb to my apartment, made my body strong and ready for some time on the farm.

Following Nan to her station wagon, I mused on how quickly my life changed in one day. I no longer felt how I did in the restaurant with Steven, which surprised me. I loved him, didn't I? Shouldn't I be more upset? Instead, I felt nothing but relief.

Staring out the passenger window, I watched the busy city fade away into the countryside and absently fiddled with the small diamond studs my parents gave me for my sixteenth birthday. While my grandmother chatted about the goings-on at the farm, the neighbors I knew of, and the ones I didn't, I searched for castle ruins off the highway.

I loved exploring the relics of the past that littered the countryside with my mother. It was something we did together during each visit.

My mother had met my father during college in Boston, and they eventually made their life together in Cary, North Carolina, where I was born. But she always insisted on taking me to Scotland every summer to stay with Nan. She said it was important that I knew my heritage and where I came from. I never had to beg her to stop at the ruins that dotted the way to the farm, and sometimes we stretched the hour-long drive to the quiet town of Cairndow into four or five.

My fondest memory of my mother was of the day she wove for me a crown of wildflowers and taught me to sing *The Rattling Bog* in the skeleton of a ruined stronghold. Her voice echoed off the disintegrating stone walls while I laughed and laughed, and tried my best to keep up with the lyrics.

Nan always said my mother had the most beautiful voice. That she could coax the most stubborn of cows out of the hills in the evening with her song. I learned a few of her favorite tunes when I was young, and although it's only been five years since my last trip with her, and my memory failed to bring them to the forefront of my mind.

But I still remember the way she would play with me. I remember the fey smile on her lips when she sang in the quiet of the ruins. Besides being with my father, it was the one place she looked truly alive. Like she was lit from within. Everyone has that one place that brings out the fire in them. That was my mother's place. I'm not sure if anyone but me ever witnessed it.

When we passed the last stretch of Loch Lomond on our left, Nan took the A83 toward Cairndow and her ninety-acre farm tucked into the hills. I felt eager to get to her home, to breathe the clean air, the faint tang of farm animals on the breeze, the mint in her garden, and lemon of her floor soap.

At twilight, we pulled onto the private drive, and I peered excitedly ahead, wanting to get the first glimpse of the white-washed stone house with cedar shakes and climbing ivy behind her well-tended garden. It seems like every visit is the first visit, each time a magical wonder for the little girl who still lives in me. I could see the fairy houses swinging in the slight breeze from the branches of the birch trees and knew there were more tucked between the mounds of flowers in the garden surrounding her home.

When I was a young girl, both Nan and my mother convinced me of the magic of fairies. They told me they lived in the homes that we made for them in the garden, and in return, they helped the bees fertilize the flowers, fruits, and vegetables during their season.

I cried myself to sleep the day I realized it wasn't true.

The moment she threw the car into park, I jumped out and skipped to the picket fence that contained the flora in front of her home. Bending over, I brushed a fallen branch off a fairy mound.

"You still have them," I marveled and turned toward Nan coming up the slate walkway that led to the porch.

She gave me an odd look. "O' course I do! Cannae be turnin' out the fairies now, can I? I'd have a right shit garden if I did." Winking at me when she passed by, she opened the cottage to me and my luggage.

I rolled my suitcases to the second bedroom, where I knew a queen bed with a white eyelet comforter and fresh lavender tucked in the crisp white pillowcases would wait for me. Wasting no time, I unpacked my clothing into the large dresser in front of the window. Through white lace curtains, I could see the barn with the hills in the distance. Nothing had changed. Here, time slowed down, and everything seemed to move slower than the rest of the world.

A kettle screamed its steam by the time I shoved my suitcases in the closet, and I padded down the short hallway into the cozy yellow kitchen. Nan was setting up tea, her back to me while she moved about in her fluffy white robe and pink pajama bottoms.

"Are ye hungry? I have some chicken salad I can fix up for ye."

I sat at the table and pulled up my legs to rest my chin on my knees. The chill night air snuck in through the partially open window, and I was glad for the thick wool socks on my feet and my mom's grey terrycloth robe I found in the closet.

With her serving tray in hand, Nan flinched when she turned around, her eyes finding mine. The tea set rattled before she caught herself and set it on the table.

"Ye looked like yer mother, sitting there," she murmured. There was a slight tremor in her voice, and she reached out for my hand when she claimed the seat across the table from mine. "I swear I felt her spirit in the room. Just for a moment."

Her words crushed my heart. Mothers should never have to bury their children.

"I miss her. You can't know how happy I was to find her robe." I brushed the lapel over my lips, feeling wretched for allowing four years to pass since my parent's funeral, and swallowed the apology that I knew she'd wave off.

But I'm here now, I thought, and squeezed her hand before helping myself to tea.

"As for the chicken salad, they served something on the plane, and I brought some snacks to munch. But this tea. I'm going to enjoy every drop," I gushed as I spooned a dollop of honey into my cup and stirred the golden sweetener into the dark amber liquid. I inhaled the refreshing aroma of the strong Nambarrie Tea before taking a sip.

"That's good stuff, Nan."

"Och, I ken how to make it better," she declared, brandishing a bottle of whiskey from her robe pocket, and deftly poured a good bit into my cup. Surprised laughter burst out of me, followed by an unladylike snort into my teacup when I took another sip.

"Mmm, that does make it better," I admitted and watched her administer the same into her own. She toasted the air.

"To ye, my dear lassie. Wit's fur ye'll no go past ye. We can only follow our path, and I am so happy that it led ye here for the time bein'." With the tip of her head, she drank her totty in one go and immediately reached for a refill.

I gave her a quizzical look. "What in the hell did you just say? Wit's for... no go... what? I've never heard that saying before."

The jumble of Scots words rolled silently over my tongue before I finished the last of my tea and patiently held my cup out for her to refill. No one rushed Nan if they knew what was good for them. She gave me a knowing smile and poised the whiskey bottle over the rim of my teacup.

"It means, 'whatever is meant to happen to ye, *will* happen to ye.'" She looked at me like she could see into my very soul, her deep blue eyes missing nothing. "Out with it, Meggie. Tell me what the *ciontach baile* did that had ye flyin' across an ocean to yer auld Nan."

So, I told her how Steven met me after work for dinner at our favorite Italian restaurant. He had seemed a little stressed during our meal, but I assumed it was because of his job. He had been working later these last few months, and since I knew how important putting in extra hours was to his field, I never gave him a hard time about it.

He'd then asked for the check before I finished my chicken—something he had never done before. We would regularly linger over our meals in the evening, sharing a bottle of wine and talking long after the plates had cleared. I asked if he had something to tell me, never guessing that he would tell me he wanted to break up right when the server placed our bill on the table. She had looked at me with wide eyes, muttered something about coming back later, and rushed back to the kitchen only to peer through the circular window at me with pity.

I told Nan about how he had secretly hired movers to pack up my things as soon as I left for the bakery that morning, and sent them to Brooklyn, of all places, in a seedy building on the corner of nowhere.

She listened without interruption, but I could see the way her hands curled around her cup and how her jaw tightened while I recapped my mortifying story.

Nan was pissed.

"And now I'm here." I laughed humorlessly into my teacup and poured the last bit into my mouth.

My stomach was pleasantly hot, and my body loose from the liquor's effects. I may regret it in the morning, but right now, after reliving the previous day… I eyed the bottle between us. Nan pursed her lips; her chin slightly jutted out in thought.

"Well," she mused. "We can either drain this bottle cursing the *bratach salach*… or we can drain it in celebrating yer freedom from him."

She lifted the bottle and looked at me in question.

I knew what she was really asking. Do I want to wallow in the past or rejoice in the possibilities of my future?

With my hand wrapped around the neck of the half-empty bottle, I filled our cups again and tapped my rim against hers.

CHAPTER 3

Meggie

S ilvery light crept into my room with the crow of a rooster I could swear was taking up residence in my bedroom.

I'm never drinking whiskey again, I vowed. My tongue felt like a furry creature had curled up and died on it. *Days ago.*

Slowly opening my eyes, I spied a water glass and two aspirin on the nightstand—that sweet woman. We got good and drunk last night, dancing together in the small yellow kitchen to an unknown song on the radio.

I lay there smiling as I remembered Nan slow dancing with the broom and insisting I take a turn. It was one of the best nights I've had in a very long time. Mindful of my throbbing head, I gingerly eased out of bed, wrapped myself in my mother's robe, and shuffled down the hallway to the kitchen.

Pastries and a pot of steaming coffee waited for me on the counter, and their aroma sang to my sleepy senses while I poured a mug of concentrated caffeine and added some cream. While I sipped, I peered out to the backyard and found Nan already tending her vegetable garden before the belly of the sun cleared the trees in the distance.

It was planting season, and she was already hard at work turning the soil for her seeds. Several of her chickens flocked around her, scratching at the newly turned dirt for grubs and other small unfortunate creatures, and fertilized the soil as they went. My Nan had a wonderful relationship with her land. It was something I always enjoyed watching. It was as though she spoke to it, or maybe it spoke to her.

Coffee mug in hand, I nibbled on a scone and stepped out onto the back porch. Folding my legs underneath me on one of the padded wicker chairs, I waited for the sun to clear the trees.

With the coffee and aspirin chasing away most of last night's effects, I stretched and waved at Nan.

"When ye're done lollygaggin', get dressed. Ye'll be gettin' right dirty today, lass," she hollered and then traipsed out of the garden towards the barn, her gardening boots covered in a thick casing of mud.

"Yes, ma'am," I quietly groaned and headed inside to change.

It seemed she had not been joking about that chicken coop yesterday.

There's something about the smell of a barn that soothes my soul. It's the earthy scent of hay and animals. Of dust motes dancing in a ray of light filtering from the hay shaft above. The soft sounds of the goat eating her grain, and the milking cow, Agnes, waiting just inside the barn doors. Her large, gentle brown eyes regarded me through thick, sweeping lashes.

"Hello, my love," I crooned and offered her my palm to sniff before I ran my hands down her neck and over her black and white flank. "Has Nan taken care of you yet, sweet girl?"

I ran my hand along her ribs and under her belly to find her udders swollen and heavy. Leaving her just long enough to fetch the stool and pail, I set to work on relieving her of her milk.

Mom had taught me how; long ago. It was my chore when I stayed here, and it was as familiar to me now as it was then. With my forehead resting against the side of her warm belly, I began the ancient motions that people have performed for centuries, the fluid movements a lullaby. Before long, my pail was full of white, frothy milk for Nan to work into butter and cheese. With my task finished, I gave Agnes a firm pat on her hind-quarters to send her back off into the pasture, knowing she'd be back the next morning for me.

~

Farm work was laborious and demanding.

We took our lunch of chicken salad and green grapes under the oak tree that shaded the west side of the barn and lounged at the stone table that had been there since before I was born, the sides and some of the tabletop covered in pale, rough moss. While we ate in comfortable silence, I gazed out on the pasture and watched the breeze dance over the long grass. The wooly highland cows lazily made their way from one end to the other, a few calves trailing behind their mothers with Agnes bringing up the rear.

"I left a full pail in the barn cooler. I'd like to use the cream in tonight's dessert if you can spare it," I told her, and popped the last grape into my mouth.

"Who am I to deny ye, lass? I've been lookin' forward to yer cookin'." She gathered up our plates onto an old serving tray. "Well, the only task left is to check on the hives in the north corner, then we can call it a day."

She nodded towards the far end of the pasture, where her newest addition to the farm sat under a grove of pine trees just before the land sloped up into the forested hillside. Nan loved a project, her latest being three honeybee hives. Declining the speed of the little golf cart, we strolled side by side along a worn path that circled the property.

When I was young, Mom and I would explore the acreage extensively. We'd play in the hidden butterfly gardens tucked in the forests that ringed Nan's land and sometimes venture off into the wilderness. So many wonderful memories danced in my mind while we stretched out our legs and enjoyed each other's silent company.

With her hives inspected and intact, Nan looked further down the path before she turned to me, her eyes sad before she asked, "Are ye wantin' to see them now or later?"

I looked down at myself, at the mud-splattered up to my knees and the dirt under my nails. Long before lunch, my hair began escaping the heavy braid that hung down my back and curled in a wild mess around my face. I couldn't visit my parents resting place looking like this. Not for the first time.

"Not now." I gestured at my outward appearance. "And I'd like to talk to them alone... if you don't mind."

She nodded in understanding and put her arm around me. Giving me a squeeze, she turned us around, and we headed back to the little white house and a much-deserved hot shower.

⌒

With a towel wrapped around my wet hair, I pulled on fleece-lined grey leggings and my favorite dusky pink sweater before padding into the kitchen. Nan was spooning the cream off the top of the pail Agnes and I had filled earlier. I immediately started pulling mixing bowls out of the cabinets and soon lost myself in the joy of cooking a simple crème brûlée to follow Nan's roast. While it chilled, I dried my hair and excused myself, taking advantage of the last hours before sunset to visit my parents.

I took not the path we walked earlier, but another that followed a stream in the shade of the woods. My destination wasn't far, so I walked unhurried and listened to the song of the nightingales and blackcaps in the trees. Funny, I felt so lonely walking the crowded city streets, yet here I felt at home with nothing but the birds for company.

Lost in thought, I skirted around a large boulder and stepped into the clearing that was my destination. Gasping, I stopped in my tracks, shocked at the scene before me.

Bluebells. Thousands upon thousands of them spread throughout the small clearing and around the angel that watched over my parents' graves. My throat grew tight as happy and sad tears warred together to blur my vision.

We laid my parents to rest in the family plot on the property with only close friends attending, and then I went back to the states the next day to continue my classes. I felt guilty for never thinking to ask how she marked their graves.

It was a beautiful statue. Her body of smooth white marble, the angel crouched with her wings stretched wide, a serene smile on her face as she looked down on her charges. Her robes fell in folds over her legs, the hem seeming to be caught by a heavenly wind.

I picked my way through the flowers to kneel between my parent's graves. Small markers set into the ground at the angel's feet displayed their names, birth, and death dates, but the foot of the angel read: *Too well-loved to ever be forgotten.*

I stayed there, silent, and still until the last of the sunlight left the glen. They did not need to hear my voice to understand my heart. Slowly, I stood and traced my fingers down the smooth arm of their heavenly guardian before leaving them to their peace.

The savory, mouthwatering aroma of slow-cooked meat greeted me when I entered the house, and my stomach grumbled loudly. In the kitchen, Nan had just set down the bottle of wine when I pulled her into a hug. Her shoulders stiffened for only a moment before her arms folded behind my back and returned my embrace.

"Thank you." I sniffed. "It's perfect."

"Och, lass. They deserved no less. A whirlwind romance those two had and their love never died down for either of them in the twenty years they were together." She discreetly wiped her eyes and took a long sip of wine before sitting down and pointed at the chair across from her in a silent command for me to sit. "Now, let's eat before yer auld Nan wastes away."

She didn't have to tell me twice. I did as she commanded and dug into the meal, allowing each bite to sit on my tongue for a moment before slowly chewing.

I inherited an honest love for all things culinary from Nan. When I was a young girl, I spent many hours in this kitchen. I learned how to crack and egg properly, make butter, and knead dough. But most importantly, I learned the fine aspects of spices and herbs. Nan's extensive garden was something to behold and envy. Never have I seen a McCormick spice bottle in her kitchen. Oh no, everything she used was fresh and bold, calling taste buds to attention. I endeavored to have the same practice in my kitchen, but for the last year, Steven had preferred to eat out instead of staying in the apartment, and my herbs often rotted before I could use them.

Shrugging off my dark thoughts, I gathered the dishes to the sink before torching the sugared pudding and topped it with a small spoonful of Nan's strawberry preserves. I watched while Nan cracked the caramelized shell. She savored her first bite and gave me an exaggerated nod, with an appropriate hum of enjoyment.

To me, that was the best part of cooking.

CHAPTER 4

Meggie

"I'm going to kill that rooster," I groused into my pillow early the next morning. It appeared he took the daily enjoyment of parking his feathered ass outside my window before dawn.

The thing about roosters is, they don't just crow when the sun rises. Oh no, they gleefully crow *all day long*. When the sun rises, when the wind blows, if they spy a buzzard in the sky or company comes calling, they'll gladly let you know when something's amiss. Because of that, I just *know* this morning's wake-up call will be a daily occurrence. I'll have no choice but to wake when he screams like a banshee.

I whipped the covers off my body and stared like a grump at the ceiling for a few moments before I dressed for another day of hard work and set off in search of a large cup of coffee. Nan has always survived on just her tea but always had a pot brewing for my mom, and now, me. It's a comfort I take every advantage of.

The week went by quickly. The fresh air and the daily temperature just kissing sixty degrees made for enjoyable working conditions. Exhausted by farm life, I fell into bed shortly after Nan retired each night, and by Saturday, I was sorely in need of a break from the mud. Lucky for me, Nan sells her honey, cheese, and eggs at the market a few towns over on the first Saturday of every month. Without complaint I happily loaded up the car for her, and before seven a.m., we were driving north toward Loch Etive.

Nan had been selling her wares at the market for the last forty years. People came from all over for her homemade cheeses and the olive oils she infuses with her herbs. Most she knew by name and greeted them like old friends, asking after their families and catching up on the local gossip.

Glad of the foresight of hitting the ATM at the airport, I ditched her the first chance I got to peruse the market and purchased a lovely hand-woven rent knitted in a dark earthy-green and blue-grey yarn. I've always loved the unique way the short, shawl-like infinity wrap crisscrossed over the chest, and kept the back, and upper arms warm.

A thistle brooch with three faceted amethysts set for the flowers caught my eye a few tables down. Its silver leaves raised in an arc, giving it a circular shape two inches in circumference. The old woman selling it took my money in exchange and flashed me a toothless grin when I thanked her for her beautiful work.

Since Nan could handle her booth by herself, I took my time with my tour of the market. It had grown over the years, and I spent the better part of two hours looking at everything. The smell of cinnamon and yeast drew me to a baker's table, and I couldn't resist purchasing a raisin loaf. Its weight and softness tempted me to rip off a piece to sample while I continued down the row of tables.

I strolled by vendors selling darned and dyed yarn, freshly sheered bags of wool, and sheepskin rugs. Another displayed every tartan color combination you could desire. Polish hens with their wildly feathered hairdos, goats, and pigs were available for purchase at the far end of the market, and I couldn't help but give each animal a little love if it allowed me to get close enough. I passed a portly man with an enormous selection of walking sticks. He was actively carving another to add to his collection, and he educated me on the species of wood he chose for their strength and elasticity. I ran my thumb over the runes his wife carved into each at half-staff to ward off evil and other such dangers a person could run into on their travels. Another woodcarver showed me his puzzle boxes and cutting boards, each polished by hand to a high shine.

Lastly, I bought a small box of whiskey-cream truffles for Nan on my way back to her booth. Unsurprisingly, her table was nearly empty, and she greeted me with a satisfied smile.

"Maybe just an hour more here, and we can pack up. Why dinnae ye grab us a wee bite from Jack over there? He has the most delicious soups," she suggested, and inclined her head toward a white canopy.

After sampling each of his four selections, I settled on his Cullen Skink, which had smoked haddock and turnips, and the Cock-a-leekie, a hearty chicken soup with bacon. My stomach growled as I navigated the crowd back to Nan to give her first choice, and we enjoyed the light lunch while happy customers snatched the rest of her goods up.

Nan's Red Anster cheese was a local favorite and had sold out long ago, but her Morangie Brie and Cambus O' May shortly followed along with the honey and eggs. Satisfied with her zippered pouch full of pounds and pence, we packed up her table and folding chairs and headed home.

～

Driving in Scotland was always an adventure. At least, for a little girl, sometimes the adventures lay in the detours. But for a seasoned local like Nan, the herd of sheep blocking the road we traveled along was a royal nuisance. Madly cursing in Gaelic and glaring daggers at the lazy sheepdog that watched unabashedly from the side of the road, she turned the car around, gripped the wheel, and stomped the gas. Tires chirping, we shot away the herd and left the objects of her frustration in the dust.

I chuckled to myself and tucked my chin in the crook of my arm that rested on the open window. I had frequently felt the same way in Manhattan when a Hollywood studio would rope off a couple city blocks. Often, those detours led me farther on foot than I wanted to go and sometimes past the smellier sections I'd been avoiding in the first place.

In Scotland, these deviations were never unpleasant for me. They brought me to beautiful places I've never seen before, ruins I'd never explored, and pools I had yet to discover.

Nan babbled about the goings-on she heard at the market when a castle in the distance I had never seen before caught my fascination. The castle was on the top of a gently sloping hill, and the loch that separated it from the highway we raced along mirrored its reflection.

"Nan, tell me about that estate up there. What do you know of it?" I asked, pointing towards the three-story grey stone structure on the other side of the loch. Its two towers stood watch over the water like proud sentinels. It looked old but with modern additions, the back side facing the quiet loch.

"Ah! That would be *Ghlas Thùr*. It means The Grey Towers. The MacKinnon's have lived there for many generations. I dinnae ken why they kept it up all these centuries. It's a large estate for one family to look after. Unlike the other castles in Scotland, they dinnae offer tours past the great hall, and even then, they watch ye like ye're out to steal their silver spoons. I dinnae ken a soul who's been beyond. The grounds are open to the public, though." She continued telling me of the hiking trails tucked into the hills.

"It's beautiful. Mom never took me there." I sighed, gazing dreamily at the structure until it slipped out of sight when we rounded a bend.

"Yer mum could have brought ye to a different ruin or castle every day of yer life, and it would take years to see them all." She raised her finger suddenly, like she had a bright idea. "Ye should spend the day exploring it tomorrow. The McTavish lad comes on Sundays to take care of the chores so that I can attend church and the ladies' luncheon. Take the day. Ye've worked hard since ye arrived, and ye dinnae want to spend good hiking weather inside with a bunch of auld crones," she teased.

I shook my head. "I don't mind, Nan. You know I like your friends." It was a weak protest, since I was already daydreaming about exploring the estate. She reached over and gave my leg a light smack.

"I insist! I'll even pack yer lunch. Although, do be careful at the caves, Meggie. Legend has stories of people exploring too deeply and never seen again. I dinnae ken that the stories hold much stock but have a care, anyway." Emphasizing her warning with a raised brow and a stern look, I could only nod my head and cross my heart.

For the first time in a long while, I felt a small thrill of excitement for adventure.

∽

I awoke to the light tapping of raindrops on my window and stretched, smiling to myself when I noted the clock on the nightstand read eight-thirty a.m. Lucky me, Nan's rooster prefers to stay in the dry comfort of his coop when it's raining.

I found Nan already dressed in her Sunday finest in the kitchen, a small brooch with the McNeely colors pinned over her heart. The pin, which was always displayed on Sundays, was a tight weave of dark green, black, and white.

"Good morning," I croaked, and filled a mug with rich caffeine and cream. "Are you going to the nine o'clock sermon?" Plopping heavily at the table, I rubbed the last remaining sleepiness from my eyes.

With a flourish, Nan swung her purse over her shoulder and plunked down a paper bag in front of me. I raised my eyebrows in question, my mouth full of coffee.

"Aye. The rain should move on within the hour, with nothin' but clear skies on after. I packed yer lunch as promised, so dinnae feel the need to cut yer hike short. Yer Granda's truck still has plenty of life left and will get ye where ye need to go, and back, safe and sound." She dug out a set of keys from a drawer and tossed them at my head. I barely caught them in time. "Be home for supper, or I'll skelp yer wee behind. Dinnae think I willnae do it." And with that, she breezed out the back door and left me blinking mutely after her.

Chuckling to myself at the thought of Nan trying to catch me long enough to smack my bum should I be late, I peeked into the bag. A small jar of honey, cheese wrapped in beeswax paper, an apple, and a thick slice of the bread I bought yesterday lay in wait for lunchtime. Simple and delicious. I brought it back to my room and quickly changed for my hike. I decided on jeans and a thin long-sleeve black shirt. After a moment of deliberation, I slipped the rent I bought yesterday over my head and pinned the thistle brooch over my heart. A bit fancy for hiking, but I liked the way it looked. Besides, there wasn't anything wrong with dressing to impress one's self.

After brushing my teeth, I braided my hair back and looked in the mirror. My bi-colored eyes stared back at me through thick black lashes, and for the first time since I arrived, I really looked at myself.

Color tinted the apples of my cheeks from my days spent in the sun. My skin was bright and glowing from the fresh air and clean food. My dark brown hair had even highlighted with strands of bronze around my face. I looked healthy. Young. Happy.

I never thought I looked unhappy before now, but a mirror never lies, does it? Turning away from the girl in the reflection, I found an old rucksack I've used before in the closet; the worn brown leather smooth and supple from decades of use. After stowing my wallet, an extra pair of thick socks, a canteen, and Nan's sack lunch inside, I set out for the truck.

She's an ancient beast, and I'm sure in her prime she was a beauty, but by today's standards, she's a rusted hunk of junk. The 1957 Ford pickup turned over without fuss; the interior smelling faintly of old vinyl, mold, and cow manure. With a crank of the gearshift, she popped into gear, and slowly coasted down the dirt driveway past the cottage. The rain was clearing, as promised, and streaks of sunlight broke through the cloud cover. With a glance at the rearview mirror, I spied Nan's rooster running towards my bedroom window, the deep green plume of his tail feathers swinging behind him in his haste.

"Not today, ye wee bastard!" I whooped out the window and eased the old truck down the lane, onto the highway, and onward toward the MacKinnon Estate.

~

The entrance to the grounds welcomed me with open, wrought-iron gates. The winding drive, paved and tidy and bracketed with oaks, escorted me for over half a mile before I spotted the grey stone of the castle ahead. Heeding my grandmother's comment of the resident's private ways, I turned the truck to the right at a fork, and into a forest, following the hiking signs.

The first hiker to arrive, I pulled in a small gravel parking area, and parked next to a map of the grounds posted to a weathered bulletin board. With my pack slung over my shoulders, I studied the map and the colored lines snaking over the topography. I decided on the moderately strenuous yellow trail because it followed the loch for a time and then a river before tying into a blue trail marked easy and returning me here. Simple enough. Eager to get started, I slipped my phone into my back pocket and headed for the trees that had the yellow plastic squares nailed to their trunks.

The forest was quiet, save for the birds and small critters foraging for food. I always liked to be the first on the trail; before human beings brought all their noise and disrupted how nature was best observed.

I walked briskly over the rain-softened path that cushioned and muffled my booted footsteps. Maybe I would be lucky enough to spot a pine marten, or at the very least, some deer.

The trail flowed downhill for a time, and my jeans brushed against the dewy ferns that reached their triangular tips over the path. Red squirrels darted ahead, chittering and chasing one another. It was late morning when I reached the loch; the water smooth as glass and so clear I could see the pebbled bottom several yards out from the shore. The trail followed the waterside for a time, and besides the occasional disruption by a car speeding on the highway across the water, it was quiet.

When I entered another forest, I slowed my pace and lost myself in thoughts of my future and my options. I didn't think I would go back to the States; there was nothing for me there anymore. Sure, I still had friends in Raleigh, but I hadn't seen them since I moved to New York. We drifted apart, and now we were more Facebook friends than anything with a *like* here or there when we shared pictures and *Happy Birthday, miss you!* posts.

And Nan was only getting older. She needed me here, and I obviously needed her. I could make a life in Scotland. Maybe in Inverness. I could invest my inheritance and open a bakery, or maybe a Bed and Breakfast.

While I kicked at pinecones, I daydreamed of what could be, and when I next looked up, I stood at the base of a clearing overrun with wild poppies. Their scarlet-petaled flowers swayed gently in the breeze in the sun-drenched meadow. Fishing my phone out of my pocket, I crouched down and took a picture of how the worn path sliced through the flowers. I did not want to forget this lovely place.

Around noon, I arrived at what I could only call fairy pools. The large basins looked like a giant had scooped out massive amounts of earth to hold caches of crystal-clear water. Multicolored pebbles lined their floors, looking like jewels in the sun.

The trail continued to the right, following the rush of a river downhill. But to my left, small waterfalls tumbled out of the hills between moss-covered boulders to fill the pools before connecting with the main river body. And because I was always on the hunt for a little piece of Scotland that maybe only my eyes would see, I veered off the trail and climbed.

This was the adventure I had hoped for.

My thighs strained the higher I climbed, and sweat quickly beaded on my forehead from my exertion of finding my footing over the loose stone and lichen-covered rock.

Then I saw them when I reached a plateau on the hill; the caves Nan had mentioned. Tucked in the hillside, the openings gaped where the incline continued.

They weren't big, just a cluster of four entrances, the largest only five feet high, and the smallest barely big enough for a dog. Long grass and ferns draped over the openings like scraggly mustaches.

Hesitating, I looked inside the largest cave: the one with water seeping from its sandy entrance, and braced myself against the cave mouth so I could stick my head through the passage. A deep droning resonated from inside the cavern, and the stone I leaned against vibrated slightly. Pushing away, I eyed the cave warily. Now I understood why there were local legends involving this place.

It gave me the creeps.

Deciding to continue up the incline so I could at least say I made it to the crest of the hill, I used the rocks around the cave mouth as toeholds and then continued to trudge up the slope. I had only gone about twenty feet when the soil gave way beneath me, and a large crevice opened under my feet to reveal the dark abyss of the cave below. Frantically, I grabbed for anything to keep me from falling in, but the earlier rainfall made everything slick. I ripped the grass and small plants out by the roots. Mud painfully shoved its way under my nails and scraped my palms with sharp, hidden rocks.

"No!" I cried, my legs swinging in the open space below me.

I could hear rocks and pebbles splashing into water below, but in my panic, I was unsure how far down they fell. The expectation of sharp stalagmites piercing my body amped my fear of falling. I stretched my right leg up to find some purchase with my boot and boost my tired body onto level ground, but the slick mud was too much, and more of the earth fell away.

"Please!" I cried out, even though I knew no one would hear me.

I was unwisely far from the footpath and the first to start the trails that morning, the closest population miles away at the castle. No one would come to help me. I knew this, and with a whimper, I slipped even farther, my chin scraping rock while I clung to the lip of the chasm. I could feel my blood make a slow track down the column of my throat.

Bit by bit, my bodyweight beat down my tired muscles, and with a scream, I fell into the darkness.

CHAPTER 5

Meggie

Consciousness returned to me slowly, my head pounding in time to my pulse, and I swallowed the metallic taste of blood. Cautiously, I tested my limbs to find my lower body submerged in a shallow pool of frigid water and felt relief that I had no broken bones. No stalagmites pierced my flesh.

With a pained groan, I wiped away the sand that clung to the side of my face and frowned when my hand came away bloody in the weak light. Shivering from cold and shock, I crawled over soft sand and loose rock out into the sweet sunshine.

I will never walk off the path again, I vowed and tipped my face up to the sun to thank God that I was not severely hurt.

Trembling, I pulled my phone from my pocket and cursed loudly at the black screen. Damn. It was just not my day. I could have sworn I had a full charge when I left Nan's this morning. After shoving the now useless electronics into my pack, I stumbled clumsily back down the hill.

Vehemently cursing wet skinny jeans and incredibly stupid ideas, I wiped at the mud and sand that coated my clothing the whole way back to the fairy pools, where I fell to my knees and touched my lips to its smooth surface. The crystal-clear water was the best I had ever tasted, slaking my thirst and coating my parched throat before I refilled my canteen. After washing most of the mud and blood off my hands and face, I tenderly probed the cut at my hairline and hoped it wasn't so deep that I would need stitches.

The sound of my growling stomach overpowered the sound of rushing water, and I wondered how long I had been unconscious. Surely it wasn't too long past noon.

I took a seat with my back against a boulder and rummaged through my scant supplies before huffing a breath of frustration.

"What I wouldn't give for some Neosporin and a band-aid right about now," I grumbled.

Blessedly, the insides of my pack were still dry since I landed on my face in the cave. Great for the pack, not so great for my face, of course. With a hard yank, I tugged off my wet boots and socks, and set them in the direct sunlight to dry out. With my pruney bare toes wiggling in the sunshine, I scarfed down the bread with a generous load of honey drizzled on it, the cheese, and the apple. Licking my fingers clean, I absorbed the heat that spread through my chilled limbs and listened to the songbirds and the lulling chorus of the rushing water.

My belly full and body warm again, I tugged on my spare socks and hoped they were thick enough to combat the damp leather of my boots. Hitching my pack on my shoulders, I turned to continue down the trailhead, only to blink stupidly at the spot I expected it to be.

The trailhead wasn't there.

Running through my memories from earlier today, I totally remembered emerging from the trail right here to this very pool.

Right?

I walked along the water's edge for fifty feet and tripped over a fallen branch before turning back. Slightly panicking, I jogged back a hundred feet. Nothing. Not even a deer trail.

The snap of a stick behind me sounded like a firecracker, and I whirled around to find two men on the other side of the river staring at me, leers upon their unwashed faces.

Yellowed, broken teeth peeked through thin lips. Long, greasy hair hung limp around unshaven faces and tattered tartans draped their half-naked bodies. The taller one pointed at me, the look on his face one I had never seen before.

Hungry. Malicious. Corrupt.

"Well, aren't ye *bonnie*..." His voice raised the hair on the back of my neck, and he took a threatening step forward. One of his bare feet entered the rushing water that couldn't have been over four feet deep. "We could have some fun with a lassie such as yerself," he snickered.

With a wave for the other to follow, he took another step, his motives clear.

Adrenaline flooded my veins, and I fled blindly into the brush at my back, instinct driving me to put as much distance as possible between us before they cleared the river.

Branches raked harshly against my face and arms like talons, tearing up my thin shirtsleeves and scratching the skin underneath. My pack bounced wildly against my back, and my keys clanged against the empty jar of honey like a dinner bell while I ran for my life through thickets and rocky open spaces before hurtling into the shadows of a forest with tall, thick trees.

The men barked at one another in rapid Gaelic while they chased after me.

"Get away from me!" I screamed.

Hot tears streamed into my hair, and I cried out in frustration when I slipped in wet leaves under the tree canopy, my blunder causing me to lose precious headway.

Get up! Get up! Get up!

My fingers clawed at the ground as I scrambled to get my feet underneath me and pushed forward, wildly scanning for some way of escape.

I chanced a brief glance behind me to find one of my pursuers hot at my heels, and the other farther back and to my left.

Spying a break in the trees, I shot to the right and vaulted over a shallow stream. My lungs hammered inside my chest, and my breath came out in labored gasps for more oxygen while I pumped my arms and tired legs... only to careen out of the forest and found myself at the base of a cliff too high to climb. To make matters worse, the damn thing curved around me on either side like a crescent moon.

They were herding me, I realized. A sob forced its way up my throat as I turned to face my pursuers.

"Nowhere to go, lassie." The tall one stepped out from the shadows thirty feet away, a knotted rope swinging from his right hand. His eyes were manic and bloodshot, so sure of his triumph.

"Ye're right where we want ye," he sneered.

Weaponless and vulnerable, I snatched up a loose rock in each hand and pressed my back to the cliff face when a rustling sounded from beyond the saplings at the tree line.

Without taking his eyes off me, the man called back to his friend with a chuckle. "'Bout time ye caught up! I was thinkin' I'd be havin' her all to me-self."

His partner then stumbled into the clearing with his hands locked on his throat and a bewildered look on his face. Blood pulsed thick and quick from between his fingers, cascading in crimson rivers down his bare arms and chest. When he opened his mouth to speak, only a gargle escaped before he collapsed to his knees and then onto his face in the grass.

The tall man swore, dropped the rope, and grabbed the dirk sheathed on his belt. Turning his back on me, he faced an unseen foe hidden in the gloom.

"Get on with it!" he bellowed, no longer so sure of himself now that he was alone.

With his full attention on this new threat, he seemed to forget about me: the helpless woman he hunted down to commit unspeakable things to.

That was his mistake.

Rallying myself for courage, I gripped the sharp stone in my hand, pulled my arm back, and threw it with all my might at the back of his head. I didn't even wait for the first stone to find its mark before I palmed the second and threw it as well. I felt a strange, unhinged joy break through my fear when the first stone connected with the back of his ear.

He grabbed the side of his head and spun around, only to take the second stone straight to the forehead. Cursing me, spittle flew from his mouth, and loathing radiated from his eyes when he took a step toward me. The sharp edge of his dirk flashed in the sun.

A primal roar resonated from the forest, and the largest man I'd ever seen erupted from the shadows, causing my attacker to turn towards the sound. With a spear in his upraised arm, he took two long strides before heaving it across the clearing towards my aggressor, his body weight behind the force of his throw.

The lance hit with such force that it knocked its target backward with a solid punch to the chest only a few feet from where I stood. Stunned, I watched its victim land hard on his back and gape up at the sky in surprise. Sucking in brief gasps of breath through his brown teeth, he pawed weakly at the spear protruding from his rib cage until his movements gradually slowed to a stop, and his bloody fingers held the spear with the loose grip of the dead.

Looking down in alarmed confusion, I stared into the sightless orbs of the dead man for a moment before my limbs began to shake. Nonsensical babble poured from my mouth while I came down from my adrenaline high, and I'm pretty sure I looked a bit like a madwoman. I certainly felt like one.

The presence of bare feet drew my attention towards my protector, and I blinked up at him dumbly while my body shook uncontrollably.

"Yer bleedin', lass." His baritone voice rolled over me, his brogue thick, smooth, and comforting.

Striking blue eyes, the color of sapphires, showed concern as he looked me over. Wavy, shoulder-length golden blond hair and a short beard of a slightly darker shade gave his handsome face a wild, barbaric appearance. Wearing only a kilt of deep blues and greens, complete with a sporran made of some furry hide and a bandolier of wicked knives strapped across his bare chest, he was a fierce presence that dominated the small clearing.

Hands raised as though he was calming a feral animal, he crept closer to me, his movements slow and smooth.

I'm the feral animal, I thought.

"Y-you killed them," I whispered, refusing to look again at the dead men. It was a sight I doubted I'd ever forget, anyway. Dead or alive, their faces were sure to haunt me in my dreams for years to come.

"Aye, that I did." He wrapped my shaking hands into the warmth of his large bronze ones and rubbed circles over the rapid pulse of my wrist with his thumbs. The soothing strokes calmed me a degree. "I heard ye scream and came runnin'. They cannae hurt ye now."

He released his hold on my hands to loom over the dead man, and with a tight grip on the spear, yanked it out of its victim. The wet sucking sound threatened to make me evict the contents of my stomach. Focusing on the wispy clouds high above while my head swam, I concentrated on taking deep breaths, and barely kept my shit together.

"What's yer name, lass? I'm Colin."

My name?

"M-Meggie. Meggie Washington. We—oh God, we need to report this. My phone's dead. Do you have one? We need to call the authorities," I babbled, struggling to form a cohesive thought.

Colin stood up from retrieving the dead man's knife and gave me an odd look before tilting his head toward the tree line. Loosely grasping my hand, he gave a gentle tug to follow and guided me back into the shade of the trees. Following some unseen path, his bare feet barely made any noise on the forest floor; every step he made deliberate and near-silent for a man of his size. I stumbled along on legs made of jelly, thanks to my mad dash thorough the forest, and made enough noise for the both of us.

With my heartbeat still hammering in my throat, I was slow on reordering my thoughts, and I found myself captivated by the beautiful contours of Colin's muscular back. By the slope of his broad shoulders and his corded arms. Every movement he made was fluid and sinuous under his sun-kissed skin, reminding me of a mountain lion that stalks its prey. A really *big* mountain lion. The top of my head barely reached his shoulder.

"Where are we going?"

He glanced down at me before pointing the bloody tip of the spear in the direction of a group of boulders lining a stream.

"I left my kills just on the other side of that burn."

"What?" I shrieked.

Firmly yanking my hand out of his, I backed up, prepared to run, fearing I traded one dangerous man for another. Colin's lips quirked up, amusement in his eyes.

"Rabbits, lass. I had to abandon them to pursue yer attackers." He continued up the gentle slope alone, allowing me the choice to follow or not.

Entirely lost and unwilling to walk alone after what just happened, I hung back and kept a healthy distance until he did indeed pick up a brace of rabbits. Slinging them over his shoulder, he winked at me as if to say; *I told you so* and headed southwest.

"'Tis no' far to Ghlas Thùr. My brother will want to ken what transpired here and send out a patrol," he called back.

"And the coroner," I muttered under my breath before I said, "You're very nonchalant for someone who just killed two people."

Colin stopped in his tracks and turned to look at me in disbelief.

"Should I have just turned a blind eye to yer plight? Would ye have preferred that?"

"No…" Overwhelmed, my eyes filled up with tears, and my voice wavered and cracked when I said, "I've just never seen anything like that—never seen death… I don't understand how you can just… *walk away* from that. I don't know how *I* can walk away from that."

Colin's features softened, and when he moved closer, I instinctively inched forward. I needed to feel his strength and confidence, because I certainly didn't have any left.

"I ken what ye're feelin' all too well, and I'm sorry ye had to see that." With the light touch of his forefinger to my chin, he urged me to look up at him. "I promise ye, I didnae enjoy killin' them. Do ye believe me when I say that?"

I heard the honesty in his voice. "Yes."

He nodded once. "Then let me take ye to Ghlas Thùr and we can disclose what happened together, aye?"

With that reassurance, I released a breath I hadn't realized I was holding.

"Thank you."

With the last of the adrenaline out of my system, my throat felt like the Sahara, and I fumbled with my pack for my canteen. Colin watched me with interest while I drank, and I offered him the half-empty container, which he sniffed curiously before taking a long swallow.

"It's a shame that it's not vodka," I joked weakly when he handed it back.

He looked at me curiously for a moment before shrugging and continued up the stream bed. We walked in silence for a long while, my mind runing loops around what just happened; a downward spiral I couldn't seem to climb out of. Shaking my head at the image of the man's dead eyes for the hundredth time, I trotted up to Colin's side.

"I didn't thank you. For saving me, I mean. I know what would have happened to me had you not come along." Looking up at him, I studied his profile as we walked. His brows drew low over his blue eyes, and his full lips thinned with anger and worry.

"They would have done horrible things to ye, lass. Things ye widnae have survived." Holding out his hand for me to take, he helped me over a fallen moss-covered log, his fingers tightening around mine slightly before letting go. "I'm just glad I got to ye in time."

"Me too."

Although I hate that it's going to cause a lot of trouble for you, I thought to myself.

Abandoning the thin trail, Colin guided me onto a rough dirt road with a thick canopy of trees. Hoofprints and deep lines that looked like wagon ruts gouged the muddy areas in thickly shaded sections. A few minutes later, we rounded a bend, and the castle came into view.

It was even more magnificent up close. The grey stone citadels looked forbidding as the keep towered above us. Two three-story wings stretched out on either side of the main body with the twin towers that gave the castle its name rising high above at either end and capped with dark brown shakes. Arrow slits ran up the thick turrets, hinting at a spiral staircase in their interiors.

It quite surprised me to see an actual curtain wall surrounding the building and couldn't believe I missed such a major detail when we drove by yesterday. A man walked along the top, his focus on our approach through a field, and his wrist resting on the pommel of his short sword. As we got closer, I noticed there were gatehouses open for entry at intervals, and we headed straight for what looked like the main entry.

Two men in light leather armor stood talking outside the largest gatehouse and openly gawked at me. One of them hissed something to Colin in Gaelic, and Colin likewise answered with a chuckle and a quip as we passed, which made the men laugh. I rushed in after him and was about to ask him to translate what they said into English when I nearly tripped over his heels and blinked in amazement at the goings-on around me.

A massive oak tree hundreds of years old held court in the middle of the center bailey we had just entered, its mighty branches spread wide, casting a thick shadow under its dense cluster of leaves. A few chickens freely roamed the enormous area while young children running around in trousers and homespun dresses kicked an oddly shaped ball. One woman in a full-length blue dress with long sleeves beat a rug with a stick, her free arm covering her face while dust billowed around her. Men in white peasant-style shirts and kilts of the same colors as Colin's busily groomed muscled horses in front of a small interior stable set against the curtain wall. One man openly gaped at my torn shirt sleeves and muddy jeans.

Through the main doors of the keep, there was an enormous open hall with a grid of exposed rafters framing the thirty-five-foot high ceilings. The largest hearth I'd ever seen dominated the wall to the left, logs piled and waiting to be set ablaze within. A thick wooden table big enough to seat twenty people stood parallel to the fireplace. Five much smaller fireplaces burned low along the opposite wall with unlit white candles on the mantles. A grand staircase with thick dark wood banisters led to the second-story balcony in the back, splitting the north and south wings. Tapestries depicting hunts and Scotland flora and fauna hung down from the rafters along the walls above the hearths, and bundled rushes sat in each corner, giving the room a spicy scent that mixed in with the lingering wood smoke.

It was odd, considering there weren't any tours happening right now, but it impressed me how this place had such an accurate historical feeling. More women of all ages in full-length dresses, their corsets tied tight, and their hair tucked under white caps, bustled around the room, assembling trestle tables and long benches.

An older woman caught sight of me and gasped, pointing weakly at my legs. Most of the mud had dried and fallen off on the long walk, but they were grimy, and I realized my boots and the hem of my jeans had left debris trailing in my wake. I quickly whispered an apology for tracking dirt into the building and hurried to follow Colin through the large room and down a darkened stairwell to the left of the grand staircase. The heavenly smell of fresh, yeasty bread drifted up from below, and I grinned with excitement the moment I crossed the threshold of the stairway. If what Nan said was true and they did not permit tours past the great hall, I was being admitted where no outsider has been in a very long time. She was going to be so jealous, and I couldn't wait to brag when I got home.

At the bottom of the steep, spiral stairwell ended in a primitive-looking kitchen. The room was long and spacious, and equipped with several medieval cooking stations in the middle, splitting the workspace in two. The heat and smoke from the cookfire disappeared up a blackened shaft in the whitewashed domed ceiling. A massive, cylindrical bread oven squatted at the far end.

Pondering over where they had hidden the modern equipment, I soaked in the details. On one side of the cookfire division was wooden shelving filled neatly with wood and metal plates, pewter and horn cups, baskets of silverware, bowls and serving platters. Pots of all sizes and bundled herbs hung on a rack above a long wooden table on the other side of the cook fires. Women chopping onions and potatoes in matching grey dresses with white aprons surrounded the table. A few young girls in braids and homespun dresses sat in the far corner, playing with sack dolls while they giggled quietly to one another. It was at the end of the table closest to us that Colin set down his burden of rabbits.

The thump of their little furry bodies coming to rest on the wood drew the attention of a middle-aged woman. Plump, with rosy cheeks and frizzy russet curls escaping her cap, she turned towards us and scowled, her hands in fists on her ample hips.

"About time ye showed up. I've been expectin' them for the stew for over an hour," she chided and gave the fluffy heap a firm pat.

My eyes widened at her gruff tone. She was obviously someone of authority here. If I had to guess, she was the head chef. They all had the same no-nonsense air about them. Some worse than others.

Unaffected by the woman's surly attitude, Colin looked down on the older woman with a devilish smirk and nodded in my direction.

"I found the lass here in a wee bit of trouble out by the cliffs. I came as soon as I could."

I caught her staring at my jeans, auburn brows hiked high, and her face a mask of judgment. I could feel my cheeks redden with embarrassment and looked down to watch dirt crumble from my boot onto the stone floor.

"Aye, I can see that." Heaving a sigh, she turned away, effectively dismissing us, and pulled a thick-bladed knife from her apron pocket.

Without warning, she skillfully hacked off the first of the rabbits' heads with a well-practiced movement. I gaped at the little head as it bounced, its death clouded eyes reminding me of the two bodies we left behind in the woods. Who the hell were these people that they lived so primitively? There a market right down the bloody highway! They never heard of chicken cutlets?

With his hand pressed lightly on the small of my back, Colin guided me through the busy kitchen and up a narrow set of stairs. The stone steps were rough on the outer edges and smooth in the middle from centuries of foot traffic. On the second story, he led me down a darkening hallway where there were thick wooden doors on one side and unlit candles or oil lamps in niches between windows on the other. Through the imperfect glass, I could see the shadowed bailey below.

At the end of the hall, we passed through open double doors and into a large, cozy room filled with old hardbound books on either side of a fireplace. Opposite the door, tall, mullioned windows nearly stretched up to the ceiling with two wingback chairs facing the view of the forests beyond. Wooly highland cowhides lay on the floor under a pair of large hand-carved armchairs turned slightly towards one another before the fire, a small table dividing them.

"Malcolm, a word," Colin said gruffly, leading me around gently by my elbow to face a man dominating a chair. A thick pelt of some unknown animal draped over his broad shoulders.

For brothers, they were complete opposites. Colin was as light as this man was dark. This man had long, silky raven hair which was tied back from a handsome, shaven face with a strip of leather. One thick brow arched with interest over warm brown eyes fringed with black lashes. He studied me curiously over the lip of his horn cup, and I felt as though I were stripped bare under his sharp focus.

Malcolm was a man who missed nothing.

"Now, where did ye find this wood-sprite?" He lounged back in his seat, a lazy smile on his face as he extended one of his large, booted feet toward the warmth of the fire.

I self-consciously ran my hand over and down my braid and realized just how many small twigs and debris I failed to pick from my hair. Wood-sprite, indeed. I brought half the damn forest into the castle with me.

"This is Meggie," Colin explained. "Two men near the small cliff to the north attacked her. They wore brown tartans, so I wasnae able to place their clan. They may have been slavers, or worse."

Slavers, what?? My eyes bugged out at the thought.

The nonchalance of Malcolm's demeanor disappeared when his smile melted into a scowl, and his long fingers tightened around his cup so hard his knuckles turned white. After draining the dark ruby contents, he placed the empty cup on the small table and stood nearly as tall as Colin. Turning towards the tall windows, he braced his arm on the outside frame for a minute, his shoulders and back stiff before letting loose a long breath.

"Are they dead?" he asked, his voice both angry and expectant.

"Aye. Without difficulty."

Malcolm abandoned the window to take my hand within his and gave me a small smile, warm and reassuring.

"Yer safe now, Meggie, and under my protection as Laird of Ghlas Thùr."

"Oh," I blurted, and looked at Colin. "This is *your* castle?"

The laird barked a laugh and released me.

"He likes to think so." Resuming his seat by the fire, Malcolm pointed at his brother. "I want ye to lead a patrol at first light. Choose eight men and share with them their task before the feast tonight."

Colin nodded and nudged me toward the door.

"Wait, don't we need to file a report?" I questioned, looking between the two men. "I mean, two people died and there needs to be an investigation."

Malcolm turned his authoritative focus on me. "Ye just did, lass."

"But—"

"—Worry naught over it. Have ye a place to stay? Kin in the village, perhaps?"

"My grandmother has a farm south of here," I explained, and noticed the light outside fading fast. "I need to get going. She's expecting me for dinner."

"Colin will escort ye. Safe travels, Meggie." He nodded and waved us away in dismissal.

Still skeptical, I made a mental note to contact the local police first thing in the morning to make sure the MacKinnon's had contacted them.

We took our time on our way out, and I soaked up every detail and facet of the castle so that I could share them with Nan. Especially the way the employees did such a good job playing at the historical reenactment.

Leaving through the arches of the main gatehouse, I followed the path I assumed would take me to my truck and looked up at Colin with a grin.

"So, do you guys put on a feast for special tours? What does a girl have to do to get a ticket to one?"

Giving me a peculiar look, he returned my grin, revealing straight white teeth.

"Although tonight is a wee bit more extravagant because of the summer solstice, the stronghold's gates are open every other Sunday to the entire clan. 'Tis the day the peasants dine with the prosperous. The tradition was started to keep morale high, form new ideas, and settle feuds. For the last two hundred years, it has worked, with each new laird keeping up with the custom. Malcolm welcomes everyone, from shepherd to blacksmith, to approach him after supper and air their grievances or share good tidings," he explained, a proud look on his handsome face. "I'm honored to serve a laird that treats everyone, no matter their station, with the same compassion and respect."

"Wow. You guys *really* get into it, don't you? Nan said this place was private, but it's not the first time she's been wrong. I can't wait to see the look on her face when I tell her," I mused and kicked a small stone ahead a few yards. "This is the way to the parking lot, right?"

"Par-king-lot? Is that where yer grandmother lives? I have no' heard of this village."

"What?" I laughed. "Come on, stop with the act." Glancing back at the castle, I tried to remember where the trailheads would be from where I stood since we weren't on the paved driveway. "It should be just down here, I think."

Marching farther down the path, I left him to follow at his own pace.

"Ye're an odd lass," he called to my back, a smile in his voice.

"No more than you, my friend," I shot over my shoulder.

The light was rapidly fading, the sun nearly below the horizon, and the woods were darkening quickly. When I stopped to peer through the foliage for a glimpse of the elusive parking lot, Colin sidled up next to me and mimicked my search.

"What are we lookin' for?" he whispered teasingly.

With an exaggerated groan, I gripped his thick upper arms and gave him a little shake. It was like trying to wiggle a boulder.

"Listen, Colin. I need to get to my truck. Can you just take me to the parking lot so I can get home? I'm filthy, there's half a tree stuck in my hair, my arms feel like a cat mauled me—Jesus, they nearly *trafficked me!* I want to go home and take a steaming hot shower. *Please.*"

The corner of his full mouth quirked up, and he stepped closer to fill the space between us. Broad hands grazed my shoulders and his thumbs lightly traced my collarbones. His touch sent shivers racing down my back, and my stomach tightened. With the way he towered over me, I had the perfect view of his muscular chest and the short blond hairs that lightly dusted the bridge of his pectorals. Tearing my gaze away, I forced myself to look him in the eyes. His stare bore into my own while he continued the gentle caress of my skin, and I nearly had to remind myself I had asked him a question when he spoke.

"I dinnae ken what a truck is, lass. Ask anything else of me. Ask me for the stars, and I'll pluck them out o' the sky for ye." The rich cadence of his voice washed over me, and his fingers slowly swept up my neck to slide into the hair on my nape.

Emboldened by the provocative way he looked at me, I blurted, "If you want me to stay for dinner, all you have to do is ask."

A blush licked its way up my neck, heating my cheeks, and Colin studied the telltale flush before shooting me a devastating smile. Untangling his fingers from my hair, he took a step back towards the castle.

"Stay," he said, his hand extended out slightly while he waited for my reply.

With my bottom lip caught between my teeth, I cast one more glance into the darkening forest, and tried to ignore the images of the dead men in my mind. I could call Nan from the castle to let her know I would be late… and I could stay, if only to make sure that Colin would meet me at the police department in the morning. I didn't want him to get in trouble—he saved my life—but this isn't the medieval times, and I was sure, with my testimony, he would be just fine.

I looked up at Colin, and even after all I saw him do today, he felt safe. That sense of safety was good and warm, and I didn't want that feeling to end.

Nan's totally going to skelp my wee behind, I thought, but took his hand anyway.

～

"Meggie would like a bath before the feasting, Mrs. Cook. I'm going to show her to the blue room. Do ye have a lass to spare?"

The rotund woman blew an errant copper curl out of her eyes and stopped stirring the large pot of what I could only assume was rabbit stew.

"The blue room, hmm? As ye like. I'll send Maeve up directly."

On the third floor of the north wing, candles and lamps were lit to combat the gloom of the evening, and I idly wondered how much Malcolm spent on candles a month. Surely, they didn't need to keep up the façade all the way up here if they didn't conduct tours. Seemed like a gross waste of money to me.

At the end of the hallway to the left of a darkened alcove where a winding staircase led up to the northern turret, Colin paused before a wooden door carved with wildflowers along the edges and pushed through into the shadows, leaving me to linger just inside the doorway. A loud snap broke the silence, followed by a shower of sparks raining down on a ball of kindling and straw in the hearth. Colin crouched over the worming embers, patiently feeding them to flame with a gentle breath. Within a minute or two, a small blaze banished the shadows and lit up the secrets of the enormous room. I entered, making a slow rotation as I took in the feminine décor.

A large poster bed with a faded blue velvet coverlet and shaggy furs stood against the western wall between two windows. In front of the fire to the right of the door, fluffy sheepskin covered the floor in front of a welcoming high-backed chair upholstered in deep blue fabric. A low tea table kept it company. Decorated cedar chests and a full-length mirror rested against tapestries depicting the countryside on the south wall. An especially pretty image of woodland animals frolicking around a naked young woman with red hair covering all her feminine parts caught my attention. The weavings covered the stone walls from ceiling to floor where there wasn't a window, creating a homey feeling I didn't know was possible in a castle. More windows lined the north wall, and around a curved wall to the left of the door was a narrow, partially hidden window. I assumed the curve was from the spiral staircase that led up to the north tower. A quick peek revealed a squat, padded bench and a view of the bailey below.

"That should chase the chill from the room in no time." Brushing his hands against his tartan, Colin lit a few candles on the mantle, further brightening the room. Oh boy. Being in this romantic room alone with him, deliciously bare-chested or not, was asking for trouble.

Footsteps and heavy breathing came from the hallway moments before two women appeared carrying a shallow copper tub, followed by several others, each toting two wooden buckets of steaming water.

This is the bath? What the hell is going on here? Shocked into silence, I stared while the women emptied their buckets into the tub set near the fireplace.

"I'll see ye at supper, Meggie," Colin whispered. Skirting around the women, he left me standing awkwardly in the middle of the room.

After they filled the sorry excuse for a bathtub and all but one woman departed, I watched her pour some kind of oil into the water before she approached me. She was petite and blonde, a few years younger than I, with a cherubic face and kind eyes.

After she lifted her hands to my wool rent expectantly, I removed it and handed it to her after depositing my pack on the floor in the corner.

"I'm Maeve, milady, and I'll be helpin' with yer bath. Mrs. Cook said someone attacked ye in the wood today. Ye're lucky Colin found ye." While she chatted away, she brushed the largest chunks of dried mud and debris from the wool into the fire. "It can be verra dangerous for a bonnie lass such as yerself to be alone in the wood, especially during a solstice." Turning back to me, she gaped at my legs. "What kind of trews are ye wearin', lass? With yer assets draped like they are, ye'll cause a scandal for sure!"

The first stirrings of unease tapped lightly at the back of my mind. No one could keep up an act like this all day long without a slip-up or two. It was too bizarre.

"They're Levi's," I muttered, and backed towards the wall. When I felt the seat of the recessed window against the small of my back, I spun around, yanked the shutters open, and searched the horizon.

There was nothing but black country under the purple sky of twilight. There were no lights save for the small torches carried by sentries walking along the top of the wall that ringed the castle. No cars raced along the highway on the other side of the loch. No ambient light from the small town I knew to be just south of here.

I fumbled with the latch of the window and swung the glass open so I could lean out. Lifting my panicked gaze to the heavens, I took in the smattering of bold stars in the sky when it was still too early in the evening to see so many. Fear tickled its way up my spine with icy fingers and pebbled my skin unpleasantly.

Reluctantly, I abandoned the window and returned my attention to the girl. The *handmaid*—not an actress—looked at me with patient expectance and gestured to the waiting tub. With cold, shaky fingers, I numbly untied my damp boots and kicked them off next to the fire to dry further. While I undressed, I ignored her slight gasp when she caught sight of my bikini briefs and bralette. Naked and abashed, I stepped into the steaming water and gingerly sat down.

With my knees tucked tightly to my chest, I resigned myself to Maeve's care, and barely felt her hands in my hair while she picked out the little twigs and threads of moss. She cleaned the dirt from under my ragged nails, trimmed the split lengths with a small pair of scissors, and scrubbed my back and shoulders. Handing me the cloth, she allowed me some privacy to finish the rest. I faintly registered the rising steam smelling of rosemary and lavender; the combination meant to relax.

It failed miserably.

Maeve kept up a constant chatter the whole time she sudsed my hair and rubbed my scalp. I made noncommittal responses, staring vacantly into the fire, and when she rinsed my hair with the last bucket of clean water, I conceded to the obvious.

I wasn't sure how it happened, but I didn't think I was in the twenty-first century any longer.

Wrapped in soft linen that covered me from shoulder to toe, Maeve ushered me to sit sideways in the wing-backed chair. There, she gently untangled the snarled ends of my hair with a wooden comb before running it along my scalp in smooth strokes, carefully avoiding the shallow cut at my hairline. After she swapped the comb for a boar bristle brush, it wasn't long before my tresses were dry, and her nimble fingers had half of the mass pinned away from my face. The rest of it she wove into an intricate braid that rested over my shoulder and secured the ends with a black satin ribbon.

"Now, to find ye somethin' more appropriate to wear," she tutted and began opening the chests.

I ignored the jab and watched her warily as she happily cooed over the fabrics she held out at arm's length. Once she laid a few items on the bed, I crept over to investigate, interest outweighing caution. Soft green silk slid through my fingers, the delicate fabric gliding smoothly against my skin. It was the most beautiful dress I'd ever seen; I had to admit. It wasn't haute couture by any means, but the stitches were fine, and I could tell it would hug the curves of the waist and breast. Maeve eagerly unwrapped me, oblivious to any modesty I may want to keep. Eager to hide my body, I lifted my arms, allowing her to slide a soft cotton sleeveless slip over my head. Next, she tied me into a corset; the boning lengthening my torso and making my small breasts sit higher, giving me the cleavage no Victoria's Secret bra had ever achieved. Buttery cream-colored stockings cinched with lace stays caressed my legs high up my thighs, and soft leather slippers protected my feet. Lastly, she settled me into the green dress. Embroidered ivy leaves lined the long sleeves and the low, square décolletage.

I glared longingly at my cotton underwear piled in the corner with my jeans and shirt and sighed. I crossed the line at wearing dirty underwear, so, it looked as though I'd be going commando.

Maeve shooed me towards the mirror with a dreamy grin, and I peered at the reflection, astonished to find a woman I did not recognize. Was it only just this morning that a girl stared back? It seemed like weeks had passed since I last stood in my grandmother's house.

"You've transformed me, Maeve. Thank you."

She beamed at me and softly clapped her hands. Ushering me out of the room, she directed me down to the great hall before the door shut in my face with a click.

With my heart hammering in my chest, I wandered down the hallway feeling both equally terrified and curious, and couldn't help but wonder if I left a piece of myself behind.

CHAPTER 6

Colin

After leaving Meggie with her maid, Colin ducked into his chamber within the barracks and splashed cool water over his face before donning a clean shirt and his boots.

"Hunting is a time to be barefoot, no' the supper table," his mother had lectured more than once. Eventually, the lesson had sunk in.

Laughter greeted him in the hall when he cut his way through the growing crowd towards the great hearth dais.

"I heard ye found yerself a wee banshee while checking yer traps today," the master-at-arms joked. Bushy, red eyebrows wagging, Magnus lounged in one of the many chairs facing the roaring fire and handed Colin a tankard of mead.

After taking a long sip, he said, "Aye, that I did. Saved her from bein' preyed upon by two evildoers. The wee thing has the courage of a cornered wildcat, I tell ye."

Colin recalled the way Meggie's lovely face morphed from terror to determination just before she let the first stone fly from her hand. Fascinated as he was, there was barely enough time to throw his spear before the miscreant set upon her again. For that, he sent up a small prayer of thanks to God for giving him the speed it took to catch up. His blood boiled at the thought of what would have happened to her if he had not been checking his snares in that corner of the wood when she raced by.

He may have told Meggie he didn't enjoy killing them, but their deaths wouldn't weigh on his conscience. Why men that took pleasure in such things were allowed to walk the earth, he would never understand. Men should cherish and protect women, not terrorize and abuse them. With a mental shake, Colin shoved away his dark thoughts and turned his focus back to Magnus.

"We're goin' out on patrol in the morn. I want ye with me and seven of yer best men. We're goin' hunting. They were too close to the keep for my liking, and they carried no supplies, which means their camp is nearby. There could be more." His announcement earned grunts of agreement from the few men gathered in front of the fire. "Tell yer chosen soon if ye dinnae have appropriate volunteers. We dinnae need them deep in their cups, and useless come daybreak."

Magnus gave a sharp nod and set out towards the barracks. Two hardened men who heard Colin's order followed in his wake.

The hall continued to fill with families, and they crowded the trestle tables the maids had assembled for the occasion. A minstrel strummed his lute while he leaned against the hearth, taking advantage of the heat. A few children gathered at his feet. From the stairwell leading to the kitchens, several women entered carrying baskets loaded with bread and stew in large pots. They passed around flagons of watered mead, and everyone took a seat.

Colin settled to the right of Malcolm's customary seat at the head of the laird's table and waved away the bold farmer's boy who hoped to snatch the vacant seat at Malcolm's left.

"The lass has decided to stay. She's in the blue room," he said, gauging his brother's reaction. Moments passed while Malcolm drank his wine and surveyed the room in silence from under his brows before settling his attention upon Colin.

"If that is what ye wish." Nodding his approval, he took a bite of brown bread dipped in the thick broth.

Colin loaded his own trencher up with stew and hungrily dug in.

Conversation flowed freely, jokes were told, stories shared, and a few villagers sought an audience with their laird. Colin reclined in his seat and was content to eavesdrop on the surrounding conversations when his brother lightly gripped his shoulder.

"Yer wood-sprite is a changeling, brother," Malcolm whispered, inclining his head toward the stairs behind him.

A changeling indeed, Colin thought while he watched Meggie descend the last few steps into the crowded hall. Gone was the bedraggled lass with the strange clothing. In her place was a captivating vision in silk. She walked with confidence, her back straight but her face soft. Standing to catch her attention, he made his way around the table and pulled the chair out for her.

"Thank you." She smiled at the spread of food. "This looks delicious."

Colin resumed his seat and watched her rip the top off of a small loaf and fill it with the stew before she leaned to the side and placed her fingertips on Malcolm's forearm.

"Thank you for the use of a room. I feel so much better without that tree stuck in my hair."

"Our mother's chamber is yers to use as long as ye need it," he affirmed.

Her hand flew to her chest. "Your mother's room…" She looked down at her dress. "Are these her clothes, too?"

Malcolm wiped his mouth with a linen napkin and nodded, rising from his seat. "'Twas Colin's decision, lass," he declared, and left the table to roam the floor and greet those who were too timid to approach him on their own.

"When does your mom return? I'm sure she'll want her space back." Meggie smoothed the silken fabric on her lap, and Colin gave her a sad smile.

"She willnae be comin' back. She died some five years ago from fever. Our father followed her shortly after." He rested his weight over his forearms on the table. "'Tis good to see her fine clothes worn again. She was a kind soul, and she would have insisted ye had somethin' lovely to wear during yer stay. Besides, if ye strutted around in those breeks much longer, I dare say there'd be a riot," he teased, and filled both of their goblets up with Malcolm's full-bodied wine.

She laughed half-heartedly, a quick *ha, ha,* and rolled her eyes. Her sass was unexpected but was a much welcome change from the blushing, quiet lasses who rarely strayed from the appropriate.

"I noticed they attracted some attention," she muttered. Setting her fork down, she leaned back and set the full weight of her beguiling eyes on him.

They were truly captivating. Surrounded by thick, long lashes, one was a deep mossy green and the other a clear morning blue. A charming smattering of the faintest freckles spread across the bridge of her small nose and the apples of her pink cheeks. He thought he could happily lose himself in that gaze of hers.

"How old are you, Colin?" she asked as she fiddled with the faceted stone in her ear, the gesture hinting at some nervousness.

"'Tis my twenty-sixth summer."

Nodding, she observed the rafters high above and touched each of her fingers to her thumbs as though she were doing sums.

"And that would make you born year…"

"Sixteen thirty-two," he said helpfully. His smile faltered when the blood drained from her face.

Clearing her throat, she repeated the present year soundlessly before draining her cup of wine and then peered into the empty flagon. Huffing annoyance, she reached across the table for his and stared into the dark red liquid a moment before drinking it all in one go.

She was staring at the empty space between them, not focusing on anything in particular, when she asked, "Have you ever been to the caves above the fairy pools, Colin? It's close to where those men came across me."

"I ken of them," he said warily, curious why she switched topics so quickly and to the caves of all places.

Many a story was told by the minstrels and local villagers about those caves—stories of both adventure and death. When he was a young lad, he dared to enter them a few times, and found nothing but darkness, damp rock, and slithering things.

"I wanted to see them, but they chased me before I had the chance. Would you take me?" Her imploring eyes locked on his own.

She could coax a fox from its den with that stare, he mused.

"If I deem the land safe on the morrow, I will take ye the day after if ye wish," he promised.

He'd promise her anything to chase that guarded, anxious look from her face.

When the meal was over and cleared away, the minstrel sat down upon the two steps leading up to the hearth and bent over his lute to play a beautiful, mournful melody. At the strum of the first few chords, the hall fell quiet.

Eager to speak to her without the table between them, Colin took Meggie's hand and led her to a bench against the wall to watch.

"Do ye ken Gaelic lass?"

"Not much, unfortunately."

Smiling at his good fortune, he slid closer to her, and their thighs nearly touched when he bent down to whisper in her ear.

Pleased that he sufficiently captivated the attention of all in the room, the minstrel began to sing his tale.

"This is the tale of a young lass that was singin' near the loch and stolen by the Morag." Colin softly echoed the minstrel's words translated to English. "Takin' her to his home in the depths, he kept her there, for he was captivated by her lovely voice. He bid the young lass sing to him each night, and as the years went by, the lass grew into a beautiful woman. The Morag fell deeply in love and found he could no' keep her captive any longer. He released her back to the shore and retreated, broken-hearted and alone, to the murky depths of the loch. But even though the beautiful woman was happy to be above the surface again, she returned each sunset to wade in the shallows and sing for him… for she also loved the Morag."

When Colin finished the story, Meggie turned to face him, her lips mere inches from his own.

"I feel sad for them," she whispered.

"Why?" he scoffed. "She's free, and he still gets to enjoy her singin'."

"Because they love one another, but they're from different worlds, so they can't be together… it's depressing." Looking down into her lap, she sighed. "I find I can imagine how they both feel."

"Och, 'tis just a story." He chuckled.

The entertainment changed course to bawdy ditties that had the room singing along and clapping, and the villagers cleared and area to dance and reel.

"Dance with me, sweet Meggie." Standing, Colin tugged on her hand and grinned when she blushed, her eyes wide. She shook her head.

"I don't know the steps; I couldn't. I'd flatten your feet if I tried, I swear."

"My feet are tough. Come," he insisted and pulled her up to stand.

She looked toward the group of revelers hesitantly before taking a deep breath.

"Fuck it. Let's go."

Laughter erupted from his chest in surprise at her speech before he led her into the fray.

She did stomp on his toes more than once, but it was worth the opportunity to goad her over it, earning himself a ribbing in return. Meggie was a quick learner, and once she relaxed, he was pleased with how spirited she became. By the third song, her lovely sable-brown hair had come undone from their pins and ribbons to bounce wildly down her back while she skipped on her slippered feet.

She had a generous laugh that was infections and well-suited. No coy, subdued giggle that fine bred ladies were wont to have, oh no. Hers was but one that came from deep inside, boisterous and with abandon.

Cheeks flushed from wine and exertion, she quickly charmed everyone in the room. With that, unfortunately, propriety had Colin reluctantly turning her over to other men that asked for a dance. Practically scowling at each who dared to claim a turn, he soon found himself alone on the perimeter of the dancing circle when Malcolm appeared beside him.

"Ye have a look on yer face that would set fire to auld Dougray if ye glowered any harder, brother," Malcolm said. With his arms crossed over his broad chest in his customary way, he followed Colin's stare towards the sixth man to dance with Meggie and huffed a laugh. "He's thirty years her senior; I doubt he's competition."

Colin grunted, unappeased.

"I thought I'd take a turn myself," the laird taunted, and then held his hands up in mock surrender before Colin's menacing glare. "Peace, brother. I jest."

"Ye better be," Colin grumbled and watched the English lass laugh at something Dougray said.

"They're only doin' it to get a rise out o' ye. Well, besides poor Donnel over there." Malcolm snickered and pointed at a youth of fourteen who mooned over Meggie like a love-sick pup while she twirled around the floor. Malcolm shrugged and scratched at the one day's growth of beard that shadowed his chin in thought. "Ye ken, I widnae be surprised if there was a certain wager on when ye'd cave and whisk her away."

Colin slowly turned an accusatory look at the MacKinnon laird before surveying the men around the room.

They widnae dare; he thought. Catching conspiring smirks from many of the men, they quickly averted their eyes and pretended to find interest elsewhere whilst covering their grins.

"What was yer bet then? Out with it." Colin sighed, and shifted on the balls of his feet. He should have known his brother would encourage something like this.

"Och, I may or may no' have placed a silver coin on the end of this verra song," Malcolm drawled.

"Yer a cheatin' bastard, ye are." Colin snarled and pointed a finger at his brother's puckish grin. "Ye'll split the winnings with me!" he called over his shoulder and pushed through the dancing partners when the last notes of the minstrel's song drifted to an end.

"Come, lass," he growled, shifting her away from yet another fellow intent on a dance and pegged him with a glare.

Booming laughter echoed in the hall as he hurried Meggie through the keep's open doors and under the canopy of the oak tree. Its thick branches stretched far and allowed a tiny bit of privacy from the prying eyes of the watchmen on the wall. Breathing hard, Meggie tipped her head back, clearly enjoying the chill of the night, an infectious smile gracing her lips.

"I haven't had this much fun in years," she breathed. Holding her arms out, she twirled slowly before him. "I shouldn't be having the time of my life, but I am. What does that say about me?"

He shook his head. "Why dinnae ye deserve to be happy?"

"Why indeed," she sighed, her words as soft as the light breeze. She stopped twirling to sway before him, the musical notes still moving within her.

The light thrown off from the torch flames played purple and orange shadows over her face as her breathing slowed and her gaze dropped to his lips. Colin's focus snapped to attention, and he took a small step closer to her.

"Ye like what ye see, lass?" he asked, his voice thick.

Her lovely neck mottled in embarrassment at being caught staring, and she turned her face away shyly. Reaching out, he cupped her cheek, urging her to look at him again, and advanced close enough to feel the heat of her body.

"I like that ye look. I dinnae want ye to ever stop."

She swallowed and sucked her bottom lip between her perfect teeth.

"You're easy to look at," she confessed and tucked a lock of hair behind her ear.

Colin tracked each movement. Every breath. She was an enigma, a lovely mixture of subdued and sultry. He never knew what was going to come out of her mouth next, and he found that he didn't want to know, for that would dilute half of what he found so appealing about her.

"I want to kiss ye, Meggie. I've never wanted to kiss anyone more." He slipped his fingers into the hair at her nape. "Would ye let me?"

Thick, sooty lashes fell fan-like over her cheeks, and her lips parted invitingly when Colin closed the gap between them. His lips barely touched hers before she seemed to shake herself awake and pulled away.

"I can't," she breathed and pressed her palm flat against his chest, stepping back. "I'm leaving soon, and I'm afraid one kiss from you wouldn't be enough."

Colin hid his disappointment with a lopsided grin.

"Would that be such a bad thing?"

"Maybe, maybe not." Her middle and pointer fingers brushed lightly over her lower lip. "But I'm not sure I want to find out."

Colin took her small hand in his and pressed a kiss to her knuckles. "Ye've put a spell on me, Meggie."

She laughed and pulled her hand away with a devastating smile that ignited an intense heat within his chest.

"And now, you're mine…" she said, her voice taking on a musical tone as she walked away from him.

He stood there, under the shadows of the oak tree, and surveyed the soft sway of her hips as she climbed the steps back into the keep to rejoin the revelers inside.

Colin was powerless at holding back his smile when he whispered, "Aye, I do believe I am."

CHAPTER 7

Meggie

I woke warm and comfortable, huddled under heavy blankets, the grey light of early morning forcing its way between my eyelids. I continued to lay there, blinking sleepily at the dark wood ceiling for a few moments before I remembered where I was.

Or more like *when* I was.

June 1658. It must have happened in that blasted cave. How, I'm sure I could ponder for the rest of my life and never find the answer to, but it seemed going back to them was my only chance at getting home. I pinched my arm for the dozenth time since last night and resigned myself to the fact that this was real.

I'd fallen through time when I fell into the cave. It was a surreal feeling, to know without a doubt that time-travel was possible, but I wasn't sure if it was excitement or dread that made my heart beat faster.

Rising from the bed, I pulled one of the blankets around my shoulders and padded on bare feet to the fireplace. Poking through the ashes, I found a few embers still alive, and after adding kindling and a split log from the niche set into the wall, the room warmed up rather quickly.

I bounced on the balls of my feet, staring at what could only be a chamber pot in the corner of the room for a good half hour before I relented, mortified. Why couldn't a garderobe connect to this room? I had no idea where it was located on this floor and was reluctant to wander around in my thin nightgown sans undergarments for anyone to see. *Third world problems*, I thought, and chuckled to myself as I took care of business.

With a tray in her arms, Maeve found me curled in the high-backed chair a short while later. She greeted me happily, obviously a morning person, and I found I couldn't begrudge her that, even though I was not. She set the small tray of tea and breakfast biscuits on the low table next to my chair. Pouring me a cup, she handed it to me before making the bed and fussed over my pillows.

"You don't have to do that," I chided.

She spun around with wide, offended eyes.

Clearly, I had made a mistake.

"The laird would be most upset, milady. He ordered me to take care of ye and take care of ye I will," she insisted with a nod of her head, dismissing my outburst. Opening one of the many chests tucked against the wall, she pulled out a few wool gowns. "They'll have to be taken in at the waist, and a few are out of style, but they're of a fine cut and will do ye in a pinch. The laird's mother was a fine lady, too, and ye'll do them proud."

I opened my mouth to tell her I was very far from a lady but thought better of it. I had to take my blessings where I could get them, and I was only going to be here another day anyhow.

Maeve chatted away about what improvements the seamstress could make to the dresses while she discreetly peeked at the unpleasant chamber pot. Laying a square of fabric that she pulled from her apron pockets over the top, she took it swiftly out of the room and returned a few minutes later to set it back in its proper place.

I nibbled a biscuit as I watched her air out the gowns, inspecting each for flaws like she hadn't just handled my pee.

Well, if she could be an adult about it, so could I.

Finished with my breakfast, I sat beside her on the bed. Maeve was a pretty girl with impish grey eyes and full, pouty lips. Light blonde hair pinned close to her neck peeked out from under a white cap. She wore a grey wool dress, much like the one she was cataloging from the chests. I ran my hands down the spun fabric, smoothing out wrinkles. She smiled at me and began to help me dress.

This would take some getting used to. I wanted to chase her out of the room and dress myself but didn't know the first thing about tying a corset, and I wasn't about to offend her again.

Once appropriately clothed, I wiggled my toes in the soft leather slippers on my feet and ran my fingers along the stitching of the dove grey sleeves. Maeve had brushed my hair and braided the heavy mass back, winding and looping the length before securing it at my nape. Giving me a once over, she nodded in approval before breezing away on some unknown task.

Unsure what to do with myself until I could get back to my own time, I wandered the many halls of the keep until I found myself in the kitchen.

"Good morning, Mrs. Cook," I chirped, greeting the plump woman as she was sorting herbs. She barely gave me a cursory glance as she continued her work.

"If ye say so. Did ye enjoy yerself last night, lass?" the older woman grumbled.

I could tell she only asked out of politeness, and I was tempted to flee her domain but decided against it. I only had so long here, and the inner workings of a seventeenth-century kitchen piqued my interest.

"I did, thank you."

Sliding up next to her, I began picking up random bunches from a large pile on the long wooden table. Comfrey, mint, oregano, and fennel were all staples in my own kitchen. I fingered a thin stalk with a wand of purple flowers curiously.

"Is this hyssop? That's a strange one for the kitchen. What do you use it for?"

The cranky cook twisted sharply towards me, and the barest of smiles tugged at her thin lips.

"Ah, the lass knows her herbs. Indeed, I use it for ailments and the like. If ye've the ague, ye be sure to come to me for a good strong draught." Shaking a sprig of rosemary at me, she prattled on.

Happy to be the recipient of herbal knowledge, I helped her sort through the pile, enjoying the mindless task. She told me of her extensive garden in the south bailey where she transplanted and cultivated many of the herbs she uses in her kitchen, and because of that effort, very little needed foraging besides mushrooms and berries.

Poking around her spotless cookery, I found the buttery filled with baskets of root vegetables. Sacks of oats, flour, and unrefined sugar lined wooden shelves and braided ropes of onions and garlic hung from hooks in the rafters. Butter sat waiting in thick clay crocks as well as aging wheels of cheese wrapped in waxed cloth. Everything neatly arranged and categorized, the room was clean and tidy.

Gently closing the door behind me, I ran my fingers along the whitewashed stone wall on my way back to the table where a serving girl busily plucked the feathers out of two geese and stored the downy tufts in a linen sack.

"Are they for supper tonight, Mrs. Cook?" I asked as she looked up from where she was tying her herbs up to dry.

"Aye. On the spit they go to roast. Do ye ken much about cooking?" She looked at me dubiously, and I nearly jumped for joy at her question.

"Would you allow me to make you something?" I hoped she would say yes as her beady blue eyes scrutinized me. I wasn't relishing the idea of wandering around all day alone.

"I run a tight kitchen." She plunked her hands on her hips, her face stern and serious. "Ye can do as ye please, but ye'll clean up after yerself or I'll box yer ears."

Nodding eagerly in agreement, I rolled up my sleeves as high as they would go and pulled my lips between my teeth to keep myself from laughing. I swear I felt my Nan's spirit in the crotchety old woman glaring at me.

"Yes ma'am. Can I make a dessert for after the evening meal?"

"Aye, if ye can manage." Waving at the assortment of bowls and baking pots, she gave me a workspace and left me to it.

Charged with excitement of trying my craft without the use of a convection oven and measuring spoons, I busied myself with planning, and the hours slipped by as I navigated the room, smelling ingredients and weighing them by hand.

I felt the stare of the cook on my back as I vigorously beat egg whites and sugar together before folding in the almonds I had ground into a powder with the mortar and pestle. After adding a small amount of blackberry syrup, I carefully spooned the mixture into a boiled pig intestine that was destined for sausage wraps.

After borrowing a silver wedding ring from one of the kitchen maids, some practice, and a few curses that shocked the sensitive ears of those around me, I was able to pipe two-inch disks onto clay plates lined with parchment paper. Sweating slightly in the warm room, I tucked a few strands of hair behind my ear that curled into my eyes as I watched over the macaron cookies baking in the bread oven like a hawk, gingerly turning the plates every thirty seconds until I was satisfied they were done.

With care, I slid the paper off the plates to cool on the table and turned my attention back to the pestle. Spooning in sugar crystals, I worked them into a fine powder. The very air in front of me shimmered like diamond dust in the early afternoon sunlight that slowly crept along the cobbled floor from the high windows, dusting my skin with its sweetness. Retrieving the sweet cream and butter, I transferred some into a clean bowl, folding in all but a small bit of the fine powdered sugar, and whipped them into high peaks until my shoulders ached and my hand cramped.

"Do you happen to have vanilla beans?" I asked the cook as she leaned over my workspace and inspected the purple-tinted puffs, her lip slightly curled up.

"Aye, a traveling merchant passed by some months ago with spices from London. The aroma is wonderful, but I huvnae a clue about how to use them. Anythin' I've made with them turns bitter and ruined," she admitted with a shake of her head, took down an earthenware jar from a shelf, and expose the dark, sticky beans nestled within.

"Yes, they're bitter in excess. You know, my mother used them to teach me about lies when I was a little girl. She had me smell the vanilla extract, which she called 'the lie,' and asked me if it smelled nice. Of course, it smelled wonderful, but the real lesson began when she poured a few drops in my mouth." I shook my head and shivered in disgust at the memory. "It was just awful, and I was shocked and upset that she did that to me. The bitterness sat heavily on my tongue, and it lingered for an hour. She told me that's how my lies taste to others, so I should never tell them. It was a lesson I never forgot."

"A wise woman, yer mother. I believe I'll be using her approach from now on," she whispered as she cast a side-eye to a group of children exiting the kitchen.

Grinning, I plucked a bean out of the jar.

"For now, I'll just grind up a small cutting, but we'll make some extract when I'm done here. All you need is whiskey, a jar, and some patience."

Pinching off the very end of a bean, I tossed it into a smaller pestle and ground it down. Wiping up the brown paste with my finger, I added it to the buttercream frosting. A taste test moments later had me moaning softly, the flavor playing tiny explosions of sweet-tasting pleasure on my tongue, and I winked at the ladies giggling at the other side of the table. I had attracted a small audience, necks craning in interest but still unwilling to get too close lest they incite the wrath of Mrs. Cook.

After rinsing out the intestine as carefully as I could in a bowl of fresh water, I spooned in the frosting and gave every other cookie a generous dollop before making the sandwiches. Setting them all together, I sifted the last of the powdered sugar over the tops of the macarons through a cheesecloth, giving them all a light dusting.

"The first one's for you," I urged, handing a completed puff to the cook. She inspected it between her fingers before taking a small bite.

"Och, this... this is…" Abandoning all speech, she cooed over the cookie and took the time to devour it bit by bit. Leaning my hip against the edge of the table, I beamed at her obvious pleasure.

"What else can ye make?" she laughed, licking her fingers one by one.

We spent the rest of the afternoon together, each of us sharing in our love of cooking while we prepped the evening meal of roasted goose with blackberry glaze and steamed carrots drizzled with honey. I recommended mashed turnips and potatoes seasoned with garlic and rosemary, and a honey-cinnamon butter I whipped up to go with her soft brown bread.

An hour before supper, she expelled me from the heat of the kitchen to clean myself up, and several calls of thanks followed me up the stairs.

My steps light with happiness at spending the day doing what I loved as well as making a friend, I slipped into the blue room and threw myself on the bed. With my arms stretched out, I watched the dust motes dance in the yellow-orange light that flooded the open window, the lazy golden swirls riding the slight breeze. It was only a few minutes later that Maeve appeared. Preceded by a soft knock and a pitcher of hot water, she nudged the door closed with the bump of her hip. If I didn't know any better, I'd think there was an intercom or surveillance cameras in this castle, because she wasn't in the kitchen, and I didn't spy her on my way up here.

"Do you have some kind of sixth sense?" I joked. Lifting my head from the furs, I watched her pour the water into the basin in the corner.

Her shoulders hiked up, and she looked at me, wide-eyed and wary.

"I am no witch, milady."

Cursing my big mouth, I hopped up from the bed and hurried to take her hand.

"No. No, that's not what I meant." Her hand shook slightly between my own, and I squeezed her fingers, trying to convey my sincerity. "I only wondered how you knew I was up here. That's all. I do not think you're a witch."

She nodded, her focus on the floor as she pulled her hand from mine and smoothed her apron.

"No harm then, milady," she muttered as she moved to the fireplace to coax flames from the coals, her shoulders stiff.

Unconvinced, I knelt beside her.

"Please forgive me, Maeve." My request was soft in the quiet room.

"Aye, milady. I forgive ye." She nodded, a small smile on her lips as she rose and ushered me to stand near the basin so that she could help me out of my corset and woolen dress.

Clicking her tongue at the powdered sugar that streaked the bodice, she smirked at me as she brushed it off.

"I heard ye impressed the cook today. I must say, 'tis no' an easy feat. She's a hard woman to please."

Mollified that she accepted my apology, I flashed a triumphant smile and stood there in my cotton shift while she pulled out another dress for the evening meal. Satisfied with her choice of gowns, she gave it a quick shake and laid it on the bed.

"That she is, but the key to her heart is definitely in her stomach, much like a man."

"Speaking of men," Maeve began as she dipped a cloth into the water and sponged my forearms, my hands, and rubbed at the blackberry stains at my cuticles. "There is talk that Colin stole a kiss last eve." After a quick peek at me from under her golden brows, she returned her attention to my nails.

I gaped at her. That was hardly a kiss. It was barely a brush of lips.

"Um… how did you hear that?"

"The guard on duty patrolling the wall last eve is married to the laundress. She told the seamstress when she picked up the lairds' new shirts this morning," she explained with a shrug.

"And I assume the seamstress told you?" I drawled, annoyed that gossip, even made-up gossip, seemed to travel just as fast here, even without the help of social media.

"Och, no. The seamstress only confirmed what I heard from the stable boy." Giggling to herself, Maeve abandoned the cloth and crossed to the bed, holding out the dress.

Shaking my head at all busybodies in the world, I decided it was pointless to correct the mistake and stepped into the buttercup yellow creation she chose for me.

White pleated lace capped the three-quarter length sleeves, tickling my forearms as I moved. Cut low and square, the bodice was plain and unadorned of embellishments save for a thick band of the same lace at the dip of my waist. A bow was tied and left to dangle along my lower back. Lace overlaid buttons fastened down my spine to close me in. With a glance in the mirror, I was once again impressed as Maeve slipped a thin strand of freshwater pearls over my head to rest low at my throat. Yet another exquisite ensemble, courtesy of a woman I would never meet. Giving a silent thanks to the woman with good taste, I sat on the edge of the bed while Maeve unpinned my hair. While she brushed out my long tresses, I leaned back into her touch, the strokes a splendid scratch on my scalp. Pinning the top up again, she braided the length in a simple plait and let it rest over my shoulder, tying it off with yet another ribbon. She left me then after bobbing a curtsey and promised to return to help me undress later.

Walking over to the open window beside my bed that faced the loch, I leaned out, the slight breeze caressing my face as I looked out on the water. The sun was low and mirrored on its surface; the slight peaks of wind-made waves washed in bright gold. There was no smog line on the horizon or con trails of airplanes. No cell towers to mar the beautiful sunset.

Tomorrow, Colin would take me back to the caves. Back to Nan. Back to electricity, to telephone wires running parallel to highways, and miles upon miles of blacktop and concrete.

Unsure why I suddenly felt regretful, I pushed those thoughts away and left for the great hall, my stomach grumbling with anticipation of a good meal.

I wasn't leaving yet; there was no sense in not enjoying this beautiful world every moment until I did.

CHAPTER 8

Meggie

"**M**ore wine, lass?"

My host held up the flagon in question. The dining hall was much more intimate tonight, with white candles running down the center of the long table set for six.

With a nod, I held out my pewter chalice, and Malcolm poured the red liquid dangerously close to the rim, grinning fiendishly at me when I gave a little squeal. I quickly sipped the excess wine before it spilled over and stained my dress.

"Och, ye cannae blame me for bein' over indulgent. 'Tis been a while since I had bonnie company at my table," he murmured over his cup conspiratorially, playfully eyeing the four other men dining with us.

I sat once more to Malcolm's left, a seat that I learned was much coveted. Next to me were Malcolm's cousins, Gavin and then Bram, with Finlay across from them. All three had golden brown hair with soft waving curls, but Bram and Finlay were the most striking. Identical twins, they both had the same bright sea-green eyes, with their hair cut in the same style; short in the back and left longer in front to sweep their brows. A playful bunch, the cousins regaled the table with their adventures. Tales wildly exaggerated but entertaining, they often finished one another's sentences with a slap on the back or a sharp kick under the table. Their booming laughter was infectious and echoed in the large room.

Laughing more at them than with them, I glanced cautiously at the quiet, dark-haired man who sat across from me. Colin and his cadre hadn't yet come back from their patrol—much to my disappointment—and in his place sat the neighboring laird's son, Baen Murray.

He was a stuffy man, a year or two older than Malcolm, in his early thirties. Inky black hair framed a face that would have been handsome if it wasn't for the permanent lift of his thin upper lip, as though he took offense to everything and everyone around him. Rarely cracking a smile, Baen sipped his ale and contributed little to the merry conversation. Shrewd brown eyes so dark they seemed black scrutinized me as we waited for the meal to be served.

Refusing to let him see me squirm, I ignored him and turned my attention toward Malcolm.

"Mrs. Cook has a special meal prepared tonight. I spent some time with her today, and we came up with a menu a bit different from what you're used to. I hope you like it."

"Do ye often perform the duties of a scullery maid?" Baen asked, his cruel, reedy voice thick with condescension.

I decided right then and there that I did not like this man. Besides the fact that he was a total douchebag, the very energy that radiated off him warned me to stay clear.

"Meggie is my guest, Baen. She may do what she will, and with my blessing," Malcolm cautioned with a piercing stare before I could muster a response.

Unruffled, Baen only shrugged and directed his attention toward the maids that appeared with trays of food.

Each woman gave me a little smile as they deposited their burden and hurried back downstairs. As I had hoped, the aroma of each dish mingled in the air perfectly.

My mouth watering, I refrained from serving myself until Malcolm took from the platter of roast goose, carved and arranged beautifully with blackberry preserves lightly drizzled on top.

While I filled my plate with a little of everything, I listened to the quiet sounds of men completely involved in their meal. Even the rowdy threesome to my left were practically inhaling what they had piled in front of them, and reached for a second helping before I had finished half of my own. Pleased and proud of this little victory, I couldn't wait to share with Mrs. Cook how the laird and his guests enjoyed the meal.

"*What* is in this butter?" Malcolm spoke out of the side of his mouth, the opposite cheek stuffed with brown bread and Texas Roadhouse inspired butter. "It's delicious."

"It's a secret recipe." Covering my mouth to hide my mirth, I caught the heavy stare of the man in front of me once more.

Baen chewed slowly, his scrutiny slithering down my neck to focus on my breasts before agreeing with our host.

"Indeed," he drawled, his gaze heavy and unwanted on my body.

His lips turned up slightly, and I broke his stare before my disgust showed on my face. Uncomfortable, my food turned to a lump of wet paper in my mouth.

In the twenty-first century, I would have just removed myself from the situation at the very least. And if I was feeling bold, I would have divested my full glass of wine in his face.

Here, in a land where men ruled over women, I couldn't do either, and I felt trapped.

The keep's main doors opened with a crash.

"My laird!"

Colin stormed into the hall ahead of nine men, all slightly bloody but seemingly uninjured, following at his heels. His wild eyes immediately found mine and held my stare for a moment as his powerful kilt-covered thighs ate up the distance to his brother's side. Knotted war braids hung down his temples; the rest of his untamed blond hair left to sweep his shoulders. Dried blood flecked his forearms and his shirt, and dirt dulled the black of his boots. His body tight with irritation, his hands clenched by his side as he stood just behind Baen and spoke to his brother.

"We found a small group of blackguards. I followed the trail from yesterday and tracked them north." He hesitated and looked at me for a moment before he added, "We left none alive."

Jesus. I wanted to ask how many, but kept my mouth shut and tried not to think about what could have happened to me had those two man caught me yesterday.

Malcolm studied his brother's face, and a wordless conversation seemed to pass between them before he turned toward the group of warriors waiting patiently at the threshold.

"Ye've had a long day. Go find yer women and let them give ye what comfort they can." With a knowing smirk on his handsome face, he saluted the group with his chalice and dismissed them. Giving their laird a curt bow as well as a firm nod to Colin, they left us to finish our meal.

"Sit, brother. Sweet Meggie here helped prepare this fine meal. It does no' disappoint."

"Problems on yer land, Malcolm?" Baen asked. Pushing his plate away, he leaned back in his chair, his focus on Colin.

Colin settled next to Finlay, who playfully pounded his back in welcome and pointed to each dish enthusiastically. I peered down the table and watched him load his plate in stone-faced silence.

"Nothing to be concerned about now," Malcolm assured his guest. Draining his wine, the MacKinnon laird peeked into my half-empty glass and smoothly filled it again before tending to his own.

Good grief, I had to be careful around this one.

"'Tis good that ye dispatch law with a heavy fist," Baen droned. "In truth, we worried our southern neighbor had grown soft with yer Sunday suppers."

Silence covered the room like thick smoke as tension radiated from the cousins. Malcolm idly regarded his guest, long fingers circling the rim of his cup like a calculating viper.

Colin's deep voice cut through the silence like a knife.

"Ye always were an arse, Baen. I can see that has no' changed since we were young lads," he drawled. Leaning over his plate, he continued eating; the corded muscled of his forearms drawn tight. It seemed as though Colin disliked the northern laird's son just as much as I did. I imagined Baen was disliked by many people, and was only tolerated because of his station as the son and heir of a more important man.

Baen let out a dark, humorless laugh and pushed away from the table.

"I will retire now. We will talk more on the morrow," he said to Malcolm, even though his focus was wholly on me. Blessedly, he left without another word or even a backward glance as he strode out of the hall.

With a clap of his hands, Malcolm summoned for the meal to be cleared, and we lingered with our wine and ale without the combative presence of Baen Murray. Even the candles seemed to brighten with his absence.

Colin reclaimed his seat across from mine and strummed his fingers on the polished wood in agitation.

"What's that snake doin' here? He's naught but trouble, although he's far preferable to his sire."

"Aye," Malcolm agreed, running his hand behind his neck and over his jaw. "But we're neighbors, and we must work to keep the continued peace between our borders."

Despite his words, the MacKinnon laird looked as though he wanted to do anything other than that very thing. I didn't blame him. After just an hour with Baen Murray, I felt like I needed to hide behind a locked door, take a shower, and gulp down a cup of Nan's special tea. I swore I could still feel his eyes upon my skin.

At that moment, Mrs. Cook delivered dessert with a proud smile on her face, and the cousins greeted her with an applause for the meal. A charming flush reddened her plump cheeks.

"So tasty, my belly is full to bursting," Malcolm boasted, and gave his food baby a pat for emphasis.

"Thank ye, my laird. 'Tis good to know when one appreciates another's hard work, although I cannae take all the credit. The lass has a good nose for her herbs." She set down the silver tray piled pyramid-style with the lavender macarons. "Lady Meggie made these in my cookery today."

Smiling at me, she bobbed a quick curtsey and retreated with a little pep in her step. Five pairs of wide, confused eyes watched her disappear down the stairwell before regarding me with interest.

"What? I like to cook," I confessed.

Waving off the attention, I plucked a cookie off the top of the small pile.

Colin exchanged a look with his brother before he reached for a cookie and popped it whole into his mouth. He chewed twice before releasing a groan and growled a string of words I didn't understand in Gaelic. He reached for two more as Malcolm and the cousins began devouring their own. I giggled to myself. It took me the better part of six hours to make eighteen macarons and these savages ate them in less than two minutes.

My single macaron sat untouched on my plate, the hungry stares of all five men intent on it. I've had dozens in my lifetime, all different flavors. In the twenty-first century, I can make them in under an hour. Here, it takes half a day.

I worried my lower lip between my teeth, knowing once I leave tomorrow, they'll have nothing like it ever again. Decision made, I painstakingly cut my cookie into fifths and passed each man a tiny triangle portion. They rewarded me with a bawdy toast by the cousins, another glass of wine from Malcolm, and a tender look from Colin.

Stuffed, slightly inebriated, and warm from the blazing fire, I excused myself to find my bed.

Malcolm stood and placed a chaste kiss on my cheek. "Thank ye for yer company tonight."

"We can do it again tomorrow," I lied, and winked at him as I headed toward the grand staircase. No doubt, I would cherish these memories when I got back to my own time.

I had just reached the top of the spiral stairwell of the third story residential wing when strong, callused fingers closed over mine. I hid my smile as the gentle touch ignited a flutter in my chest.

"I will never understand how someone so massive can be so silent," I teased and turned to find Colin looming over me as he ascended the last step, his face unreadable in the faint candlelight.

Reaching up, I ran my fingers down the tangled braid resting against his temple and over the tiny specks of dried blood that dotted his right cheekbone. Upon seeing those dark flecks, my smile faded.

"I'm glad you're safe," I whispered.

"Ye worried about me?" His mouth turned up in a seductive grin, and he slowly stalked forward, giving me no choice but to retreat.

My breath hitched, his height making it impossible to look at his face without craning my neck, as close as he was. His presence nearly overwhelmed me, and my thoughts jumbled as I tried not to imagine what his powerful body was capable of.

"Only a little," I taunted. Gently holding him back at arm's length, I stepped backward in the darkened hallway.

His muscled chest leaped to life under my fingertips as he continued forward, guiding me to the decorated door of the blue room one step at a time. A soft growl hummed low in his throat, and I felt the vibrations of it under my fingertips when my back pressed against the polished wood. His arms came up, caging me in, his fists on the door I leaned against.

"What are you doing?" I gasped, anticipation heating my cheeks.

His intense stare bore into mine, holding me captive.

He smelled of the forest and of the sea. The pine and salt scent of him drifted around me as he leaned in. My hands, no longer holding him back, dragged down his chest in defeat when he pushed ever closer. I gripped his shirt on either side of his thick torso, and noted the muscle warm beneath my knuckles. He dipped his head until his mouth was mere inches from mine.

"Ye were in my thoughts all day, lass, and ye worried for me only a wee bit?" he purred, ignoring my question.

One of his hands slipped toward the hair at my nape. Gripping my braid, he wrapped it once around his wrist and tugged my head back gently. His face was so close to mine, his gaze burned a trail slowly down my face, only to lock on my parted lips.

He was going to kiss me, and I knew I would allow it, too seduced to stop him.

I whimpered when he boldly ran his tongue once along the seam of my lips, his breath sweet from dessert.

It was not nearly enough.

My hands took on a mind of their own, tugging him closer, and my breath came out in shallow pants while I squeezed my thighs together. I'd never been so aroused by a man in my life, and he'd barely touched me.

"I've always been a terrible liar," I said, my voice husky in my own ears.

Anticipation turned into impatience, and I lifted my lips to his, straining against his hold on my braid. He pulled farther away, punishment for my hasty retreat from him last night. I glared at him, and the corner of his mouth pulled up in a sly smile.

"Kiss me," I demanded.

Abandoning my grip on his shirt, I slipped my hands underneath the hem and reached around his back to lightly score his skin with my nails, urging him closer to me.

"*Kiss me.*"

I felt victorious when his smile faded and his eyes grew dark and hooded. He watched me, an intense, near feral look on his face, and with deliberate slowness he lowered his lips to mine.

A low groan rumbled in his chest when my mouth freely opened to his advances, and his control broke. His tongue plundered my mouth, both of his hands now cupping my face, while he devoured me like a man starved.

It was the most amazing kiss I had ever experienced, and I whimpered once more when he tore his lips from mine. Both of us were breathing heavily as we stared at one another in the shadowed hallway.

"Meggie," he murmured, swallowing hard, his jaw clenched tight. He opened his mouth a few times as if to say more, but shook his head, and his focus dropped back to my mouth. Pressing his thumb down my lower lip, a silent demand for them to open, he captured my mouth again. His beard rasped deliciously against the softness of my cheeks. He trailed kisses along my jaw, down my neck, and lit fire to my skin.

I wanted—I *needed*—more. This taste of him was not nearly enough to satisfy his touch. It was an instant addiction.

I ran my hands along his powerful arms, his shoulders, and his chest. His muscles bunched under my exploration. Abandoning my face, his rough hands traveled up and down my silhouette until they gripped my hips.

Bending at the waist, Colin kissed the top swell of my breast, only to still, and his body jerked back slightly in surprise. Drawing away from me, he licked his lips.

"Meggie. Is that…" He dropped his head down again and his tongue eagerly darted out to lap at the soft skin between my breasts. "Is that *sugar*?"

Laughter bubbled out of me, and my hand flew to my mouth as I remembered the powdered sugar that had shimmered in the surrounding air earlier. "Yes?"

"Hmm. Do ye often dust yer skin in such a way?" he teased, and kissed my neck and nipped my earlobe, a smile in his deep voice.

"No," I sighed. My eyelids drifted closed. "But if it gets me this kind of attention, I may need to start." Rubbing my cheek against his short beard, I sought another kiss.

He pushed even closer, nestling one of his powerful legs between my thighs. Pulling the ribbon from the end of my braid, he let it fall to the floor. Quickly, he unraveled the rope and allowed my thick tresses to fall around my shoulders and over my breasts in waves. He rubbed a dark lock between his fingers and lifted it to brush the ends over his lower lip.

"I want this beautiful hair draped over my chest," he said boldly, his lustful focus on my mouth, leaving me little wonder of what he meant.

Dear God, no one's ever said anything like that to me. With my heart beating wildly, and my hormones fighting my every move, I firmly pushed him away before I did something I'd regret. My finger poked the middle of his chest in warning, and I reached for the latch of my door.

"Goodnight, Colin," I whispered, a flirtatious smirk on my kiss-swollen mouth. I backed slowly over the threshold and memorized the carnal look on his face before I closed the door.

Leaning my forehead against the cool wood in the dark, I willed my breathing to slow and ran my fingertips over my kiss-swollen lips. A light knock a minute later had me jumping back in surprise. As much as I wanted him, I was going back to my own time tomorrow and drew the line at amazing kisses.

"Milady, may I come in?" Maeve's voice drifted through the thick wood.

Equally disappointed and relieved, I opened the door to reveal the handmaid holding a candle and a pitcher of water. Colin was nowhere to be seen. She dipped a curtsey before breezing past me, a knowing smile on her face.

"Well, well, well." She cast me a sideways glance and lit the candles on the mantle, dispelling the darkness of the room as I bolted the lock. "If that wasnae the wickedest kiss I've ever seen. I thought he'd swallow ye whole for a moment there," she teased. Fanning her face with her hand, she let out a dreamy sigh while she poured fresh water into the basin.

Jeez, was nothing private in this castle?

"I don't kiss and tell," I simply stated, and spun away to hide my crimson face.

"Och, ye dinnae have to tell me a thing. I saw it all."

CHAPTER 9

Colin

He stared at the door in shock when it clicked shut and had half a mind to break it down to pick up where they left off.

This lass will be the death of me, he thought as he adjusted himself and took a deep, ragged breath.

Meggie's sweet mouth had been so eager and passionate. Her body fit into the hollows of his own, like she was molded just for him.

A feminine throat cleared in the gloom, and Colin spun towards the noise when Maeve strolled down the shadowy hallway, her brow raised haughtily.

"And just *what* do ye think ye're doin' besides attemptin' to ruin the lass's reputation?" she hissed.

Rolling his eyes, he muttered a curse on nosey females and stalked down the hall. Maeve's soft giggling chased after him before she called out for her mistress.

As much as he was irritated, left wanting as he was, she was right. Meggie was not a tavern wench that would toss up her skirts for any man with a coin, and he would not treat her as such.

Back in the great hall, he found his brother sitting alone by the fire.

"Ah, there ye are. I wondered if I'd see ye again this night." Malcolm snickered into his cup when Colin claimed the padded chair beside his.

Resting his elbows on his knees, he rubbed his face roughly before smoothing his beard.

"No' by choice. The wee hellcat left me in the hallway for Maeve to find," he complained, and scowled at his brother's eruption of laughter. Surveying the way flames licked at a newly added log, he let out a long breath.

Malcolm drained his cup, set it aside, and grunted his agreement.

"'Tis probably best she did." His long legs stretched before him as he reclined in the chair, the leather cushioning creaking as he shifted his weight. "Now, tell me what ye found on yer hunt, brother. I ken there is more to be said."

"Much more," Colin confessed. "But I wish that was no' the case."

Wrenching his thoughts away from the beauty sleeping above them, he recalled what he found in the hills.

They had made good time, his nine companions armed and waiting for him at the gatehouse shortly after the first cock crow. Magnus had chosen his cadre well; all eight warriors seasoned and eager for the task at hand. They all knew what they were hunting, and kept a brisk pace through the fog and early morning mist while they followed Colin to the small clearing at the foot of the cliff.

Scavengers had torn the bodies apart, their remains scattered and shredded. No less than they deserved, *Colin thought.*

From there, he followed Meggie's trail for fifteen minutes to the north. Her fear was apparent in the way she had fled from her pursuers. Heedless of dangers, self-preservation was her only goal. Silently seething at how far she had run until he had heard her, his anger heated when he ran his fingers over the tracks.

She fell here, and ripped at the underbrush with her hands to regain her balance. A piece of her shirt hung torn from a dead branch there.

His warriors followed him wordlessly as he navigated the dense brush and open fields until they arrived at a burn downriver from the fairy pools and the very caves she had asked him to take her to.

Crouching low to the ground, Colin scrutinized the prominent track of Meggie's peculiar boot prints that stomped up and down the hill along the water's rocky edge.

Why was she pacing? What was she searching for? *he wondered. Dismissing those questions, for the time being at least, he waded through the rushing water and easily picked up the footprints of his quarry. They were careless with their steps, unhurried and unconcerned on who they may come across on land that was not their own. In Colin's experience, men like that were either very dangerous or very stupid.*

Colin read the soil, moss, and grass like a man possessed. Their prints wandered through the woodlands and pastures as though they were searching for something... or someone.

The fog long ago burned away and the sun nearly reached its zenith as when they pushed through a thicket and finally spied their prey.

The camp was on the top of a low hill thirty yards away among large boulders, with five crude tents circling a smokeless fire. Colin and his group of warriors lay in wait, downwind and in the cover of shadows, patiently checking their weapons or weaving their war braids.

As they watched and waited, they learned the movements of the camp. Magnus counted seven men. Four sat around the fire eating as they talked with one another and two lazed in the sun, leaning against a low boulder, their backs to the thicket. A skinny, seventh man patrolled the outer ring of the camp, paying more attention to the largest tent than his surroundings.

The wind was in Colin's favor, and a soft breeze flowing towards them conveniently carried with it the sounds of the camp. He was contemplating approaching the men civilly when he heard a muffled female cry that someone cut off prematurely. Colin's skin prickled down his spine at the sound.

Magnus gripped his shoulder tightly. He wasn't the only one to hear it then.

"Eight," he whispered, and received slow nods of confirmation in reply. There were at least eight men and one female on the hill above them.

Colin slid his sword from its scabbard and palmed his dirk, the weight of them familiar and welcome. An extension of himself. The soft singing of nine other deadly honed blades as they left their leather sheathes was music to his ears.

Upon the hill, more cries came from the tent, calling the attention of the sentry. Colin and his warriors watched from their shaded cover as the man rushed to open the entrance flap and laugh maniacally before ducking inside. The six others in the camp hadn't seemed surprised or bothered by the cries and laughed amongst themselves.

Colin clenched his teeth as any consideration of extending a civil conversation burned away.

Rage saturated Colin's blood, pumping into his muscles, and h erupted from the cover of the wood. Magnus and his men followed close behind, and spread out on either side of him like a V of geese. Trusting the wind to carry away the sound of their approach, their long, powerful strides ate up the distance. Lunging up the slope, they roared in unison when they entered the perimeter of the camp.

The two men leaning against the rock didn't have a chance, and the snick of Colin's blade opened their throats before they could pull their own weapons to defend themselves. He left them grabbing uselessly at their exposed windpipes while their life's blood rushed from gaping maws to soak their chests.

The four men around the fire had more warning. Flinging down their unfinished food, they quickly armed themselves by the time Magnus and the rest of his men entered the camp circle.

Leaving their deaths for the others, Colin turned toward the largest tent where two men had just exited. One was naked save for his long shirt. Dark eyes crazed, his greasy black hair hung in a tangle around his unshaven face. He held up a rusty short sword, and waved it before him.

Through all the filth, Colin thought he looked vaguely familiar, but quickly brushed the thought away. There was no way he knew this man.

The sentry stood behind the naked madman. His fearful focus was transfixed over Colin's shoulder while he watched his comrades fall one by one around the fire, and Colin witnessed the moment the sentry realized he would share the same fate. A dark spot appeared on his trouser leg, and a telltale puddle of terror formed around his bare foot. A moment later, he turned to flee, and practically slid down the hill in his haste to escape.

"Gunn! Farlan!" Magnus barked when he came to stand in line with Colin. His bloody dirk pointed at the retreating figure of the camp's sentry. "Bring that feckin' coward back alive."

Both men laughed darkly and loped down the hill to fulfill their order, calling out taunts and promises of bloodshed towards their prey.

Whimpers drifted from the tent as Colin stood before his foe. With his feet spread slightly apart and his knees bent, he waited patiently for an opening to end the foul creature in front of him.

"She's mine; I found her," the man spat. His wide, wild eyes darted from Colin to the group of soldiers that circled him. "Ye cannae have her!" he bellowed and swung his sword in reckless arcs; a measly attempt to keep them from advancing closer.

"Enough," Colin growled.

Closing in on the space between them, he deflected a wild swing at his head with his sword. Sparks showered upon the ground from the impact, and Colin neatly plunged his dirk into the soft belly of his opponent.

Rancid breath expelled from between thin, chapped lips before the man fell to his knees. Blood dribbled from his mouth when he looked up. Baring his stained teeth, he began yelling incoherent curses, hatred and madness further darkening his features.

Colin pulled his sword arm back, and with a force that started from his hips, swung his steel, severing the man's head from his shoulders. A warm spray misted one side of Colin's face before the body crumpled to the ground.

Slow and steady, he wiped his weapons on the back of his adversary's soiled shirt before sheathing them at his belt. Stepping over the body, he gently peeled back the flap of the tent and peeked inside. The tent reeked with the scent of fear, and a small, shaking form huddled under a pile of matted furs.

"Lassie," he whispered. "Ye're safe now."

Colin knelt patiently at the tent's threshold, heedless to the sharp rocks that dug into his knees while he waited. Some time passed until a pair of large, fearful brown eyes revealed themselves. His pulse racketed once again with fury. She's only a child, *he realized. Battling to keep his features calm, he ground his fists into the dirt.*

Her wee face revealed swollen and purple bruising from temple to jawline, and her thin bottom lip split in the middle. She couldn't have been much older than her first bleeding. So young. She should still be innocent in the ways of men.

"Ye're safe," he promised, and held out his hand. "Ye ken who I am?"

She nodded once, the dip of her chin nearly imperceptible. Colin managed a small smile.

"Then let me take ye home," he pleaded. "Let me take ye home to yer Da."

She stared at him for some at his outstretched hand, and Colin was prepared to wait as long as it took for her to decide he was not there to harm her. He'd wait all night if he had to.

Then finally, hesitantly, she wrapped her frail body in a thin blanket to hide her nakedness and reached for him. As delicately as he was able, he scooped her up and cradled her against his chest. Standing slowly, he faced his warriors. They cursed, their wrath reigniting, and she buried her small face into Colin's neck as if she could hide from the world. More purple bruises wrapped around her pale wrists and upper arms, stark in the sunlight.

"That was too quick a death for the likes o' him," Banner snarled, his face full of rage. He gave the headless corpse a swift kick. "She's my own daughter's age."

Menace rolled off the men in waves while they glared downhill at the scout trying to escape the iron grips of Farlan and Gunn, the efforts of his scrawny body useless against the enormous warriors. Dragged up the rocky slope, his bare feet were bloody from fleeing over the sharp rocks.

The gutless wretch sobbed and pleaded for his life as soon as they tossed him roughly to the ground in front of the weapons master. He knelt there, in the spreading blood of his comrade, his hands outstretched and palms up.

"What's yer name, coward?" Towering over the snake in the dirt, Magnus's smooth voice carried over the ridge.

"Name's C-Crom, m-milord," he stammered, snot dripping from his hooked nose, and fell silent. That is, until he noticed the shivering bundle in Colin's arms, and his anxiety renewed itself.

"I never touched her, I swear it! I'm innocent!" he howled.

"Lassie. Did this man violate ye?" Magnus asked in a gentle voice Colin had never heard him make before.

Her face pressed harder into Colin's neck, and her hands wrapped around his shoulders with surprising strength before nodding her head. Hugging her closer, Colin gave a nod to Magnus and began carrying her down the hill. Picking his way around the rocks and brush, he found himself humming a lullaby his mother had sung to him when he was a wee bairn.

They slipped into the shelter of the trees when the screaming began.

Colin turned his haunted blue eyes upon his brother and raked his hair away from his face in frustration.

"Before he died, he confessed to traveling with those men for the last few months, taking *wives* to share amongst themselves. They discard them in shallow graves when they either die of injury or from taking their own lives to escape their fate." He gripped the wooden armrest so tight it groaned under his strength. "The lass is the daughter of a shepherd, a tenant on yer land no' but a mile from where they camped. When we returned her to his care, he told us she had gone out in morn with the sheep, and he didnae ken she was missin'. She's only seen twelve summers."

Malcolm brooded as he stared into the fire, his dark brows drawn low and his mouth tight with anger.

"What kind of laird am I that I cannae keep my people safe from monsters like that?"

"'Twas no fault of yer own, brother." Colin clutched Malcolm's shoulder and gave him a firm shake. "They came down from the north. From Laird Murray's land." Refilling Malcolm's chalice, he downed the contents and rose from his seat. "I assume ye'll be visiting the family in the morn?"

"Aye."

Colin left Malcolm with the dying fire and his thoughts, knowing that when his brother was in the mood to brood, there wasn't much that could lift his spirits until he was good and ready.

A fire burned low in the hearth in Colin's chamber. Two buckets of warm water and a small cake of soap atop fresh, folded linens waited for his use. Grateful for the forethought of the castle maids, he undressed and left his soiled clothing beside the door before kneeling as close to the heat of the flames as he dared. Scrubbing himself with the fragrant soap, he lathered his beard and hair before submerging his head fully into a bucket. Water sluiced down his body onto the stone floor when he stood and vigorously dried himself off. Piling more logs on the fire to dry the stone floor with its heat, he slid naked between the white sheets of his bed. Plush furs settled over a wool blanket, their weight a welcomed comfort in the chill evening.

Laying there with his arms behind his head, Colin thought of the part of the campaign he kept from his brother… about what he found on their journey back to the keep after they returned the child to her family.

The men were in high spirits on their trek back, roughhousing and ribbing one another. The need for silence and seriousness over, and it wasn't long before their chatter of battle and prowess morphed into talk about women: The sloe-eyed beauty at the town tavern, the lass with flaming red curls in the keep's laundry, and Gunn's fair-haired sister, much to his dismay at her being the object of his comrades lusty thoughts.

"The English lass is a fine sight for the eyes, too," Farlan said, and a chorus of agreement echoed his assessment.

"Aye." Colin stopped on the other side of the burn that led to the fairy pools. "And the wee thing can curse better than any o' ye on yer best day." Laughter erupted from the men, filling the valley with their howls as he gazed upstream. "Take a rest a while; I'm goin' up for a look."

Leaving them to pass around the last of the salted meat, he climbed the gentle slope of the burn alone until he came across the prominent prints of Meggie's boots. They passed over themselves several times as she ran back and forth along the water's edge. Taking his time, he followed them up to the pools where an apple core covered in ants lay discarded by a boulder near one of the larger basins with smooth multicolored pebbles in its depths. Bypassing the pools, he climbed along the tumbling water that fed into the main river body, and followed her trail.

Her tracks were clumsy, even a novice could read her trail from how she disturbed the shale and robbed the stones of their moss caps. But Colin knew her path; he'd been there dozens of times as a young lad, and apprehension coiled in his gut when the caves came into view.

There were handprints and deep indentions in the damp soil at the entrance of the largest cave, hinting that she had crawled out of the gloom. Stooping into a crouch, he entered the cave and allowed his eyes to adjust to the darkness before continuing deeper… and found the end of her tracks at a shallow pool fifteen feet inside.

No. They began *there.*

His breath echoed in the cavern as he swiped his finger on a flat rock and scraped at a dark smear of dried blood. Bewildered, he left the cave, rubbing the blood flecks between his fingers, and stepped back out into the early evening light. He searched the surrounding area for more prints, his mind racing while he turned the evidence over in his mind, again and again, unable to comprehend what his eyes were telling him.

Why would she tell him she'd never been to the caves when she so obviously had? And there was the question of how her tracks originated inside. He mulled over his pondering in silence when he rejoined his men and hurried home, only to have jealousy burn hot as a forge in his chest when he found Baen Murray staring brazenly at Meggie's breasts while she ate.

She's mine, *he thought.*

Those unspoken words lay heavy on his tongue when he took his seat at the table and devoured the most delicious meal he had in a very long time. His Meggie was gifted in the kitchen, so it seemed. And when she generously divided her only sweet to share with his family, leaving nothing for herself, his heart swelled.

When he followed her upstairs with every intention of demanding why she had spoken falsely about the caves, she disarmed him when she lifted her sweet lips and brazenly demanded a kiss. All thought of confronting her eddied out of his head and he couldn't resist—

With a groan, Colin turned his face into the pillows with frustration and willed sleep to find him.

He would need his rest, for tomorrow, he promised to take the lovely liar to the caves. *Again.*

CHAPTER 10

Meggie

I awoke with trepidation thick in my gut, and the nauseating feeling only solidified as Maeve dressed me. A plain, lightweight blue wool blend wrapped my body in its warm embrace, its only embellishment a thick satin ribbon the color of smoke tied at my waist.

I stood there in nervous silence, my thoughts full of Colin and his sinful kisses warring with my need to return to my own time. To Nan, who was surely tearing the countryside apart trying to find me.

Once alone, after Maeve departed the room with a cheery wave, I grabbed my pack from where it waited patiently under the bed and stuffed it with the freshly laundered clothing I arrived in. I would put them on when I got back to 2019. Pausing in the threshold, I took one last look around before pulling the door shut and set off to find Colin. Unsure of where his room was or if it was even on the same wing as my own, I navigated the many halls and stairwells until I reached the kitchen.

Mrs. Cook greeted me warmly, her cheerful smile denting her plump cheeks.

"Ah! There ye are, lass. I was wonderin' when ye'd be comin' down. I wanted to thank ye again for yer fresh ideas. Despite our northern guest darkening his door, the laird was most pleased," she boasted and set a plate of breakfast biscuits next to a teapot on the table.

I plucked a cookie from the tray and chewed my lower lip in consideration before I spoke.

"Baen's not a very nice man."

The cook's gaze flicked to mine a moment before she nodded her head in grave agreement.

"I cannae imagine anyone raised under his sire's harsh thumb would grow to be kind," she murmured as she pulled bowls off the shelving and set them with a clang on the long table. I blinked at her.

"His father *beat* him when he was little?"

"I widnae put it past him. A child learns to be cruel from heavy hands. They dinnae become that way on their own." Her eyes grew sad. "Struan Murray is a cruel Laird. No' kind to his people... and he wasnae kind to his wife, Baen's mother, who died when he was a young lad. Rumor has it that Lady Murray fell down one o' the stronghold's many stairwells in the middle o' the night. 'Tis said her body was so battered from the fall that she died before dawn from her injuries... but no' everyone believes it."

"That she fell?"

Mrs. Cook shrugged. "Many believe someone pushed her. Or somethin' worse. Maybe that's the reason the laird never married again. What sane woman would have a wife-murderer for a husband?"

Jesus. To be raised by a man who killed his mother—

"No wonder Baen is so... dark."

Nodding again, she measured out flour, sugar, and yeast, her eyes wholly focused on her task until she said, "Just... stay out o' Baen's way while he's here, lass."

I wanted to tell her I'd rather jump naked in a frozen lake than spend any amount of time with him, but said instead, "I promise, Mrs. Cook."

"Och, ye'll call me Iona, ye will." Patting my cheek with flour dusted hands, she gave me a joyful smile, her eyes crinkling at their corners.

And just like that, our gloomy conversation was forgotten, and in that moment, I found I did not want to say goodbye to this prickly woman who had dulled her thorns for me.

"So, are ye plannin' to take over my kitchen today?" she asked as she mixed her ingredients and added eggs and milk.

"Not today, I'm afraid. Colin promised to take me to the fairy pools."

"Romantic place, that." A wistful look transformed her face as she worked the mixture. "Why, when I was a few years younger than yerself, a lad took me to those very pools." Her cheeks pinkened, obviously reliving the memory before her mouth turned down in sadness.

I knew that look.

"What happened to him?" I asked softly.

"He died… a few weeks before we would marry. It happened during a skirmish with a neighboring clan. My fearless Broderick gave his life defending our laird from a killing blow. He saved the life of Malcolm's father at the price of his own." She stared unseeing at the far wall before taking a deep breath and turned her glassy eyes upon me. "And since there was no other man for me, I guess ye could say I married the kitchen. That's why they call me Mrs. Cook."

"I'm so sorry, Iona," I said in sympathy.

How much love she must have shared with that man to forsake any chance at love with another. She shook her head, and the few curls that escaped her cap bounced as she kneaded her dough.

"I was verra angry with him for many years for leavin' me. Then Malcolm and that rapscallion Colin were born and invaded my black heart. I have never been prouder of Malcolm. He's the finest laird that ever was, thoughtful, cunning, and true, and if it was no' for my Broderick's sacrifice, he would never be. Who is to ken what would have become of the MacKinnon clan had his father died that day in the hills?" She threw a few punches on the dough for emphasis and then smiled wistfully. "So, ye enjoy yer day at those pools."

I blinked back the heat that crept up behind my eyes from her sad story and busied myself with pouring a cup of tea.

"Well, it's not the pools I'm interested in so much as the caves in the hills above," I said nonchalantly, and startled when her head whipped toward me so fast, I wondered how it didn't roll right off her shoulders.

"What in the blazin' hell do ye want to see those caves for?" she demanded as she tossed a rounded loaf down on the floured table to rise.

Shocked by the rapid change in her demeanor, I leaned back on my stool and swallowed the truth that was unwise to share.

"I'm just curious," I lied.

She narrowed her shrewd eyes and leaned forward, invading the space I just vacated. Her penetrating glare rooted me in place as she surveyed me a moment before turning away and grunted in indignation.

"Nothin' good comes o' those caves, lass, but ye seem to have made up yer mind. Off with ye then," she grumbled.

Her disappointment was thick in the air when I thanked her for the tea and fled the kitchen, my eyes downcast, and hustled up the stairs. The slap of my feet against the stone steps and the jingle of my pack bouncing against my lower back echoed with finality.

I hated the dishonesty that seemed to pour out of my mouth lately. I could almost taste the bitterness of vanilla on my tongue, and I swallowed reflexively. Shame and regret weighed down my shoulders when I realized the last thing I would ever say to her was a falsehood, even though the truth would have made me look madder than a wet sack full of polecats.

But I couldn't go back. I couldn't explain myself.

Better to leave it, I thought as I quickly crossed the quiet hall, and barely stopped in time before I collided with a muscled chest.

Strong hands grasped both of my arms above my elbows, steadying me, and I looked up into the cruel face of Baen Murray who had just come down the grand staircase. Attired from head to toe in black, Baen was not nearly as tall as Colin or Malcolm, but still seemed to tower over me from a three-inch difference. It was his bearing that intimidated the hell out of me. His iron confidence that made me feel small and helpless.

"Excuse me," I said breathlessly when I tried to pull away.

He kept his grip on my arms a moment longer than appropriate before releasing me.

"Good mornin', Meggie," he purred with a leer, and I sidestepped him with a tight half-smile. "Where are ye rushin' off to so quickly?"

Damning the manners my mother taught me, my steps faltered, and I turned back to face him. The corner of his lips turned up in a small, patronizing smile and his head tilted to the side with interest, reminding me of a wolf assessing its prey.

"I'm going for a walk," I answered quickly

"Allow me to accompany ye then," he said smoothly. He hooked his thumbs into the belt that secured his black kilt and lazily stalked me, his boots echoing in the empty hall with each step.

The space between me and the kitchen grew as I backed up towards the keep's main door and the safety of the busy bailey beyond.

"Um, thank you, but Colin has already promised to take me."

I felt like a cornered hare and nearly whimpered when my backpack pressed up against the keep's thick door. Refusing to show him my back, convinced he'd pounce as soon as I turned around, I fumbled blindly behind me for the brass latch.

"Colin." His lips tightened with frustration for the briefest moment before they morphed into a devil-may-care smile that failed to reach his eyes.

Holding my stare as though he dared me to scream, he closed the distance between us and reached behind me, his face so close I could smell his breath. The loud snap of the latch cracked the silence in the quiet hall and he pulled open the other side of the door I wasn't leaning against. Bright morning sunlight washed over his face, illuminating nearly imperceptible scars I hadn't noticed before on his cheek and hairline.

"Another time then," he crooned in my ear as though he were telling me a secret.

I didn't even bother forcing another smile before I slipped out the door. The sound of his chuckle, full of dark, cruel promise, chased me down the stairs and into the bailey. Risking a quick glance to assure myself he had not followed, I passed under the branches of the great oak and into the small stable tucked against the curtain wall.

The nervousness of my encounter with Baen slowly dissipated when I entered the shadowed, peaceful sanctuary filled with the muffled thumps of heavy hooves and the effortless movements of gentle giants. Strolling down the swept cobbled thoroughfare that ran the length of the stable, I peeked in on the six beasts within their stalls, and their long, curious faces regarded me with interest when I passed by.

In the last stall on the right, a large sorrel mare popped her head over the half-door and waited, rather impatiently, for me to reach her. She tossed her reddish-brown head and nickered as if to say, *hurry up, why don't you?*

"Hello there, beauty," I cooed, and extended my palm up to let her take a sniff before I ran my hand over the side of her velvety lips and the length of her face. When I curled my fingers around the base of her ear, she leaned into my touch, and her eyelids grew heavy as I caressed her in long, smooth strokes. I stood there for a long while, her breath warming my belly, and was content to spend my entire morning meditating with the smell of fresh hay in my nose and the docile beast enjoying my attentions.

"Ye'll spoil her rotten if ye keep that up much longer," Colin said lightly, and came to stand at my side. He patted the animal's neck affectionately like one that was comfortable around horses does.

"How long have you been watching me?" I sighed, an amused smile playing on my lips. Once again, he'd snuck up on me without a sound.

"Long enough to be jealous." Leaning down, the tip of his nose caressed the shell of my ear, and that side of my body ignited with goose bumps.

I will miss him, I realized. Something in my chest gave a little lurch at the thought.

"Why dinnae we take Una here on our adventure today?"

"Can we?"

With a nod, he left me long enough to grab a thick padded blanket from down the hall, and laid it over the low door to her stall before leading her out. She waited, untethered and patient, while he secured the makeshift saddle over her back with a length of oiled leather. Taking my pack, he tied it on the pad over Una's rump with thin leather laces before leading her out to the courtyard with a crisp whistle. Her steps were light and quick, her tail lifted and flicking with obvious pleasure at being included. With a lightness belying his size, Colin mounted the enormous horse with ease—an impressive feat considering there were no stirrups to aid him.

"Ready, Meggie?" he asked as he offered me his hand.

Well, if that wasn't a loaded question.

With a gentle but firm grip on my forearm, he hoisted me onto the saddle pad between his muscular thighs. My legs dangled awkwardly to one side, throwing off my balance, and after I bent my knee closest to Una's withers, I could face forward comfortably and leaned some of my weight against Colin's chest. With a soft grunt of approval, he gripped the wiry mane in front of my shin with his right hand, and his left curled around my waist to hold me tighter against him when he squeezed with his lower legs. At the command, Una plodded swiftly through the gatehouse and out to the eastern field that hugged close to the curtain wall.

We rode in silence for a long while, past gardens and paddocks, enjoying the warmth of the sun on our faces as it burned away the last wisps of the morning fog. Colin expertly guided Una northward through wildflower-filled meadows and craggy hills covered with globes of purple heather. The lilac scent of them was heavy in the air as he pointed to this and that, telling me about the land, and some of the battles fought between clans generations ago.

Anxiety curled its cold fingers around my gut as we came to a river, followed it uphill, and passed the spot where the two men chased into the wilds. Memories of my terror strongly resurfaced, the echo of dread thick in my tummy. Even Colin had grown strangely silent.

Leaving Una to nibble at the long grass growing near the pools, Colin helped me down and tugged on my hand to follow.

"Wait! My pack." Stretching on my tiptoes, I tugged on the ties of the saddle pad.

"What do ye need it for? The caves are naught but a few minutes' walk." Reaching above me, he pulled the long end of a knot and my pack fell into my arms.

"I just do," I mumbled as I slipped the leather straps over my shoulders. He observed me with suspicion before shrugging and left me to follow him up the hill.

Relieved he hadn't pushed for more of an answer, I lifted the hem of my dress and began my ascent. Stumbling up the hill, sharp rocks hidden under a thin sheen of moss poked painfully at my arches and the sensitive bend under my toes through my soft leather slippers. Breathing heavily because of the the cursed corset Maeve had stuffed me into, as well as the incline, I fought the urge to lean over my knees when I caught up to Colin.

Resting his shoulder against the mossy rock face between two cave openings, he crossed his thickly muscled arms over his chest and watched me take in our surroundings.

Everything was different. A thick cover of bright, springy moss dotted with small five-petaled flowers replaced the ferns and grasses that draped the cave mouths in 2019, and a few birch saplings stood among the grass and rock farther up the hill in the area I had fallen through.

"Are they everything ye thought they'd be?" There was a tone to his voice I couldn't decipher.

"Yes and no," I panted as I neared the largest cave, and steeled my nerves to enter.

Would it hurt? Would I remember everything that had happened in the last three days? I flat-out refused to think that I could possibly end up even farther back in time.

Gritting my teeth, I reached for his hand and clasped it within mine. Hot tears of fear and loss pricked the backs of my eyes.

This isn't fair, I thought.

"Thank you for everything, Colin."

Squeezing his hand, I brought his knuckles to my mouth and placed a kiss upon them. Memorizing the curious look on his beautiful face, I willed myself to never forget this man as long as I lived, and quickly ducked into the cold, damp darkness before I lost my nerve.

With my arms stretched out, I shuffled through the throat of the cave until my vision adjusted. Minimal light seeped in through the entrance behind me, the shadows only growing thicker ahead. The steady drip of water echoing from deeper in the cave mingled with the sound of my breathing and the rasp of my slippers on the wet sand.

Squatting down at the spot where I had woken half-submerged in water, I looked up to find a rocky ceiling above me where there should have been a gap revealing the blue sky. Alarm prickled the back of my neck when I spied bats slumbering above where the crevice should be, their furry little bodies tucked into cracks in the stone as they waited patiently for dusk.

No, no, no!

"I'm stuck here," I whispered hopelessly in the dark. Fisting a handful of wet sand, I threw it into the shallow pool as my throat restricted and tears welled to spill down my cheeks.

For the last two days, I had hope of returning to Nan, and those hopes were squashed in a second at the sight of the intact cavern above me. My chest tight, I fell back on my butt in the damp, and burying my face in the fabric of my skirt, I cried in the gloom.

Colin's soft footsteps on the sand announced his presence.

"Why do ye cry, lass?"

I pulled the fabric away from my face to find him crouched beside me, and another hot flood of tears blurred my sight. My lips trembled as I waved a hand towards the rock above me, as though to answer his question, and wiped my face with my forearm.

"I can't get home."

"What do ye mean?" He cocked his head, looking up at the bats.

"I mean, I have nowhere to go. I'm all alone."

Sobbing once again into my skirt, I felt a light touch on my shoulder, one of support, before Colin rubbed my back in big, slow circles.

"Ye're no' alone. I cannae say I understand what's goin' on, but I'm with ye, and ye have a place at the keep for as long as ye like." His deep voice was soft and calming while he continued to comfort me.

I sat there, long after my clothing was soggy from both my tears and the damp earth, and the start of a chill burrowed into my bones from the subterranean waters. On unsteady legs, I led the way out, feeling defeated and saddened, and trudged to the streambed to rinse my hands and splash the icy water on my swollen face.

"Meggie," Colin said, waiting until I turned to face him. He looked frustrated and confused as he continued, "I came this way after my patrol yester-eve." He bent to pick up a few pebbles and threw them one by one into the burbling water. "I followed yer tracks. Ye said ye'd never been to the caves before."

I blinked up at him, rooted in place, and his sharp stare contradicted his gentle voice when he said, "Ye lied to me."

His statement made me flinch, and my mouth fell open slightly when I quickly shook my head. Not to deny my lie, but to deny the hurt I saw plainly in his face.

"I had to."

"Why? What made ye feel the need to lie about somethin' as simple as having been here before?" Arms crossed over his chest, he towered above me. He didn't trust me; that was clear enough.

Shoulders slumping, I bit my lower lip and dipped my hand inside my pack for my hunter-green wallet. The fake gold dachshund charm attached to the zipper glinted, swinging in the sun. Colin eyed me suspiciously as I opened it.

Please don't freak out, I prayed, and took a deep breath.

"My name is Meghan Aurora Washington." My voice wavered when I slipped my driver's license from its little pocket and handed it to him. "I'm from the United States of America—but I think it's only made of colonies right now. I boarded a plane two weeks ago and came to Scotland to visit my grandmother and help her on her farm while I figured out my life. I saw your castle when we were driving by, and she told me to take the day for myself and hike the grounds."

In silence, he fingered the small card, studying it. His thumb traced over the picture of my face, and he tilted it to-and-fro when the holographs flickered. Taking his reticence as an invitation to continue, I sucked in a breath and hoped with all hope that he would believe me.

"I went off the trailhead and fell through a crack above the caves. When I crawled out, I wasn't *there* anymore... I was *here*. I'm not even *born* yet. I'm not born until 1997." My voice cracked when I finally said it out loud.

Covering my face with one hand, I hugged myself with the other and spun away from him. I knew I sounded insane, and I didn't want to see the look on his face confirming he felt that way.

He was quiet for a long while. So long I almost thought he had left me when he spoke.

"I had wondered how yer tracks originated in the cave. It was a question I asked myself a hundred times and had no answer for. Look at me, Meggie... *Meghan*." I dropped my hand and turned to look up into his deep blue eyes when he gripped my shoulders. "I'm unsure how ye got here, and I dinnae ken how to send ye back, but ye are *no' alone*." He drew me against the warmth of his chest, his arms circling my shoulders, and rested his chin on the crown of my head. I gripped his shirt, and the relief that he believed me combated with the sadness I felt in knowing I'd never see Nan again.

Pulling away, I took back my ID and stowed my now useless wallet in my pack.

"What am I going to do here, Colin? I have no skills. No family— my Nan was all I had left for family. I know nothing about this time."

"Aye, ye have a lot to learn. But, in the meantime, ye'll continue to stay at the keep and under MacKinnon protection. 'Tis where I want ye, and since ye need a home, 'tis the best place for ye to be. And, if ye felt the urge to make another one o' yer delicious sweets, ye widnae hear any complainin' from the likes o' us. In fact, many would encourage ye to do so." Snickering, he grasped my hand and began descending the hill. Sliding on some loose rock, I winced and shook myself free of his hold.

"Let me put my boots on. I'm going to either break a toe or break my neck in these slippers." Before I could remove my pack, he spun around and scooped me up from behind my knees, holding me tightly against his chest.

"I can walk, you know," I squawked, and flung my arms around his neck, praying he wouldn't drop me.

"Och, I'm sure ye can, but that would rob me o' this small pleasure." Pleased with himself, he agilely navigated all the loose stones down the hill and didn't put me down until we got back to Una.

On our way back, Colin was quiet while I numbly watched the countryside slowly pass by and was so deep in my thoughts that I practically jumped out of my skin when he broke the silence.

"What's a plane?"

"Oh. Well, a plane is a metal machine that flies people long distances in the air. Higher than the clouds." I held my arms out as though I had wings. "Higher than an eagle."

"How is that possible?" he sputtered, clearly thinking the idea asinine. "'Tis as though ye told me I'd float if I swam with my armor on." Scoffing, he shook his head adamantly. "Ye're jesting."

Clearly, I wouldn't be able to convince him today, and leaned back against his broad chest, Una's lulling gait making me drowsy with the sun beating down upon us.

"What's a truck?" he blurted.

I suppressed a smile when I realized he must be mulling over all our past conversations and recalled how I was looking for it on my first day here.

"It's a metal machine on wheels that takes a person, or many persons, from place to place. Some of them can go over two hundred miles an hour." I glanced behind me and realized he did not know how far a mile was. "Believe me when I say we could get to Glasgow in an hour."

"*Glasgow*... now I ken ye jest, lass. I'm no' an idiot."

~

With Una groomed and back in her stall, I followed Colin down to the deserted kitchens to scrounge up a late lunch. With a plate loaded high with fresh bread, cheese, summer sausage, and berries, he led me up to the library while I carried a flagon of watered wine and two horn cups. The windows were open, allowing a warm breeze to drift through, and fluttered the pages of an abandoned book left open on a writing desk. While Colin set our meal on the table between the two chairs in front of the cold hearth, I flipped the book closed and grimaced at the cover. *Macbeth*. I will sorely miss my science fiction and spicy romance novels.

Joining Colin, I reclined in my chair and looked up at the painting displayed above the mantle of a proud, handsome, dark-haired man who stood behind his lovely wife. She wore a secret smile, serene and mysterious. Familiar. Her mass of blonde curls had escaped their pins, wreathing her angelic face.

"Who are they?" I asked.

"My parents, God rest their souls," he said as he looked up at the painting affectionately. "My father was a good man and laird. Beloved by our people. His first wife was the daughter o' a highland laird in the far north. Theirs was an arranged marriage with no love between them, although they made it work. Sadly, she died in childbirth a year later when she brought Malcolm into the world. Two years went by before he met my mother by chance, while he visited a neighboring clan. Our father took one look at her and knew... she was it for him. He cared naught that she was the daughter o' a miller, who was reluctant to let her go. Her father had promised her in secret to another, ye see. When she told our father that she was against the match to the unknown man, he stole her away and married her, for he was hers and she was his."

Colin leaned back into his chair, his eyes soft, and the corner of his mouth quirked up when he continued the story. "They had a love that was envied by anyone who saw them together… ye see, to ken her was to love her. Elsbeth was her name, and she had an open soul, welcoming and warm." Raising his horn cup, he toasted the painting and took a long sip before continuing, "She was no' Malcolm's mother, but she loved him as though she was. She's half the reason he's the man he is today."

That's why she looked familiar. It was Colin's mouth, Colin's eyes staring back at me from the oil on canvas.

"That's very romantic. She sounds wonderful. I'm sorry you lost her. Both of my parents died four years ago, and it's still fresh."

Hugging myself, I ran my palms lightly over my arms, brushing off old ghosts and new ones. Colin angled his body toward me, the look on his face sympathetic but earnest.

"Losing a parent is hard for everyone, but they live in our memories. The more we think o' them, the longer they live on inside us."

I surveyed the painting a moment longer before nodding in agreement. Picking apart a piece of oat bread, I thought of Nan. It pained me to think of her searching for me, and never finding me. She already lost her only daughter. I remembered all too clearly the way she had wailed like her heart was being ripped from her chest when we buried them. She had clung to me so tightly I could barely breathe when the minister gave a nod to lower their caskets into the ground. Her anguished face haunted me for weeks.

Goose bumps spread their way down from my scalp as I realized she wouldn't have my body to lay to rest… because my body no longer existed after I fell through that hole in the hearth. I would be worse than dead to her. Would she bury some of my belongings next to my parents amongst the bluebells to give herself some closure? Would ever stop searching? The thought of her all alone made my throat tight and my eyes burn. She didn't have anyone left to hold on to.

The full impact of my disappearance hit me like a punch to the gut.

"I need some time alone." My voice broke.

Grabbing my pack, I hurried from the room before he could reply and wiped angrily at the fat tears that rolled down my cheeks. Deep guilt and regret lashed barbed whips at my heart. Nan had told me to stay away from those caves. She *told* me, and I still had to go climbing above them. This was not the adventure I wanted when I went off the trailhead. And now she was alone.

In the privacy of the blue room, a sob broke free when I slapped the deadbolt in place and sank to my knees. Pressing my hand on my chest, I gulped down air as I came to terms with the fact that I was trapped in the seventeenth century. Worse, the only person I loved in the world would think I was dead, and there was absolutely *nothing* I could do about it. It was the deepest sense of helplessness I've ever experienced next to my parents' deaths.

Eventually, I made my way to the bed, shedding my slippers and nearly shredding the ribbons that contained me in my dress. Leaving it in a light blue heap on the floor, I slid between the cool linen sheets and cried myself to sleep.

~

The soft rapping of knuckles on wood seeped into my consciousness, and I found the room flooded with the golden hues of late afternoon light. Pulling my knees up to my chest, I yanked the blankets to my chin and stared at the tapestry of the Scottish landscape across the room.

"Milady," Maeve's muffled voice drifted through the door. "Milady, are ye well?"

Sighing, I roused from the bed and crossed the room, wearing only my linen shift, my hair wild, and my eyes puffy. Slipping the bolt back, I returned to bed when she entered.

"Will ye be takin' dinner with the laird this eve, or should I make yer excuses?" she asked as she looked down at me with compassion.

"Make my excuses, please. I'm not hungry."

She dipped a quick curtsey and left me alone to glide back into the oblivion of sleep.

Full darkness had settled, and a chill crept in through the open windows when she visited me next, a tray with tea and a candle in her arms. Wordlessly, she lit the tapers on the mantle and a fire in the hearth after shuttering the windows. Her capable hands coaxed some flames within minutes, warming the room.

"Mrs. Cook sent up a sleepin' draught for ye. 'Tis chamomile tea and a good bit o' whiskey as well as valerian root," she explained while she poured me a cup.

My hand shook as I took it from her, the hot totty making me think of that evening with Nan only a couple weeks ago. My lower lip trembled, and I took a long sip, the liquid burning its way down my throat in more ways than one. I chased a cough away with another swallow and drained the cup before handing it back to the stricken handmaid.

"Another?" she asked, her eyes wide.

I nodded, my face red as I tried to hold back my tears.

She quickly filled my cup again and watched me drink it down before I turned away and buried my face into the pillows. With my belly warm from the liquor that did little to dull the sadness in my heart, I curled onto my side. Maeve tucked blankets around me, smoothed my hair away from my tear-stained face, and then quietly left with a promise to return in the morning.

Listening to the crackle of the fire, I watched the shadow flames dance on the wall as I mourned.

"I'm sorry, Nan," I whispered to the empty room a moment before the valerian root's effects dragged me under.

CHAPTER 11

Colin

"Just yer ugly face this eve?" Malcolm gripped the back of Colin's neck and shook him affectionately before sitting down heavily at the head of the table. "Where's that bonnie lass of yers?"

"She'll be takin' her supper in her room, if she takes it at all."

Leaning over his mug of mead, Colin thought of the moment Meggie fled from the library. The poor lass.

Malcolm speared him with an accusing glare. "What did ye do, brother?"

"Nothin', although I wish it was that simple. Meggie received word that her grandmother had passed from this world. She was her last kin; she has no one else."

Colin figured that was a good excuse for her reaction to the day's events without disclosing the truth. Sipping his mead, he leaned back in his chair to make room for the serving girls when they deposited roast chicken, boiled potatoes and turnips, and grainy brown bread in front of them. The fare was nothing like what they had feasted on the previous eve, much to his disappointment.

"She has a place here," Malcolm declared, and lightly pounded the edge of the table in his typical laird-like fashion to emphasize his decree.

"I told her as much. I'm no' wantin' her to be anywhere else," Colin admitted as he filled his plate and began nibbling on a chicken leg.

Malcolm nodded in agreement. "Aye, I see the way ye look at her. The whole bloody keep sees."

Colin rolled his eyes and focused on his meal until the chair in front of him filled with the unwelcome sight of Baen Murray.

"Pardon my tardiness," Baen said, not looking the least bit apologetic as he filled his own plate and poked at the plain fare with his knife. "Too bad the English lass spent the day in the wood and no' in the cookhouse. Come to think of it, I have need of a new kitchen wench, and ye have a cook already in residence. Perhaps I'll take her off yer hands."

Reclining in his chair, Colin refused to rise to the bait that was dangled in front of him. Since they were young lads, Baen had always been the jealous type and quick to prey on things that were not his.

Lairds typically fostered their male children out to neighboring clans, leaving them for months at a time to forge allies and learn the politics of their neighbors. When it came time to take on their role as laird, they were better prepared to continue relationships with their neighbors on a personal level. Being a second son did not exempt Colin from accompanying his older brother.

The year the MacKinnon brothers fostered at the Murray keep, Colin forged a deep hatred for the Murray's only son. It seemed Baen had taken on a personal vendetta against him, although he did not understand why. Malcolm protected him when he could, Colin being five years younger than his instigator, but he could only shelter him from so much. Besides, the physical beatings would come upon him in the keep's dark hallways, not just the training yard.

Memories came unbidden of the day ten-year-old Colin found the fledgling nightingale.

They were going to return home that day, and Colin was eagerly awaiting their father's arrival when he found the young bird in the bailey, stuck in the loose hay piled outside the stable. Being a soft-hearted boy, he'd picked it up. Cradling it in his small hands, he headed for the gate to release it within a small copse of trees close to the wall.

"What do ye have there?" Baen taunted, pulling at Colin's hands for a look.

Before Colin could hide the feathery bundle, Baen seized the bird and snapped its neck with a hateful grin before handing the limp body back. Colin's eyes had burned with tears and loathing while he watched Baen laugh cruelly as he strutted back up to the keep.

Angus MacKinnon found his son crying in the shadow of the curtain wall, the earth underneath his bare knobby knees freshly turned and his fingers blackened from mud.

"What are ye doin' out here, lad?" The MacKinnon laird knelt in front of his son and listened through the sniffles and hiccups while Colin told him of the dead bird he had buried in the cold mud with his bare hands.

"I hate him, Da," Colin railed, and pounded the stone of the curtain wall with the side of his small fist.

"Aye, I can see that ye do." Angus MacKinnon ran his scarred fingers down his dark beard and studied his youngest son with kind eyes. "What do ye plan to do about it?"

Colin's head snapped up in shock at his father's words.

"There's nothin' I can do! He's bigger than me," he scoffed and hung his head again.

"Today he is." His father nodded in agreement.

Pulling his son up to stand before him, he brushed the dirt off his knobby knees and the wiped the tears from his smooth cheeks. Gripping Colin's skinny arms with battle-hardened hands, he looked at his son levelly.

"But one day, ye'll be bigger than he. 'Tis up to ye if ye also want to be bigger than him in here *as well." He poked Colin's bony chest over his heart. "And decide if ye will use yer strength to prey… or to protect."*

His father had not been wrong in his prediction. At sixteen, Colin sprouted to six feet, and honed his body through swordplay and hand-to-hand combat with the garrison's men under the watchful eye of Magnus. At twenty, he stood solid at six foot six and filled out his frame, keeping the quick reflexes of his youth and attaining a vigor that rivaled seasoned warriors. Now, at six and twenty years he was nearly twenty stone, unmatched in strength and stamina, and considered the MacKinnon clan's finest warrior.

Colin picked up his tankard and took a long swallow. Smacking his lips, he swirled the dark liquid, and smiled hollowly at his childhood enemy.

"Just because ye cannae keep women in yer stronghold does no' mean ye can pilfer ours."

"'Tis no' pilfering if she comes willingly." Baen's voice dripped with arrogance and challenge.

"*Willingly.* That's a word I dinnae think men above our northern border understood." Colin leaned forward, his forearms resting on the table, his features smooth and calm as the man on the other side of the table radiated tension. Malcolm watched the volley of conversation, ready to interject if he needed to.

"And just what is *that* supposed to mean?" Dark brows drew down over onyx eyes as Baen glanced between the two brothers.

Malcolm cleared his throat. "The day ye arrived, Colin tracked down a group of men that have been terrorizing the countryside. They'd been stealing lasses to take as wives, raping and beating them. Some no older than children. My men put one of them to question, and he said they had come from yer territory."

"And?" Baen scoffed and glared openly at the Mackinnon laird.

Malcolm returned his stare and shrugged. "And they're dead. Feasts for the crows, thanks to my brother. Ye had no complaints o' this?"

"No' a one." Baen smoothed a palm down his black shirt and wiped his mouth with his napkin before tossing it on his plate. "An unfortunate turn of events, but as ye said, they are dead and cannae do any more harm."

Colin nearly smelled the deceit and cast a look to his brother, who gave an imperceptible shake of his head. They would not be talking further of this, at least in their present company. If Laird Murray allowed his people to be preyed upon by monsters, then Colin could only pray for them. He did his part by ridding the earth of their vile presence.

Obeying his brother's silent order, Colin dismissed the topic and said, "Ye're invited to train with the men on the morrow, Baen. 'Tis been a while since we took a turn with blunted weapons."

Baen stood and took advantage of being able to look down his nose in contempt since Colin remained sitting.

"I leave at first light. Another time perhaps." And with that, he grabbed his tankard and turned on his heel after a quick nod to Malcolm, bidding them goodnight.

"That was disappointing." Colin sighed and ran his fingers through his hair when the pretentious gait of the northern heir disappeared down a corridor. "No' that I wanted him to remain here with us."

Malcolm chuckled into his cup. "He's no' taken ye up on yer kind offer to spar since ye embarrassed him when ye were nineteen." Malcolm closed his eyes and lifted his chin into the air, a look of pure satisfaction on his face. "A pity we will never see the likes o' that fine sight again."

Colin grunted his approval and recalled the fateful day he bested his childhood enemy.

He had practiced his swordplay tirelessly for years with his father's men to prepare himself for the next inevitable confrontation with the neighboring laird's son. It was on that memorable day at The Gathering that it finally happened.

The two brothers were touring the merchant stalls after a morning of teasing lasses and entering in games now that Colin was of age to partake in them all. While Malcolm stopped to inspect a young black stallion, Colin spotted Baen handling a year old filly roughly. The old trader wrung his weathered hands at the way his property was being treated, unwilling or too fearful to voice his concerns to a laird's son. Two other men were with him, laughing as Baen held onto the filly's lead and poked at her reddish-brown chest with a stick to make her rear up. Her head raised as high as she could hold it, her fearful eyes rolled wide as she watched the stick come at her again and again.

Hands clenched and body tight with repressed anger at the treatment of such a beautiful animal, Colin stepped forward before Malcolm could react and gripped a handful of Baen's shirt between his shoulder blades. Catching him by surprise, Colin yanked Baen backward and flung him off balance towards his two companions. With her lead free from her tormentor's grip, the young horse bolted straight through the rickety fencing, and the merchant made chase after her.

"How dare ye!" Baen snapped, flinging off the arms of his comrades that had kept him on his feet.

"Easily. Ye weigh less than a milkmaid," Colin taunted. "Still terrorizing gentle souls, I see."

Baen laughed darkly. Puffing out his chest, he held his arms out wide, one hand still gripping the thick stick he'd been using to jab the horse.

"Still upset about that little bird? Been cryin' about it all these years?" He twirled the dark shaft of wood around as though it was a sword and glowered at Colin. "I think ye forgot yer place as a second son. A second son birthed by a peasant no less," he spat.

Malcolm stepped forward to intervene, but Colin waved him away and allowed Baen to size him up. Swallowing the rage that surfaced with Baen's insult towards his mother, he seized a pitchfork leaning against the flimsy picket fence and brought his foot down on the shaft, snapping the three tines off the end. With his grip tight on his wooden weapon, he schooled his facial expressions and waited for Baen to make the first move.

He did not need to wait long.

With an angry yell, Baen lunged for him, aiming for Colin's temple.

Tap, tap, tap, tap.

The sharp sound of two sticks colliding in rapid succession echoed off the makeshift stalls and canvas tenting in the valley, thus gathering the attention of several people. Feigning frustration, Colin only defended himself, yielding ground… and led Baen around the corner to where he spied the swine earlier.

Tap, tap, tap, tap.

Baen's companions hollered their enthusiasm as they followed, elated at how their man had the obvious upper hand. Malcolm followed casually behind, arms crossed over his chest, and his head tilted to the side as he watched with amusement.

Tap, tap, tap, tap.

Colin allowed himself a few shows of weakness, parrying strikes slower and slower as he led his adversary right where he wanted him. Baen was so intent on his victory; he didn't expect the abrupt attack.

Tap, tap, CRACK!

Colin's arm came down with a powerful blow. Sidestepping and pushing forward now, several strikes in sequence, he quickly overwhelmed his childhood rival while Baen tried desperately to evade the blows.

Tap, crack! Tap, crack!

A frightening smirk broke across Colin's face as he feinted a strike to the top of Baen's head, forcing the man to raise his arms up to block a blow that would surely split his skull... and unwittingly opened his belly up to a swift front kick.

At the impact, a glorious whoosh of air escaped from Baen's shocked mouth, and he tumbled over the back of a large sow to land with a loud squelch on his back in the wet mud.

Laughter erupted around them from the crowd that had gathered to watch the spectacle. Baen lay there as he tried to suck air back into his lungs, unable to speak. But Colin could read the hate radiating from his eyes well enough. Turning, he glared at Baen's fellow men, hand still gripped tight on the broken pitchfork. Wisely, they averted their eyes and ducked around him to help their laird's son up from the cold black mud.

Leaving the trio, Colin returned with his brother to finish his deal with the stallion, several onlookers thumping his back in congratulations along the way.

"I hope it was worth it, brother, for ye've just made yerself an enemy," Malcolm warned as he threw his arm around Colin's shoulder with brotherly pride.

"He made an enemy o' me a long time ago."

Thankfully, the old man had recovered the filly and tied her securely to a post. Her long legs still danced skittishly with agitation and nervousness.

"I'm sorry for damaging yer property, my friend," Colin said as he extended the broken pitchfork. The man took the stick and watched as Colin dug a copper from his sporran.

"No, no. I cannae accept." Shaking his head, he curled Colin's fingers around the currency. "I'm grateful ye helped me. Ye're a good man, like yer Da." Bowing slightly, he walked away with Malcolm toward the black stallion.

Colin reached out to the shaky horse. Murmuring calming words to her, he ran his hand down her neck, rubbed her shoulders and her flank, and worked her flesh until her tremors subsided. Eventually, her head drooped, and she took weight off her back-hind hoof, proving to Colin she was well and truly relaxed.

"We're finished here, brother."

With a firm grip on the spirited black's lead, Malcolm made for the direction of the MacKinnon camp, and Colin gave the filly one last pat before following.

"Wait!" A rough yet gentle hand latched onto Colin's elbow, and he turned to find the old man holding the filly's lead. "Her name is Una. I want ye to have her." His wrinkled face turned towards the horse kindly before offering Colin the weathered leather strap.

"Thank ye, but I cannae accept a gift for doing what was right," Colin said, and interrupted the old man when he opened his mouth to insist. "But I will happily pay her fair price."

Shaking himself out of his memories, Colin drained his cup of wine and nodded at Malcolm.

"Aye, a pity, but I'm no' sad to see him go. I ken it will be too soon before he darkens our door again."

Sweat dripped down the hard planes of his chest and down the hollow of his back as he swung the heavy claymore onto the shoulder of a wooden dummy. The striking impact traveled up the metal, making his limbs sing and his muscles shake from exertion before he worked the blade out of the thick wood. The clang and wooden knocks of practice weapons filled the south bailey as the garrison's men kept their skills sharp and their bodies strong.

Breathing heavily, Colin discarded the claymore on a rack and wrapped his fingers around the smooth handles of twin hatchets. Tossing one lightly into the air, he let the weapon rotate once before catching it, and launched it at the head of his wooden target. The hilt vibrated slightly from the impact, and he let the second one fly, burying it in the belly. Retrieving them both, he then made slow work of whittling the wood away bit by bit, both arms swinging in a measured, flowing dance taught to him years ago. Neck, torso, arm, leg, repeat. His body flowed around the movements as his hair escaped from its tether to fall around his face, and he lost himself in the physical activity, the burn of his muscles, and the breath in his lungs. *In and out, in and out—*

"That's the fifth dummy ye've murdered these last three days, lad."

Colin halted his swing a hairsbreadth from impacting the splintered wood. Glancing over his shoulder, he found Magnus standing behind him with his ruddy arms crossed over his barrel chest and his copper brow cocked in fascination at the object of Colin's focus.

"Now, what did they do to deserve yer wrath?" Magnus asked, nodding toward the pile of discarded wood heaped against the wall. Once assembled to resemble a man, they would now fulfill their lives as kindling.

Colin pointed one hatchet toward the north end of the keep.

"She's cloistered herself in her chamber for neigh on five days, Magnus." Stalking toward the rack, Colin set the hatchets down before turning back to the weapons master. "I dinnae ken what to do for her."

Magnus rubbed at a week's growth of beard and scratched under his chin as he followed Colin's gaze to the far end of the keep.

"So, that's what has ye haunting my domain. Ye huvnae trained this hard since yer mam died." Shaking his head, his fiery hair shone like a beacon in the sunlight. "I heard the lass lost the last o' her kin. That would be verra grim news for anyone."

"Aye. I only wish I could help her." Colin shoved his sweaty hair away from his face.

His breathing returned to normal as they walked toward the well where he could drink his fill of the crisp water. The air was warm and humid, with a strong wind blowing from the east; a sure sign of an impending storm even with the absence of clouds in the sky.

"Ye've offered her sanctuary here, lad. There's no' much else ye can do but wait. Women are soft o' heart, and ye need to allow her to grieve on her own terms. I ken ye have a strong fondness for the lass. Be there for her when she's ready." Giving Colin's shoulder a pinch, he winked before saying, "Now go have a bath; ye stink worse than my auld boots."

Colin chuckled and lightly punched Magnus's chest. "Aye, I'll do that."

Ducking into the barracks, he swiped a cake of soap before strolling towards the loch and his favorite bathing spot, where a massive, flat rock stretched like a thick finger out into the depths. A pile of flat, smooth rocks lay heaped at the deep end beside pits worn into the stone from decades of laundering heavy plaids.

Discarding his boots and belt, Colin peeled off his short hose and clutched his plaid around his hips as he waded into the cool water. With a sharp inhale, he quickly plunged into the water up to his neck, and the heat of the sun and training quickly leached from his body, refreshing his mind. Grabbing a laundering stone from the pile, he kneeled in the shallows of the submerged boulder and began the momentous task of washing first his stockings and then his plaid. With the woven fabric stretched out on the rock, he painstakingly rubbed out every bit of soiling before wringing the tartan out and draped it over the scrub bushes that lined the banks of the loch in the sun. Using the rest of the soap, he lathered his hair and beard, relishing the scent of juniper that filled his nostrils. A rustle and childish giggling in the bushes drew his attention, and he spun toward the shore.

"Get on with ye, ye wee rascals!" Colin roared, his arms raised over his head and fingers curved in like claws.

A group of children burst from the foliage and ran up the hill towards the keep, their laughter fading with them. Standing waist-deep in the water, he caught his reflection and chuckled before dunking under the surface and rinsing the ridiculous vision of himself covered from neck to crown in puffy white suds. A fearsome beastie, he was not.

After scrubbing his body with the rest of the soap and a smooth rock, he swam out to deeper waters and floated on his back. The few inches of water closest to the surface were warm and inviting. Slow, deep, and even breaths kept his chest afloat as he spread his arms out and stared up at the clouds that had started to roll in.

Like all his thoughts lately, they drifted to the beautiful lass in the blue room and how she looked when he found her huddled in the dark cave. She had buried her face in her skirts while her shoulders shook with wracking sobs.

He'd been angry and disappointed with her for lying to him. For saying she had never been in the caves before. And when she tried to explain, at first, Colin thought she was a little mad when she babbled about made-up countries and confusing things he'd never heard of. But the stiff, glossy rectangle gave him pause. Someone drew her image onto the bottom left corner with surprising detail, and the magical sketching that flashed multicolored in the sunlight had him listening closely to her words. He mulled over her odd speech and even stranger sayings as the truth rang clear.

She had planned to leave him; he realized. She had kissed his hands in goodbye, planning to disappear and never see him again. Bitter hurt had poisoned his heart for a long moment before he placed himself in her position. When he did, any anger and bruised feelings he felt melted away as he reassured her of a home with the MacKinnon clan and brought her back to Ghlas Thùr.

After he had shared the story of his parents, he witnessed profound grief twist her features, and she ran from him before he could catch her hand. He had then hunted Maeve down and made the excuse of her grandmother's death to keep Meggie from having to explain anything. The knowledge of her coming from a distant time was hard enough to wrap his own mind around when provided with evidence. A silly lass like Maeve and other God-fearing folks would have had her tried as a witch, or worse.

Leaving his frustrations to drown in the deep, he swam back to the shore, wrapped the still damp plaid around his hips, and strolled back to the keep with his boots and stockings in hand.

CHAPTER 12

Meggie

A soft knock at my door pulled me from a dreamless sleep and I opened my eyes to see Maeve slip into the room with her tea tray and a soft smile.

"Mornin' milady," she whispered as she placed the tray on the small table before crossing the room to the west windows.

She looked at me with brows raised in question, her hands poised on the shutters. I nodded for her to open them and winced when the grey morning sunlight filtered into the room.

I had been adamant about leaving the windows closed, content to sulk in the darkness for the last... week? Had it been that long? My chest felt hollow, and my eyes dry, scratchy, and spent. I didn't believe I could even summon a tear at gunpoint.

Finally, I was all cried out.

Pushing myself up, I rubbed my face roughly and squinted at the growing brightness of the room before touching my hair. I could feel the greasy strands standing up in ugly cowlicks on the crown of my head.

I had felt this way once before. After my parents died. For two weeks, I mustered up the strength to attend my classes, but that was the extent of my daily routine. I spent the rest of the days curled up in their bed; the shades drawn and the lights off, surrounded by their smell and possessions. I never even turned on the TV.

Licking my lips, I was aware of my body for the first time in too long.

"May I have a bath, Maeve?" I croaked, my voice foreign to my own ears.

Eyes wide, she nodded enthusiastically. "I'll have hot water sent up right away."

I slipped my arms into the blue robe she held open for me and slumped down on the edge of the bed as soon as she left the room. My body was weak from misuse, and my mind foggy from lack of food and general daily stimulation.

Clearing my throat, I stood on weak legs and padded to the chamber pot I had grown to rely on. It had kept me from prying eyes, as I was unwilling to visit the garderobe down the hall while I mourned the end of my old life and came to terms with the birth of my new one. I vowed to myself, once I became human again, I would never use it another day.

Catching sight of myself in the mirror, my hand drifted up to my neck as I stared into the polished looking glass. Yup, I looked as awful as I felt. Maybe even worse. Dismissing the haggard creature that stared back, I drooped into the blue chair and nibbled a biscuit in silence until a troupe of women came in with buckets of hot water and a hammered copper tub that they set between the dead fire and my bare feet. This tub was deeper than the much shallower one I used my first day here. One side was higher than the other, the lip gently curved. The perfect place to rest my head as I soaked. After pouring steaming water into the tub, each woman dipped a small curtsy before leaving the room. Most of the women, ages ranging from sixteen to forty, I recognized from the kitchen, but a few I hadn't yet met. Maeve skipped in last with her arms full of creamy linen, a woven basket stuffed with cork-stoppered glass bottles, and a clay bowl. Once the last of the women departed with their empty buckets, she closed the door, flitted over to the tub, and dropped the linen on the floor next to my chair.

"Mrs. Cook was verra glad to hear ye wanted to bathe," she said, and motioned for me to stand, lightly holding onto my fingers for support.

She pulled off my robe before lifting my dirty shift from the hem up and over my head, leaving me naked and shivering to step into the tub and the steaming water. The tub wasn't long, and I would have to sit with my knees bent, but I didn't care. I was more than happy to be submerged past my hip bones.

Gingerly, I lowered my body into the water, and the sharp heat licked at my skin almost painfully when I sank down. Settled against the tall side, my long hair floated on the surface and lapped against my barely covered breasts with every breath I took.

"She worried about me?" I asked hoarsely.

Maeve's head popped up from digging in her basket of bath salts and oils, startling me.

"O' course she was! She even threatened a few times to check on ye herself, but I was able to keep her away," she chirped, and I smiled at the vision of Maeve standing up to a fire-breathing Iona.

Once I acclimated to the heat, I let out a sigh and focused on the way it seeped into my weary bones and ignited some life back into my soul.

Dipping the bowl into the water, Maeve ladled the rose-scented liquid over my head before lathering my long tresses from root to end. I tipped my head back, and the wonderful sensation of her nails on my scalp made me shiver. Once my hair was clean to her satisfaction, she handed me a square of cloth and a small soap cake that smelled faintly of heather before she gave me space to wash in relative privacy.

And because I couldn't help myself, I asked, "Did anyone else ask after me?"

"No," she answered as she pulled the linens off the mattress.

Thankfully, her back was facing me, and she didn't see my face falter. I hugged my knees closer to my chest and berated myself for asking. No doubt Colin thought I was some wackadoodle since I locked myself away for a week.

Sullen, I watched Maeve fluff the furs at the foot of the bed and shake the thick wool blanket out the window before she turned around.

A devilish smile adorned her pretty face as she said, "But, I should tell ye… there's been many sightings in the past week o' a certain golden beast, pacin' just outside yer door like an angry badger. If he's no' trainin' with the garrison's men or bathin' in the loch, he's prowlin' the hall or watchin' the stairs, waitin' for ye to appear for the evenin' meal."

Confusing feelings wrestled in my chest as I thought about Colin. Relief and elation that he'd been wanting to see me clashed with the guilt I felt over that very relief.

When the water cooled, Maeve held out the soft linen wrap for me as I stood from the tub and she rubbed me dry. My skin felt fresh. The scabs on my arms from the incident in the woods healed during the last week, and left faint lines of new, pink skin behind as the only proof they ever existed at all. I fingered the spot on my head that had bled when I fell into the cave and found it smooth and healed.

I felt slightly reborn.

"What shall we do with ye today?" Maeve asked while she combed out my hair.

"I think I'll spend some time in the kitchen. Maybe Mrs. Cook will allow me to make something for dinner tonight. I need to be active. My brain feels like someone stuffed it with cotton."

"Aye, I believe she will."

She hummed a lilting tune while braiding my damp hair in three ropes, pinned them in an elegant knot at my nape, and dressed me in a light grey frock. Before shooing me out of the room, she tied a white lace-lined apron around my waist. I immediately shoved my hands into the deep pockets. Feeling some nostalgia for my oversized hoodies, I vowed right then and there to learn how to sew so I could make one for myself.

My slippers made little sound as I navigated the hallways toward the busy kitchen, where Iona's gruff voice bellowed up after three children. Nearly knocking me off my feet, they tore around the corner of the spiral stairwell, their impish faces covered in what could only be chocolate sauce, and scampered past me without a backward glance.

In the cookhouse, freshly harvested green vegetables covered one half of the worktable, and loaves of bread sat to rise on the other. Iona had her back to me and muttered angrily to herself while she pounded dough.

"Get away, ye wee scunners!" The cook whipped her head in my direction, prepared to chew the ear off a child brave enough to enter the kitchen again so soon, before a smile broke through her scowl. "Lass! I'm so happy to see ye out and about."

Her smile faded to a glower when her eyes locked on the lower half of my dress. Peering down, I found the object of her scorn where dark brown smears from little chocolaty fingers streaked the delicate lace.

"Savages, the lot o' them," she growled, and wiped her hands roughly on a towel.

"It's just chocolate. It will clean."

To appease her, I took off the garment when she asked for it, and she promptly handed it to an eager kitchen maid who hurried off to the laundress. Seemed like a big fuss for such a small mess, but I didn't comment and settled tiredly on a stool next to her workstation. While I drew designs in some spilled flour with the tip of my finger, I watched her shape the last of the loaves and score them three times with a knife.

"I'm happy to see ye're feelin' well, Meggie. I heard about yer grandmother. She'll be dining with the angels from now on." She nodded to herself, her expression sad. I'm sure she thought of her young Broderick in the same light and imagined a place where she would reunite with him in death.

"Thank you, Iona. I found myself in a bad place for a while." I drew looping daisy petals in the soft white powder before swiping my hand through the design. "But it was time for me to be among the living again." Striking my hands of flour, I looked along the table. "What needs to be done? I want to be useful."

"Those greens need washed and rooted, but the scullery maids can do that. No, ye can help me forage for mushrooms. Some fresh air will do ye good and we still have a few hours yet before I start on the laird's noon meal. Come."

She handed me a clean but tattered white cotton apron, a basket from a shelf, and guided me to the south bailey, skirting the few warriors that were busy sharpening various weapons. The high pitch whine of whetstones on steel filled the courtyard.

Against the grey stone of the castle, her herb garden, neatly-arranged and well-tended, sat where it would get the most sun beside a well. Mounds of chives, thyme, mints, and oregano sat in dark, damp, freshly turned soil. Garlic shoots waited patiently for harvest between the herb mounds. Large fuzzy petals of a sage plant and fine-needled rosemary reached high behind the shorter mounds. A bog myrtle sat proudly in the middle of the garden, its honeyed scent on the breeze warding off the pesky midges. I smiled sadly at the sight of the long-leafed bush. Nan had one in each of her gardens and regularly tucked the leaves into her bra and behind her ear in the summer months to keep the insects away while she weeded.

Following Iona through a gatehouse, we wended down a path along the wall toward the sounds of farm animals. A squat barn sat near to the curtain wall, a few fenced paddocks filled with horses stretching around it.

"Ho, Earie!" she called through the open double doors, and with one hand on her hip, she waited for a skinny old man to shuffle out of the shadows.

His white hair was thin, with nearly all of it missing on top and the rest sticking out at all angles, much like Albert Einstein. He had the most wrinkles I'd ever seen on a face, and when he grinned a me with a gap-toothed smile, I couldn't help but smile back.

"'Tis been a while since I seen the likes o' ye. Ye've come for the pig now, huvnae ye?" Earie's voice was so hoarse, and his brogue was so thick, I understood him more from reading his lips than I did from hearing his words.

"Aye. I depleted my truffle stash and need to forage. We'll be back with him by noontime."

She followed him into the barn and reemerged a few minutes later with a large, hairy hog in tow. She barely had to tug on the braided leather strap that connected to his thick collar as we made a beeline through the field towards the forest in search of oak trees and the fragrant fungi that grew near their roots.

"I've never seen a truffle hog before. Did you train him yourself?" I asked as I hurried after the black and white pig, who grunted and snorted his pleasure at being freed from his pen.

"Aye. Wee Hammy here was destined for my ovens until he broke from his pen. Earie found him deep in the forest feasting on the verra thing he hunts for me now."

I barked a laugh. '*Wee*' was the last word I would use to describe the three hundred pound hog.

"*Hammy?*"

She grinned as we hustled behind him.

"Well, what else do ye name a pig?"

A quarter-mile later, I felt exhilarated and caught my breath when the pig stopped and sniffed between two roots of a large oak. Iona fell to her knees and shouldered Hammy out of her way. She clawed at the soft ground and brushed dead leaves and bracken away to reveal the round, bumpy orbs hiding underneath.

"Good pig!" she cried out and handed him a well-deserved treat before she stood up and brushed off her skirts.

I peeked into her basket, where six small truffles rolled around the bottom.

"Can I gather the next batch?" I asked, excited to be part of this little adventure.

"As long as ye push him out o' the way in time. He's a quick one," she lectured, and tapped his rump lightly with the leather rope to get him to move on. I nodded enthusiastically as I took it from her and trotted behind him, ready to pounce the second he stuck his nose in the ground.

A short time later, I got my chance. The moment he nuzzled the ground, I threw my weight like a linebacker against Hammy's hairy side and barely budged him even an inch. From behind me, Iona howled with amusement, and infectious laughter bubbled out of me while I fought against the pig and clawed at the ground. My efforts were rewarded when I dug a large black sphere from beneath the earth, followed by two small ones.

I turned to Hammy, whose slimy mouth was open and waiting for a treat, and popped one of the smaller globes into his maw before I used his shoulder to pull myself up. Proudly, I displayed the largest truffle to Iona as though the ugly, bulbous mushroom was a golden nugget.

She wiped her cheeks with the corner of her apron, her eyes twinkling.

"Och, I huvnae laughed that hard in years, watchin' yer wee self tackle that pig."

I giggled at my own expense and urged Hammy on to the next root system, feeling much lighter than I had when I woke up. Who would have thought a romp in the woods with a pig would fill me with the sense that everything was going to be just fine?

A couple hours later, we returned to the keep arm in arm with a full basket of black truffles, chicken of the woods, cep, and wood blewit mushrooms. In the cookhouse, I lightly swept the dirt from the fungus and stored them in the buttery for use in the next few days. The truffles we strung with thread and hung high above the ovens to dry.

"Can I make us an omelet for lunch?" I asked when my stomach let out an obnoxious growl.

My mouth watered, and my belly cramped painfully in demand for something other than the whiskey-laden tea I had been living on for the last week.

"Only if ye make one of… whatever that is, for the laird. He takes his noon meals in the library."

With an eager nod, I snatched a copper pan from the rack and set it over the coals that still burned low from breakfast this morning. While it heated, I chopped up a few mushrooms and a large portion of an onion. Tossing the onion bits in, I caramelized them with butter while I cracked eggs into bowls—four for Malcolm, two for each of us. Moving about the room, I found some cream, added a spoonful into the eggs, and beat them vigorously until they were thick and fluffy before folding the mushrooms and a portion of the onions into each.

Adding a pat of butter Paula Dean would be proud of into the copper pan, I waited for it to melt, and rotated the pan so that every inch of it coated evenly before I poured in the egg mixture and jiggled the pan to keep the eggs from sticking. Without my modern-day spatula, I slid the partly cooked eggs onto a plate before flipping them back face-down into the pan. Placing two thick slices of cheese on one side, I folded the eggs over with a wooden spoon and transferred them onto a clean plate. In a small bowl, I mixed truffle shavings with butter and spread a thin glaze over the finished omelet before topping it with fresh parsley.

Handing Malcolm's lunch to Iona, she sniffed the plate, her russet brows raised high as she set it on a tray next to some buttered toast and ordered it up with a serving girl to the hungry MacKinnon laird. She helped me make the next two before we sat down together at the far end of the table to enjoy our well-deserved lunch.

"Where did ye learn to cook like this?" Iona asked between bites.

I wasn't sure how to answer that, or how much I should reveal about where I came from. It didn't seem wise to be honest, as I doubted they had culinary schools in this time, but it was hard to lie to this sweet woman who had befriended me in this strange land. I cleared my throat and took a long sip of water.

"My grandmother loves—loved to cook. She taught me a lot of what I know."

Not a lie, not the full truth, but she was the one that opened the door to my chosen career. I spent many summer days and evenings in her kitchen as a little girl, first just licking the batter from silver beaters and unsuccessfully cracking eggs. It wasn't long before she handed me her favorite recipes and left me to it while she sipped her "special tea" and observed from the kitchen table as she knitted. She also paid for my culinary training. I owed a lot to Nan, and it hurt my heart to know that now I would never be able to repay her.

Iona lifted her blue eyes from her meal and reached across the table to grip my hand, her plump fingers squeezing mine.

"Yer life is here now. Yer no' alone," she whispered kindly.

Tears pricked the corners of my eyes. Colin had said that very thing to me when he held me in his arms. I sniffed, banishing my tears, and squeezed her back before settling my hands on my lap.

"Thank you. I'm glad to have you for a friend."

Iona beamed at me, and her eyes crinkled at the corners.

"Me too."

〜

I sat patiently in the blue room—now my room—and waited for Maeve to help me dress for dinner. I'd spent the entire day with Iona, and although my thoughts had drifted to Nan on more than a dozen occasions, the sorrow I felt over the last week failed to resurface. I was still sad to never see her again, and probably always would be, but her memory did not drag me back under the black cloud that smothered me in the days prior.

In the peacefulness of my room, I gave myself a silent vow to survive in this remarkable place. Not just survive but *thrive*. I had access to a kitchen I was welcome in and grateful people to make food for with the fresh ingredients Nan raised me to use. Sure, I would miss my KitchenAid Mixer, microwave, and non-stick cookware, but I found I loved the challenge of figuring out how to get the same effect without the luxury of electricity or silicone.

Propped up on the recessed window ledge, I pulled my knees against my chest and rested my forehead against the cool glass. Its greenish hue gave the world a dreary cast as I scanned the rolling countryside beyond the loch. Dark clouds had rolled in a few hours ago and misted the air with impending rain. The wet season had made its presence known and would permanently scent the air for the next few months. Days like this made me glad to have a warm, dry kitchen to spend long hours.

When I was a young girl, I always thought there was magic in Scotland. It was something I could almost feel on my skin while I frolicked in the woods or swam in the many rivers and lochs. That feeling blessed me with a rampant imagination, although most of it was thanks to Nan and her fairy houses, and my mom with her tales of fair maidens in castles, enchanted pools, and toad trolls.

But never had I imagined *this* was possible. To sit here and see the world before we ruined it. I was seeing the earth almost a hundred years before the Industrial Revolution. Even the air I pulled into my lungs was different. Cleaner. Sweeter.

A soft knock announced Maeve's bubbly face as she entered, carrying the lace apron free of fingerprints.

"Did ye have an enjoyable day, milady?" she asked, even though I was sure she knew full well how I spent my every hour.

With a nod, I hopped off my perch and gave her my back so she could finish undoing the dozens of buttons that ran up my spine. I had given up on them myself, having only undone three before my fingers cramped, and I resigned myself to wait for help.

"I did, very much. I spent too long in this room alone."

She brushed streaks of flour from the sleeves, and her brows furrowed as she picked a few bits of dark soil and tree bark off from the hem that I had missed from our truffle hunt. I only shrugged at her questioning look, plastering an innocent smile on my lips before I washed my hands in the basin and wiped my face and neck down with a soft, damp cloth.

After choosing a cream-colored silk dress with light golden cuffs, Maeve tied the corset enclosure at my back, and after poking through a jewelry box, lifted a delicate necklace of aquamarines with a silk ribbon enclosure. My hair had become ruffled after my wrestling match with Hammy and a day spent cooking, so she let it all down to brush before braiding it, and secured it at my nape with a few twists. Lastly, she brandished buff-colored slippers from one of the many Mary Poppins chests, and then dabbed rose oil behind each of my ears before nodding in satisfaction and left for her supper.

A peek at my patinaed reflection showed some life had crept back into the wan face of the bedraggled woman I was this morning. My cheeks had color, and the light blue jewels at my throat brought attention to the differences in my eye color.

I had lost weight. My cheeks were slightly hollow and my collarbones more pronounced from a week of tea and whiskey as my only sustenance, but thankfully I no longer looked like I had one foot in the grave.

A young girl in maids' garb was busily lighting the oil lamps in the alcoves between windows when I passed her on my way to the great hall. The hem of my dress whispered lightly against the polished wood floor with each sway of my hips, and in my eagerness to see Colin again, I had to slow myself down from a jog—*twice.*

I knew he was aware that my self-confinement was over—Maeve told me so herself when she handed me the single blue petaled flower he sent her to gift me.

He gave me space today, which I was grateful for. The time I spent with Iona had been a welcome buffer between those depressing days I spent grieving my grandmother's absence, and the joy I knew I would feel at seeing him again.

My steps were quick and light as I descended the grand staircase and found my hosts in deep in conversation. Colin caught sight of me first and stopped mid-speech. His sapphire-blue eyes snapped to mine before they drifted from my head to my feet, taking in the changes of my body before he gave me a sad, understanding smile, and lifted his eyebrows as if to ask, *are you alright?*

Settling into the empty chair across from him, I nodded shyly before taking a sip of wine.

"I'm glad to see ye, Meggie," Colin rumbled. Leaning back in his chair, he held my stare. "And I've been told ye had yer magic fingers in tonight's meal—"

"—Och, ye missed the noon meal she made for me, brother," Malcolm boasted as he reached over to shake Colin's shoulder.

I snickered, remembering how Malcolm howled my name and thundered down the kitchen stairwell when Iona and I were cleaning up our lunch dishes. With a manic grin on his face, he had picked me up around my ribcage and swung me around, promising me his favored warhorse if I would just make him one more folded-egg-with-cheese-in-the-middle. He then parked himself at the long table and watched me fulfill his request like an overgrown hobbit waiting for a second breakfast.

"That is a shame," Colin said, and glared at me in mock jealousy over his mug of mead while the kitchen maids set the dinner platters on the table.

The lid of the largest earthenware pot was removed with a flourish to reveal the tender beef roast soaking in a red wine and bone broth reduction. Beside it, mushroom caps lay among large hunks of carrots with wilted sprigs of thyme and rosemary. Another bowl held creamy garlic mashed potatoes next to a basket of yeast rolls. I watched as the men leaned forward, sniffing at the fragrant steam that rose from the braised beef, and wasted no time in filling their plates haphazardly while I made a small mound of potatoes in the middle of mine. Next, I arranged the beef and carrots on top of the fluffy mound before spooning the thick broth in an elegant crescent on the plate. Happy with my presentation, I speared a small bite and brought it to my mouth, savoring the way the flavors coated my tongue while I chewed the tender meat.

"What?" I asked when I looked up and found my plate the object of fascination and bewilderment by both men. Colin shook his head slightly in what could only be wonder, his lips turning up in the corners.

"Everything is just so… put together," Colin blurted. "Would ye arrange my meal like that sometime?"

Malcolm nodded enthusiastically, with his mouth full, and pointed down at his plate in agreement. I shrugged my shoulders and beamed at them.

"If you'd like. I won't be able to make it pretty if I fill your plate like you have, but you can always serve yourself a second helping."

They looked pleased with the compromise and turned their attention back to their own food, the clink of silverware on the metal plates our dining symphony.

"Ye've done it again, lass." Malcolm leaned back in his chair to rub his stomach as he sang my praises. After sipping from his mead tankard, he pointed it in Colin's direction, the amber liquid barely contained as it sloshed up the side. "I speak for us both when I say ye're welcome here for however long ye decide to stay. Hopefully, for a verra long time."

Saluting me, they both drained their cups.

My belly warm, and my cheeks flushed from the wine, I looked down at my lap and nodded, emotional over their declaration.

Thumping his empty tankard on the table, Malcolm rose from his seat and excused himself, leaving us alone in the great hall. The sun had set long ago, leaving the room dark save for the soft, romantic candlelight. In the quiet hall, my skin felt tight under the weight of his gaze, and I bit down on my bottom lip to keep from squirming. This man made me ache with longing to touch him—to be touched by him—and that terrified me as much as it excited me.

"Come with me."

His deep voice rolled through the silence as he stood and walked around the table to pull my chair out. Black leather pants hugged his muscular thighs, his white shirt left untucked. My heart rate sped up at the thrill of those three words. Heat licked up my neck and my stomach tightened when I looked up at him.

"Where are we going?" I asked as I placed my fingertips in his warm palm.

"The library. I thought we could end the evening with a game."

Intrigued, I agreed, and with my hand tucked into the crook of his arm, he guided me up to the cozy library with the tall windows.

Embers were still burning low in the hearth under a thick coating of light grey ash and caught a new log in flames quickly. While Colin lit a few fat, white candles to illuminate the corners of the room, I busied myself with pouring some wine into two horn cups. Rain began tapping a light rhythm on the glass just as a few far-off pulses of lightning lit the dark hills outside.

He maneuvered the two cushioned chairs before the fire to face one another with the small table between them and then lifted a heavy chess set down from the top of a cabinet. With care, he placed it on the smooth wood surface of the table. I felt a mixture of relief and disappointment at the barrier between us, but handed him a cup and took the seat with my back to the open double-door.

"Have ye played before?" Colin asked hopefully while he tidied up the line of black pieces.

I nodded and ran my fingers down the thick side of the wooden base. Every inch of the dark, oiled wood was carved with delicate depictions of craggy mountains, castles, and pine trees.

"My father taught me when I was a little girl. I'm not good at it at all, but I enjoyed playing with him."

I lifted the king and studied his heavy weight in the candlelight. These pieces were not the cheap plastic moldings I had played with as a girl. Creamy, ivory tusk was chiseled and shaped into the likeness of a squat old man with beady eyes and a sword resting over his knees as he sat on his throne. He stared back at me from underneath his crown. The rook depicted a man standing behind a full-length shield, his square teeth biting the top rim with a wild look in his eyes. The knight was a man with a spear in hand, mounted upon a horse draped in a covering to hide the legs. Bishops stood tall on either side of the royals with their staffs in one hand and the other held up as though they were giving the last rites. Pawns were just spheres, all relatively the same size with a flat bottom to keep them from rolling.

I found the queen to be the most peculiar. She sat upon her throne with one hand cradling her face, the other resting in her lap as though she was bored and dismayed with her company. She held no weapon, just her crown. The strongest player on the board, yet she looked so fragile with her lack of armament.

"These are beautiful. What are the black pieces carved from?"

"Jet. 'Tis been in the family for many generations. My father taught me as well, and I'm no' good either." Winking at me, he leaned forward to advance one of his pawns forward two spaces. "They carved the ivory from walrus tusk. 'Tis one of our few great treasures."

I peeked behind me towards the open doors and the darkness of the hallway before turning back to whisper, "In my time, ivory is illegal in many countries. Poachers have hunted some species into extinction simply for their horns and leave their carcasses behind to rot in the sun." I looked at the pieces sadly. "In Africa, the last living male white rhino received an armed guard until his death just last year. There are two females left, but they're the last of their kind, and when they die, there will never be another."

It was not lost on me that in the seventeenth century, there were probably thousands of white rhinos wandering the African planes. I lifted the knight and shook it in the air gently before advancing it over my line of pawns. "So, I say these pieces are beautiful, but they're ugly too."

Colin regarded me quietly a moment before he too slid his eyes toward the open door.

"I'm sorry, Meggie. I ken how badly ye wanted to go home," he murmured as he moved another pawn up one space to make room for his bishop to run free.

"Thank you. I suppose I could be worse off, though. Here I am, with a roof over my head and a warm welcome when I could be dead. What were the odds you had been in those woods that day? And close enough to hear me?" I tapped my fingernails on the side of my cup before taking a long swallow. "I thought about that day a lot the last week, and I know I'm so very lucky you found me, Colin. Even luckier that you believe me... I owe you my life."

He shook his head slightly and stared into the flames with a haunted look on his face. "Ye owe me nothin', lass. I was glad to do it. Would do it again a hundred times."

"Well, I'm grateful all the same."

We sat in silence for a while, taking turns moving our pieces over the hand-carved checkered squares of stone and bone.

"What's it like... the future world?" he whispered as he leaned over the board, his eyes no longer somber but lit up with curiosity. "I guess it's very similar to this chess set. Beautiful... and ugly." Taking a deep breath, I gathered my thoughts. "We rely a lot on our technology in the future. That technology has allowed us to build the most amazing creations. Buildings so high that when it rains, most of them are hidden above the clouds. Bridges can span miles over waterways... we have tunnels that allow us to travel under the ocean, and we built a rocket that took a man to the moon."

Colin's face twisted from fascination to disbelief mixed with fear.

"That's no' possible," he whispered. "Is it?"

"The moon landing happened decades before I was born, and there's more than a few skeptics that deny it ever happened, but yes, it's possible, and they go several times." Emptying my cup, I held it up for a refill. "And I wasn't lying about the machines. The truck and the plane? They exist—or at least they will. And they can do more than just carry you from place to place. When we made machines, the world really changed. What used to take ten men all day to do, a machine could do in minutes. It became all about efficiency... all about money and the bottom line." I thanked him for filling my cup and moved my second knight forward, placing it in danger of his queen, but guarded by my pawn. "Because it's all about wealth, we'll start to kill the environment. We'll do it in the name of economics. For jobs, you see. There're so many people who need the income, so where do we draw the line? And that's where we move into the ugly. Animals choke on the garbage we dump in the ocean and on the side of the road. We need enormous water treatment plants to filter our drinking water. We put chemical preservatives in our food to make it last longer because we hold more food in our pantries than we really need. Half the time, it's not even used by the expiration date, so it ends up getting tossed to rot in a landfill for the next hundred years."

Colin looked at me sadly.

"Ye said there's beauty. Where is the good in yer world?" he asked as he slid his queen across the board to take my knight.

Palming the horse, he saw his mistake and cursed, lightly smacking the table in frustration. I smiled wryly. So, he wasn't lying when he said he didn't play well. Taking his queen in my possession, I rolled her between my palms, the jet cold and smooth from centuries of use.

"We have national parks which are protected chunks of wilderness you can visit. Our art is pretty amazing. It's no longer just sculptures of people and animals, portraits and landscapes. There's a woman in my country that can *see* music—literally see it in her mind's eye, and she's able to paint it on canvas to share with the world. I wish you could see them. They're truly amazing."

He captured one of my pawns and advanced on his bishop, smiling slightly.

"And the food, you know that to be true." Winking at him, I watched his smile grow. I'm sure he was reminiscing on the macarons. "The music too… there's a genre for everyone. I know you have no idea what these things are, but the invention of the electric guitar, turntables, and sound booths make anything possible… or at least they will in a few hundred years."

"What else?" he asked as I moved a pawn and thought for a moment.

"The dancing. I believe some performances could move even a hardened warrior like yourself to tears."

Colin looked skeptical, but instead of denying the possibility, he studied the board a moment before moving his knight toward my queen. I moved my bishop to intercept.

"But saying all that, the only thing I really miss is my grandmother—and toilets! Ugh. I'm not even going to expand on that luxury, but seriously, you're missing out. Indoor plumbing is one of man's greatest inventions, if not *the* greatest invention. Imagine having a room dedicated to bathing, and all you have to do is turn a knob, and hot water rushes out of a pipe to fill your bathtub in a matter of minutes."

Sighing heavily, I gave the modern toilet's absence the moment of silence it deserved. Resting my chin on my fist, I watched as Colin moved a pawn up two spaces… and freed up the clear shot from his bishop to my king.

"Checkmate."

I sat up straight and stared at the board to find that if I moved my king anywhere else; he was in danger from Colin's rook, knight, or pawn.

"Well, damn."

I didn't even see it coming; I was so involved in describing the twenty-first century. He chuffed a laugh and grinned like the Cheshire cat, pleased with his win and not above a little gloating.

I glared at him playfully. "I think you used my distraction to your advantage. I thought men from this century were supposed to be chivalrous."

He shrugged his massive shoulders and reached across the table to tip over my king before leaning back in his chair with his legs stretched out under the small table.

"I'm happy ye're here, Meggie. I ken Mrs. Cook is. Ye've soothed that auld woman. Many others have tried, and all have failed until ye showed up lookin' like a wee bog monster."

"I did *not* look like a bog monster."

Hiding my elation that he was happy I was here, I feigned indignation at his description of my appearance that day. In truth, a bog monster is probably *exactly* what I looked like, but he held his hands up in surrender and laughed.

"Whether ye did or dinnae, ye've thawed her, and for that, we're all grateful."

"You like her," I stated.

Tucking my feet under my thighs, I enjoyed the heat of the wine in my belly and the flames in the hearth. Sitting with him was comfortable and so enjoyable, I imagined I could sit here all night with him as my only company.

"I do, though I terrorized her as a young lad, always sneakin' into her domain to steal a sweet or two. I used to pretend she was a giant, and if she caught me, she'd gobble me up." Chuckling to himself, he shook his head as he described his childhood adventures.

"Now, Mrs. Cook doesnae like bairns to spoil their supper, so sneakin' in and out successfully without yer ears gettin' boxed had its own set of challenges. Malcolm always took the brutish way he usually does, tearing down the stairs as fast as his legs could carry him to pull a snatch-and-grab before she could catch him."

I tipped my head back and laughed, having already witnessed Malcolm MacKinnon running down the stairs to snatch *me* up and then beg for another omelet a moment later. I'm sure as a young boy, he was even faster, without the bulk of a grown man's body slowing him down.

"And you? How did you steal your sweets?"

"I learned to be patient," he explained, his deep voice smooth and sultry as he slowly walked his index and middle finger along the edge of the table between us. "I learned to be quiet. How to be invisible in an open room and how to use my surroundings to my advantage. It didnae matter if it took me five minutes or twenty; it was the thrill of being caught that drove me."

"*That's* how you're so quiet. I noticed, back in the woods, how you could walk and not even snap a twig."

He nodded, finishing his wine, and refilled his cup as well as mine, emptying the flagon of the last few drops. Down the hall, I could hear faint murmurings as doors opened and closed. It was getting late, but I didn't want this night to end.

"Aye, the sneaky practice in the cookery eventually bled into my skills as a hunter, and then as a warrior."

I tilted my head. He was not boastful like I expected, but solemn, simply stating a quiet fact. The terrible memory of one of my attackers grabbing his ravaged, bloody throat came unbidden into my mind. I shivered and yearned for the day when I could forget that gruesome sight.

"The man in the woods," I whispered, and rubbed the skin at the base of my throat.

"Aye. He didnae ken I was behind him until it was too late." He met my stare levelly. "Does that scare ye, Meggie?"

My pulse drummed under my fingertips as memories of those two men played back in sharp detail. *They* had scared me. The lecherous look in their eyes disgusted me. What they had planned for me, had I been alone and vulnerable, was enough to make me want to vomit. Had anyone else been in the woods that day... I doubt they would have chosen to risk their lives to save me, a total stranger.

"I know it should... but I feel safe with you."

I felt more than just safe with this man. I felt protected, cherished, and wanted. Whenever he was near, my body reacted intensely to his voice, his touch, his smell.

"It pleases me to hear that." Draining his cup, he stood smoothly from his chair and extended his hand. "'Tis a late hour. I'll walk ye to yer chamber."

I let him pull me gently to my feet and lead me through the candlelit hallways, his warm hand clasped around mine. All too soon, we stopped before the beautifully carved door of the blue room, and he reached for the latch, pushing it open on near-silent hinges. Excitement curled in my belly as I looked up at his handsome face, the shadows making him seem even larger.

Watching him in fascination, he held my stare as he lifted my hand to his mouth and pressed his lips intimately against my palm. The short whiskers of his beard were a new, delicious tickle against my skin, and I had to fight the urge to curl my fingers against his cheek.

"Good night, lovely Meggie," he murmured against my skin.

Pulling away, he left me standing in the doorway to watch him disappear into the gloom.

CHAPTER 13

Meggie

I relaxed on one of the stools at the prep table in the kitchen and winced as I watched four children try again and again to snatch a pastry off a tray. They were failing miserably. The puffy raspberry-and-cream pastries I taught Iona to make earlier this morning were just too enticing for them to quit after the first failed try. The cook wielded her wooden spoon as though she were a fencing champion, and their stubborn little fingers were red and angry because of that sharp aim. After a minute I was beginning to think she was enjoying it and stood to put a stop to their torment before she started drawing blood.

These kids could certainly benefit from a lesson or two from Colin. Their strategy was lousy.

"Enough of this." I laughed. "You'll each wash that pile of pots there before you have a taste. Go on."

Wide, innocent eyes met mine and bounced back and forth as they took in my eye color. Hope bloomed on their faces a heartbeat later and they dashed to the pile of dishes, scampering off with their arms full.

With a smirk, I looked down my nose at Iona. "If I learned anything from my Nan, it was not to waste free labor." Snatching two pastries from the pile, I cut each in half for when the dishes returned clean. "Or at the very least, cheap labor."

"Hmph. I guess there's some truth in that."

Grumbling to herself, she placed the rest of the pastries on a top shelf, far out of reach from thieving hands.

Returning to my stool, I sipped my tea and contemplated what to do with my day when I felt a finger travel softly down the side of my neck. Squeaking, I whirled around, spilled my tea on the stone floor, and almost toppled off my perch by the time I found Colin grinning playfully as he claimed the stool next to mine.

"I'm going to put a bell on you!" I hissed, unsure if my elevated heart rate was because he surprised me, or just because he was near.

Probably a bit of both.

His golden hair was still damp from a bath, the curling ends soaking the collar of his white shirt a light grey. His long, muscular legs were once again covered in leather and his feet were bare. He smelled of soap and pine, a combination I loved instantly.

"It willnae work," Iona snapped as she placed a few pastries on a plate and set them in front of Colin with a motherly glare. "I tried that when he was but a bairn, and he *still* managed to scare years off my life on several occasions."

I covered my smile with my hand when Colin shrugged, unrepentant, and took a bite of his pastry.

"Mrs. Cook made those this morning," I blurted. "Do you want some milk?" Hopping up, I filled a small cup with the fresh, creamy liquid and handed it to him.

"Och, delicious, but dinnae give any to the laird, Mrs. Cook. He's gettin' fat," he teased with a wink. Making quick work of his breakfast, he took his dishes to the designated counter.

I snorted at the thought of anyone calling Malcolm fat. Sure, the MacKinnon laird didn't have the defined bulk of muscle mass Colin had, but who did? I wouldn't say Malcolm had a dad bod, but he certainly lacked a warrior's physique. Besides, he was more of a scholar than a warrior, and I would bet money that he spent more of his time in the library than he did anywhere else.

At that moment, four children ran into the kitchen with clean bakeware and eagerly shoved them under the cook's nose for inspection while they turned their hungry gaze on their prize waiting for them at the far end of the table.

"Ye dried them too, I see." Iona waved her hand at the pastries before she sighed heavily. "Motivated by yer stomachs, the lot o' ye. Take yer sweets and dinnae return for more this day."

They settled the clean pots on the shelves with enough noise to rival a marching band before their eager fingers snatched at the goodies. A moment later, they disappeared up the stairs in a herd of grey fabric and unruly curls, the sound of their giggles echoing off the stone.

"I hope that bought me a day of peace," Iona groused, and marched off in the buttery's direction.

I snickered to myself and smoothed a wrinkle in my skirts. Maeve dressed me in lavender today and swept my hair away from my face with silver combs. The rest hung down my back in a thick plait with the ends wrapped in a white lace ribbon. Black leather slippers protected the white silk stockings she cinched at my thigh with lace stays. I had to admit, I felt beautiful in these dresses, so different from my usual jeans and cotton T-shirts. The lack of underwear still felt incredibly bohemian and a bit hedonistic, knowing everyone else around me was also sans their knickers... including the man beside me. I felt my face flush at the thought and pulled my bottom lip between my teeth.

Colin ran his finger lightly down my cheek, noting my blush, and said, "Ye're lookin' verra bonnie this morn. Would ye like to ride with me to the village? Bram and Finlay need to pick up some supplies, and I ken ye want to see more than just the inside of these walls."

All thought of Commando Colin and his sinful leather pants disappeared in a puff of smoke—almost.

"The village? Absolutely!" Elated at the opportunity to explore my new home, I jumped up and quickly deposited my empty teacup with his plate before rushing back to him.

Shooting me a dazzling smile, he took my hand and tucked it into the crook of his elbow before leading me up the stairs. I looked back to find Iona watching us as she set down sacks of flour and sugar in preparation for baking the day's bread. Her features gentle, she gave me a brief wave before we disappeared from her view.

Dashing up to my room for a cloak, I secured it below the dip of my throat with the silver frog-clasp and pulled the wide hood over my head to protect my hair from the weather. Stepping through the keep's main doors, I was met by a light mist that thickened the air around me, and fat drops of collected condensation dripped on my hood when I walked beneath the oak tree. I found Colin already seated on Una with his tartan draped over his shoulders, and his feet no longer bare. Clasping my forearm, he pulled me up without difficulty to sit in front of him.

"Ready for a wee journey, Meggie?" His arm tightened around my waist, and I nodded eagerly, barely containing my excitement.

Una responded to the click of his tongue and trotted through the gatehouse. Bram and Finlay were waiting just outside the wall on their twin greys, their chocolate-brown hair curling tightly in the mist. Colin's cousins seemed delighted at my presence and wasted no time in sharing stories of when they were young boys.

"Remember the day ye slipped that massive beetle in the cook's apron?" Finlay crowed, his boyish chuckle filling the air around us.

It didn't take me long to notice that the most noticeable difference between the twins was that Finlay was a bit of a ditz, louder and quicker to laugh than his more subdued mirror image. The two of them rode on either side of us, volleying a constant chatter. I twisted in Colin's arms to look up at him in shock that he would do such a thing to my friend. Sheepish but unapologetic, he shrugged and stared straight ahead at the wide, muddy path flanked with ash and oak.

"She never found out it was me, either," he said with pride before shooting me a warning look.

"Oh, I'm surely not telling her." I laughed and leaned back against his chest.

As we rode east for a mile or so, I soaked up the tales of their childhood until the forest thinned into an open field. To my delight, a town came into view, nestled in the bowl of a shallow valley. Three well-traveled roads, not including the path we were on, also led into the hamlet, causing me to believe it was an important crossroads to the area. I wondered if the town was still around in the future. I didn't remember driving through it on my way to the estate.

The short church steeple rose proudly in the middle of the town, making me believe it was the first building erected, and the people followed, laying down roots and making their homes and businesses around it. Long, squat, mud and stone huts with steep thatched roofs outlined the eastern edge along a lazy river that curved around half the town. Sturdier and more sophisticated one and two-story stone and mortar buildings clustered around the perimeter of the churchyard.

We could hear the high-pitched clang and ping of a blacksmith hard at work long before we entered the town, and the men guided our horses to a small stable near to the smithy. Colin helped me down before speaking to a young boy in Gaelic, and passed him a coin, as well as Una's lead rope.

"This way, Meggie."

Striding away from the stable, Colin left me to follow in his wake between houses and small private gardens toward the center of town. Finlay and Bram trailed close at my heels.

In the town proper, hard-packed dirt and gravel served as roads and walkways between buildings. Shaker signs hung above some doorways with either painted pictures or words in Gaelic describing what I may find inside.

I absorbed the surrounding sights, enchanted. The smoke of peat fires permeated my senses, as well as boisterous laughter that rolled out of a two-story tavern. A young girl with bouncing blonde curls crossed our path while she chased a flock of grey geese through the street with a stick.

When Colin ducked into a building with the word *Spiosradh* painted in flowing white lettering above the door, I slipped through after him and immediately identified the aromatic scent of cinnamon and clove. Peering curiously around his large frame, my eyes adjusted to the watery light that filtered down from small windows in the loft. Dark floors and even darker brown shelving lined on all four walls and were stuffed from top to bottom with sacks, clay jars, small wooden boxes, and tall cylindrical glass containers with elaborate toppers. Only the heavenly smell of herbs and spices offset the building's gloomy interior.

A spindly woman with hair the color of walnuts and a pinched face sat behind a table labeling vials. She greeted Colin by name.

"What can I do ye for? Rosston just brought a shipment back from York," she boasted and gestured to the shelves behind her.

Colin smiled kindly at the woman, but turned towards me and said, "I assume ye know what our cookery is lackin'. Gather what ye need, and I'll be back shortly."

With a nod to the woman, he left me with my task, and I introduced myself. My American accent obviously surprised her, but she quickly mastered her face and introduced herself as Nessa. She proudly told me she had owned the shop with her husband for the last thirty years, hauling back spices from Inverness, Edinburgh, and even some of the British cities, supplying the locals with the savory and sweet.

A cheery fire burned in a corner hearth, not only to provide warmth but to keep the room dry, preserving the life of the seeds and leaves. The heat of it forced me to discard my cloak, and I laid it over the back of a chair before taking a turn around the room.

Iona's kitchen wasn't entirely without spices, but I quickly found a few that would complement what she already had, and I eagerly began pulling the little pots down, hunting for the best options.

Nessa followed me around as I handed her my choices.

"Are ye the new cook, then?" she queried.

I glared at the tidy, painted writing on a tin jar and wished I understood Gaelic. It was a good thing I knew most spices by scent. Black cardamom pods were my first exciting find, as well as Spanish saffron, the orange-red fibers potent in their small glass vial. I could use cardamom seeds on both meats and sweets and the saffron with fish... Nessa's question finally seeped into my consciousness and I pulled my nose out of a jar of dried lemon peel.

New cook? My good mood deflated at the thought of Iona being pushed out of her position.

"Um, no… I'm only here to help." I stumbled over my answer as Nessa gave me a small patronizing smile and took the jar of lemon and a sack of star anise from my outstretched hand.

"That's good to hear," she said, depositing the sack on the table. "Since Iona's made her life in that cookery."

My back stiffened at the not-so-subtle warning, but decided not to rise to the bait. Turning back to the shelving, I continued my perusal, very much aware of the woman who stared a hole between my shoulder blades.

"Yes, well, she has nothing to fear from me, I assure you."

You're a stranger in this land, Meggie Washington. You should expect some people to be wary, I coached myself. Clearing my throat of the tension I felt, I turned a bright smile her way, and determined to change the subject, asked, "Do you have nutmeg?"

Colin returned to the shop ten minutes later to find me ready to go with measured amounts of dried lemon peel, cloves, nutmeg, star anise, cardamom pods, a small vial of saffron, a bundle of cinnamon sticks, and two small envelopes of coriander and basil seeds. The latter I planned to grow in Iona's herb garden. All were snug in a small wooden crate.

Digging out coins from his sporran, he placed them into Nessa's open palm one at a time. Slipping them into the pocket of her apron, she spoke a few words in Gaelic, a tight smile on her mouth. Colin's brows drew down slightly as he looked down at the older woman.

Whatever she had said, it had not made him happy, and I did not envy her to be on the receiving end of his glower.

"*I mo bhean san àm ri teachd,*" he growled in response.

Nessa's eyes popped wide and slid to mine in a slight panic.

Without another word, Colin grabbed the crate and tucked it under his right arm. His left hand settled on the small of my back, and firmly guided me out the door and away from the speechless shopkeeper.

"Nice to meet you," I said sweetly to Nessa's blanched face when we left her store.

Outside, the mist still hadn't let up, and I quickly pulled my hood over my hair. Bram was waiting outside and took Colin's burden of spices. The clay and glass containers clinked together in the transfer.

"Those can't get wet," I said, pointing at the crate. He immediately covered it with his plaid, the tightly woven wool thick enough to shield the dried vegetation and seeds from the mist.

Satisfied, I looked up at Colin. "What did you say to her?"

Ignoring my question, he crossed his arms over his tartan covered chest and looked down at me with both irritation and concern. Somehow, I knew the irritation wasn't pointed at me.

"Was she rude to ye, Meggie?"

"No. She only asked me if I was here to replace Mrs. Cook," I confessed, wanting to hear what he thought of it.

He scoffed and shook his head as he took my arm and led me down the damp road. When he didn't comment, I pushed the subject while he steered us around puddles, mud, and horse dung.

"I'm not... right? I can't replace Iona."

"No, lass. As much as we've all enjoyed the fruits of yer labor, ye're no' destined to fill her post. That's no' why I brought ye here today."

Relieved, I followed him into a tavern. The smell of beer and whiskey, as well as roasted chicken, greeted us with a puff of warm air.

"What is my destiny, then?" I countered, melancholy because I surely didn't know.

Colin only gave me a roguish smirk, which told me absolutely nothing. He pushed his way through the small, crowded tavern towards one of the few small tables in the back by a window where I spotted Finlay already seated in the corner, a wrapped parcel before him.

The creaky wood floors of the tavern were slightly sticky and smelled strongly of fermented fruit. The stench made me slightly nauseous, but I could handle it. I've smelled worse.

The tavern patrons were loud and already tipsy, even though it was only early afternoon. Taking a seat with my back to the door, Bram staked the chair to my left, his back to the window, leaving Colin to sit on my right. Toeing the crate to the relative safety under my chair, I looked around.

A grizzly old man with white hair and a missing eye under bushy brows tended his bar, cleaning tankards and horn cups with a piece of fraying cloth. Earthenware jugs and small tapped barrels resting on their sides lined a counter behind the bar, and a set of stairs led up to the second floor behind them.

"Why, hello there, lads," a throaty voice purred.

Spinning in my seat, I witnessed a buxom brunette with exotic looking, up-tilted eyes and pouty lips run her knuckles affectionately over Finlay's shaven cheek. Her touch elicited a wicked grin from him as he pulled her down to perch in his lap.

"What will ye have, sweet Meggie?" Bram asked me.

I looked at the three men nervously. My days of ordering a glass of Pino Grigio with a grilled chicken Caesar were long gone.

"Um, whatever you're having?" I squeaked.

Finlay hooted and ordered *a dram and a pint all around* as he caressed the serving wench's curls. She winked at him and hopped up to fill his order.

Leaning toward Colin, I silently beckoned him with a look, and he leaned close enough for me to whisper, "What exactly is a dram and a pint?"

"A small measure of scotch and a pint of ale," he answered before standing up to greet a monster of a man with a weathered face and the biggest arms I'd ever seen.

They spoke most conversations around me in Gaelic, something that relieved and irritated me since I only knew the swear words, courtesy of my grandmother. My ears *always* caught those.

A natural-born people watcher, my concentration flitted from person to person until they noticed my stare and I was forced to look away. Being the only woman in the tavern besides the curvy beauty serving us, I was already calling the attention of the locals, and because of that, I reluctantly abandoned my survey to face my three companions. It was hard to be the watcher when you were the one being watched.

A minute later, four tall glasses of dark ale accompanied by four short horn cups filled with swirling honey-colored scotch arrived at our table.

Ho boy, this was going to be dangerous, but when in Rome… Following Colin's lead so I didn't look like a professional shot-taker, I gulped down the liquor, and the burn of it raced down my throat to sit in a pool of fire in my belly. Blinking tears from my eyes, I pulled my pint of ale closer and took a small sip to chase the biting aftereffect of the single malt with its fruity taste.

"Good lass!" Finlay barked. Saluting me, he stood to push through the growing lunch crowd toward three men playing cards on the other side of the room.

Bram rolled his eyes. "I'm no' in the mood to pull him out o' any trouble today." Grumbling into his tankard, he glared daggers at Finlay's back before grinning at me when he caught me looking at him. "Dinnae worry overmuch, lass. Finlay can handle himself on most days."

I looked between the two of them dubiously before returning my attention to the amber liquid in front of me. Never having had ale before, I found I liked it. It wasn't the hoppy, slightly watery body of Stella Artois, that's for sure, but it was crisp and sweet and tasty. I took another sip.

"What else do we have to do here?" I asked Colin.

"I have an order ready from Norval at the tannery… Although, that may no' be somewhere ye would enjoy visiting." Leaning on his forearms, he scanned the tavern slowly, his body relaxed but his focus alert. It wouldn't surprise me if he always knew where everyone in the building was at every given second, even those that stood behind him.

Along the length of the bar, men sang an awful, tuneless song in Gaelic about a "bonnie whore". They draped their arms over one another's shoulders, and swaying back and forth, their warbling becoming louder, causing me to raise my voice.

"Why not?"

Colin studied me a moment before answering.

"Have ye a strong stomach, Meggie?"

Well, that didn't sound good. I eyed him cautiously. "I'd like to think so." I lived in Manhattan for a year, for Christ's sake. I've smelled things no one should be subjected to.

Beside me, Bram snickered and drained his glass. Lifting it, he caught the barmaid's eye and held up three fingers.

I peered into my half-empty pint, took a deep breath, and prepared myself to finish it by the time she brought the second round. Bram's eyebrow cocked up as I began my tried and true, sloth-slow beer guzzle. Mindful that none escaped to drip down my chin, I plunked down the empty glass moments before the second order arrived.

Pleased that I accomplished that small goal, I wiggled a little dance in my chair and swiftly picked up one of the three drams that had just arrived. I shot both men a smug look before disappearing the fiery liquid into my belly. They looked at me with their brows hiked high. Neither of them touched their horn cups yet.

Trying hard but failing miserably to suppress the full-body shiver that raced down my spine, I quickly washed away the sting of the alcohol with my fresh ale and met Colin's rapt stare. His mouth slowly curved into an encouraging smile when he picked up his whiskey.

"I've never had ale before," I admitted with a small hiccup.

Both men looked at one another before they both leaned back in their chairs and roared with laughter. I couldn't help but feel that I was the subject of a joke when Finlay sauntered back to his seat, his face set into a scowl as he scanned the table.

"Which one o' ye *bataichean* stole my dram?" He glared accusingly at his twin. "I saw ye order three, brother."

Oh. I could feel a blush creep up my neck to mottle my cheeks as Colin and Bram turned amused faces upon me. I cleared my throat and licked my lips.

"It seems *I* am the bastard," I confirmed, my face hot from embarrassment as well as the two shots of hard liquor in thirty minutes. No wonder they looked at me with such shock!

This round was not meant for me.

All three men howled with amusement when I sheepishly slid the pint across the table towards its rightful owner. Finlay waved the pint away and reached for my hand to lay a quick kiss on my knuckles before making his way to the bar.

"You two could have warned me," I sniped.

"Ye snatched it up so fast, we didnae have the chance." Bram chuckled before tipping his whiskey back and laid its lip down on the table. Colin teasingly offered me his dram and snickered when I shot him a halfhearted glare.

I nursed my second ale, content to listen to them talk about the upcoming Sunday supper happening in four days. Having drawn the short stick for that evening, Bram would be on guard duty and was sorely upset to miss the entertainment. Colin was due to set his rabbit snares in the forests and meadows to help support the many mouths to feed.

My thoughts blurred pleasantly together when Colin plunked some coins on the table and stood to leave, extending his hand to help me out of my chair.

Oh my. I gripped his fingers hard to keep myself steady, and the full effect of the last hour slammed into me.

"Um, I made a mistake," I muttered, belatedly realizing Scot ale had a vastly different alcohol content than the watered-down American beer I was used to.

Colin looked down on me with knowing patience. Directing Bram to grab my crate of spices, he steered me toward the doors and the cool mist outside.

"I think I'll pay auld Norval a visit on the morrow. Let us be gettin' ye back to the keep," he murmured as we exited the tavern.

"I can still go," I protested. Only slightly swaying, I laid my hand on his forearm. I hated being *that* girl, ruining plans all because she couldn't hold her liquor.

Colin peered through the grimy window to see Bram collecting Finlay from the bar and explained, "Meggie, the tannery is a foul-smelling place where the tanner processes animal pelts into leather with pig dung. I dinnae wish to take ye there as ye are."

"Oh." I swallowed and nodded in understanding. "Can I come back with you tomorrow?" I asked hopefully. I didn't get to explore nearly as much of the town as I had wanted to. My disappointment must have been evident on my face because he ran the rough pad of his thumb along my cheek and agreed.

"Aye. I'll bring ye as long as the weather holds out," he promised, and I found my focus drop to his lips.

Flushing with desire and my blood alcohol level, my body hummed with the memory of how he seduced me against my bedroom door. I yearned to feel his hands in my hair and his thigh pressed between my legs again.

Closing my eyes, I leaned forward on my tiptoes to kiss him when the cousins burst loudly from the tavern and effectively doused my daydream like a bucket of ice water. With a devilish smirk, Colin smoothly tucked me against his side and I practically floated back to the stables, his arm a welcome weight on my shoulders.

Una nickered at our approach, happy to see her master. Colin gave her an affectionate pat and vaulted on her back before he eased me into the snug space between his thighs. A few lengths ahead of us, the twins quietly talked to one another as they led the way, my spice crate safe in Bram's lap.

A late fog had rolled in, smothering the land in misty white and grey as we passed through the field and entered the woods. The thick blanket of swirling vapor amplified the forest's sounds while cloaking it, giving the path we rode along a magical, yet eerie impression. I could hear the birds in the trees and the squirrels as they raced over last autumn's fallen leaves, but I couldn't see them.

Leaning back against Colin's chest, my body both hypersensitive and numb from my over-indulgence, I concentrated on every movement he made behind me. The rise and fall of his chest. The way his leather-clad thighs rubbed against mine. When his bearded chin would lightly brush the top of my head in tune to Una's gait. Focused so intently on these rhythmical movements, I almost missed the lazy stroke of his thumb on my hip.

My lips parted, and mind dumped out all thought to zero in on that one delightful touch. My breathing shallow, I waited, silently begging for him to do it again. One minute turned into two, and I began to think I had imagined it when his hand slid leisurely over my waist to rest on my belly, his fingers making achingly slow, featherlight circles over my navel. My breath hitched, and I let my head fall back against his shoulder with a soft sigh.

The fog grew heavier as we rode deeper into the forest, and our companions quickly became faint silhouettes farther down the path. Tugging Una's mane, Colin commanded her to slow down and allow the distance to stretch until we couldn't see them at all.

Shifting behind me, Colin dipped his head down and grazed his lips over the shell of my ear, evoking a soft whimper to escape from me. Goose bumps erupted over my skin, and my spine arched at that touch. Resting my hands on his thighs, I gripped the supple leather tightly.

"Meggie," he crooned. "Such sweet sounds ye make, and all o' them just for me."

Halting those soft flutters over my belly, he ran both of his hands firmly along my hips and the tops of my thighs before entwining his battle-hardened fingers with my soft ones. All the while, he pressed kisses up the column of my neck.

I arched further into his touch and tilted my head so that he could taste more of me. I wanted him to taste *all* of me. He was everywhere: his muscled chest at my back, his thick legs on either side of me. The sensation of his powerful body wrapped around mine was deliriously exciting and infinitely arousing.

He dragged his right hand back up my leg, each finger pressing with delightful pressure, catching on the fabric of my skirt as they went up, up, up, and dipped daringly into my bodice to palm my breast. His calloused fingers sent pulses of pleasure straight to my core as they trapped and rolled the hardened bud of my sensitive skin.

Catching my throaty moan within his mouth, and his tongue stroked my lower lip, seeking entrance.

"Let me in." His voice was rough, mirroring my desire as his sapphire eyes searched mine and tasted my lips once more.

Unable to deny him, I opened my mouth to receive his kiss, thrilled at the low growl he made when I sucked lightly on his tongue and grazed my teeth over his flesh. I was even more delighted at the growing bulge at my backside. And because I was tipsy and feeling quite naughty, I wiggled my bum a bit.

"Wicked lass. Be still," he grumbled against the corner of my mouth a moment before he abruptly withdrew from my breast.

I nearly whimpered at the absence of his hand and tried to twist around to claim his lips again. Gripping my hips, he dug his fingers into my flesh hard enough to stop my movements, the compression firm but not unwelcome. His breathing was as ragged as my own when he pressed a kiss to the hair above my temple.

"Meggie, I—"

"—Colin!" What could only be Finlay's voice cracked the silence followed by a muffled thump and a hiss. "Ouch! What did ye do that for?"

Colin stiffened and muttered something about premature death, and nudged Una onward at a trot. His arm snaked around my waist, anchoring me to him as we propelled forward through the mist. Hastily, I covered my hair with my hood, and we found the twins just outside the forest with only the field separating us from the keep. Through the fog, I could barely discern the massive stronghold and its towers.

Finlay was busy rubbing his shoulder, scowling at his twin, who was glaring right back at him. Colin didn't slow Una as we quickly passed them by, much to my relief. I didn't want either of them to see how flushed I was, even though I knew Bram was well aware of why we fell back.

Once in the center bailey, Colin lowered me onto the steps leading up to the castle's main door.

"Go on in, Meggie. I'll see ye at supper," he said gruffly before turning Una away toward the stable and his awaiting cousins.

I stood there a moment, shocked at his cool dismissal, a complete opposite from the passion he showed me in the woods. Feeling confused and slightly discarded, I turned on my heel and entered the keep. My soggy slippers left footprints on the stone and wide plank flooring as I rushed up to my room. Upon entering, I immediately noticed the smell of lemon, and found Maeve and another girl I didn't know polishing the posters of my bed.

"Oh, I'm sorry." Turning to leave but unsure where to go, I began to pull the door shut when Maeve called out for me.

"Can I help ye out of yer wet garments, milady?" she asked sweetly as she ushered the other woman out of the room with a wave of her wrist.

I nodded gratefully and unclasped my cloak, which she took and dropped on the floor by the door. She quickly stripped me out of my damp slippers and stockings. The dress she heaped upon the cloak to be laundered.

Once she wrapped me in a dressing robe, she took down my hair and left to fetch some tea. I ran my fingers through my locks to find most of it in snarls. The mist had attacked and killed any smoothness, curling it into a wild, frizzy mess. Plopping down in the plush chair, I finger combed most of the knots out before twisting the length into a topknot on my head.

Sober, hungry, and perplexed at the swift change of Colin's demeanor, I waited patiently until Maeve returned with the promised tea along with a small plate of cheese and fruit beside the little pot. While she chose another gown for me to wear, I eagerly stuffed a handful of early whortleberries into my mouth and made a small goat cheese sandwich with the two tea biscuits.

"Mrs. Cook was siftin' through the crate ye had brought back from the village." she said idly as she shook out a gown of midnight blue wool. Laying it on the bed to air out, she found fresh, snowy-white stockings and blue slippers to compliment it.

"Yes, Colin was kind enough to gift me with whatever I needed to add to her supplies." In my sleeveless cotton shift and robe, I walked around the curved wall towards the only eastern-facing window. Perching a hip on the ledge, I nibbled on the cookie sandwich and looked down on the bailey.

Light rain had beaten away the fog, and the north and center baileys below were empty save for a few people rushing from one shelter to the next. Then I saw him exiting the stables, the man who had held me so passionately on horseback a short while ago.

Colin's white shirt soaked up the rain as he crossed the yard, his hair hanging in curling ropes around his face. As if sensing my stare, his eyes snapped up to mine for only a moment before he disappeared from my view under the canopy of the oak tree. He hadn't looked happy to see me at all, and I quickly stepped away from the window, more flustered than I was when he left me at the steps of the keep.

I do not like this feeling, I thought to myself when Maeve beckoned me forward so that she could begin taming my hair. She pinned it up in a fashion that let some of the shorter locks fall loose around my face. Dipping her hand into the water basin, she ran moist fingers over the loose strands and urged them to spring up in curls. She then chose a beautiful necklace to grace my neck as well as a matching bracelet. Seven thin strands of freshwater pearls wrapped around one another like a rope, and connected to an ivory oval disk with a thistle carved delicately in the center. The sight of it sparked my memory as I ran a fingernail over the famed flower of Scotland.

"Maeve, what happened to the clothing I arrived in? And specifically, my thistle brooch?"

"It's polished and safely tucked in with the rest o' the jewels, o' course," she chirped as she pulled silken stockings up each of my legs and secured them with a length of lace tied high on my thigh.

I had worn a garter belt once, just this past February. A gaudy, expensive Valentine's day piece from Victoria's Secret. I found I vastly preferred this soft ensemble to the scratchy polyester that had clung uncomfortably to my torso.

"And my... trews?"

She turned away to grab my dress, but not before I caught the comical curl of her lip and widened eyes.

"They're at the bottom of that chest," she said reluctantly, nodding at the smallest one in the far corner, and held open the beautiful gown.

When I stepped into the sea of blue fabric, I had to pull my lips in between my teeth to keep from laughing at her honest reaction to my jeans.

Still hours before supper, I decided to visit the library, hoping to find a book or two to fill my time. A low fire smoldered in the hearth to chase away the damp that crept in from the single-paned, mullioned glass of the many windows that lined the far wall. Although they allowed ample light in the room for reading, even on a gloomy day like today, they did little to keep the room warm without the help of a fire.

Strolling into the quiet room with my hands clasped lightly behind my back, I didn't see the man in one of the high-backed chairs facing the window until he stood and closed his book with a thump. A scream ripped its way up my throat and I nearly jumped out of my skin before I recognized the MacKinnon laird.

Breathing heavily, I clutched my throat, torn between laughing and glowering at the dark, handsome man staring at me humorously with his thick brows hiked high on his forehead.

"You scared the shit out of me." Wheezing, I patted my chest and tried to calm myself. Malcolm tilted his head curiously and took a quick glance in the direction of the back of my skirts.

"It's a figure of speech," I said quickly.

"I do hope so. I'm rather fond o' that rug," he teased as he returned his book to the shelves. "Ye're welcome to any tomes in this room, if ye're of a mind to read. Most o' them are in English."

"Thank you. I would like that very much." Examining the leather-bound spines, I found that they rarely advertised the titles, and I had to pull them out one at a time.

Malcolm cleared his throat behind me and I turned to find his face soft as he said, "If ye're anything like our mother, ye'll find what yer lookin' for on the shelves closest to the windows."

With that, he strolled out of the room, and pulled the doors shut for my privacy.

Thankful for the time alone and freedom to snoop, I hurried to the far shelf and pulled out one book after the other. Most were Shakespearian plays, including *King Lear*, *Winter's Tale*, and *Twelfth Night*.

A Christopher Marlowe play named *Dr. Faustus* caught my eye for a later read, as well as *The Duchess of Malfi* by John Webster. But it was the worn, thin book tucked under a small silver box that captured my attention. It was Aemilia Lanyer's *Salve Deus Rex Judaeorum*. The book opened easily in my hand to the third page, the chapter titled, *To all vertuous Ladies in generall*.

I smiled at the old-world spelling and carefully flipped the delicate pages to find the book compiled of eleven poems and letters. Claiming the wide upholstered chair Malcolm had vacated, I tucked my feet under my butt and settled in to decipher the thoughts of a woman born over four hundred years before me.

The light rain on the windows was a tapping staccato as I sat curled up, the little book in my lap as I labored to unravel what I was reading. I was starting to believe I had a female's reading of *The Passion of the Christ* in my hands, when a gentle knock pulled my attention to the door.

"Pardon the intrusion, milady." A woman I had seen a few times in the kitchen poked her head in between the library doors. "I was told ye were up here and to fetch ye for supper."

"Oh, I didn't know it was so late, thank you." Extending my legs slowly to the floor, my knees protested at being bent for so long, and my feet tingled with the renewed blood flow.

Returning the book to its place under the silver box, I took a moment to lift the lid. What I found was not anything I expected. Only a lock of curly blonde hair tied with a thin blue ribbon and an unremarkable pebble the size of a small acorn sat inside the red velvet lining. Slightly disappointed I did not find it filled with gold coins or some other exciting treasure, I replaced the lid and headed for the great hall.

My stomach growled loudly in its demand for something weightier than the berries and biscuits I devoured earlier, and I found myself more than fashionably late when I arrived at the great hall. The serving girls were filtering out to return to the kitchens, just having left the platters of brown rolls, two braised chickens in a mushroom white wine sauce, and roasted beets sprinkled with goat cheese.

"Sorry I'm late. I lost track of time," I explained when I took my usual seat across from Colin.

Gavin, who I had met on my second night here, rose to help me into my chair before settling back down beside me. Bram winked at me from across the table through the aromatic steam rising from the bowl of mushrooms.

"Ye arrived with perfect timing," Malcolm said reassuringly as he filled his plate and then my own. "I take it ye found a book to yer liking?"

"I did, thank you," I said, content to be served. I did not feel like making art with my meal today, too hungry to want to take the time, and was happy to be served.

Iona and I had talked over the menu this morning while I instructed her on making the breakfast pastries. Taking my first bite of chicken, I found she did a wonderful job braising them in the bread oven instead of roasting them over a spit. She had been reluctant to try it, but after some encouragement and more than a little teasing, she trusted me, and stuffed the cavity of two chickens with mushrooms and bundles of herbs wrapped in thread. On the table, the meat had fallen clean off the bones when the men served themselves.

I felt the weight of Colin's stare on me as I focused on my meal. I had not yet looked at him since coming down to supper, and when I finally mustered the courage to meet his gaze, I found the same unreadable look on his face. Averting my eyes, I reached for my wine.

"And how did ye enjoy yer first visit to our village, Meggie?" Malcolm's deep voice rumbled.

"Ye'd be wise to guard yer chalice," Bram muttered under his breath.

My face heated at his comment, but I smiled respectfully toward the laird and nodded with enthusiasm.

"Colin was thoughtful enough to introduce me to the woman who deals in spices. We brought back several new ones to add to the buttery and enhance the foods that you already eat." I peeked across the table to find Colin still watching me, although his gaze had softened a degree.

"That is most welcome," Malcolm replied. The other men grunted in agreement as they cleaned their plates of every last morsel.

Conversation turned to the running of the barracks and any disputes that needed to be addressed that couldn't wait until Sunday. I sat quietly and looked everywhere but at the man in front of me, studying the tapestries or the ironwork of the rushlights and candelabras. I measured the time by how much the candles burned down.

A maid served dessert in individual wooden bowls filled with sweetened cream whipped into soft mounds over last season's preserved blackberries and raspberries. I dipped my spoon into the bowl, catching equal parts berries and cream, and noted the way the tart berry battled with the sweetness of the cream on my pallet. I would most definitely make baked French toast with these preserves in the near future.

Unable to finish it all, I pushed the bowl away and dabbed at my mouth before asking to be excused. Malcolm nodded and bid me good night as Colin rose from his chair.

"I'll walk ye to yer chamber," he declared brusquely. Nodding in deference to his brother, he walked around the table to tuck my hand over the bend in his arm.

My skin thrummed where we touched as he steered us from the great hall and deeper into the keep's many corridors, candlelit hallways, and stairwells in uncomfortable silence. It seemed like eons had passed before we arrived at my bedroom door, and when we finally did, he did not release me. I tugged lightly, futile against his considerable strength.

"Um…" I swallowed, searching for words. "I'm not sure what I did to upset you—"

"—Upset me?" His eyes widened as he released my hand and took a step back. "Ye have no' upset me. Far from it." His words were hoarse with emotion, and he reached for me only to pull away and rake his hands through his hair. We stared at one another for a long moment before he rasped, "Ye beguile me, Meggie."

My mouth popped open.

"I don't... I don't understand." My heart felt like it was going to hammer out of my chest with anticipation of what he may say next.

I was not disappointed.

"Ye cannae possibly ken how much I want ye. How I want nothin' more than to bury myself inside ye right now. My very *bones* ache with wantin' ye. Yer in my mind day and night, either wishin' ye were by my side or lookin' forward to the next moment I can see ye. Touch ye." He stood there, his face intense as his eyes searched mine, his hands fisted by his sides. "And ye feel the same for me."

"Yes," I breathed, emotion thick in my throat when I realized how much he desired me.

Closing the distance between us, he finally allowed himself to touch me, to cradle my face in his battle-hardened hands. He swept his thumbs over the apples of my up-tilted cheeks and bent to rest his forehead against mine.

"Ye are a stranger to this land, but I cannae think o' any reason but fate that led me to find ye." His deep voice was rough with sincerity, and his words tore at the walls of my heart.

"That makes a lot of sense," I whispered, elated at his revelation, and pulled him closer to feel the strength of his arms wrap around me. I soaked in some of that strength and pressed my face against his chest. Breathing in his sharp, piney scent, I reminisced about frolicking through the woods and long hours spent exploring the forest behind my Nan's farm, and smiled when I realized Colin smelled of adventure.

He smelled like home.

"I'm glad ye agree." He stroked my back, content to hold me while I processed his words.

But something still nagged at me, and I pulled away slightly to look up at him.

"If you feel this way, I don't understand why you dumped me off at the steps. And you looked angry when I saw you from my window."

He sighed before answering and rubbed a hand over his brow.

"Because as much as ye delight me, sweet Meggie, ye frustrate me."

I cocked my eyebrow at the backhanded compliment, and he smiled apologetically.

"Ye misunderstand. Havin' ye all warm and receptive to my touch... I lost focus. Anyone could have seen... it would have ruined yer reputation, and that would have been my fault."

"But Bram obviously suspects—"

"—He *suspects*. But suspectin' and seein' are two verra different things." His handsome face hardened again, but not in anger like I had mistakenly thought. It was frustration. Like the frustration I saw in his face as he said, "I willnae touch ye that way again."

I opened my mouth to protest, but he stopped me with a finger to my lips.

"No' until we wed, if ye'll have me."

Oh... *Oh.* My ears hollowed out at those words and my mind drew a complete blank. The ability to speak left me completely while I replayed his last sentence over and over in my mind, and while I stared dumbly at him, he stepped in close and calmly fingered a curl at my temple.

"I have searched for a lass that makes me feel the way that ye do, and here ye are, in the most unlikely of ways," he continued, his voice soft. "I dinnae ken what magic brought ye here, but I will ever be grateful for it."

Footsteps echoed down the hall, and he stepped away from me. The empty space felt as big as a canyon. Catching my hand, he brought it to his lips and pressed an intimate kiss to my palm. His eyes bore into mine.

"Think on yer answer, Meggie. I will see ye in the morn."

I watched him prowl down the hallway before slipping into my darkened room. Rushing across the floor to throw open a window, I welcomed the cool, damp air that flowed around me. A wide smile broke over my face as I inhaled deeply and committed the joy and anticipation that raced through my body, mind, and soul to memory.

Through my elation, a small wisp of sadness pressed against the chambers of my heart when I remembered I could not share this experience with Nan. I could only take comfort in the fact that I knew what she'd say, because she said it to me the night she picked me up from the airport.

The whiskey bottle was nearly empty after an evening spent dancing with broomsticks and purging Steven from my mind.

Without warning, Nan grabbed my shoulders with a strength I didn't know she had and said, "Meggie, the heart kens what it wants. It does no' matter if it's been an hour or a year. When ye find that person who makes yer soul sing, ye hold on to them with all yer might, and ye dinnae let them go. Yer mother was lucky to find that with yer father. I thought she was mad when they eloped scant weeks after they started dating, but when she brought him home, I saw the love between them, and I understood."

She kissed my forehead, her thin lips trembling slightly and her blue eyes glassy with tears as she thought of her daughter.

"Dinnae ye dare settle until ye find yer soul's equal."

On the third floor of Ghlas Thùr, keeping one foot on the floor, I leaned out into the open air, and closed my eyes. The light rain hit my face as I sent out a message into the universe, one I had to believe Nan would somehow receive through time and space. I clung to the hope that there was a possibility of bringing her closure, making my presence here easier.

My thoughts were simple and concise as I grinned up at the clouds and beyond.

I found him, Nan.

CHAPTER 14

Meggie

I awoke at dawn, warm under my blankets, to the nagging of my bladder. Cursing the lack of modern plumbing, I donned my dressing robe, cinching it tightly at my waist, and quickly padded down the deserted hallway for the garderobe. Pushing through the thick wooden door, there was just enough light filtering in from the high, slatted windows to brighten the spacious room. There were neatly folded linen squares on the bench and fresh bundles of lavender and rosemary in the corners. A sprinkling of hay dusted the floor, keeping the room dry and the air fresh.

The first day I used this room, I steeled myself for the worst, but was pleasantly surprised to find the seventeenth-century version of the toilet vastly better than a twenty-first century Porta Potty.

The rest of the castle's residents were rousing when I slipped back into my room, more awake than I wished to be. Instead of crawling back into bed, I poked at the banked coals. Enticing a few flames to lick at fresh kindling, I added a length of wood to warm the air. Unshuttering my windows, I let in the light and rejoiced over the lack of rain clouds in the periwinkle sky.

Colin would take me back to the village today.

I stepped into a dove-grey dress with front buttons I could do up myself and began impatiently pacing the floor while I waited for

Maeve. I did not have to wait long. Every inch a morning person, she breezed through my door with a chipper smile and styled my hair in an intricate braid in record time. Excited, I rushed down to visit with Iona and found her slumped at the table, massaging her temples.

"What's wrong?" I asked quietly as I sat beside her.

"Och, lass, ye're up early today. I'm in a bit o' pain, is all, and we're out of valerian root and meadowsweet," she explained, her voice soft and breathy. I frowned and rubbed her back, running my thumbs along her spine with slight pressure.

"If you haven't made the laird's breakfast yet, let me do it," I offered.

She waved her hand toward the buttery without a word, and I gave her one last rub before I left her alone to fulfill my task.

I knew Malcolm had a bowl of porridge every day, like the rest of the keep's residents and garrison, but the thought of making something so bland for the man who welcomed me into his home without question did not appeal to me. After I filled a cauldron with oats and water over a low fire for everyone else, I skipped happily around the scullery maids as I gathered bowls, butter, eggs, cream, and a loaf of yesterday's bread. I cut the latter up in thick slices after I placed a pan over hot coals to heat. A short time later, I had four fat, fluffy slices of buttery French toast neatly arranged on a warm plate with honey and raspberry preserves drizzled over the top.

"He's probably pacing a track in the floor by now, but I'm sure he will forgive the delay." Iona smiled weakly at me as she directed a serving girl with the toast upstairs.

Grinning at the visual of Malcolm pacing like a hungry black panther, I laid two more slices on the hot, buttered pan when Colin appeared at the bottom of the stairwell.

"Whatever ye're cookin', I want some. I could smell it as soon as I entered the great hall." His smile faltered as he took in the miserable look on Iona's face. "What ails ye?" She opened her mouth to reply when he interrupted her. "Besides me," he goaded.

She huffed a laugh, wincing at the movement, and peered up at him with heavy-lidded, reddened eyes before she replied, "An ache o' the head is all. I'll be fine."

"She's out of her herbs. Is there somewhere we can get more in the village?" I asked as I flipped the toast over.

Colin looked down at her with concern. "Aye, that we can."

Sliding onto the stool across from her, he folded his muscular arms in front of him and settled in to watch me work. I could feel his focus burning between my shoulder blades like a brand as I took care to arrange his meal, much the same way I did Malcolm's. Pleased with the presentation, I turned to find his hungry eyes lift to mine. I gave him a dazzling smile when I set his plate down in front of him, and then the two smaller portions for Iona and myself.

"Yer a sweet lass." She managed a smile as she picked at it.

"Maybe the sugar will help you until we get back," I said as I turned to clean up my mess.

"Leave it for the children, Meggie. They'll come sniffin' around here soon enough, and it would be best if they had a task."

Finding that a great idea, I perched on the stool next to Iona and tucked into my meal, soaking up their praise on the most American breakfast I could have ever made. It was only missing maple syrup and the vanilla extract, but the beans still had a few more weeks of soaking in their whiskey baths before they would be useful.

Funny how, on the day I arrived here, I was pondering the idea of running my own bakery or bed and breakfast. I had to admit that this was a fine alternative. I could not deny that I enjoyed being here, that I felt more alive than I ever have in this beautiful, simple place. Sure, the hole in my chest still ached when I thought about Nan, but it was getting better each day. And besides, it did me no good to dwell on the things I had no control over.

I looked forward to making the most of my life here.

With yesterday's mist and rain gone, the village gave off a different feeling as I strolled down the primary thoroughfare at Colin's heels, happy for him to guide me while I took in the sights.

Women lined up along the river's edge as we rode in. With their skirts tied up around their hips, they crouched bare-footed in the shallows. They sang and laughed together while they laundered their linens and spread them out over mounds of mauve-colored heather to dry in the sun.

Children herded small flocks of sheep and goats in pairs through the fields, heading up to the hills. I could tell they took their tasks seriously, tapping long sticks on the ground to keep their charges moving. A few men were busy mending a thatched roof, hauling bundles of sticks and straw up with rope. During the rainy season, it looked like the locals took full advantage of a clear day, and many of them worked together to get the most done.

The herbalist's store was on the other side of the church from the stable, and I was slightly breathless and a bit warm from keeping up with Colin's long strides when we arrived at her door. It was hot, despite the swift valley breeze; the bright sun burned away the cooler morning temperatures long ago. Colin knocked three times and waited until a short, middle-aged woman with white hair opened the door and greeted us with a smile.

"Welcome," she said with a respectful nod, her voice high-pitched and scratchy.

We entered the one-room home, the ceiling low and a small bed tucked against the wall opposite of the hearth. A worn table, strewn with roots, leaves, and berries, dominated the center of the room.

"Have ye come for more self-heal?"

"Aye. As well as valerian root and meadowsweet."

Colin waited patiently, bent slightly at the waist to keep his head from hitting the low rafters while she gathered his requests from the chest tucked under a table. She handed him three small linen sacks before advising him to transfer the herbs to glass as soon as he could to keep them fresh longer.

"Thank ye, healer." He placed a few coins in her hand before ushering me out the door.

"What is self-heal?" I asked as we walked back the way we came, the church grounds just ahead.

"A purple flower we mix with goldenrod and butter to speed up healing if we injure ourselves in training or after a battle. The barracks are running low, and we will need a ready supply at the Gathering." His fingers brushed mine as we walked side by side, but he did not grasp my hand like I wished he would.

I lifted an eyebrow, intrigued.

"Gathering?"

We walked at a slower pace around the perimeter of the church ringed with a knee-high stone wall. The building was quiet, its stained-glass windows gleaming in the sunlight. Willow trees swayed in the breeze over a few moss-covered tombstones like shrouded crypt keepers.

"Aye. Tis a five days ride to the east. Clans from all over gather to trade and begin or renew alliances. Malcolm sits in on many meetings with other clan chieftains during the first few days. There are also competitions between the warriors of each clan. Weapons, fists, horsemanship—"

I perked up at this information and whirled around to grab his hand.

"The Highland Games?" I squealed, beside myself with excitement. He looked at me oddly and shook his head in confusion.

"I dinnae ken those games, but the Gathering has many to participate in." His thumb brushed over my knuckles, and I glanced around before I leaned in closer to him, my voice low.

"No, the Highland Games are famous Scottish competitions in the future. Maybe they started out like the gatherings you have now? I've always wanted to attend them, but they're held during the school year, and I was always back in the States by then."

"Then ye will come with us."

I bounced on the balls of my feet with glee at the opportunity, and Colin looked down on me adoringly as he squeezed my fingers.

"How about a visit to the blacksmith before the tannery?"

At my eager nod, he laced my fingers through his, and we slipped between two houses, heading toward the harsh clamor of metalworking.

The forge glowed brightly, as though it refused to be outdone by the sun's bright light, and I recognized the man with the tree trunk arms from the tavern yesterday. He was busily pumping more oxygen with the bellows into the hungry blaze of the forge, his back a massive spread of muscle that bunched and shifted beneath the fabric of his dark shirt.

"Ho, Kerr," Colin called when we stood outside the blacksmith's ring of tools, anvils, and worktables.

The giant of a man peered over his shoulder. His short brown hair curled around his ears with sweat, and he nodded at Colin in acknowledgment before he turned back to the heat of the forge.

Grasping the rod with thick leather gloves, he impaled it within the coals before he rested the red-hot end over an anvil and pounded it mercilessly with a hammer. The high-pitched ping of metal beating metal made my ears ring, and I slapped my hands over them, taking more than a few steps back. Colin did the same.

A few minutes later, Kerr took the rod, now looking slightly more bladelike, and plunged it into a bucket of water. It instantly boiled and hissed, spitting out steam. Discarding the unfinished blade and his work gloves on a table, the massive man lumbered over to us while he dug wads of waxed wool out of his ears.

"Good day." He smiled shyly, his dark eyes expressive and kind. I guessed him to be in his late forties, but I could have been wrong. Between the constant heat from the forge baking the skin of his face and hands, and the strength he needed to use his heavy tools slowing his speed, he could have been a decade younger.

"A verra fine day," Colin agreed. "Meggie here is new in residence at Ghlas Thùr. I thought she should meet the most talented blacksmith in Scotland."

A deep, charming blush mottled Kerr's cheeks. Mumbling his gratitude, he waved us toward a workbench under the sloped shelter of a three-sided shed, its roof just high enough that neither Colin nor Kerr had to stoop.

Dirks, daggers, swords, and stilettos in various stages of finish sat strewn over the rough sawn table. Intrigued, I ran my fingertips down the cool metal of a small dagger, the wide double-sided blade six inches long, and the handle; a naked rod. It was unfinished, its edges dull and unpolished. Kerr shuffled behind me and picked up the weapon, his movements smooth and confident as expected of a man who makes his livelihood forging them.

"I'm afraid I know nothing about swords and knives. Outside of the kitchen, at least." I was pretty positive they'd laugh if I told them about the dinky pocketknife I kept in my purse.

Kerr waved off my ignorance and motioned to the dull blade in his hands.

"The key to a good weapon is balance." His low, rich voice captivated me as he ran his blunt fingers lovingly over the metal. "The way it is now, 'tis imperfect, the blade heavier than the handle."

Demonstrating what he meant, he rested the dagger mid-length over the bridge of his finger, and the killing side immediately dipped below the rod of the naked hilt.

"Right now, the difference in weight is no' much, but when finished with oiled wood or wrapped in leather strips, it will no' fail its bearer."

He handed it back to me, and I laid it over the bridge of my finger like he had.

"How do you choose how it's finished?" I asked, intrigued by this gentle giant. He lifted a thick shoulder and jerked his chin toward Colin.

"For a warrior, I'd wrap it in leather cords to keep an easy grip, even when covered in enemy blood. Plain, with only the edge honed with polish, the rest of the metal dull to keep any light from reflecting. It would become a weapon for stealth."

A vision of Colin wielding the small dagger, sneaking soundlessly behind his prey, flashed through my mind as Kerr took the dagger from me and set it down with the rest before palming a thin stiletto.

"This is a lady's blade," he said, wrapping my hand around the handle.

Twisted like a unicorn's horn under my grip, the haft was elegant even in its rough state. From pommel to tip, it was about fifteen inches long.

"Why is it so much longer than a man's?" I inquired as I awkwardly held the weapon out in front of me.

"A lady's blade is thin but strong; the metal folded several times to keep its strength. 'Tis forged this way to slip easily between the ribs because ye're made so much weaker than a man. Ye simply dinnae have the brute strength that is needed to deliver a killing blow through the chest with a thicker weapon."

I blanched at the thought of ever having to kill, especially in such close quarters. My father taught me the fundamentals of handguns when I turned eleven, and even entered me in competitions when I showed some talent. But shooting at a paper bullseye at twenty yards differed vastly from taking a life with a sliver of steel. Oblivious to my discomfort, Kerr continued the lesson and ran his finger over the flat of the blade.

"'Tis long to extend yer reach, to deliver the most damage possible when it enters the belly. Ye may only have one chance to maim yer enemy, or at the verra least, slow him down long enough to escape."

I swallowed the saliva that collected in my mouth as I stared at the weapon in my hand. This was no culinary knife. Wicked enough in their own right, chef's tools were meant to chop vegetables or filet fish. They weren't designed for killing.

With my awkward grip on the stiletto, I doubted I could ever do something like that to another human being... but hadn't I had thrown that rock at the man in the glen with the intent on hurting him? What else would I have done if Colin hadn't come? If I had possessed this weapon, it would have provided me with protection and given me a means to fight off my attackers. Would I have used it? A small shiver rippled down my spine, and I set the stiletto down on the workbench.

"Kerr has other talents besides weapon-making," Colin said to me before turning to his friend, who was once again bashful at the praise. "Would ye show my Meggie where yer true talents lie?"

Inwardly preening at those possessive words, I bit my lower lip to keep from cheesing like an idiot.

Kerr's earthy brown eyes shifted to mine before motioning us to follow him to his home; a modest two-room building behind the forge.

The first thing I noticed were the wood shavings on the floor, followed by the fresh, spicy scent of cedar and cypress. The shavings crunched beneath my slippers when I stepped into the living area, and I soaked up the visual feast that was his humble home.

"Wow," I whispered, awestruck, as I looked up.

Intricately carved wooden birds of various sizes and species hung from the rafters by thin strands of yarn and leather. The birds gently swayed on currents of air that our entrance into the room created, their wings outstretched in perpetual flight. Nightingales, crested tits, and starlings were but a sample of the many species suspended in mid-flight. There was even a lifelike golden eagle perched proudly on a beam, looking down on me.

Birds were not the only subject of Kerr's talented fascination. A scene of mythical creatures pranced along the mantle above the hearth: unicorns the size of my hand, a troll hiding under a stone bridge, a dragon with its wings spread wide and its mouth opened to show rows of sharp teeth. The mantle face itself he also etched and polished into a panoramic mountain scene.

Grinning like a little girl, I bent to inspect a life-sized bear cub standing alert in the corner, its chubby belly jutting out. Kerr had worked black ink into the reddish-brown wood, darkening places to give it shadow and personality. A shelf beside the door held several sizes of stylized wooden boxes, their lids fitting perfectly and their corners seamless from being carved out of a solid log.

"These are wonderful. Amazing," I gushed over the carvings and took the time to look at each beautiful piece.

Children's toys of warriors and dogs, horses, pint-sized swords, and shields sat in a large woven basket under the table. A padded chair stood before the hearth, a pile of raw wood beside it. They were odd pieces, knotty, weathered, and bundled along with small slabs of oak, maple and elm, each a different color and texture. Clean, dry roots peeked out from between. Scattered tools of his trade spread over the table: wooden-handled short-blades for whittling, rasps, chisels of all sizes, corkscrews, and a two-handled saw-like knife.

"Ye've been busy, Kerr," Colin marveled, captivated as he turned over the carving of a pine marten with its adorable forepaws resting on a stump and its perky triangle ears alert. "Where do ye find the time?"

Kerr shoved his hands in the pockets of his wool trousers and studied his birds.

"I find I dinnae need as much sleep as I used to—only three or four hours most nights. There are many hours before dawn and, since they'd run me out of the village if I began work at the forge before sunup, I use the wee hours to do quiet things like this." He lifted his large hand and brushed the underbelly of a falcon above his head. "Or sometimes I walk the land at night when I'm restless, no matter the weather. I like the peace. No' much of that to be had at the forge."

I felt a kindred spirit in this unassuming hulk of a man, and almost overlooked the body of a mountain cat carved from light yellow wood, its hind legs and tail peeking out from under a throw blanket on the chair. Picking it up, I inspected it further. The predator crouched low on its haunches as though stalking its prey, a front leg reaching out to take another step closer.

"This reminds me of you," I murmured to Colin and ran my thumb down the length of the polished wood before setting it down. "I thought you moved like a mountain lion the day we met."

"Oh?" Male pride shone on his face, and I rolled my eyes at his vanity.

I should have told him he looked like a warthog to knock him down a few pegs, I thought to myself, and bit my lip to keep from laughing.

Unaware of my inner thoughts, Colin scanned the room, and when he found what he sought, plucked the object off a windowsill. His back to me, he inspected it for a moment as though to make sure of his choice before handing me the long-legged, delicate creature.

It was… not what I expected.

Confused, I gave him a questioning look and traced the perfectly arched neck and alert ears. A doe was not how I saw myself. If given the choice, I would choose a bird to represent for my free spirit or a wolf for my loyalty and love for my family… but never the slender, frail creature in my palm.

"The doe is a calm, shy soul. Tender and lovely. But more than once have I seen one lash out when cornered, killin' the wolf or hound that hunts her with a well-placed strike of a sharp hoof… or in yer case, a well-aimed stone or two."

A small, mollified smile pulled up the corners of my lips.

I could be a deer, I thought, and took one last look around before placing it on the table with the mountain cat guarding her.

"Thank you for sharing this with me," I said to Kerr, who bowed his head slightly and led us back out into the bright sunshine.

～

The growl of my stomach drove Colin into the tavern, where he bought a fresh loaf of brown bread, some cheese, and a bottle of ale. After sending the stable boy up to the castle with the herbs for Iona, he guided me to the river upstream from the village and settled us on a flat rock under the shade of a silver birch tree. The hem of my grey dress fanned out around me as I nibbled on the heel of the loaf and enjoyed an unhindered view of the shallow valley and the river that snaked its way north. Tufts of purple heather clumped around large boulders whose northern stone faces were covered in moss and lichen where it was safe from the glare of the sun.

Settled across from me with one knee tucked against his chest, Colin scanned the ridge of the hill to my right, allowing me the opportunity to study his profile. The sun glinted on his hair, highlighting the wavy golden strands, and kissed his tanned skin.

"You haven't asked me much about the future, besides when we played our game of chess." I snatched up the brown bottle of chilled ale between us and took a long sip.

"The only piece of future I care about is yers," he murmured. "And after ye spent so long in yer grief, I was loathing to pester ye to speak about a place that may bring ye such pain again."

I cleared my throat, slightly embarrassed that I shut down for so long. "Yeah… I'm sorry about that—"

His blue eyes sliced to mine, his expression serious. "Ye willnae apologize for that. *Ever*. Ye lost all ye had, all ye loved, in one moment. Everyone is allowed to grieve the way they need to." He huffed a humorless laugh and ran his hand through his hair. "I went off for days after my mother died… I missed her funeral and everythin'. I kenned Malcolm would be furious with me; our father was sick too, ye see. But I could no' bring myself to come back for it. I could no' watch her go into the ground." He stared off at nothing, his eyes unfocused as he thought back on that dark time, and then shook his head. "I arrived just in time to witness our father's passing. And then it was Malcolm's turn to make a fool o' himself."

When he didn't elaborate further, I looked away and nodded, having had my fill of death-talk.

Taking a deep breath, I steeled my nerves to broach a subject that did not thrill me to begin.

"Since we're in a sharing mood, there are some things I need to talk with you about." His head tilted to the side as he gave me his full attention. "Where I'm from, things are… different." I searched the skies for the right words and worried the bottle of ale in my hands.

His eyes were alight with mischief while he watched me squirm. "What do ye need to tell me, lass?"

"Well, I need to explain how different… *women* are in the twenty-first century. Ways a man in this time would find shocking."

I swear I watched the wheels in his head grind to a halt for a moment before he sat straighter and his eyes dipped down to my pelvis and back up again. A look of profound confusion and worry passed over his face, and he opened and closed his mouth a few times, reminding me of a fish out of water. I watched him curiously for a moment before it occurred to me what must be going through his mind and burst into laughter. My cackle echoed off the hillsides, and I wiped my eyes clear of tears.

"Oh my God, Colin. Not *that* kind of different!"

"Then what do ye mean?" His cheeks mottled with red, but he looked relieved as he accepted the ale from me. I snorted and giggled once more over the ridiculousness of our situation before attempting twice to smooth my features.

"I meant that we are independent. My parents raised me to care for myself in all aspects of life. In my time, women run companies, own property, and are heads of households. We are free to speak our minds without fear of physical repercussions and live our lives the way we choose… and it's also not required to hold on to our virginity until marriage either." I blushed furiously but powered through. "I just want—*I need*—you to understand I didn't grow up in a world where men rule over women." Taking a deep breath, I drew my shoulders back and straightened my spine before I said, "And I cannot marry a man who won't respect that. Respect *me*."

I would be his equal or nothing at all.

Understanding washed over his face, and my gut loosened its iron grip on my lingering anxiety over his reaction to a modern woman.

"My life would be dull indeed if I married a biddable lass without her own mind or aspirations," he said quietly. Unfolding his legs to stand, he pulled me up with him and his thumbs stroked the soft skin on the back of my hands. "Meggie, I am verra much aware that ye are different and educated, and the fact that ye are, delights me. I promise no' to clip yer wings but to help ye soar."

"You don't care that I'm not a virgin?" I asked suspiciously. All my historical romances had virgin brides. He tucked a strand of hair behind my ear and kissed my forehead lightly.

"I think that yer new life began when ye crawled out o' that cave." He swept an arm out, sending my gaze toward the countryside and the puffy clouds that smudged the horizon. "Are ye no' a virgin in these lands?"

"I guess so."

Colin shrugged, wrapping me in the cage of his arms, and rested his whiskered chin on the top of my head. "Then nothin' else matters. I want to marry ye. Even more so now, if I'm bein' honest."

His chest vibrated with his words, and the last of my worries left my shoulders light as I circled my arms around him and wove my fingers together across his lower back.

A cool breeze blew from the western hills, bringing with it the fragrant smell of heather. It tugged at the hem of my dress and teased at my hair with invisible fingers.

I looked up at Colin's face, and my heart swelled with joy at the thought of living a simple life with him.

No, it wouldn't be simple at all, I realized. He was the promise of adventure, of life spent in the wilds, and of explorations in a barely civilized world.

I was forever part of that world now.

Unable to contain my smile, I reached up to curl my fingers into the hair at his nape and said clearly, "Then my answer is yes."

⌒〜

The tannery, far downriver from the town, the slaughterhouse, and a grove of yew trees, was as foul as Colin described.

We hurried past two large vats of limey water close to a diverted part of the river, the noxious odors uncontained and free to assault the senses of the tannery's visitors. I held my sleeved arm over my nose when we rushed past wet hides with lingering patches of hair waiting for the next process. Black flies, drunk on the foul stench, flew around like fighter pilots to buzz in my ear.

There were four smaller vats filled with hairless hides in a less offensive liquid farther down the path before we veered up the hill and into a sparse forest. Well above the flood line, we skirted three pits dug into the earth where the sharp, acidic smell of bark mulch drifted up from the massive holes to clear my sinuses of the stench below.

"I feel the need to thank you for using your better judgment yesterday," I wheezed, spitting the vile taste out of my mouth as I followed behind him and waved a fly out of my face. His broad shoulders jerked as he chuckled.

"Aye. In truth, I expected ye to turn tail and hie back to Una at yer first breath o' the vats."

At the top of the hill, we came upon a whitewashed stone house with a thatched roof under the shade of two gigantic oaks. The premises were tidy and well-kept; even the dirt swept clear of debris. In a primitive outdoor kitchen, racks of small fish stood over a smoking peat fire. To the right of the house, a thatched awning continued off the roof above the workspace, protecting everything underneath it from the elements. The peat fire gave off no sparks, allowing it to burn safely under the flammable shelter. Racks of stretched hides leaned against the house, and I assumed that was where they would complete the final stage of becoming soft leather.

A waifish girl of about thirteen rounded the corner from the back of the house carrying a sloshing pail of water. She smiled shyly when she caught sight of us and set the bucket on the counter before smoothing her bright copper hair.

"Good day, Colin." Blushing, she studied her feet bashfully and peeked curiously at me from under her copper brows. "Da is down the way finishin' up in the dung vats. He should be back any moment."

"Thank ye, Nighean. I'm here for the laird's order. Is it ready?"

She nodded enthusiastically and ran into the house, eager to be of help.

A whistling tune drifted up the hill, followed by its composer. A rail-thin man with copper hair and a shaven face, the tanner wore a thick leather apron stained from many years of use over his kilt and soiled shirt. The acrid smell of pig poop hung on him like a second skin, stuffing itself up my nose.

"Ho, milord! I'm glad to see ye on this fine day," he said in a voice that was hoarse and guttural from many years spent working over a peat fire.

Nighean skipped up to her father's side, her arms loaded with supple leather in shades of fawn, buff, and dark brown tied together with thin strips of leather. She beamed up at Colin in utter devotion as she hefted up the heavy hides in her skinny arms.

Colin handed the tanner a small pouch of coins and accepted the large bundle.

"I thank ye, lassie." She blushed once more before racing back to her chores, and Colin said to the tanner, "Norval, this is my lady, Meggie."

Curling his fingers around my shoulder with his free hand, Colin told me that it was Norval's capable hands that made all the leather purchased for the keep. Norval puffed out his chest, proud of his work. I reached over to feel the hides, and found them all to be buttery soft and suede-like, easily rivaling all the overpriced handbags in Manhattan.

"Six generations o' knowledge in tannin' milady," Norval boasted, and tapped his temple with a grin that deepened his crow's feet.

"It will be good to see another familiar face on Sunday," I said honestly, thankful to meet another friendly member of the Clan MacKinnon; even if he smelled so bad, my eyes stung.

"Ye dinnae want to miss this one, my friend," Colin said with a hint of pride, and tucked me closer against his side.

Norval studied us a moment before his brows rose high in surprise, wrinkling his forehead. Gallantly, he took my hand, and placed the barest kiss on my knuckles. It was all I could do to allow the contact and keep the smile on my face while I mentally added hand sanitizer to the growing list of things I missed.

"This news pleases me, but I will keep it to myself. 'Tis yers to share," Norval said as he straightened, releasing me. He looked at his daughter, her back to us as she worked, and let out a sigh. "Joyous news indeed... but I'm afraid it will break many hearts."

After we bid the tanner goodbye, I led the way back to where we left Una. Practically sprinting upstream past the lime vats, I plunged my hands into the river once I was certain the water was clean. Grabbing handfuls of fine sand, I scrubbed off what could only be poop residue off my fingers. *So gross.*

Satisfied I was clean, I climbed to my feet and brushed debris off the damp fabric of my skirt, now a darker shade of grey at the knees. Colin handed me a square of white linen from his sporran to dry my hands, and I absently noted the delicate yellow flower embroidered in one corner.

"I'm sorry," I murmured, handing the handkerchief back to him.

He chuckled and took my hand—the one Norval did not touch—and threaded his fingers with mine. Without a stench to run from, we walked at a more leisurely pace the rest of the way to where Una waited for us.

"He smells right awful, I understand perfectly." He cringed, drawing a laugh out of me. "Remember when I told ye the tannery was full o' dung? Well, count yer blessings we didnae walk past *that* particular area. I nearly vomited the first time I smelled them."

"I had forgotten until he showed up," I admitted, and ran my thumbnail along his palm, causing him to tighten his grip. "I hope my face didn't give me away."

"Dinnae worry overmuch about it. The lime and peat smoke burned away Norval's sense of smell long ago. The lad that courts sweet Nighean will have to be a braw lad indeed. He'll need a strong constitution for that apprenticeship. Since she's Norval's sole wean, she'll need to marry a man strong enough to take over the trade, or the clan will be needin' to find a new tanner."

It saddened me to know that Nighean's father's need for a successor would basely drive her choices in suitors, and I almost said so when Colin continued.

"But there will be young men aplenty at the Gathering lookin' for apprenticeships. I'm certain she will have a thing or two to say on who they bring back with them."

"He'll be going?" I asked and imagined what the Gathering would be like when we reached Una.

"All the village merchants make the journey, even Norval. Kerr will have a whole wagon loaded up high with his weapons and return with a chest full o' coin. In times of peace, like it is now, the Gathering is the major source of income for many people."

Mounted upon Una's back, Colin lifted me up to sit between his thighs and wrapped an arm around my waist.

"I want to make ye happy, Meggie," he said, his lips pressed to the top of my head.

Surprised by the change of subject, I twisted around to look up at him and found sincerity staring back. His thumb traced the line of my jaw until his hand cupped the back of my neck. That simple touch coaxed a flush to my cheeks, and I wondered if anyone else ever experienced such an instant magnetism with another person, because this yearning I felt just *looking* at this man—it overwhelmed me.

"I want to make you happy, too," I said and then drew his lips down to mine. It was sweet and sensuous, and I imagined we looked a bit romantic while we kissed on horseback by the bank of the river.

All too soon Colin broke away, leaving me breathless, and with the click of his tongue, Una took off towards the castle. This time—and much to my disappointment—when we traversed the forest that divided the keep from the village, Colin's hand did not wander.

This was going to be a *very* long engagement.

CHAPTER 15

Colin

His bare feet sunk into the underbrush of the forest. His balance perfect, he flexed his toes in the soft, damp moss.

Afternoon sunlight filtered through the tree canopy to dapple the ferns and moss-covered rocks in golden splashes. Clad only in a kilt with a quiver of white fletched arrows resting snug against his bare back, he stalked his prey through the forest.

He had been hunting since the previous day, and already there were seven large hares tied to a high branch back at his small camp. He'd checked each of his snares that morning to find them fruitful before carefully stowing the braided leather cords away to use another day. His efforts meant his clan would eat heartily tomorrow, and that was worth spending two days in the wilds with only his thoughts for company.

There was an arrow nocked in his bow, primed and ready to draw and fire, and among the thick ferns and the darker shadows of a mighty oak, Colin crouched down low; his body motionless, save for his shallow breathing. He'd been stalking the two-year-old buck for the last few hours, slowly closing in as the animal unknowingly made his way closer to death. Colin could hear the steady huff of the beast's breathing when it nuzzled the earth in search of mushrooms and roots, and the dull thud of its sharp hooves striking the soft soil with each step.

In the treetops, the birds had long since continued their song. They were used to the predator's presence in the wood, and thus, not warned his prey.

The buck took five steps closer, it's head still low to the ground. Colin began to move, his mastery over his body steady and measured as he ever so slowly raised his bow. He only needed the buck to come a few steps closer, and there would be no risk of error. The huffing grew louder, and he could hear vegetation grinding between teeth. One more step—Colin emptied his mind of everything besides his aim as he fluidly stood from his crouch, punched the bow out before him, and let his arrow fly.

With each kill he made to feed his clan, he felt a small sadness at having taken the life. Today was no different. The birds all quieted as though sitting in judgment of him; the forest eerily silent except for the rustling leaves and the soft grunting of his prey. He propped the bow against the thick trunk of the oak and advanced swiftly, sliding his hunting knife from its sheath. The arrow had struck true, but the beast was still alive, and struggled on his deathbed of moss and leaves. Loathing to prolong its terror, Colin knelt at the buck's back. Smoothing a firm hand down its sleek neck, he murmured soft words as he slid his blade into the heart.

After field dressing the deer to preserve the meat, he hefted the considerable weight over his shoulders and trudged the mile back to his camp.

Sweating from carrying the fourteen-stone buck, he lay the deer down and rinsed the blood and sweat off his back and chest in the burn that ran next to his camp before packing up.

Experience taught him never to kill more than he could carry. When he was a young lad, he took down a twelve-point elk with no way to get it home. He had raced miles back to the keep in a panic to enlist help from men much stronger than he. But when they went back to retrieve it, the carrion birds had already claimed the kill. Colin's face heated at that remembered shame.

Feeling somewhat rejuvenated after slaking his thirst, he unwrapped the litter he always brought with him if he was hunting anything much bigger than a hare. The two long, springy lengths of wood connected by a span of oiled leather had served him well on many occasions. With the buck and hares secured, they weighed it down considerably, but it was better than carrying them on his back. Gripping the smooth wood handles, he headed west, dragging his burden behind him, and left two deep grooves in the earth as the only proof of his presence in the forest.

The sun was red and low on the horizon when he entered the bailey. Handing the deer carcass off to be butchered and its hide delivered to the tannery, he lumbered his exhausted body to the kitchens. The yeasty smell of bread and stew permeated his senses, as well as the sounds of women busy with their tasks. Strangely, they laughed and sang while they prepared for the gate opening tomorrow and the evening's meal.

Bewildered, Colin leaned against the white-washed wall to watched the merry bunch of women. Never had he seen the scullery maids in such good humor while they worked. Especially in the presence of the forbidding cook, who, he noted, was humming along while she shoved bundles of herbs and potatoes into the cavity of a chicken. Children sat on a blanket in the far corner, polishing candlesticks and silver platters without fuss or rush. Their little tongues poked out of the corners of their mouths in concentration while they buffed and rubbed.

"Ah, there ye are. Come, set them here," Mrs. Cook trilled, waving at the free space on the table next to her before she closed the chicken up in a covered pot and shoved it in the bread oven. "Have a seat, lad, ye look dead on yer feet."

"I cannae soil yer clean cookery," Colin protested as he set the hares down in bewilderment, and wondered why she hadn't already chased him out with a broom. The cook did not suffer an unclean body in her kitchen, something he had witnessed on several occasions.

"Ye may sit there long enough to drink a restorative tea before ye bathe."

She pointed firmly at a stool before washing her hands in a basin filled with soapy water. Drying her hands on her apron, she disappeared into the buttery. Two women at the far end gave him a knowing smile and giggled to themselves as Colin sat there in confusion.

Minutes later, Mrs. Cook plunked a steaming cup of fragrant tea in front of him, the dregs of the dark leaves dancing in the water while they steeped, as well as a cake of soap that smelled of pine and juniper. His skin positively itched with the need to wash away the accumulation of two days' worth of dirt, grime, and blood, but he made himself sit there until the tea was gone. Only then did the cook give him a firm nod before handing off the empty cup to a child to clean, and Colin left the unusually cheerful kitchen behind to head to the loch.

As promised, Meggie helped deliver a plate of food, artfully arranged by her hand, to the brothers and Bram that evening. In the center of each plate lay a neat pile of mashed turnips with a choice slice of roasted chicken, and a sprinkling of finely chopped parsley. Three small roasted carrots bridged one side of the mound, a sweep of thick gravy on the other.

She accompanied the maids from the kitchen to serve them.

"I asked them to bring up the rest in a few minutes once you've conquered and devoured these small portions," she teased as she settled her linen napkin in her lap.

Earlier, on his way to the hall, Colin caught her in the shadowed main-floor hallway.

She smelled so sweet, with her freshly washed hair caught up in a black beaded net, that he couldn't help himself but to wrap her wee body in his arms and breathe in her scent. She immediately snuggled into his chest.

"I'm glad you're back. I've missed you, but I need to help Iona," she said breathlessly as she both pulled him closer and pushed him away. Her eyelids were

heavy as he kissed her lips, once—twice—her thick lashes fanning out on her cheeks.

"Ah, the source o' her good moods." He growled low in his chest, pleased that his future wife had made such strong, positive changes in her short time there. "Have ye told her about us?"

Meggie shook her head and leaned up on her toes for another kiss.

"I haven't told a soul. Can't say it hasn't been hard, though." Carding her fingers through his damp hair, she lightly scratched his scalp, eliciting a groan before she quickly kissed him one last time and rushed away. He watched her retreat, her white lace gown glowing faintly in the shadowed hallway.

Colin stared in awe at the arrangement placed in front of him. A minstrel, who had arrived a day early for the Sunday supper, softly played his violin from his chosen place near the hearth. The entertainment he would provide Malcolm during the next two days would be his only payment for his meals and a warm bed at night.

"I dinnae think I can eat it," Bram confessed. "'Tis too… well, 'tis verra bonnie, isn't it?"

Meggie's laughter echoed off the high walls before she lightly slapped his arm and picked up her fork.

"Here. I'll show you how it's done."

Bram shot Meggie a droll stare but watched her display her fork in his face and slowly, as though he was a child, demonstrate spearing a small amount of turnip and chicken. Dragging them over the gravy, she made a big show of placing the fork in her mouth.

"If you willnae eat it, Bram, I will," Colin said, and reached across the table to snatch the plate, only to have it slide out of his reach.

"*Ith thu fhèin, co-ogha*," Bram snarled good-naturedly and threw up his arm to create a barrier between Colin and his plate.

"I *will* eat my own," Colin grinned and glanced over to Malcolm's plate to find it already cleaned of even the gravy. "Christ, brother. Did ye even taste it?"

The MacKinnon laird shrugged and filled Meggie's chalice to the brim before she could cover it with her hand.

"Och, Meggie, my dear, ye'll have to learn to drink like a Scot if ye have any hope o' survivin' us," Malcolm warned, reclining back in his chair.

"Ho, the lass can drink, and swipe yer own from under yer nose while she's at it," Bram blurted, unable to keep the story to himself any longer. "We watched her disappear two pints and drams *each* in under an hour, and she cannae be but eight stone."

"Nine stone." She sniffed, glaring at Bram while he laughed at her expense. "And for the record, I didn't know that second round wasn't mine."

Malcolm appraised her thoughtfully and asked, "Who was it meant for?"

"Finlay," Colin answered, no longer able to keep a straight face for her benefit.

"Mmm." Malcolm nodded and patted Meggie's hand. "Dinnae belittle yerself over it, lass. Finlay has pinched his fair share and it was bound to happen to him someday. Although, I'm sure he didnae expect a wee thing like yerself to enact retribution."

Meggie sighed and sipped her wine when focus toward the platters the maids set down along the table. Famished, Colin heaped a large portion of everything onto his plate and bolted it down in record time. The salted meat, cheese, and hard bread he ate that morning had long since burned away, and he was ravenous after dragging his kills back to the keep.

"Did you enjoy your hunt, Colin?" Meggie asked when she pushed her empty plate forward and tucked her half-empty chalice closer to her body to protect it from his brother's watchful eye.

"Parts of it," he said wearily, and leaned back in his chair. The weight and warmth of the food in his stomach amplified his exhaustion and clouded his mind. "My efforts were rewarding but tiresome." Mismatched eyes studied his face with sympathy.

Exhausted, Colin turned his heavy, bloodshot eyes toward his brother and asked to be dismissed.

"Aye, go find yer bed before ye need someone to carry ye there." Malcolm smirked. "Magnus will expect ye for training at sun up. He says ye're gettin' soft."

Colin rolled his eyes at the notion of anyone calling him soft and made a mental note to prove it to the weapons master in the morn, as well as be present the next time Malcolm trained.

"Aye, well, I'll join ye for the noon meal after he whips me into shape. There are things we need to discuss."

Colin's aching muscles protested when he pushed the heavy wooden chair away from the table and stood. With a nod to his brother and the touch of his lips to Meggie's knuckles, he bid all three good night and trudged heavily out of the hall. He would have liked to have escorted Meggie to her chamber, but she was still bright-eyed, and he was unwilling to pull her away from good company just to satisfy his wants.

The stairs seemed like too much of a challenge, anyway.

Colin found his private room in the barracks warm and his bed inviting as he stripped out of his clothes, slid between the sheets, and fell into a dreamless slumber moments later.

⌒⌄

The blunted training sword rushed over his head in a whisper of parted air as Colin ducked and made a series of counterstrikes on the behemoth of a man who was his training partner.

Nearly seven feet tall and twenty-eight stone, Wallace MacKinnon was formidable and would be unbeatable if it weren't for his massive size. His ugly, brutish face, with a nose that had been broken several times, twisted into a scowl when Colin landed the flat of his blade with an audible smack on his belly. Red-faced, he turned on Colin with an angry roar that echoed off the keep's walls.

Colin kept his features neutral; his concentration wholly fixated on his opponent's shoulders and hips for the minute changes and subtleties that foretold of the next attack, or where he could place an unguarded strike.

With a bellow, Wallace swung his practice sword down with a mighty force intended to smash Colin's skull. Raising his weapon defensibly above his head, Colin caught the blow close to the hilt on the rain guard, and before the larger man could pull back, Colin twisted and stepped away to the right, catching his opponent's weapon with the cross-guard. With a soft grunt, he ripped it from Wallace's meaty hands and jerked the giant dangerously off balance. The sound of metal skittering over sand and gravel caught the full attention of the other men in the bailey, and they all turned in time to watch Wallace fall to his hands and knees like a mighty ogre in the dirt.

"Training is useless if ye are no' given the opportunity to learn and adapt." His father's voice resounded in Colin's head, and he took a few steps back to allow Wallace to reorder his thoughts. The large man huffed, weaponless save for the ones God blessed him with, and heaved himself back up to his feet.

"Dinnae let him get his arms around ye, lad," Marcus warned.

Re-centering his considerable weight over his thighs, Wallace sneered at Colin for a moment, a strange glint in his eye, and then flung a handful of sand aimed straight at Colin's face.

Forced to close his eyes, Colin felt a mixture of pride at Wallace's forethought and trepidation at his vulnerable situation. The tiny projectiles peppered his face, lodging themselves in his lashes, and made it impossible for him to open his eyes without painfully blinding himself. Instinct had him wanting to retreat and brush the sand away, but his discipline overpowered the urge. He had other senses at his disposal.

Time seemed to slow while he grounded himself. His feet absorbed the pound of heavy footfalls on the earth, forewarning the impending attack. Tilting his head, he heard them coming from his left instead of the head-on approach he expected, and focused on Wallace's labored breathing and the soft whoosh of displaced air as massive arms closed in around him. Left with only enough time to angle his blunted sword and shove its rounded edge into the soft flesh under Wallace's jaw, Colin applied just enough firm pressure to crane his head back.

Were they in battle, with weapons honed to a wicked edge, Wallace's head would have fallen from his shoulders before causing any damage to Colin.

With a growl, Wallace thumped Colin's upper arms, acknowledging his defeat.

"I thought I had ye," he harrumphed and shook Colin's shoulders with brotherly frustration.

"Aye, so did I," Colin admitted.

After brushing off as much of the sand as he could, he allowed Wallace to guide him toward the water trough by the far wall where he dunked his face fully beneath the surface, and the crisp water washed the rest of the kernels and dust away. Seasoned warriors gathered around to comment on their duel, and commended Colin's quick thinking and Wallace's use of his surroundings.

"That's cheatin'," a green lad of twelve muttered to his partner about the use of sand when they resumed sparring with their wooden swords.

"That's called *survivin'*, lad," Magnus said sternly, his red hair a blazing corona in the sun. "In battle, ye use whatever ye can. Ye lose yer weapon, ye find another. I dinnae care if it's a handful o' rocks or yer grandmam's knickers."

The younger members snickered at the thought, but the older, wiser weapons master whirled around and jerked one offender up by his shirt front.

"Ye think me funny? I could murder ye with the shirt yer wearin' right now," Magnus drawled, his eyes intense and wild with promise.

The youth's face drained of color and he stuttered an apology while his toes sought the ground three inches beneath him.

Colin glanced at the arc of the sun, and judging it time to make his way up to the library, passed by Magnus when the older man began to demonstrate the finer points of strangling to the green-boys with a spare cloth.

As he expected, Colin found Malcolm deep in concentration over a book; his long, leather-wrapped legs stretched out towards the cold hearth. A wolfhound lounged at his feet. The windows were open to let in the warm breeze, and the air was clean and earthy and smelled like the freshly tilled fields outside the wall.

"Brother," Colin said as a way of announcing himself.

Malcolm waved lazily at the seat to his right—the seat Meggie had occupied while they had played chess. Colin waited patiently until Malcolm closed his book with a soft whump.

"Yer warriors are gettin' smarter. Wallace nearly had me."

Malcolm grimaced, having been on the receiving end of the brute himself a time or two.

"But still undefeated, which is as it should be. We cannae have the MacKinnon Eidolon bested by his own men," Malcolm jeered. Playfully swiping his book in the air as though it were a sword, he rose from his chair to replace it on the shelf.

Colin scowled. "Ye ken I hate that title," he grumbled.

Malcolm shot him a glare as he settled back in his chair.

"That title ye despise strikes fear in the hearts o' men all over Scotia, Colin. Embrace it. Ye earned it," he barked and pounded his fist down on the table between them before his dark features softened. "Now, what is it we need to speak about?"

A bashful smile threatened Colin's lips. "Meggie consented to be my wife," he said softly, gauging the unreadable look on his laird's face. "And I would verra much like yer blessing."

Malcolm's face morphed from polite interest to profound happiness as he reached across the table and squeezed Colin's forearm. "Aye, ye have my blessing. Ye have the whole damn clan's blessing."

"Thank ye, brother." Relieved, Colin settled further into his chair and basked in the happiness he felt with his laird's support in his choice of a wife.

It was one thing to want a lass; it was another to have the blessing of his laird. Even though Colin was the younger brother, Malcolm could still use his marriage to tie an alliance. To be bound to a stranger he did not love was not a fate he wished to have, but he would honor it as his duty if that was what Malcolm decreed. But with the laird's acceptance and approval of Meggie, Colin's love and devotion to his brother grew all the stronger.

"The lass belongs here." Malcolm said with a firm dip of his chin and a jab on tabletop with his middle and forefinger. "Besides, I fear alone what our cook would do if Meggie ever left. She's been… *happy*."

"Och, ye noticed? I thought I arrived at the wrong keep last eve."

"How could I no'?" Malcolm scoffed. "I heard singin' drift up the stairs the other day. Singin'! I spotted the wee urchins scrubbin' pots in the courtyard and replacin' rushes. The maids greet yer betrothed as though she were somethin' between a queen and a friend… I dinnae ken what magic the English lass cast upon the keep, but we are in her debt. Iona Cook has been sour-faced for over thirty years, barking and sniping at any bit o' imperfection or disorder." Malcolm shook his head ruefully. "Our father resigned to her surly moods because o' the sacrifice her man had made for him; a courtesy, I continued after his death. I had no hope that her iciness would thaw."

Colin was of the same thought. Meggie had indeed warmed the grumpy woman to the benefit of all. In that respect, she was indispensable to the clan.

Soft footsteps and the telltale clinking of cutlery on a serving tray preceded the approaching scullery maid with their noon meal.

"I had word that yer intended was in the kitchens earlier," Malcolm whispered and rubbed his hands together with anticipation. "I cannae wait to see what she has in store for our bellies today."

The maid bobbed a curtsey when she reached the library threshold and set down the heavy tray with a flirtatious glance at the laird, bestowing him with a generous view of her bosom before she retreated from the room. Colin raised his eyebrows in question.

"Haud yer wheesht. Ye're no stranger to the soft thighs of a maid," Malcolm taunted and sniffed at the covered dishes between them.

"True." Colin lifted the lid in front of him and frowned at what he found. Malcolm removed his as well, and raised his lip slightly when he revealed a mirror image on his plate.

"What do ye suppose it is?" Malcolm asked as he poked at the thick disk of charred meat that sat on one half of a toasted bun. Two thick strips of bacon settled crosswise over the meat and topped with a piece of melted cheese. Thinly cut circles of raw onion sat on the other half of the bread. Colin shrugged and stared dumbly at his plate. A pile of slim, crispy spears sat in a golden pile dusted with what he knew to be salt and pepper and a few other spices he couldn't name by sight.

"Maybe we need to assemble it further?" Colin pondered, and placed the bread with the onion on top of the meat. Malcolm followed suit. They both lifted the heavy, stuffed roll that dripped with grease to their mouths and took a tentative bite.

"*Iosa Crìosd*," Malcolm cursed. Tipping his head back, he chewed slowly; his eyes closed in bliss.

"Dinnae take the Lord's name in vain, brother," Colin chided out the side of his mouth. "Although, I must agree."

They ate together, the rest of their conversation morphing into grunts and hums until they sucked the last of the grease from their fingers and converged upon the golden spears. Their grunts then turned to laughter when they realized they were eating fried potatoes dressed in sprinkles of garlic, truffles, and grated cheese.

"Meggie feeds ye every day?" Colin asked, making a mental note to insist his brother train more often. The Mackinnon laird struck an imposing figure, but Meggie's cooking was sure to truly make Malcolm into what Colin affectionately called him behind his back.

"No' every day, but when she does, it always surprises me," Malcolm said with a pat of his belly before he grew serious. "It will be best if ye wed before we set off for the Gathering, ye ken. I assumed she would want to accompany us before yer welcomed news, but if ye wed her before she's presented in front o' the other clans, it would be much easier to protect her. 'Tis no secret that Meggie's a bonnie lass, and I doubt ye'd take kindly to wolves sniffin' after her skirts—which ye ken they will if she goes without the strength o' yer name."

"I had no' thought o' that, but it does seem the best course," Colin agreed and wondered if Meggie would want to marry him within a fortnight. Something told him the idea would not be as well-received as he hoped.

"Good." Malcolm beamed. "Then I will announce the good news this eve."

～

Villagers and crofters filtered into the great hall with the setting of the sun. Colin sat stiffly among the collection of men gathered around the warmth of the low burning fire. He idly listened to Wallace rehash their earlier duel to Finlay and Gavin, and anyone else who would listen.

"I blinded him, and he *still* had his blade at my throat as if he kenned precisely where I would be," Wallace complained. "I dinnae ken how he does it."

Finlay laughed at the bewildered look on the giant man's face and pointed at Colin with his mead tankard.

"The Eidolon does no' need sight to see. All who have sparred him ken this for a fact."

There were murmurs of agreement from each of the men. Lenny, Arol, and Calan had all been on the receiving end of a sound beating in the sparring ring by Colin, who sharply nodded once to acknowledge their respect. Surrounded by his clansmen, Colin took a long drink of his mead and thought about the day he learned what it meant to be humble.

Long ago, when Colin came into his maturity, he realized his body was capable of many wonderful and awful things. He swaggered through the barracks, feeling very self-important, and boasted of his few conquests.

The MacKinnon laird overheard of his youngest sons' egotism, and the very next day, he visited the sparring grounds unannounced. Without a word, he picked up a wooden practice blade, called out a challenge, and soundly pummeled the arrogance out of his youngest son in front of his fellow men. When Colin was prone on the dirt with blackened eyes, a split lip, and more bruises on his body than he'd ever experienced, the MacKinnon Laird knelt, grabbed his son's ear, and twisted with enough pressure that Colin gasped and looked up with more than a little fear.

His father's words were only loud enough for him to hear, but they were deafening all the same, and dripped with disgust and disappointment.

"Yer strength is a gift, Colin, but yer arrogance will only weaken ye. These men are in awe of yer capabilities, yet ye toss their admiration and shortcomings in their faces. Be better."

Embarrassed and humbled, Colin limped into the hills that night and did not return for eight days.

A profoundly different man returned.

Stepping over the keep's threshold, Colin found the great hall filled with kin and clan for the Sunday supper. He walked without swagger, his eyes lowered. Repentant. With his lip healed and his bruises faded to a sickly yellow-green, the room hushed when he approached their laird. And in front of everyone he knew and loved, Colin knelt and lowered his head to rest on his father's forearm.

A subject before his king.

"I will be better," he vowed and counted his heartbeats until he felt a reassuring touch on the crown of his head and his father spoke with a hint of respect in his voice.

"Then take yer seat. Yer mother was worried."

Relief washed over him as he raised his head and met his father's eyes to find fierce pride and fatherly love within.

Colin felt his anxiety grow as he shook off his memories and scanned the growing crowd for Meggie. She was not in the kitchens when he finished eating with his brother, and neither was she in the library, her chamber, or the stable. Even Maeve, who had her nose in everyone's business, did not know where she was.

Colin tapped his thumb on the armrest of his chair. He needed to talk to her before Malcolm made their betrothal known.

The scullery maids arrived into the hall with stew pots and roasted venison, followed by children carrying baskets of brown rolls and crocks of butter.

"Let's eat, cousin," Finlay crowed and bounded down the few steps to claim a chair at the laird's table.

When Colin stood to follow, a blur of jade-green silk caught his eye at the foot of the grand stair, and he turned to find his betrothed weaving her way between the settling crowd, her beautifully mismatched eyes locked on his.

"There she is," Malcolm's voice boomed from where he appeared at Colin's side. Grabbing Colin's hand, he motioned to Meggie impatiently to join them on the dais. A look of confusion and curiosity passed over her features as she sidled closer.

"Brother, wait—" Colin hissed, pleading silently to stall the announcement he knew Malcolm was about to make.

Ignorant of his brother's beseeching look, Malcolm helped Meggie up the two steps and bellowed for silence. As the room fell quiet, Colin looked at Meggie apologetically. There was nothing he could do now.

"Clan MacKinnon, I welcome ye," Malcolm said clearly. "For two hundred years, we open these doors to share in yer good tidings, celebrate new life, and mourn the passin' o' yer loved ones. Today is no different, for I have joyful tidings to share with ye this night." Malcolm beamed and turned a proud eye upon Colin as he maneuvered Meggie to stand in front of him.

Her look of confusion melted into maidenly embarrassment, and she smiled shyly when Malcolm folded her small hand into Colin's large one before he stepped a pace away.

With open arms, the laird's voice rolled over the people that were near-silent with anticipation. "And I am happy to share that this woman will have my brother to wed."

A deafening cheer nearly shook the rafters. Tankards pounded tables and booted feet stomped the stone floor. Meggie's free hand flew to her mouth, and she laughed, leaning a shoulder into Colin's chest.

"I guess they approve," she said with amusement and turned her radiant gaze upon him, unaware that behind her, Malcolm was motioning for silence.

"With the Gathering in a fortnight, they will wed Saturday, with a feast following," Malcolm said enthusiastically and held his mug of mead high while the clan cheered their approval.

Colin felt Meggie's back stiffen under his hand and dread prickled his throat when her brows pinched together. She looked up at him in accusation.

"I'm sorry," he whispered, and gripped her hand tight, hoping she heard his sincerity. "I tried to find ye."

With shoulders drawn tightly back, she nodded stiffly, her mouth frozen in a smile that lacked its usual warmth. Pulling away, she left Colin standing on the dais alone.

Feeling like twelve times a fool, he breathed a heavy sigh and followed in her wake to secure her in the chair on Malcolm's left before he claimed his own.

With his trencher filled with fragrant rabbit stew laden with chunks of carrots, onion, and potatoes, Colin watched Meggie stab her meal as though it were still alive. Brazenly holding his stare, she jabbed her two-pronged fork into tender pieces of meat and looked away from him only long enough to thank the well-wishers that shared their table with a tight-lipped smile. Twice he attempted to explain, and twice she pursed her lips and made it a point to speak to either Malcolm or Bram, denying him the opportunity. By the end of the meal, neither of them had spoken a word to one another, and Meggie seemed to harden further with each glass of wine.

Colin's worry abated as his irritation grew. If she wouldn't let him explain, then she could wallow in her anger for all he cared.

A fierce strumming of a lute reverberated behind him as the minstrel played a few chords, demanding the attention all musicians crave. Twisting in his seat, Colin pretended to ignore the seething beauty behind him while the minstrel told his tales. When the trestle tables were cleared and pushed against the walls to make room for dancing, Meggie stood abruptly.

"I need some air," she grumbled, and turned on her heel for the open doors.

"Allow me to escort ye." Smoothly rising from his seat, Colin rounded the table and she shot him a glare when his fingers closed around her arm.

"I don't think—" she began haughtily, only to have Colin tighten his grip and propel her forward.

"Ye think too much, lass. Maybe ye should try *listenin'*, if yer pride will allow it," he hissed as he guided her through the throng of dancers, past the heavy wooden doors, and into the chill of the night.

Meggie didn't fight him, but walked stiffly with her pert nose in the air until they were inside the deep shadows and relative privacy of the stable. With a jerk and clench of her teeth, she freed herself of his grip and folded her arms tightly over her chest while she glowered at him from beneath her brows.

Pacing in front of where she stood, Colin took a deep breath to steady his temper before he said, "Ye cannae be mad at me for somethin' that was beyond my control. Malcolm only decided when I asked for his blessing, and ye were nowhere to be found to warn ye. I searched everywhere I could think to look—" He halted his steps when a dreadful thought occurred to him, and he searched her face for a sign of forgiveness. He found none.

"Do ye no' want to be my wife, Meggie?"

Flinching at his blunt question, her shoulders sagged a little, and her chin dipped down.

"I do…" she trailed off, hugging herself tighter.

Colin nearly fell to his knees with relief at her swift change in attitude.

"I cannae read yer mind, but 'tis obvious the thought of marryin' me is unsettlin' to ye. Or… would it be the time frame that vexes ye so?" Leaning back against the wall, he waited for her worries to pour out, and it wasn't long before she launched into motion.

"It's just… well, it's my life, and no one consulted me! No one considered my thoughts and feelings! And… well, I thought we'd have more time. Maybe a year or two…"

Colin blinked dumbly at her as she stood before him, a defeated and worried look on her face.

"*A year or two*," he sputtered. "My God, woman, why would ye want to wait that long?"

"Well, that's how long engagements are, of course. A lot of planning goes into a wedding, and we've only known one another for two weeks," she squeaked and stared at him as though he were daft.

"No' *now* they dinnae, lass," he stressed. Abandoning the wall, he settled his hands on her arms. Smoothing the silken sleeves of her dress, he kissed her forehead lightly, and felt reassurance when she leaned into his touch.

"Malcolm decided on us bein' wed before the Gathering, and I agreed to it without yer consent—but no' because I dinnae care for yer feelings. Ye must understand, Meggie, if ye went to the Gathering a free woman, ye'd be sought after by every lad and auld unmarried man between the hills, and Malcolm would drown in proposals before the sun went down on the first day."

A dark, finely arched brow quirked up in disbelief, and she glared up at him skeptically. A bemused grin tugged at the corner of his mouth as he ran the pad of his thumb over the pout of her lips.

"I can see ye dinnae believe me."

"I don't know what to think." She slipped her arms around his ribs and rested her cheek over his heart.

"Somehow, I find that hard to believe," he said wryly as he ran his fingertips lightly down her back on either side of the thick plait of her hair. "Where were ye this afternoon? I cannae believe I would have missed ye."

Meggie looked up at him and answered with an apologetic shrug. "I heard there were piglets in the barn. I spent the day cuddling them with Earie."

Colin chuffed a laugh at the thought of Meggie buried up to her hips in hay with the sow and her brood.

"Well, I didnae think about searchin' the barn, but from now on, it will be the first place I look," he promised, before growing serious. "'Tis been a short time, our courtship, but I feel somethin' fierce for ye, Meggie. It frightens me, to be truthful, but I have thanked God every day since He sent ye to me."

"I feel it too," she whispered with a slight nod.

Colin could have joyfully crowed at the moon to hear those words, but bent his head to pepper her cheek and neck with kisses instead, making her sigh.

"I want to make ye a promise, Meggie." He took her face in his hands and angled her chin up, so he could better look at her. In the shadows, he couldn't make out the colors of her eyes, but in them he saw a desire that mirrored his own.

Meggie licked bottom lip, drawing his attention away from her eyes and asked, "What promise?"

Colin stared at the perfect pout of her lips when she asked her question and couldn't help himself but to lean down to slant his mouth over hers. The little moan she released when he delved his tongue between her lips had the same effect as throwing oil on a flame. The frantic need to feel her body flush against his overpowered the fragile tether he had over himself. With a quick movement, Colin grasped her by the waist and spun them until he had her back pressed flat against the wall.

Her breathy laugh and the way her eager thighs wrapped around his hips was nearly his undoing. With her fingernails scraping his nape, Meggie returned his kiss without hesitation and grazed his top lip with her teeth before she sucked lightly on his tongue.

Iosa Crìosd, this woman—The sound of heavy footsteps on sand startled him out of his lustful daze, and he wrenched his mouth away to look out the stable doors.

"Colin, what—"

"—Someone's comin', lass."

"Um, not yet, buddy." She choked on a laugh but didn't protest when he disentangled her legs and set her on her feet. Worried of being spotted so close together in such an intimate setting, Colin fled to the other side of the hallway and tried his best to look nonchalant.

"You're crazy." Meggie whispered mockingly from where he left her.

When it comes to ye, Colin thought.

A guard strolled past the door a moment later, ignorant of the tryst within the stable, and disappeared as quickly as he appeared. Loosing a breath, Colin rubbed his hands roughly down his face and said a silent prayer of thanks for leather breeks. No doubt he wouldn't be able to return to the hall for an hour if he were wearing a kilt.

"So, um… that wasn't a promise," Meggie said, her eyes twinkling with mirth.

Colin couldn't contain his chuckle. "No. No, that wasnae what I meant to do, but I couldnae help myself. Yer just so damn beautiful."

Meggie smiled a little wider and crossed the stable floor, her arms extended, and wove her fingers within his.

"You looked like someone was about to catch you with your pants down," she teased and then whipped her face towards the door, her eyes and mouth open wide with fright as though she saw a ghost.

Colin rolled his eyes when she began laughing anew.

"I didnae look like that."

"You sure did. Deny it all you want, but it's true." She squeezed his fingers. "Now, what were you about to promise me?"

Colin studied the way her smaller, scarless hands fit with his own.

"Well, besides the renewal of my previous promise no' to touch ye 'till we're wed—" She opened her mouth to protest and he shook his head adamantly. "—No, Meggie, ye have only yer devilish tongue sucking to blame. A man can only take so much."

Biting back her retort, she rolled her eyes half-heartedly and grumbled to herself before she asked, "What's the new promise?"

Colin took a step closer.

"I promise I willnae make decisions that affect ye again. I will always talk with ye—always seek yer opinion. I promise I willnae leave ye in the dark or make decisions that are for ye to make." He brought their joined hands up to his lips and kissed them. "Meggie… I *never* again want to see ye look the way ye did when ye thought I betrayed ye. The announcement of our betrothal should have been a joyous moment for us, but it wasnae… all because I didnae think to look in the bloody barn."

Meggie pushed against his chest at his weak joke, but smiled and nodded.

"Thank you, Colin."

A much happier Meggie returned to the hall with him; her fingers curved into the bend of his arm and her footsteps light. And this time, when his clansmen took his future wife to dance, Colin did not feel jealousy.

CHAPTER 16

Meggie

I stood patiently on a small wooden dais while I was measured and draped in the softest moon-white satin and delicate lace. Four women, Maeve among them, twirled around me while they bickered excitedly about the shape and fall of my wedding gown.

Caitrin, a seasoned seamstress in her middle years, barked orders at her two young apprentices, Blair and Lioslaith. The two girls practically fell over one another while they hurried to outdo their rival. The withering look she gave me when she placed a pin at my waist hinted their behavior was business as usual. Suppressing a giggle, I bit my bottom lip and extended my arms out for the thirtieth time. Maeve perched on the edge of my bed and looked at me dreamily.

"Och, ye're a vision," she sighed. "Bonniest bride I ever saw, but dinnae tell my sister I said so." She wagged her finger at Blair in warning.

"You have a sister?" Embarrassed that I'd never thought to ask about her family in all the days she had been tending to me, I vowed to find out more about my sweet handmaid.

"Aye, she's heavy with her first bairn. She's the reason I willnae be goin' to the Gathering this year. She needs me by her side." There was a mixture of disappointment and excitement in her voice.

The seamstress placed one more pin into the hem at my feet before stepping back to eye her work. Undiscouraged at the quick timeline Malcolm had given, Caitrin had shown up early in the morning with Maeve. Roused from my bed, she gave me only enough time to rush to the garderobe and choke down a biscuit before they directed me upon the dais. And since I had only found out about my impending nuptials twelve hours prior, I left the decisions up to Caitrin on the agreement that the gown would be simple. Pleased that I bestowed my trust in her expertise, she wasted no time in draping me with bolts of fabric she pulled from an enormous chest that someone had delivered to my door earlier that morning.

"What's all this?" I asked Maeve after she lugged the last of the three new chests into my room and immediately took out a length of lovely pink linen, complete with a delicate rose brocade. Tenting it over her blonde hair, she spun around the room.

"Why, 'tis yer dowry o' course," she quipped. Oblivious to my confusion, she continued to pick through the contents and cooed over the yards of beautiful fabric.

"But I don't have a dowry," I argued.

I didn't have parents here. I was an orphan with no property or belongings of my own. Essentially, I was destitute. Frowning at that personal realization, I said a quick prayer of thanks that the caves hadn't spit me out during the bloody crusades. As my mother would often say, "It could be worse."

Maeve spun around and gave me a queer look before motioning around the room.

"O' course, ye do. Colin has given ye all his mother's possessions. 'Tis only right that ye have them."

Speechless, a lump formed in my throat at the mention of the woman I most desperately wanted to meet, and then solidified with the fact that I never would.

My thoughts jerked back to the present when Caitrin snapped her fingers and pointed at the full-length mirror. In a flurry of movement, her apprentices immediately dragged it over and tilted it just right so I could see what six hours of handiwork had wrought.

My hair, still mussed from sleep, failed to diminish the flattering cut of the unfinished dress that hung becomingly on my body. White lace over a creamy satin started low under my collarbones, leaving the very tops of my shoulders bare. Fitted sleeves ended just above my elbow with a thin satin cuff, and pleated lace ruffles continued in a fall down my forearm to make it three-quarter length. The skirt fell in a waterfall of bustled satin hemmed with lace.

Not simple in the slightest, but it was perfect.

"Thank you, Caitrin. It's beautiful."

She beamed at my praise and carefully peeled it from my body without disturbing the pins, or drawing my blood, and carried it carefully out the door; her two competitive assistants following close on her heels.

⌒

Iona greeted me with open arms, folded me against her bosom, and kissed both of my cheeks. Crowing her happiness at my impending nuptials, she tucked me onto a stool and set a plate heaped with soft rolls, herbed goat cheese, and cold chicken in front of me. I was busy stuffing a second roll into my mouth when I felt the air stir at my back, and I cast a glance to my left to find Colin lowering onto the stool beside me. A devastating smile graced his face when I tried unsuccessfully to hide my full cheeks.

"Ye look like a wee squirrel movin' her winter store," he joked, and stole the last piece of chicken from my plate to pop into his mouth. My face heated at being caught eating like a slob, but I shrugged, swallowed, and sipped some tea before replying.

"I was starving. Who knew being fitted for a wedding gown would work up such an appetite?" Reaching for his hand, I speared my fingers through his and memorized all the calluses and scars that marked him as the warrior he was. "Thank you."

"For what?" He tilted his head, and his fingers danced with mine to cause little butterflies to unfurl in my chest.

"For everything, I guess." I lowered my voice to say, "Actually, I was just sitting here thinking about how lucky I was to be welcomed to stay the day you found me in the woods. Any other laird would have turned me out on my ass—"

"—Malcolm's a romantic, lass. He kenned the way I felt about ye the moment I told him ye were in my mother's chamber."

"Malcolm's a romantic?"

"Och, I've found him with *Romeo and Juliette* in his hands more often than any other tome. Years ago, when I found it fun to needle him, I thought it would be humorous to hide it away."

"What did he do?"

"Well, after he tore the library apart, he overheard Bram and I laughin' about it in the trainin' yard." The whimsical look on Colin's face twisted into a scowl. "And later that night, I found every single one o' my weapons dulled from his retaliation. Took me two days with the whetstone to get them sharp again."

I grimaced. "I think you probably deserved that if you knew it was his favorite."

Colin spun on his seat to lean his back against the thick table and tilted his head in contemplation.

"Maybe. But I did learn a valuable lesson that day."

"What?"

"Malcolm's an eavesdropper."

I barked out a laugh, and he grinned at me.

"I think the better lesson would be that Malcolm likes to even the score, and then some."

"Ye only say that because I didnae tell ye that I kept his precious Juliette from him for another month after he pulled that stunt."

I shook my head and watched Iona pound her fists into dough at the far end of the table when a thought occurred to me and my smile slipped into a frown.

"What is it, lass?"

"You said Malcolm's a romantic… but *Romeo and Juliette* is a tragedy."

With calloused fingers on my chin, he urged me to look at him and said seriously, "We aren't."

I held his gaze for a moment. "You're right, that's a silly thought. But there has to be another reason besides Shakespeare why he allowed me to stay."

Colin tipped his head slightly from side to side in thought.

"I think Malcolm enjoys yer company—and yer cookin'. We all ken ye're too refined a woman to have come from a life o' servitude, but the laird willnae keep ye from doin' what ye love. He learned at a young age that people should be allowed to do what makes them happy, no matter what it is." He paused and smiled at me sadly before he said, "Our mother enjoyed the harvest. There was nothin' our father could say or do that would keep her out o' the fields come autumn. Eventually, he gave up and let her go without complaint. She returned to the keep at the end o' the day, dress ruined, and her skin scratched from fingertip to elbow... but she loved it, and there was a look o' satisfaction on her face for days after. Because o' her, Malcom willnae keep ye out o' the cookery if that's where ye want to be."

I nodded, feeling immensely better, and decided not to question my good fortune again.

"Speaking of your mother, are you sure you want me to have all her things? Maeve told me I should have them, but it feels a little weird."

It was one thing to borrow the dead woman's clothes, but to own them was another. Colin regarded me thoughtfully, his sapphire eyes gentle as they scanned my face. Shifting from my eyes to my lips, they finally rested on our entwined fingers.

"My mother would have loved ye, Meggie. Yer thoughtfulness o' others, yer passion and humor—that ridiculous laugh." He grinned when I tried and failed to show offense.

"My passion, huh?"

"Oh, aye." His face smoothed into sensual sincerity. "We will never bore one another, I promise ye that." He looked around and judged the two scullery maids at the end of the table, and Iona, now over by the cookfire, far enough away to chance whispering, "When my mother died, all her possessions became mine... and when we marry, all that I have will become yers. I want ye to have them. Ye came to this world a stranger, with naught but the clothes on yer back. It pleases me to ken I can give ye somethin' to call yer own."

Later that night, while I looked out at the black countryside and the stars that stretched all the way to the horizon, I thought maybe it was luck that brought me here in the first place.

～

It poured the next three days, the dark sky angry and brooding, and did its level best to drown those who wandered into its clutches. I spent most of my time, when I was not with Caitrin for fittings, in the warm, dry kitchen with Iona. A surplus of baking goods arrived last week in preparation for the Gathering, and she explained to me how she made the clan money in the market by selling baked goods, laboring day and night the week before.

Turning over ideas of what I could contribute, I settled on my childhood favorite. After begging a few pounds of sugar and some potato starch, I grabbed a cauldron and a wooden paddle and began making a large vat of sweet, sticky syrup. My knowledge, acquired from working in a bakery that made simple syrups, caramels, and ganache from scratch, made my task easy.

After I weighed out approximate measurements, I brought the clear liquid to a boil. The lack of a candy thermometer was my biggest handicap, but I hovered over the pot like a mother hen. Feeding the fire underneath, I stirred the syrup until it was at the soft-ball stage. To be sure, I tested a small spoonful in a cup of water, fresh and chilly from the well, and was satisfied when the syrup kept the shape of a soft opaque orb when submerged in the water.

While the syrup cooled in the corner until I could transfer it into corked bottles, I mulled over my game plan for the next day and decided a trial run was in order.

In a new cauldron, I combined half of the still-steaming syrup with more sugar, starch, butter, salt, and raspberry glaze, and brought it all to a boil. On more than one occasion, Iona peeked into the roiling vat of translucent sweetness but refrained from asking questions.

Once I heated the new concoction up to hard-ball stage, I buttered five metal platters and ladled a thick, runny glob onto each one. After allowing them to cool for fifteen minutes, I enlisted the help of Iona and three scullery maids.

"Now, smear some butter on your hands so that it doesn't stick," I ordered, and laughed at the confusion on the women's faces. "Well, go ahead; it needs to be worked by hand before it cools too much."

"Ye've never failed me before, but… well, I dinnae understand how one can eat this," Iona complained as she poked at the clear mixture that had spread itself out on the platter.

"Where's your faith in me?" I chided, and then showed them how to fold the mixture on itself a few times to make a long rope. "Now fold it end to end, like this. Good. Twist it like you would ring out a towel… and now fold the ends together again. Just like that!"

Slowly, the saltwater taffy became increasingly opaque and pale pink with each pull and twist, growing tougher the more it cooled. Without waxed paper to separate the candies traditionally, I had one of the girls grind some sugar into a fine powder. When the taffy was fully cool, I cut a piece off and rolled it between my palms to make an inch sphere before tossing it in the sugar bowl. Once coated to keep it from sticking to anything, I made four more spheres and gave one to each woman. Unsure, they waited for Iona to taste hers first before raising their own to their lips, and watched one another for their reaction.

At first, they were quiet, chewing their candies slowly, their lips pursed. Suddenly, Iona's face split with pleasure, and she laughed around the candy in her mouth while she made a cutting motion at her neck.

"We're no' selling bread this year, lassies!" she whooped.

Gripping my buttered hand in hers, she praised my Nan in heaven for teaching me her craft and their good fortune that I had found my way to the MacKinnon clan.

Later that evening, while a storm raged outside, Malcolm, Colin, and the three rowdy cousins chatted excitedly about the Gathering while they waited for dessert. I had given Iona specific instructions to serve three pieces of taffy to each man so that we wouldn't have a free-for-all. When the tiny portions were placed before them, the cousins frowned, their brows drawn low as they looked suspiciously at the pale pink orbs.

"What are they?" Gavin asked as he picked up one and took a sniff. "It doesnae smell like anythin' at all."

But, as a recipient of many interesting lunches, Malcolm was not so untrustworthy, and immediately shoved one into his mouth. All eyes were on him as he chewed, his face wiped clean of any emotion while his jaw worked. Swallowing, he turned toward me with total seriousness and said in a rough voice, "I've changed my mind, lass."

The table fell silent as they watched the exchange.

"About what?" I squawked, stunned and baffled as to why he would look at me in such a way.

"I'm sorry, Meggie, but ye'll no' be marryin' my brother on Saturday. Ye'll be marryin' *me*."

"Malcolm!" Colin glared at his brother, his face furious at the betrayal.

Speechless, I scrambled for a polite way to tell the laird *hell no* when his cheek twitched. No longer able to keep up his farce, Malcolm snickered and waved off Colin's indignant look.

"I jest, brother. Dinnae growl at me… but if yer smart, yer first request as her husband should be to make these sweets—*daily*."

I giggled into my hand when the twins immediately argued over the food *they* would request if they were to steal me away—the list was obnoxiously long and strangely detailed. Beside me, Gavin wisely stayed silent after Colin cuffed Finlay lightly on the back of the head just for mentioning breakfast in bed, and I almost died from laughter the moment I caught Malcolm stealing one of Colin's candies when he wasn't looking.

I nearly died a second time when Colin accused Finlay of the thievery.

Only after I gave up one of my own sweets was the crisis averted, and while they ate, I told Malcolm of my and Iona's plan of replacing the sale of bread with the taffy at the Gathering. To my delight, he agreed enthusiastically. Pleased and slightly proud to have his support, I felt the first stirrings of importance and an ability to truly take part in life here. I could help my new family prosper.

Family. Yes, that's what this is—what they have become to me. The feeling of comfort and profound joy was so overwhelming that heat pricked at the backs of my eyes.

The last four years since my parents' deaths had been so very lonely. And I hadn't felt lonely for even a moment since coming here. My heart squeezed with both pain and delight at the realization, and I had to swallow back a sudden surge of emotion that threatened to wash me away.

"Ye're tired," Colin murmured from where he now crouched beside my chair. "Let me walk ye to yer chamber."

Blinking the moisture from my eyes, I placed my hand in his and allowed him to escort me upstairs. On the third floor, the hallway was dark and silent, with only a few candles lit to chase away the black night. When we arrived at my room, he didn't open my door like he had every other night he escorted me.

Thinking he was going to kiss me, I gasped when he gripped my arm instead. Propelling me to the right of my door, he herded me into the little alcove where the spiral stairs led up to the turret above. A single fat candle sat in a niche, doing little to light the area.

"Colin, what—"

Looking up at his face, I found his eyes dark and possessive as he positioned me against the stone wall. Curious about where this was going, I allowed him to pin my arms above my head with one hand on my wrists.

"What are you doing?" My breathing ratcheted with excitement as I beheld the warrior towering above me. His hungry, carnal stare drifted down my body even as he kept space between us.

"I thought you said you wouldn't touch me again," I challenged breathlessly, and clutched my thighs together. Warmth pooled in my belly at that heated stare.

Wordlessly, he dragged the fingertips of his free hand over the swell of my breast and down the side of my rib cage.

"It appears I have lied." A roguish smirk played on his lips before he leaned to the side and blew out the flame, effectively cloaking us in darkness.

Frozen with anticipation, my skin came alive when I felt his hand skim over my belly and veer up to cup my left breast. Through the fabric, his thumb made a hard arc over my budded nipple. Swallowing a whimper, I struggled to free my hands, aching to touch him in return.

"No, sweet Meggie," he purred, his mouth mere inches from mine in the dark.

"Why not?"

I was panting and dug my nails into the palms of my hands while my body arched toward his. His soft lips pressed against mine for the briefest of moments before his teeth closed over my lower lip, silencing further protest.

I had expected a chaste kiss like the ones I had gotten the last few evenings when he walked me up here, after which he would hurry away from me before I could reach for him. Now, it seemed, he wanted more.

"I have to touch ye," he implored. His deep voice was harsh, and his brogue thick, as though he were grasping for control. "Just... let me touch ye, please."

"Okay." Leaning back against the cool, rough stone, I waited, my pulse a loud drum in my ears.

Blinded in the darkness, I searched for any sign of movement in front of me, but the night was too black, and he was too large. His body blocked any pulse of lightning that flashed in the hallway. Our heavy breathing mingled with the sound of the storm and rolling thunder in the hills.

Taking my wrists, one in each of his hands, he lowered them to press my palms flat to the wall just below my hips, and firmly held them as he finally, sweetly, kissed me. Too soon did he break away.

"You're a tease," I complained. My body was aflame with frustration. After weeks of nearly chaste kisses, I felt as though I would combust if he didn't *touch me.*

I could hear his answering smile when he said, "Dinnae move away from the wall, lass." He squeezed my wrists firmly in emphasis. Oh?

"What happens if I do?" Because pushing my warrior's boundaries was most definitely something I wanted to test.

Abandoning my hands, he gripped my hips, and I felt him lower to his knees. Kneading the muscles of my thighs, he rested his forehead just under my breasts.

"I'll stop."

His baritone warning carried straight to my core, and my face heated when I realized what he had planned. Yes! My entire body went loose and tight with expectation.

Chilled air curled around my stockinged ankles as he inched the hem of my dress from the floor and felt his way up my stockinged calves. Rucking up my skirt, he raised my right leg and hooked my knee over his shoulder to reveal the most private part of me. His beard, tickling my thigh when he leaned closer, caused a shiver to race up my spine.

The first stroke of his tongue on my soft folds practically buckled the one leg I had left to stand on, and my hands flew off the wall to steady myself.

He stopped. Why did he stop? My thoughts were hazy, and it took me a moment to realize I had woven my fingers tightly through the locks of his soft hair. *Right.* Immediately releasing him, I slapped my palms back against the stone wall with a loud smack, and Colin's shoulders jerked under my leg as he chuckled.

"That's a good lass. Dinnae move them again." I felt the vibration of his words at my core a moment before he lapped at my entrance and hummed with approval.

Oh my God.

With all my weight on one leg and my hands pressed against the wall, I had little control as his left hand palmed my ass and the other hand wrapped in the fabric of my skirts and hip. His tongue made deliciously quick sweeps over my clit, and he worked my body into a fever pitch so quickly I began to tramble with my impending orgasm within a minute.

"Colin," I pleaded, my voice strained as he sucked on me. I needed *more,* but if I moved my hands, he'd stop, and there was no way in hell I was moving them even an inch.

Emboldened with need, I dug my heel into his back. Pushing myself off the wall and closer to his sinful mouth, I felt what little restraint Colin had over himself dissolve away. He gave the globe of my ass one last squeeze before he slipped one finger, then two, deep inside me, and then groaned low in his throat when my inner walls gripped him.

With a whimper, I ground myself shamelessly against his mouth while he licked me, seeking the pressure I needed. Focused on the way his skillful fingers stroked the little bundle of nerves inside me, my pleasure rose to euphoric heights, and I cried out when an explosion of energy ripped through my body. Thunder rumbled outside, muffling my voice, and I felt the stone at my back tremble.

Panting, I struggled to reorder the world around me. Never had I experienced such bliss. It was all I could do to remember how to breathe.

"I've never felt—wow. Just... *wow.*"

Lowering my trembling leg from his shoulder, he rested his head against my belly and stroked the backs of my thighs while he waited for my breathing to return to normal. Only then did he release the fabric of my dress and stand.

"Can I touch you now?" I asked, my voice breathy and my hands still fused to the wall.

"No, Meggie."

"Why not?" I pouted. "I want to make you feel the way I feel right now."

Colin brought each of my palms to his lips and rubbed at the puckered indents caused by the rough stone with his thumbs.

"Because if ye touch me there willnae be any stopping." Walking backward, he tugged me along on wobbly legs to my bedroom. "*When ye touch me*—and ye can be certain I cannae wait for that day to come—I want it to be all night, and forever." He bent at the waist to kiss me, his tongue hot in my mouth and tasting of my body. I moaned at the loss when he pulled away.

"When ye touch me, I want ye to be mine, as I am already yers."

"But I am yours." I protested.

"I'm glad to hear it, but my answer is still no."

I sighed heavily. "If you were any smaller, I'd attempt to persuade you."

"I dinnae doubt that for a moment." A pulse of lightning illuminated his smile. "Good night, my Meggie. I cannae wait to marry ye," he whispered and pressed the prudish kiss I had expected earlier on my cheek before he strode away down the dark corridor.

With a stupid grin on my face, I pushed my way through the door only to have my heart drop into my stomach to find Maeve waiting for me. Her saccharine smile had a look of feigned innocence.

"And *where* have *ye* been, milady?" she inquired with her usual sweetness.

"Um." I just knew I was seven shades of red, and damn her to hell, but she let me stand there sweating for an excuse before erupting with girlish laughter.

"Now, ye cannae imagine ye're the first lass to find herself in that particular shadowy alcove, can ye?" Giggling, she began unbuttoning my dress, followed by the laces of the confining corset. I frowned at her words when they sunk in.

"You?" Cringing, I wanted to kick myself for asking. I didn't want to know about Colin's past lovers. After what just happened between us, the thought of him with anyone else made my stomach sour. Especially if one of them was serving as my ladies' maid.

"Mhmm," she hummed as she took my dress away.

Wilting, I berated myself for having such a curious mind and advised myself that in the future, I should not ask questions I did not want to hear the answer to.

Shaking out any superficial wrinkles, Maeve hugged the dress to her chest and sighed, fluttering her lashes up at the ceiling.

"Finlay is a fine lover."

"Finlay?" Relief so thick, it made me lightheaded, passed over me as I sat down in my shift before the fire.

And then I learned that even though *I* may not kiss and tell, Maeve surely didn't have the same restraint.

~

During the final three days leading up to my wedding day, I made four more small batches of taffy, all with different flavoring, and taught the girls how to make it on their own. Concentrated syrups pressed from ripe summer berries, concentrated peppermint tea, and vanilla gave a wide range of tastes. Iona planned on making as much as she could before we were to set off.

My irritation at Malcolm's surprise announcement at the Sunday supper was water under the bridge as far as I was concerned, and I began to behave as was typical of a bride in the days leading up to her wedding day. As in, I cursed time when it moved so slowly it seemed to crawl in reverse, only to panic when I found the day over and that much closer to Saturday.

The next two evenings after supper, when Colin walked me to my room, I expected him to take me to the darkened alcove and was disappointed to find he had reverted to monkish pecks on the cheek with a gentle good night.

It was in front of my room on the eve of our wedding day—after two games of chess and too much ale—that I boldly grabbed a handful of his shirt before he pulled away. He looked down on me with wicked delight as I closed the distance between us with a bold step.

"What is it ye want, sweet lass?" he crooned; his mouth quirked up seductively as his attention locked on my mouth.

"More than that sorry excuse of a—"

His mouth swooped down on mine, and he picked me up to push me firmly against the carved door, rattling the thick wood on its hinges. Wrapping my legs around his hips as much as my skirt would allow, I gasped at the thick bulge contained within his leather pants. With a groan, he plunged his tongue inside my mouth, plundering and conquering. His fingers dug into the flesh of my ass, and I ground myself against him brazenly, hating the layers that separated us.

Tearing his mouth from my lips, he glared at me and drove himself closer as though he wanted me to feel all of him. He was beautiful, with his lips swollen from my kisses and his hair mussed from my fingers, which were purled through his dark-gold locks. His muscled chest expanded with each heavy breath, mimicking my own. Slowly, he unhooked my legs from his waist and gently lowered my feet to the floor.

"Get some sleep," he ordered as he walked away and spoke over his shoulder. "For ye willnae be gettin' much tomorrow night, and many nights thereafter."

Oh my.

"You promise?" I called down the hallway after him. His dark, rumbling laughter was my answer.

Somehow, someway, sleep did not elude me.

CHAPTER 17

Meggie

I spent the morning of my wedding down in the busy cookery after flatly refusing Maeve's rather unpleasant suggestion that I keep to my room in seclusion. Iona was the next best thing I had to a mother, and she seemed more than happy to fill the role. That was, until she began an awkward explanation of what I should expect on my wedding night. I bit my lip to keep from smiling when the plump woman turned a deep shade of scarlet and fumbled over the appropriate words. Taking pity on her, I confessed my mother had already warned me of *'passionate male urges'* before she died, to which Iona let out a relieved breath.

Red wine and rosemary braised beef, and slow-roasted chicken were on the menu for the evening's feast, along with the usual staple of potatoes, carrots, and brown rolls. With Iona in full control of dinner, I whipped up two omelets stuffed with soft cheeses, caramelized onions, and bacon, as well as toast slathered in honey-butter, and sent it upstairs to Malcolm and Colin in the library for lunch.

While I sipped honeyed dandelion tea, Maeve descended upon the kitchen in a pique, and dragged me away. Herding me towards the stairs, she jabbered on about how I was *"the only bride in all the land who would rather gossip and knead dough than ready herself for her future husband."*

For the next three hours, Maeve scrubbed, plucked, brushed, and buffed me from head to toe. The abnormal attention was strange at first, but after a few minutes, I relaxed and enjoyed the extra pampering. She dressed my hair with silver combs, gathering the tresses away from my face, and secured the rest of the heavy mass low on my nape.

Wrapped in my dressing gown, I stared at the white dress that hung from the rafters in the far corner. The sight of it brought forth images of radiant brides on the arm of proud fathers, and I found a part of myself feeling a little hollow. Regardless of whether or not I had gone through the caves, I would have had to walk towards my chosen husband alone, but that did not make it any easier.

With dampened spirits, I thought of my dad as I stepped into the gown, and imagined to myself what he would say to me while Maeve tugged and smoothed the silk and lace until it lay to her satisfaction. A quiet knock at the door signaled it was time for my carriage to take me to the church in the village.

"She's ready," Maeve called out. Giving me a little wave, she exited through the door that revealed Malcolm waiting on the other side.

Dressed in a jacket and vest, with the MacKinnon clan colors of blue, green, and black wrapped around his hips, he stood tall with a gilded sword and dagger sheathed at his belt, and one of his hands tucked behind his back. I nearly sighed at the sight. There was nothing more handsome than a Scotsman in full regalia.

"Well, don't you look sharp," I said, surprised but pleased by his visit.

"And ye… such a bonnie bride." He gave me the once-over before guiding me toward the mirror by the small of my back. Standing behind me, his warm brown eyes locked with mine through our reflections. "But something's missing," he said and settled a thick silver necklace around my neck a moment later.

It was beautiful, with alternating emeralds and sapphires the size of robin's eggs set in square silver settings. The weight of it rested along my collarbones.

"It's perfect," I whispered.

Although Malcolm had never commented on my peculiar eye color before, the necklace that now warmed on my skin told me he noticed, and thought them lovely. Spinning around, I placed my hands on his broad shoulders and stood on my tiptoes to kiss to his cheek.

He blushed charmingly and motioned toward the hall.

"Shall we? Colin will have my bollocks if I make ye late."

I beamed at him. "Well, we can't have that, can we?"

With my hand tucked in the crook of his arm, Malcolm escorted me through the nearly deserted hallways and into the great hall that someone had decorated with garlands of wildflowers, and fragrant heather. White pillared candles stood ready to be lit on the long tables. It looked like a fairytale wedding venue.

"Ye're an English lass with no kin," Malcolm said frankly when we reached the bottom of the staircase and crossed the hall towards the keep's thick open doors.

My chest pinched slightly at the reminder as we left the shadows of the keep and stepped into the bright sunlight where a massive black warhorse stood waiting patiently with a young groom.

Malcolm squeezed my fingers. "So today, I would like the honor of standing in for yer father, as yer brother."

⌒﹏

Idly playing with the thin gold band that hugged the fourth finger of my left hand, I watched my husband covetously from across the great hall as he laughed with Bram.

With our wedding feast over and long since cleared away, dozens of revelers danced in the space separating us while they celebrated our union. Joyously flushed faces spun around in a blur of MacKinnon tartans and twirling skirts, coming together, apart, together, apart. The music, a mixture of drums, clapping, and two string instruments that resembled a violin filled the great hall, urging the dancers to move faster. My feet idly tapped the stone floor as I split my attention between the dancers and Colin, and I thought of how fate brought me here.

"What's that look?" Malcolm inquired. He lounged contentedly beside me on the ornate wooden bench near the great hearth, his mead tankard resting on his thigh.

The Laird MacKinnon, my father for the day and now my brother for the rest of my life, had shepherded me to the church on his beast of a horse. I couldn't have put into words at that moment how much it had meant to me, but Malcolm knew when he dried my tears in the shade of the ancient oak.

"Happiness, I hope." Giving him a small smile, I resumed my study of Colin while he talked animatedly with his cousin.

He looked so handsome, attired in his jacket and clan-colored tartan. He had his hair pulled away from his face, and his beard brushed free of its usual wildness.

I still couldn't believe he was mine.

"I could no' have asked for a better woman for my brother, Meggie," he said seriously while he studied the level of mead in his tankard. I glanced sidelong at the dark man in my company and caught a shadow of longing pass over his face.

"Why are you not married?" I blurted. The wine and wedded euphoria coursing through my blood blurred my usual firm line of propriety tonight.

Malcolm flashed me a tight-lipped smile before he let loose a heavy breath and leaned closer, lowering his voice.

"Because for many years I have said that I would marry for love or no' at all," he said sadly. "If I could find a love match within the Scottish nobility as our father had wanted for me, it would be ideal. But the noble daughters of Scotia can be spiteful, spoiled creatures. If I had it my way, I'd keep Colin as my heir rather than tie myself to a woman I could no' love. But I also dinnae care to spend my life alone."

Shocked at his honesty and what was probably a rare glimpse at his romantic side, I rested my hand on his forearm and said softly, "You are a wonderful man, Malcolm. Promise me you'll never settle for anything less than requited love."

His brown eyes met mine intensely before he nodded and emptied his tankard, as though sealing a pact.

For the next hour, I danced with Colin, and every one that claimed their rightful turn with the bride. That is, until my husband effectively put a stop to it by throwing me over his shoulder and carried me up the grand staircase. The villagers and men and women of the castle howled with amusement at the groom impatient for his bridal bed. Laughing as well, I merrily waved at the mirthful crowd while I bounced along on Colin's shoulder, causing more hilarity that followed us long after we were out of sight. In the deserted third-story hallway, he set me down on my feet and kissed me soundly in the silence.

"I'm sorry I interrupted yer dance with Bram, but if I had waited any longer, they would have escorted us up themselves," he whispered against my lips.

Walking me backward, he continued kissing me, and at the door to the blue room, he gently removed my hands from the lapels of his jacket.

"Is this our room now?" I asked, my eyes heavy with lust, and my lips numb from his kisses and wine.

"Aye, but Maeve's waitin' to help ye out of yer gown. Dinnae take long, *mo ghràidh*." His eyes roved down my body as he spoke, setting my skin on fire.

I almost said to hell with Maeve and to hell with this dress, but at that moment the door opened behind me, and Colin stepped farther down the hall.

"Come in, milady," Maeve whispered, and ushered me into the candle-lit room. She had me out of my dress, priceless necklace, and undergarments in record time. Shoving a glass of minty water into my hands to sip, she dipped a cloth in a steaming basin and wiped my bare skin down with warm, lightly scented water.

"You're the best bridesmaid, Maeve." I giggled as I swayed slightly on my bare feet. She shot me a vivacious smirk and winked at me.

"O' course, I am," she quipped and held out a new floor-length lace dressing gown with satin cuffs. "Caitrin made this especially for ye this night."

Slipping my arms through the wide sleeves, I tied the satin sash and blushed furiously at the see-through fabric that did little to hide my exposed skin. Grateful that Maeve had thought of all this special attention, I made myself sit still on the corner of the bed while she slipped the pins from my hair, allowing it to tumble down my back. Then she brushed the length until it shone in the soft candlelight.

When she finished, she pulled back a tapestry on the wall that separated my room from the next, and revealed an ornate door I did not know was there. After knocking twice softly and unlocking the bolt at the top of the door frame, she rushed to gather my dress and carried it out through the main door, leaving me alone in just my skin and a few panels of filmy lace.

The metal scrape of a sliding latch announced the opening of the strange door, and I stood quickly, clutching the lapels of my gown closed when Colin ducked through the low entrance.

Bare-chested, he wore his kilt low, drawing my gaze to his muscled stomach and the deep V between his hips. He looked larger than life in this room. My warrior husband. I've seen him shirtless many times, but here, alone with me, it felt different. Intimate.

"Like what ye see, wife?" His voice was deep and rough as he came to stand before me.

He had asked me that once before, on my first night here under the oak tree. It seemed like years had passed since then.

I continued my blatant perusal of his body and nodded once. Swallowing, I clutched the filmy dressing gown in tight fists, suddenly shy. With a light touch, he trailed his fingertips from my elbows to my shoulders before burying his hands in my unbound hair. The pads of his fingers pressed deliciously against my scalp, and my eyelids fluttered closed when the calming pressure morphed into a gentle tug, coaxing me to tip my head back and receive his kiss.

Gradually, the hypnotizing stroke of his tongue against mine allowed me to loosen the death grip from my gown, and I began exploring the contours of his body. My palms brushed against the short blond hairs on his chest, the globe of his shoulder, the soft skin over his ribs. Withdrawing his hands from my hair, he palmed my breasts, stretching the lace over my peaked nipples.

"This needs to go." Yanking at the satin sash, Colin let it fall from my waist and parted the gown in one smooth movement.

Stock-still, he drank in the sight of my naked body, a primal, ravenous look on his face. Emboldened by his hungered stare, I shrugged my shoulders, and the fabric slid down my arms to land in a pool of white on the floor.

"Do you like what *you* see, husband?" I did not recognize my voice, low and husky as it was.

His eyes snapped back up to mine and sparkled with desire.

"Ye ken that I do, yer beautifully made."

Thrilled by his answer, I grinned, and he advanced, crowding me. I backed up a step. Another. Then another. When the backs of my knees hit the edge of the bed, he wrapped his arm around me and lowered us both down into the softness of the furs. My legs opened for him automatically, and he rested his hips between my thighs; the weave of his kilt and his arousal underneath rubbed against my core.

Holding the weight of his torso on his forearm, he traced the bridge of my nose with a finger and then slipped it between my lips.

"I imagined what ye'd look like a thousand times, but I never imagined ye as perfect as this."

I melted with his words and bit down on the pad of his finger before running my tongue over the small hurt. He groaned softly and tracked the movement of my tongue from under heavy lids.

"That lovely mouth will be the death o' me."

"Maybe," I teased, and ran my fingers under the belt that secured his kilt while I slid my bare feet over his calves. "But why am I the only one naked?"

He barked a laugh. "Why, indeed?"

He rose to stand at the foot of the bed, and that lazy, perfectly male smile on his lips melted away when he focused on the thighs that had closed in his absence. Boldly, I let one of my knees fall to the side, and my face burned with the thrill of my wantonness. Colin's fingers stilled on his belt buckle.

"Don't stop," I whispered, and allowed my other leg to drop with deliberate slowness, revealing my core. I knew how aroused I was, and I knew he could see it by the look of desire on his face. Never have I ever been looked upon in such a way. As though the mere sight of me was the only sustenance he needed.

Abandoning his belt, Colin lowered to his knees. Gripping my hips tightly, he tugged me roughly to the edge of the bed, pulling the furs I weighted down along with me. His fingers flexed with the first, slow drag of his tongue, and I cried out at the pleasure that tingled along my inner thighs. With my legs draped over his arms, I felt his control slipping while he licked me, and I writhed with every flick of his tongue.

When my stomach began to quiver with the first stirrings of my approaching climax, he stood up swiftly and jerked his kilt off his hips. Panting, I devoured the sight of his thick cock and the way it jutted out proudly before he covered me with his body. Poised at my opening, he smoothed my hair away from my temples and then lifted my hips. Watching my face, he pushed slowly into me, inch by inch. My eyes fluttered closed, and my neck arched when he was seated fully inside. He stilled, allowing my inner walls to adjust to his intrusion, and ran his lips over the corner of my mouth, the sharp line of my jaw, and then the pulse in my neck.

Then he began to move.

Never had I experienced sex like this. Colin seemed to worship my body with his own, thrusting ahead with long, deep strokes that reached my womb. I murmured soft words of encouragement and propelled my hips forward to better satisfy my need for him. Heat bloomed in my core, and I moaned at the delightful friction he was causing with his pelvis, burning hotter and hotter until my orgasm barreled down my spine. With my body gripping him, Colin's strokes became frenzied, and he pounded into me with abandon, milking my release further until he found his own culmination and spilled himself deep within.

Wrapping his arms around me, he rolled onto his back, pulling me along so that I was astride him. Chest to chest, we caught our ragged breath. With my head tucked under his chin, I stared at the tapestry of the young woman surrounded by woodland creatures; a lone witness watching over us from her place on the wall.

Blissfully happy, I snuggled into the rise and fall of his chest and nearly purred when he ran his fingers along my ribs with smooth, soothing strokes. Within minutes, heavy exhaustion pressed down on my mind like a weighted blanket, and I fell asleep listening to the thump of his heartbeat.

Several times that night, Colin woke me, sliding into my body and leaving us breathless and spent only to do it all over again. I feared I would never tire of my new husband's cravings for me, even if I never slept again.

⌒

The feeble grey light of early morning pried its meddlesome fingers between my eyelids, and I woke to find myself warm and cozy. Colin's long, thick limbs wrapped around me from behind. His chin rested on the top of my head.

Someone likes to cuddle, I mused. One of his arms had banded around my chest, the other supported my head, and a muscled leg wedged between my own.

Slowly, so as not to wake him, I tried to slip from the bed only to have his arm tighten around me, pulling me back. I yelped in surprise when I felt his teeth close on the sensitive span of skin between my neck and shoulder. Spinning around in the blankets, I found him grinning playfully, stretching like the mountain lion I had likened him to, his eyes hooded and twinkling with mischief.

Oh no, I knew what this was.

"You're a *morning person*," I snarled. Rubbing my eyes, I fell dramatically onto a pillow and wondered how I got saddled with Mr. Bright-eyed-and-bushy-tailed when I felt like a cranky toll troll.

"And ye, sweet wife… are no'," he said with a sleepy smirk on his face and placed a kiss on my forehead.

"Not when a great hulking beast kept me up all night," I grumbled, trying my best to sound grumpy while my traitorous face grinned hopelessly when he lazily palmed my breast and his lips grazed my collarbone.

"Mmm. Well, this beast finds ye so temptin', he's more than willin' to face yer wrath," he crooned against my neck while he rolled my nipple between his fingers and pressed his hardening cock against my thigh, displaying just how *temptin'* he found me.

Not one to argue with firm evidence, I threw my arms around his neck and basked in his lazy, thorough attention.

Sometime after the sun was high in the sky, I realized being married to a morning person wasn't so bad after all.

CHAPTER 18

Meggie

It took five long, hard days of travel before our caravan of fifty crested the last hill, and I finally beheld the spread of tents and temporary structures that made the Gathering. Our little procession had an escort of twelve guards: MacKinnon laird and five others riding in the lead, with the rest bringing up the rear. I learned quickly that Magnus, a rough-looking man with wild red hair, oversaw all the warriors, save my husband, and since he was staying at the keep, Colin would be in charge of the garrison's men until we returned.

The village merchants also traveled with the castle residents for safety as well as fellowship. All in all, the caravan was orderly and worked with an efficiency only years of traveling together achieved, and our pace was smooth and without hiccups, if not ridiculously slow.

I broke up the agonizingly long hours spent on the back of my horse by riding in the wagon with Iona, napping in the safe cradle of Colin's arms, or walking along the roadside foraging for blackberries and edible mushrooms to add to our traveling rations.

I longed to break away from the group to explore the forests that dripped with bright green mosses. To discover its treasures. But the schedule would not allow for personal voyages, and I was left to daydream instead.

It was that first night of travel, while we camped in a field alongside the road, that I discovered what the sky truly looked like when the horizon was void of ambient light from cities, neighborhoods, and baseball fields. While Colin erected our small tent, I had gawked at the pulsing arc of greens and purples of our Milky Way galaxy and the thick smattering of stars in the heavens within and around it. I had seen pictures in books and on the internet, of course, but as I gaped up into the cloudless sky and saw it with my own eyes for the very first time, I felt so small and insignificant. My short life was just a blink of time under the heaviness of the time-eternal high above.

"There's no way I'm going in that tent when we can sleep out here and see *this*," I argued, much to Colin's amusement. Placating me, he made our bed of furs and wool blankets on top of the short grasses not far from the rest of our party.

It was there, cuddled close together, that we looked up into the heavens, that I told him in hushed whispers of the Milky Way, the planets of our solar system, and the trillions of galaxies far, far away. My head cradled on his bicep, he played with the end of my braid, looking up with fascination.

"And even with all that, I still found ye."

My throat tightened at his words as I tracked the path of a shooting star meeting the end of its long journey. A momentary scar in the sky where it burned up in the atmosphere.

"Yes, you did," I whispered.

I laid there listening to the peepers in the trees long after Colin's breathing evened out and mulled over the secrets of the universe, pondering why fate would give me such a gift. Why would it go to so much trouble to bring me to *him*? By the time the moon had traveled half-way across the sky, I still had no answers. Only a deep sense of appreciation.

Late into the night, when my eyes grew heavy as anvils, I wondered if anything would ever dampen this euphoria I felt. I hoped not, but in the morning, I had my answer while I cursed everything in sight for the next two days, miserable and sodden as I was.

Low clouds had moved in and opened up above us while we slept to maintain a steady, lingering drizzle that chilled the air and froze the bones in my body. Sometime after lunch, the thick wool cloak I wore conceded its battle against the damp, and traitorously welcomed trickles of moisture to run down my neck to soak into my traveling dress.

"Ye're of a foul mood, wife," Colin noted while I rode sideways in front of him. With both of us wrapped up in his thickly woven plaid, I huddled against him for warmth and glared miserably at the passing of the countryside from under my brows.

Lifting my face, I scowled at him, beyond irritated that I seemed to be the only person affected by the rain. A drop of water dripped from the tip of his nose when he looked down and it hit me square between the eyes. He barked a laugh at my expense, unmoved by my string of muttered profanity.

"I'm adding an umbrella to my list," I grumbled, and angrily wiped my face before tucking my hooded head back under his chin.

We rode between a supply wagon and a group of warriors; Finlay and Bram among them. The grunts of oxen pulling at their burden and the merry singing far at the back of the caravan distracted me as I closed my eyes and attempted to imagine sun-drenched white-sand beaches in hopes to will some warmth back into my toes.

"What list is that?" he asked, pulling the plaid tighter when the rain came down harder. Fat drops pelted the hood of my cloak and caused Una's ears twitch with irritation.

"Just a list of stuff I miss… from my time. Creature comforts."

Grouchy and miserable, I didn't elaborate further, and we fell into silence until we made camp when the rain blessedly left our traveling party—and most importantly, *me*—alone.

Grateful for the waxed canvas that protected our spare clothing, I changed with the rest of the women in the relative privacy of a rowan grove. After I wrung out the water from my dress and hung it on a low branch to dry as much as it could overnight, I headed straight for the nearest fire to thaw out the rest of the way.

An hour later, my hands and cheeks toasty warm and my belly full of bread and deer jerky, I sought out my husband and found him finishing with the assembly of our tent beneath the canopy of an oak tree. Within, the thickly padded pallet of furs promised a comfortable night's sleep and beckoned me to curl up among them.

With a light smack on my butt, Colin inclined his head towards the tent and said, "Get in. Ye huvnae stopped shiverin' all day."

Eagerly, I crept through the loose flaps of the tent and melted into the furs, the exhaustion of my miserable day finally catching up to me. Colin had chosen a thick, mossy patch to make our bed, cushioning my aching joints. I dozed to the sound of the sentries' footsteps and muted conversations around us, and it was fully dark when Colin slipped into our tent. It wasn't until he wrapped his arms around me that I allowed myself to glide into a dreamless sleep.

Blessedly, the rain did not plague me for the rest of our journey, and I was better able to appreciate the scenic views. On the fourth day, I had spied an unmanned watchtower atop a hill: one thick turret encased within four high walls. The fine hairs on the side of my neck and my arms lifted. Memories sprang up of my mother and me, singing in the hollow of an old ruin when I was about fourteen. We had laid down in the middle of a broken cylinder, the tops of our heads touching, and relaxed in the tall green grass that grew within. I had seen it from the road and begged her to stop so we could explore.

I halted my horse, a gentle-spirited chestnut gelding named Jodee, and stared up at the watchtower while the caravan trundled slowly along. The last time I had been here, it was crumbling, and half the height it is now, the walls only a faint outline along the foundation, their stones long since stolen or scattered down the hillside.

I looked at the terrain differently after that.

⌒‿

Around noon on the fifth day, I was in better spirits as I rode Jodee, and kept pace beside Iona's wagon. I listened politely while she told me of her duties and then adamantly refused my proffered help. I shrugged, undeterred. She'd cave, eventually.

The kitchen women had been very busy while I spent the first few days of married life locked away in the blue room with Colin. We did not venture out much, not even to go down for dinner, preferring to eat our meals before the fire. When we emerged two days before we were to set off for the Gathering, it shocked me to see how much they had made.

Three hundred pounds of pastel-colored taffy loaves, ready to be cut and powdered as we needed them, were tucked safe beneath a waxed tarp in her wagon.

"We'll make more coin with less effort selling these sweets than we would have with bread," Iona explained cheerily and patted the covered crock of powdered sugar resting safely between her feet: the key ingredient to keeping the spheres shaped for sale.

"How many people do you think will be there?" I asked, unable to picture the event in my mind.

"Thousands. Look for yerself, lass." With a grin, she encouraged me to trot ahead to the top of the hill. Giving sweet old Jodee a tap, he lumbered along, and I stared in awe of the sight spread before me when I reached the crest.

Slightly shorter than Central Park, the sun beat down on a shallow valley about a mile wide and two long, with a forked stream dividing the valley into three uneven sections. The largest division, on the west side of the stream, was used purely for clan camps. From Jodee's back, I could clearly decipher where one clan territory ended and another began by how their tents and shelters surrounded their main cook fires. Wagons and livestock were stationed and penned along and between small groves of birch trees. They spread each campsite tidily over an acre or more, filling the section without overcrowding it. In the middle, a large canvas pavilion was at the midpoint of being erected.

On the east side of the stream, the second-largest section was a market divided in two for livestock and goods. Tents, rough lean-tos, and even a few ramshackle buildings spread across the grass dotted with large pine trees and small clusters of birches. Animal pens and enclosures filled with pigs, horses, goats, cows, and sheep lined up along the southern edge near the creek after it forked.

South of where the stream forked was the smallest section; the gaming field. The southernmost division was a triangularly shaped half-square mile with an interesting-looking depression in the middle. Devoid of any scrub vegetation or trees until it turned to a dense forest at its southern side, it was the perfect spread of land to hold competitions.

We parted the sea of busy people and our party navigated south through the campground, the pathways between clan sites plenty wide enough for wagons. Tartans of all colors were displayed proudly and worn by all, and I absently noticed the men I traveled with were all wearing their kilts. No leather pants today.

The MacKinnon camp, in the same place each year, was near the southeastern edge, close to where the stream forked and within sight of a stone bridge leading to the bazaar. Birch trees and large boulders flanked the site, affording us some privacy from our neighbors. Prime real estate in such a crowded, busy congregation of people.

Wasting no time, Iona began inspecting the clay-and-brick oven used over the previous years and started barking orders, sending for water and birch bark to kindle the cookfire. Most of the wagons had peeled off from our group and continued to the market area, Kerr among them. I had learned that most merchants, especially those without a spouse to accompany them, would sleep in the market, making their beds under their wagons or in their shelter with their unsold wares. Because of that, our camp would be composed of only the castle residents and guards.

Colin helped me down onto shaky legs. The last few hours on Jodee left my lower back aching and my feet asleep. Shaking some life back into my limbs, I looked up at my husband's serious expression and raised my brows in question.

"Ye'll wear this at all times, wife. Dinnae be without it." He draped a thin length of plaid about six inches wide over my shoulder and tied it loosely to rest on the opposite hip like a beauty pageant sash. I looked down, the MacKinnon colors of blue, green, and black stark against my dove-grey traveling dress.

"Why?" I tugged on the fabric to fall across my chest more comfortably, dismayed that I would have to wear another layer in the heat of the day, even as insignificant as the sash was.

Scotland summers were mild compared to what I was used to, but wrapped in floor-length wool, even with cloud cover, was stifling. Already, the hair that escaped my braid curled around my face, and I felt an overwhelming need to air out my skirts.

"It marks ye as married and as a MacKinnon. And ye willnae wander without a guard if I am no' with ye." He wrapped his hands firmly around my upper arms to convey his seriousness, his face dipped down to my level. "Ye *will* heed me on this."

"Jeez, okay. I didn't know it would be dangerous," I grumbled, concerned now even as it irritated me to be ordered around. Colin's features softened, and he pressed a kiss to my forehead.

"A precaution is all. No' all here are our allies, and I need ye safe."

Pacified by his reasoning, I nodded in agreement and watched him march away. Pointing at various gradients of the hills, he stationed the first watch to keep us and our belongings safe from thieves and unwelcome guests. Gavin told me that thievery was rare, at least at the camps, and with an armed guard or two always on watch, I could understand the rarity.

Five other women besides me and Iona came from the castle, all married to men of the garrison. Three were the scullery maids I had come to know well: Lorna, Janet, and Annabel. All three were busily toting buckets of water to fill a large cauldron already positioned over a fire. Crissy, a healer, was stripping linens in preparation for injuries she expected to happen. And then there was Bradana, one of the keep's laundresses, busily stacking the firewood between two birch trees. She was in her thirties, beautiful, with dark brown hair, high cheekbones, and bright blue eyes. I thought those eyes were going to pop right out of her head when I began helping her stack wood, and she insisted I relax in the shade instead.

Whatever. There was plenty more I could do.

Snatching up an extra bucket, I made it halfway to the little waterway before Bram caught up to me. Deftly plucking the pail from my hand, he tossed it back towards the camp and began steering me upstream.

"Ye'll be no help to them, lass, as a lady and Colin's wife," he murmured and pointed towards the market. "Why dinnae we explore a bit and leave the rest to mind the camp, eh?"

Peering over my shoulder, I caught Colin's watchful stare as Bram guided me away.

Fine. They could all sweat without my help.

"Colin told you to get me out of the way?" I snapped as I stuck my nose in the air and quickened my pace. My dress swirled around my feet as I marched over the grass. His long legs kept up with my pace easily.

"Och, never. He only mentioned ye would like to acquaint yerself with yer surroundings and that I was to accompany ye," he explained flippantly, his sea-green eyes dancing with amusement.

We walked upstream, parallel to the gaming field along the burbling water, and neared the stone bridge that led to the market section just above where the stream split at a large boulder. Although many clans arrived before ours, most merchants were still setting up, and I could see large groups of people ambling down and between the hills, heading for their designated campsite. Slowing my pace, I strolled with Bram down the rough lines of the bazaar, noting the tents I would visit when all was in place and ready for sale.

"Where will Iona's stall be?" I asked as I waved away a thick cloud of peat smoke from my face.

"Och, I believe she'll bully a spot close to the burn with easy access to the camp. There willnae be a busier soul than she this week, and she willnae be wantin' to waste the time to travel between."

As we explored, he walked just behind my right side, content to let me choose our direction. His right hand rested lazily on the hilt of his sword while he casually looked around. Bram's focus lacked the intensity of my husband's, but I doubted he missed much and would quickly spot any hint of a threat that got too close for his liking. Colin wouldn't have left me in his care otherwise. Still, I couldn't imagine what danger would lurk between stew pots, piles of wool, linen, and pottery, but I was grateful for his company.

The more ground we covered, the more I wished we had more than three hundred pounds of taffy. Besides pies and honeyed rolls, there wasn't anything resembling modern-day carnival food. I kept expecting to catch a whiff of funnel cake on the breeze but was only met with the savory scents of stews, roasted meats, and yeasty bread. When our stomachs grumbled, Bram purchased two bowls of hearty chicken soup in bread bowls that we ate with flat wooden spoons under the shade of a Scots pine.

"The games start the day after tomorrow. Ye'll be wantin' to see yer man in action, I'm sure," Bram said as he polished off the remainder of my bread bowl and returned our spoons to a bin for someone to wash—hopefully—and re-use. With a jerk of his curly head, he steered us back towards the camp a half-mile away.

"What competitions are *you* entering?" I asked, curious.

The yard had gotten busier since we started our tour a couple hours ago, making our trek back slower but still enjoyable as the sun made its slow decent. I spied a silversmith as well as a woman selling small kegs of beer and ale, tables covered with candles, jars of jellies, honey, and pickled vegetables. Some merchants sold straight from their wagons, forgoing a table altogether. I ran my fingers over soft mounds of carded wool and embroidered linens while I listened to Bram list off the competitions he planned to enter.

"But I'm mostly lookin' forward to the hammer throw. 'Tis the perfect sport for these long arms." Proving his point, he extended his tanned limbs to their full wingspan, and the cords of his muscles stretched under his rolled-up sleeves. "And then there's the tuggin' of the rope, which is the most fun, pitting clan against clan. I do believe we will win again with that brute Wallace on our side." He chuckled and pushed his hair off his forehead.

I snorted in agreement. "You're all giants to me."

To my relief, a thick cloud passed in front of the late afternoon sun, dropping the temperature to a more comfortable level as we left the market behind and found an organized camp. Iona had the oven heated, and a large haunch of some unfortunate animal spitted over coals. The tents, arranged in a wide semicircle, were far enough away from the fire and near the little thicket of birch and boulders.

Settling down on one of the logs and stones surrounding the firepit, I told Iona about the food I had seen available for purchase.

"We're going to make a killing selling that candy," I said proudly. Tying a blade of grass in tiny knots, I waved off her confusion at my modern speech. "It's a good thing, I promise."

Beaming with excitement, she rushed off to the market where her stand was being erected across the water.

⌒ᴗ

I awoke shortly after sunrise to the god-awful sound of bagpipes echoing across the land. With a frustrated groan, I reached for Colin, only to find the spot he should occupy empty and cold. I missed him. Married not even two weeks, and his absence felt like a missing limb. I wondered if I would feel that way when we were old. I hoped so, and snuggled under the thick wool blanket and heavy furs. Alone, I watched the canvas of our tent brighten as the sun climbed higher in the sky, and the sounds of the camp became more animated.

My traveling apparel made dressing without Maeve easy. She packed four, in shades of blues and greys for me to choose from, and thick-soled leather slippers that wrapped and tied around my naked ankles. Buttons ran up the front and boning, sewn into the bodice, replaced the need for a corset. Without Maeve to braid my hair, I had made sure to bring my hair tie and faked a twisted bun high on my head to battle the heat. It would be a day worth crying over when the rubber band snapped, but until then, I planned to use it all week long.

I wolfed down a bowl of porridge around the fire with Lorna and Anabel before enlisting a guard, a fearsome man named Gunn, to escort me to Iona's table in the market. She had, just as Bram predicted, acquired coveted space along the gently rushing water. In full view and with easy accessibility, the thick boughs of a pine reached overhead, promising shade when the sun hit its zenith.

"Don't even think about sending me away," I warned and plopped down on one of two stools to slice into a taffy loaf resting on a metal platter. Iona glared at me with feigned irritation and attempted to dismiss my guard.

"I cannae leave her, Mrs. Cook. Colin would have my bollocks if I did," Gunn explained, but didn't feel the need to hover, and walked a few yards away to stand vigil as he leaned against the rough trunk of the pine. Iona rolled her eyes but said nothing of my armed guard and began coating the spheres I made with the powdered sugar.

"I think we should make some free samples," I suggested. Slicing some balls into sixes, I rolled out blueberry-sized portions.

"*Free?* Why in the blazin' hell would we give these away for free?" she squawked, her features displaying a mixture of horror and disgust at the thought of giving something away for nothing.

I laughed and reminded her of her first impression of the candies.

"If we give them as gifts to our fellow vendors, *they* will spread the word about how delicious they taste and where to find us. Trust me. Word-of-mouth is a powerful thing."

We made a hundred portions, powdered and ready for distribution in a clay bowl as the thoroughfares filled with people. Waving at Gunn to follow, I set off, leaving Iona behind to mind the booth.

Much to my surprise, many were wary of my gift, confused that I didn't demand payment of some sort. I had to resort to leaving a sphere or two in front of several vendors and, after pointing out our general location, moved farther down the row.

When my bowl was empty, and we arrived back to Iona, she turned from the small group of people on the other side of her table and looked at me with a stunned expression.

"I've already gone through the first loaf," she whispered to me as she accepted a few coins from a man.

"That's a good thing!" I squealed. Digging another wrapped brick from the trunk under our table, I sliced into it to make more powdered spheres.

Within two hours, we ripped through thirty pounds of candy, called in for reinforcements, and even raised the price. By the end of the day, we had only a hundred pounds left. Iona stared at the two heavy pouches of coins Gunn wordlessly carried back for us just as the sun withdrew over the gentle upward fold of the valley.

Her face was a mask of disbelief when she said, "We made more coin today than we would have selling bread the whole week."

I wrapped my arm around her shoulders and gave her a squeeze.

"Next year, we'll bring twice as much," I promised.

Dinner was a boisterous affair, full of laughter and stories told around the fire while we ate. I especially enjoyed Finlay's stories. My cheeks were already aching from laughter as he began a retelling of last year's tug-o-war victory.

"And we were so close to getting' pulled over the line, ye see, when bawface Wallace here had a thorough-cough from the stress, and with him being first in line, the rest of us would have choked on the stench if we allowed ourselves pulled any farther." Finlay stood behind where the enormous man sat. Gripping his meaty shoulders, Finlay shook him roughly, and Wallace's face turned beet red. "So, the only thing to be done—was win!"

The men roared with laughter, all talking over each other at once, either insisting Wallace have the same place on the rope or threatened him with murder should he pull the same stunt again.

I turned to Crissy in confusion. The red-headed healer hid her grin behind her hand as she chuckled at the story.

"What's a thorough-cough?" I asked softly, not wanting to call attention to myself. For a moment, I thought she wasn't going to answer until she shrugged and leaned in close.

"'Tis a cough followed by a fart, milady." She made a sickly face and shuttered before leaving me to refill her cup. Wishing I hadn't asked, I caught sight of Colin a few minutes later and watched him make his way through the circle towards me.

"Where have you been?" I asked curiously after he lowered wearily beside me and settled a round of bread filled with brown stew in his lap. The sky was purple with twilight, but there was still plenty of light to see the smudges of exhaustion under his eyes.

"Standin' guard with Farlan while Malcolm met with the other lairds. They meet several times over the week, and the first day is always the most stressful. 'Tis a tedious job of long hours standin' sentry." He tucked into his meal and relaxed a bit after I kneaded the muscles in the middle of his back. "That feels good. Tell me, what did you do today? See anythin' excitin'?"

"Nothing terribly exciting, but I learned what a thorough-cough is just a short while ago."

Colin rolled his eyes and grumbled around his stew, "Finlay loves tellin' that bloody story."

"He did tell it exceptionally well." I laughed. "But my day was good. It wasn't nearly as taxing as yours, but we were very profitable at the market, and I think we'll sell out by noon tomorrow."

I clapped my hands softly while I shared the news, a giant grin on my face. He leaned over and kissed me quickly after tucking a wisp of hair behind my ear.

"I'm proud o' ye, wife," he said reverently. "We're lucky to have ye."

"You bet your ass you are."

And then I leaned in for another kiss.

CHAPTER 19

Meggie

"What the fuck is wrong with you Scots?" I groaned and yanked the blanket over my head in an unsuccessful attempt to muffle the dreadful music. It sounded like the bagpiper stood directly outside the canvas walls of our tent, and at that moment, I couldn't help but think of Nan's rooster.

Colin's inquisitive fingers slipped around my midriff to trace lazy designs under my navel and then picked at the pesky linen shift I wore.

"Ye dinnae like bagpipes, *mo ghràdh?*"

He tugged the blanket away from my face, and I looked up to find him smiling down at me, his hair in wild waves and his eyes still heavy with sleep. I shook my head, all my focus on his wandering hand that leisurely lifted the hem of my shift.

"What are you doing?" I demanded, trying my best to look serious, and stopped him from advancing further. I could hear footsteps outside our tent as the camp roused from sleep. Abandoning my shift, he rolled onto his back only to pull me across his chest and ran his fingers through my unbound hair, gently untangling the snarled spots with infinite patience.

After he combed all the knots out, I sat up and looked down at him. "What does that mean? What you just called me. You've said it once before."

"*Mo ghràdh?*" One of his golden brows raised up, and he pinched my butt, earning a squeak from me. "Means bog monster."

"Ugh." I rolled my eyes and slapped him lightly on his chest. "I should have known."

Colin's mirthfulness sobered, and his sapphire gaze roamed over my face thoughtfully. I narrowed my eyes down at him when his mouth curved into a small, secret smile.

"What are you thinking about?"

"Ye. Always ye, my bonnie bride." He reached up to bop my nose and pouted adorably when I batted his hand away.

Scooting away from him, I wiggled into a dress and fastened the buttons in record time.

"Are you spending the day with Malcolm again, or will I have some time with you?"

"I'm all yers today, lass." He wagged his eyebrows, and I shook my head and bit my lip to hide my smile at his not-so-subtle hint. There was no way in hell I was having sex in the middle of a camp filled with warriors. Sorry, buddy.

"You're not entering any competitions today?"

"Not this day." After wrapping his kilt around his hips and tugging a shirt over his head, he inspected both of the wickedly sharp daggers sheathed at his belt before he ducked out of the tent and held the flap open for me to follow.

Fog hung heavy in the air as we huddled around the fire, steaming bowls of porridge with blueberry preserves and cinnamon in our hands. The last mournful note of the unknown bagpiper drifted over the valley when the sun peaked over the hillcrest.

And so began the third day of the Gathering.

After only a few hours spent touring the playing fields at Colin's side, I learned that there was an irrefutable distinction between that of a fighter and a true warrior.

The cocksure, boastful creatures that flaunted their muscles much like a male peacock displayed his feathers were the fighters. Sure, they were strong, and I had no doubt that someone trained them to handle weapons from a young age. I'm sure they had come out the victor in more than a few tavern brawls… but for all their posture and pomp, they lacked the unique darkness that emanated from the seasoned warriors.

It was the deep knowing and menace that rolled off their shoulders like a shroud of thick smoke as they walked. I practically felt it brush my shoulder when I walked past them, and after watching a few competitions, I could easily identify who had killed in the heat of battle, and who had not.

They noted the shadows, and their surroundings; chin tucked, brows lowered slightly—a veritable threat to anyone who may dare challenge the space they occupied.

It was the same expression Colin wore.

There, surrounded by a sea of testosterone, the man that stood beside me was not the same man who I woke up with this morning. This man was different, though he looked exactly the same.

As we walked through the crowds, Colin used his own body as a buffer, preventing me from being bumped or jostled. Any man that looked at me a moment longer than necessary quickly found themselves the subject of Colin's sharp focus and wisely found something else more interesting in the other direction. Twice he ushered me away from a crowd moments before a brawl erupted. It was as though he knew what people were going to do before they did. Or maybe he was just more observant than most. Either way, I allowed myself to enjoy the chaos around me and trusted Colin to take care of the rest.

Finlay impressively bested all in archery by splitting his opponents' arrows straight down the shaft. Serious for once, he wielded his bow with discipline, confidence, and sinuous precision; his sea-green eyes brilliant as he focused intently on his target.

Finlay did not simply hold the bow. He *became* the bow.

We had just finished cheering on Banner, who finished second in an all-out quarter-mile horserace, Bram in fourth, when I felt a strange flush start at my knees and race up my back. Goose bumps followed the surge, even with the heat of the day. Whipping my head around, I searched the sea of onlookers as they dispersed and headed for the next event. I've experienced that foreboding rush of energy before on more than a few occasions when I walked the less savory streets of New York City.

Someone was watching me.

"What is it, Meggie?" Colin asked. His hand curled protectively around my ribs and pressed me closer to his side. The young couple standing beside us looked at me strangely before they walked away.

Reluctant to worry Colin over something as silly as a feeling, especially with him already wound so tight, I stroked his midsection and gave him a little smile.

"It's nothing. The wind brushed my neck wrong, is all."

He didn't look convinced but guided me over the now empty racetrack, the soft grass under our feet eaten up by heavy hooves to reveal the dark soil below.

We shared half of a roasted chicken and a soft loaf of bread under the popular canopy of a small pine grove just on the other side of the stream from the market. Claiming a spot on the thick carpet of needles around a low, flat rock, we devoured the meal and licked the grease from our fingers. Cool, crisp ale washed it down; a vintage from the south, if the peddler was to be believed.

"Will we have time to visit the other side of the market before sundown?" I asked.

It was a strict MacKinnon rule to be back at the camp by sunset. No exceptions. When Malcolm reminded everyone on the first day, I expected some irritation or push-back from some men and felt surprise when the order was well-received with firm nods of agreement. When I asked Colin the reason for the curfew, he told me that on two separate

Gatherings, when he was just a baby, a few MacKinnon men were found dead with their throats slit after being away from the camp at night. They did not find the murderers, of course, and Colin's father had decided from then on that there would be a strict curfew for everyone staying at the camp. A rule Malcolm continued to enforce.

"Aye, I believe so." Helping me to my feet, he led me back to the market with my hand wrapped snugly within his.

Instead of using the stone bridges that spanned the brook in sporadic intervals, Colin preferred more direct routes, like marching right through the water that reached his knees or jumping from one stone to the next. Today, with me in his arms, he waded through the chilly water, keeping me well above the gently churning surface.

The merchants along the far northeast quadrant of the market closest to the tree line were the last to arrive, some having finished their journey from wherever they came from early this morning.

Besides the bottle of wine bought as a gift for Malcolm and heirloom seeds for myself, I also purchased a small silk sachet embroidered with flowering vines for Maeve to stuff with herbs and keep her clothing fresh.

There was a blacksmith with not even half the talent as Kerr, his rough weapons and shoddy armor displayed on a rickety table. The most interesting find was the portable tabletop grindstone I thought Iona could use. I made a mental note to drag her up here to look at it tomorrow.

When we came to a break between stalls, I spied another trader tucked between trees, oddly surrounded by unoccupied space and a tent set up a little deeper in the woods. A woman in a faded black dress was bent over, rummaging through a trunk, her wild, mousey brown hair a riot of curls and tight waves that hid her face. Bundles of herbs and little bottles lined her table, and I tugged on Colin's hand to head her way, only to find him rooted to the spot he stood.

"No, Meggie. That's the *seann bhuidseach.*"

"What is that?" I asked warily. She didn't look threatening at all as I watched her pull small bundles of lavender out of her trunk.

"The auld witch," he breathed, and tried to guide me away. Pulling out of his grasp, I crossed my arms and glared at him playfully.

"You're such a weenie. Witches aren't real. She's just a woman, Colin, and she's not even old," I mocked, amazed that the brave man before me feared an unarmed woman surrounded by herbal remedies and oils.

"This one is, lass. Dinnae go over there." He looked so unnerved I almost let it go. Almost.

Curiosity piqued, I spun on my heel and hurried towards the pseudo witch before he could catch me, calling out a quick hello when I neared her table. Her arms now full of sage bundles, the woman turned to greet me, and I quickly realized why Colin had pegged her for a witch.

Glacier-pale irises ringed with a line of dark grey seemed to burrow straight into my soul. Her focus on me was so intense that I wouldn't be in the least bit surprised if she knew which direction my blood flowed beneath my skin.

"Hello and welcome. I am Vanora, midwife, and healer."

Her voice was as smooth as aged bourbon, low and throaty. Neither beautiful nor ugly, she was instead rather striking and unforgettable. A thick patch of white hair grew out from her side-part, framing her face with tight, icy waves. Her skin was a pale, unblemished porcelain with the barest of crow's feet lining her eyes the only hint of her mature age. Thin, rose-petal lips curled up to reveal white, straight teeth.

Waving a graceful hand over the table between us, she asked, "May I interest ye in my oils and salts for yer bath, milady? Or maybe a sage smudge to drive away ill humors?"

I felt Colin ease behind me, and I tore my gaze away from her weighted stare. I had the oddest feeling of being stripped naked with all my secrets written on my skin that she could read at her leisure. Suppressing a shiver, I politely picked up a few long-necked bottles. Heavenly scents of heather, peony, and sweet pea flooded my senses when I plucked open the cork stoppers.

"They smell amazing; no one else has anything like this here," I said, and inhaled the rich scent of rosemary and mint mixed in with a bag of salts. "Colin, come smell this." But he only watched the woman as though she were some boogeyman ready to drag me off and chew on my bones.

"Yer no' from around these parts, are ye?" Vanora probed. Flatly ignoring Colin's warning-glare, she took my hand and began administering oil that smelled like lily of the valley onto my skin.

"Um, not really... I mean—no—I'm not from around here," I stammered and watched her rub the oil into my cuticles. Her hands were hot, the difference between our temperatures shocking but soothing.

"Yer other hand?" Releasing me, she waited for me to offer the other. Colin shifted impatiently.

"Sure, thanks."

She watched me with those piercing eyes while she spread the oil to my skin, running her thumbs along the pressure point on the meaty part of my hand and the fine lines of my palm.

"Perhaps... from verra far away?" Her stare flicked up and over my shoulder, measuring the man behind me before returning to study me further.

"You could say that," I snorted. "Thank you. That felt wonderful."

My hands felt softer than silk, and I plucked up a peony oil before looking over my shoulder. Colin plunked down the amount she asked for on the table and quickly began steering me away, his hand splayed across my back while he urged me forward.

"Before ye hurry off, I must ken... how *did* ye come to be here? The stones? The caves? Or perhaps maybe the pools in the far north?" she called at my back.

The tingle of apprehension tickled the back of my throat, and I spun around, clamping my teeth tight. *She couldn't know. Could she?* I thought as the hair on my scalp lifted.

"Let's go," Colin growled. I could tell he was moments away from throwing me over his shoulder and bolting for the safety of our camp.

Vanora laughed darkly and leaned over her hands braced on the table between us. Her hair fluttered around her in the breeze. "Ye think ye're the *only* being to pass through to a time no' their own? There have been many before ye, and many more will follow."

"*Haud yer wheesht, witch,*" Colin snarled. He stepped in front of me; his hand wrapped menacingly around the hilt of his dagger. Peeking around his torso, I watched the woman's smile melt into a scowl at the name.

"Peace, warrior. I mean her no harm. 'Tis been an age since I met a walker. The last time I was a young lass of fourteen... but I remember." She looked sad as she spoke, and I had a feeling the person's fate wasn't a happy one.

But I had to know.

"What happened to them?" I murmured, and tried to sidestep Colin, only to have him throw his arm out. He would not let me get close to her again.

"Witch trials." She shrugged. "Yer were luckier than she, findin' a warrior to protect ye... and the lass didnae ken how to get back."

I shook my head in confusion. "But she couldn't go back. I tried."

"There's *always* a way back. The sun must only be in the right place in the sky, on the right day." The blank look on my face must have portrayed my confusion because she rolled her eyes and looked at me like I was slow in the head. "Did ye no' travel on a specific day or night on an equinox or solstice?"

My memories raced. Of walking along winding fern-lined trails, past the fairy pools, and then coming across the caves around lunch-time. The roaring vibration when I peered into the darkness of the cave. And then Maeve telling me it was dangerous to be a woman alone in the woods, especially during a solstice—

The solstice. The longest day of the year. Was it that simple?

"Summer solstice," I whispered. "I fell through at noon."

It felt like a lead weight had settled in my stomach, and the chicken I had eaten threatened to come back up. I heard Colin's quick intake of breath when the woman nodded.

"And now ye ken how to go back if ye so choose." She rounded the table and took a few steps closer. "But ken this, lest ye try. Ye cannae bring *him* with ye." She motioned toward Colin. "I dinnae ken why or how, but every walker goes somewhere different. While ye'll return to yer rightful time, *he* would end up in another, forced to wait months to return and possibly lose years. Dinnae chance that."

I looked up at the grim lines on Colin's face, and after a quick nod of his head, he propelled us away without another word.

We hurried back to the camp in silence, each of us wrapped up in our own thoughts when the curve of the sun touched on the hilly horizon. The sky was washed in bright, orange light, the long, skinny underbellies of the clouds painted pink. Moving with the flow of the crowd, we followed the beaten paths between tents and shelters to exit the market via a bridge.

My stomach churned as I mulled over what Vanora had said.

I could go home... but how could I possibly do that when I felt like home was right beside me? A place within my chest lurched at the thought, and I looked up at Colin. He averted his face, but not quick enough for me to miss the sorrow in his eyes and the grim set of his mouth.

"Colin," I said desperately when we passed Finlay on watch.

"No' here, lass. Please."

He left me to sit on a log and accepted an overflowing trencher of stew for each of us from Iona.

The camp was boisterous and merry around the fireside. Everyone ate and drank deeply of dark ale, recounting the games to those who hadn't been able to attend, and above, the sky darkened to dusk.

Listening to the music flowing from the camp beside ours, I pushed the stew around but couldn't even manage to take one bite. Colin seemed to stare into his untouched meal as though it was telling him the secrets of the universe. If it was, he didn't like what he heard.

"I can't eat." I sighed. "Colin, I... we need to talk about this. Please, talk to me."

He ran his hand back and forth through his hair several times in frustration before he stood up and led me to our tent. It was dark inside, the only light coming from the campfire far away. Once barefooted, with my legs folded beneath me on top of our pallet, I reached for him. I needed to feel him close, to have his arms around me… but he had barely followed me inside.

He sat back on his heels near the entrance, his shoulders slumped, and his head bowed.

"Colin—"

"—I'll take ye back to the caves on the autumnal equinox. I'll send ye home," he murmured, his voice hoarse and lifeless.

"What?" My throat tightened, and I stared in shock at his dark silhouette.

"I said, I'll send ye back." The desolation in his voice broke my heart.

"But I don't want to go back. I want to stay here with you." Devastated, I could barely make out the shaking of his head in the gloom.

"Ye have a list, Meggie, filled with things ye wish ye had. Things I cannae give ye. Ye can have them again."

Anger and irritation burned within me. He had the audacity to make a decision—*this* decision—without consulting my feelings first. He *promised* me he wouldn't do that.

"You *stupid* man," I hissed, and crawled over to him to grab his face between my hands. "None of those things would be worth it if I can't have you too."

My heart gave a painful lurch when the pad of my right thumb disrupted a line of moisture on his cheek, and I felt my own eyes fill with unshed tears.

"I'm not going anywhere," I promised, and knew I had never spoken truer words in my life.

Without warning, he wrenched me against his chest and buried his face against my neck. One arm wrapped tightly around my ribs, the other pressed lengthwise along my spine as though he was anchoring me to him. I let him hold me for a long while, unwilling to pull away even though I couldn't draw a full breath. Spearing my fingers into his hair, I held him just as tightly.

"I need ye, Meggie," he whispered against my skin as he ran kisses along my jawline.

Nodding in agreement and surrender, I pushed him away just long enough to unbutton the bodice of my dress.

Acutely aware of the number of people on the other side of the thin canvas and of Bram's soft footfalls while he walked the perimeter behind the row of tents, I found I didn't care.

A very new kind of thrill had me pressing my thighs together when I slipped my arms out of their sleeves and let the dress fall in a heap on the ground; Colin's shirt and tartan discarded beside it. In the dark, he lifted the hem of my shift. His calloused fingers brushed over my bare skin like a brand as he lifted the gauzy fabric over my head. My freed breasts immediately pebbled in the chilly night air. Wordlessly, Colin lay me back on the furs and stretched out beside me, his torso propped up on his elbow instead of getting right to it as I expected. Instead, he began a gentle exploration of my skin.

His fingertips brushed up and down my waistline and along the sensitive skin under the swell of my breast. I arched beneath his touch and began panting when he lightly pinched the peak of my nipple. His touch made me shiver, and a soft moan escaped my mouth. The feather-light pressure on the apex of my thighs had me gasping.

"Careful, wife." I could hear the smile in his voice as he continued his teasing. "Someone may hear ye."

I wasn't convinced that he would care in the slightest if they did.

Sitting up, I pushed him onto his back and straddled his waist. His thick erection bobbed against my lower back, ready and waiting.

"You like to tease," I purred, an grinned like a minx in the darkness. Reaching between my legs, I wrapped my fingers around his length and reveled in the sound of his ragged intake of breath.

Guiding him to my entrance, I was more than ready as I slid his thick head against my cleft, priming him for entry. His hips surged up, searching, *reaching*. I would not allow it. I rose higher on my knees until he settled. Small punishment for him to pay for thinking he could send me away.

Planting my hands on the bridge of his chest, I leaned back slowly and took him within my body an inch or two before retreating, again and again, never letting him advance further than I allowed. His muscles leapt under my palm as he struggled for control underneath me. His fingers clamped down hard on my thighs.

Well, well, well. Now I know why he draws it out. It's empowering, this control I have over his body's reactions, not to mention erotic as hell. Bending down, I slid my tongue into his mouth at the same time I tilted my hips and took him deep into the heat of my body, invading him while he invaded me. I swallowed his low groan along with mine as he stretched me wide.

Sitting up straight, he followed me, and urged me to move with his hands on my hips. The angle and pressure of his body gliding against mine, both inside and out, were almost too much. With my head tipped back and my hands on his knees, I concentrated on how our bodies joined while I moved against him.

Faster and faster, I chased my orgasm while he closed his mouth over my nipple and sucked on it, hard. Surprised at the sharp, exquisite pain, I forgot where I was and cried out. My release raced through my body, and sunbursts of red and white bloomed behind my closed lids.

Dimly aware of the laughter and cheers of the clansmen around the fire, I held on for dear life when Colin flipped me onto my back and plunged himself deep inside, pounding hard; my legs draped over the outside of his forearms. Hypersensitive and at his mercy, I began shaking again in the throes of a second orgasm, and my inner walls gripped Colin's cock tight.

"*Iosa Criosd*, Meggie," he muttered breathlessly against my mouth as he pumped his hips wildly before stilling, spilling himself deep inside me. Spent, he tucked me against his chest, my big spoon. The chilly air licked at the thin sheen of sweat on our bodies.

"Definitely not going anywhere," I said dreamily, and Colin chuckled, pressing a kiss to my shoulder.

We stayed up long into the night, wrapped up in one another, a serene peace between us with my decision to stay in the seventeenth century.

Before meeting Vanora, I had accepted the fact that I was stranded in time. But now I could choose—I had a *choice*—and I chose him. And I would choose him every day, every season, every year, for the rest of our lives.

I didn't want to be in a place where he didn't exist. I couldn't go back knowing he was long dead and buried, while I still had decades of life left to live, and I couldn't chance going back for even a short time because I didn't know if I'd ever be able to return.

I felt that choice bond us further while I lay in his arms, and would always be grateful that I insisted on talking to the witch in the woods.

CHAPTER 20

Meggie

D ay six was committed to games, and since all clans were encouraged to participate, there were no meetings between leaders.

I stood beside Malcolm within the thick, swirling mist and fog. Picking mercilessly at my fingers, I watched the furious display of male prowess during the warrior's championship. Eighteen clans had entered their best warrior, each hoping that their man would conquer all others, and for the last hour, I'd watched the ranks whittle down to six, including Colin.

"Dinnae be nervous, lass. My brother has won the last four years. He'll claim victory again," Malcolm boasted with confidence as he gripped the flimsy fence that divided the spectators from the fighters.

The fighting area was an eighty-yard round grassy depression that allowed those in the back of the crowd to see easily over the heads of those in front. At first sight, I wondered if the area had been hand-dug and shaped, but when the first teeth-jarring clash of weapons echoed off the hills, I had forgotten to ask. We packed the whole circumference of the circle with people, shoulder-to-shoulder, and jostled for space. Children sat on excited father's shoulders, and babies squalled along the outer edges.

No one missed the Warrior Championship if they could help it.

Last night, after the drawing of short sticks, they rounded up a small fortune to pay Finlay and Gavin for staying behind with Iona to guard the camp. Bram told me that *the paying of the guard* was a MacKinnon tradition for as long as anyone could remember.

Rolling my weight from foot to foot, I abandoned my cuticles to shove my hands deep into my armpits. To say I was nervous was an understatement. I was terrified, and no amount of reassurance, even if it came from Malcolm, was going to fix that.

"I can't help it. That man just broke his opponents' *arm*," I hissed. "In *two* places! It looks like a goddamn noodle!"

Dark grey clouds hung low, giving the stretch of earth before us a baneful appearance from the heavy mist, and made it hard for me to decipher what I saw on the field. The screams and cheers of the spectators ratcheted my anxiety more than anything. For the moment, Colin wasn't in my line of sight, but I knew he was out there in the fog, waiting with the other contestants on the far side of the ring. Waiting for his next round with another monster of a man.

Judging by the crowd, I learned that Colin was a bit of a favorite, often receiving applause from many other clans when he fought. And watching him fight was nothing short of amazing. Where his opponents bellowed and snarled while they swung their blunted steel swords, Colin barely made a sound save for a quick inhale or exhale of breath. He moved so fluidly, each advance and retreat designed to bring his opponent in close before quickly and decisively ending the round with a powerful strike. After winning the first few rounds, I noticed my husband didn't celebrate his victories like the other men did. Instead of strutting around the ring with his weapon raised over his head, he chose only to acknowledge the man he had beaten before ambling away until it was his turn to compete again.

"He's up next," Bram murmured from my left.

"Aye, two more, and the MacKinnon Eidolon will triumph once again," Farlan said from behind me, his focus wholly on the field.

I looked curiously back at him and the rest of the clan that flanked us. I had heard that name shouted from the crowd a few times today while Colin fought.

"Why do you call him that?" I didn't like it. Colin was a man, not a nightmare.

"Because that's what he is, milady. The phantom in the night. Six years—"

Bram pegged him with a glare. "—She doesnae want to hear—"

"—She should ken who she married," Farlan snapped and folded his arms in across his barrel chest.

A chorus of agreement rumbled around me. Bram shook his head, in an obvious disagreement with the rest of them, and stared straight ahead.

"Go on," Malcolm said, giving Farlan leave to continue his story.

Out on the field, ghostly shapes of men beat the crap out of one another with steel while Farlan spoke behind me.

"Six years ago, a band of raiders plagued the land. Where they came from, I dinnae ken, but they slaughtered, and they plundered, and they soon found themselves in MacKinnon territory where they murdered a family—every member but their eldest wean of ten summers. He showed up half-frozen at the keep's doors well before the sky began to lighten. He told us he was in the woods when they attacked, and that's the only reason he survived. Seventeen men wiped out that family of sheepherders, and then they decided to take a wee rest before they continued to their next conquest. They didnae ken they missed the lad, and they thought they were safe to tarry."

All conversation around us fell silent, intent on the story. Deep in the fog, I could see a new set of men striding out onto the field. I could make out Colin's smooth gait. Saw his sword held out slightly by his side, the tip down, ready and waiting.

"That day, most of the seasoned warriors were away with our laird, leaving his eldest son, Malcolm, in charge until he returned. We lacked the numbers to take on seventeen bloodthirsty raiders, so Malcolm did the only thing he could and sent word to his father for aid."

The two warriors in the field moved closer to our section of the circle. Colin drove his opponent hard, flustering him, and rained down blow after bone-crushing blow. Farlan spoke while we watched the warriors fight, the *clang, clang, clang* of clashing metal amplified by the moisture in the air.

"And *that* cocksucker…" Farlan pointed at my husband with a humorless chuckle just as Colin hooked his foot under his opponent's ankle. We all heard the loud *whuff* of lost breath when the man landed hard on his back, followed by the roaring cheer when Colin ran the flat of his sword across the man's neck, winning the match.

Farlan spoke over the applause. "Colin didnae tell anyone what he was doin'. He just marched right out to the loch, covered himself from head to toe in mud, and ran in the dead of night loaded with weapons to the shepherd's hut in the hills."

My skin pebbled while I watched my husband help the man he had beaten to his feet. His breathing was shallow, as though he hadn't just won his ninth match. He did not look our way before strolling back into the mist.

"Our laird had received the message and arrived back to the keep by noon the next day. By then, we realized Colin was nowhere to be found, and his weapons also missin'. The sentries didnae even see him leave. The bastard eluded even his own men." Farlan cleared his throat in a way that made me think *he* was on watch duty that night. "We wasted no time after that, and rode thirty-strong into the hills toward a line of thick smoke.

"We found the bandits that would have been on watch duty first, face down in the mud and dirt, their throats slit from ear to ear. No' one of them had drawn their weapons… as though they didnae ken he was there before he struck, and by then, well, it was too late.

"There were five more bodies closer to the cottage. They had met their end while takin' a piss in the middle o' the night with either a dagger in the chest or an arrow through their throat. And the rest… the rest he burned alive in the cottage whilst they slept, and he offered no mercy for the few that attempted to escape out the window."

I spun around, wanting to call Farlan a liar. Horrified by his story, I refused to believe that my sweet, adoring husband was capable of something so dreadful. I willed him to say he was joking, but he did not.

Malcolm leaned down, his face full of understanding as he spoke. "Colin told me, after keeping silent for neigh on three days, that it was the sight of the dead bairn that drove him to such lengths."

My stomach soured with dread at his words, and I shook my head. Not for the acts Colin had committed, but for the baby who died such a terrible death. For the mother who probably watched her children killed.

This beautiful world that I had fallen in love with had a dark side I didn't want to comprehend.

Malcolm went on. "The bandits massacred that family and left them all discarded in a heap in the woods. We found Colin sitting beside them, covered in blood no' his own, holding that deathly still bundle… I'll never forget that sight as long as I live." Malcolm's eyes unfocused for a moment before he said, "I ken that it's no' what ye wanted to hear, Meggie, but I thought it best ye heard it from us. Dinnae think too harshly o' him."

My eyes brimmed with tears as I stared back at the MacKinnon laird. I wanted to tell him I understood. I truly did. But I didn't trust sound to come out of my mouth. Turning my blurry focus back on the field instead, I stared out into the mist while another pair of unknown men battled against one another.

"That is why he's called the MacKinnon Eidolon," Farlan said softly. The group of men around us nodded and grunted agreement. "He's the ghostly shadow in the dead of night… and an absolute horror on the battlefield."

I watched Colin with a new perspective as the mist and fog finally dissipated and left us with a unobstructed view of the circle. The last four warriors would fight in groups of two in tandem, the winner of each battling for victory shortly after.

"See how he doesnae make any unnecessary movements?" Bram whispered when the battle began. He had a death-grip on the woven sapling barricade. "See how he barely tires. How he outlasts most men."

Colin's body surged forward in a quick, calculated movement. His sword flashed down, then up so fast his competitor barely shielded the first strike in time, only to find Colin's blade pressed to his neck. His opponent conceded defeat with surprise in his eyes a heartbeat later. A few cheers echoed off the hills, but most spectators stayed silent, waiting for the final match.

"One more, brother."

I barely heard the words from Malcolm's mouth as we all stared raptly at the last two warriors.

The McRoberts champion was a mountain of a man with a heavily muscled torso and thighs I would have bet money on were twice the size of my rib cage. A thick, black beard rested on his chest, and his midnight hair was short and sweaty from the day's performances. Colin stood motionless, twenty feet away while he waited. His war braids hung limply against his temples, his golden hair dark and curling from the humidity and the last hours of exertion.

Both men looked terrifyingly intimidating. Bare-chested, they sized one another up from under lowered brows. The McRoberts gave a subtle nod that he was ready, and both men raised their weapons, advancing upon the other.

The crowd was deafening as the first sharp clang of clashing metal rang through the air, and the two leviathans performed their deadly dance. They swung their swords so hard I worried about the damage they would do if they broke through their opponent's guard and landed the blow.

All too soon, Colin looked to be tiring, his blows weaker. My heart attempted to crawl up my throat when he stumbled slightly backward, and his opponent closed the gap between them.

No. No, no, no!

I couldn't get enough air into my lungs when fear seized control of my breathing and I swayed on my feet. The McRoberts was growing more confident, more violent with each step forward, and I feared all the things that a man that size could inflict on a body.

Bones could break. Internal organs could rupture—

I jumped when a strong hand gripped my shoulder and gently shook me out of my panicked thoughts. Malcolm's deep voice curled inside my ear.

"Watch, Meggie. *Watch*," he stressed. I glanced sideways at him and it surprised me to find an excited grin stretching his lips. Completely enthralled with the men in combat, he did not look even the least bit worried.

I refocused on my husband just in time to see him shift to the left, dodge a downward blow, and kick the backs of the McRoberts' knees. The dark man landed hard, and I imagined I felt the earth shudder at the impact. In the blink of an eye, Colin slipped behind the McRoberts' back, and rested the tip of his sword in the pocket of flesh above the man's collarbone, poised to plunge it into his lung.

Malcolm and the surrounding men shouted in celebration of the defeat. Tearing through the crude fencing, they rushed their clansman, my husband, who was clasping forearms with his fellow warrior.

Left alone on the sidelines, emotionally reeling and a bit light-headed, I quickly lost sight of Colin when a sea of bodies surrounded him, and decided to take my time until the pig-pile of Scots calmed down before I sought him out. I had only taken a short step toward the celebrating group when I felt a flush of heat race from the backs of my knees and up my spine.

The telltale feeling of being watched had returned.

Instinctively hiking my shoulders up, I slowly turned in a circle, searching for the source.

Where are you hiding, creeper?

Then I saw him, twenty-five feet to my right, dressed in black.

His cropped silver-fox hair and short silver beard failed to hide the loathing in his face. Cold, coal-black eyes radiated menace while he surveyed my body from under thick, dark brows. His thin lips twisted in a sneer that looked faintly familiar… but I had never met this man.

It couldn't have been more than a few moments from when I first saw him and when I finally shook myself free of his hostile, hateful glare. Spinning on my heel, I rushed towards the protective circle of my family, my bones vibrating with the urgency to put more space between the stranger and me.

By the time I reached Bram's side to point him out, the man vanished into the dispersing crowd, and I decided to let it go.

I stayed very close to my family for the rest of the day.

CHAPTER 21

Colin

There was no sweeter feeling in the world than to wake up with Meggie's rump planted firmly against him, warm and soft. Colin looked over his wife's pleasing form in the gloaming while he waited for the bagpiper to announce the sun on the horizon on the last day of the Gathering.

He was eager to be back at Ghlas Thùr and civilization. He didn't want his wife to bathe in the woods with the other women of the clan. Although she never complained and was happy enough to get clean, he would rather she soak in hot, scented waters behind the privacy of a thick wooden door; not in the wilds for anyone to come across.

Most of all, he wanted to be back where he was anonymous... or at least where no one gawked at him. He'd had enough attention in the past week to last him until the next Gathering.

At least this year, he'd arrived as a married man.

Thankfully, Meggie had gone to the market with Bram that first day they arrived, and she did not see him hiding in his tent from advantageous fathers seeking a match for their unwed daughters. Had she, he imagined she would have laughed herself hoarse and needled him mercilessly for days after.

Meggie turned toward him in her sleep, hiked her leg over his hips, and draped an arm over his chest to snuggle closer. Colin winced at the slight weight. His body was still sore from the competition and would be for a few more days. His chest, sides, and arms had glorious blooms of violet and midnight-blue bruises from glancing blows and well-placed elbows. The pinkie of his left hand had jammed terribly during the last match as well, which prohibited him from entering the bare-knuckle boxing matches, much to his wife's relief.

Later that day, Malcolm had forbidden him to be seen without a shirt on until they were well on their way home, with no chance of being seen by outsiders. "*I cannae have my best warrior, the Eidolon no less, to be seen wounded as a mortal man*," he had said, and then gave him the evil-eye until Colin reluctantly agreed.

His brother liked people to think of him as invincible. Colin thought it was ridiculous. No one lived forever. A man aged and died like any other, their bodies susceptible to damage, disease, and time.

The canvas above him brightened further, and the first mournful wail of the bagpipe screamed through the quiet, sleepy valley. The wee thing in his arms huffed in irritation, wiggled higher on his chest, and smooshed her face against his neck.

"I will not miss that," she pouted against his skin.

Colin stroked her disheveled hair and grinned. He loved the personal challenge of chasing her churlish moods away. She was a cranky wee beastie in the mornings.

"And what *will* ye miss?" He tickled the soft span of skin at her waist. She didn't answer, but he could feel the apples of her cheeks push against his jaw. She was smiling.

"Will my shy wife miss the carnal relations we've had out here for anyone to hear?" he teased, and her head popped up, her lovely face an unconvincing mask of seriousness.

"No," she said with a stern glare, and then blew several strands of her dark, silky hair out of her face.

"Och, a bonnie liar, ye are." He reached up to tuck her hair behind her ear and then placed a kiss upon her stubborn nose. "And as much as I'd enjoy reminding ye, there's much to do before we can start our journey back."

Leaving her to dress at her leisure, he dressed and strode out barefoot to await a large bowl of porridge. Colin noticed that many of the villagers already had their remaining wares packed and their wagons lined up around the camp perimeter. He was also happy to note all the wagons were light, if not empty, save for personal supplies.

Kerr's wagon was especially devoid of items of his trade. He knew from past Gatherings that a full chest of coin would be in the false-bottomed section of his wagon concealed underneath his belongings. The large man was busy handing out the last of his toy swords, daggers, and shields to any child in sight, preferring to give them away than storing them until next year. Colin mused that the wide grins upon their faces were payment enough. Delighted squeals and laughter filled the area, and the young band of ruffians tore down the muddy path and back to their rightful camps, swords swinging in the air.

"Trade was good this year," Mrs. Cook said when she handed Colin a bowl of steaming porridge. "Unfortunately for our journey back, it was too good since there are no more stock animals to buy. We'll need ye to hunt."

Colin nodded as he tucked into his meal. "Aye, just tell me when, and I'll ride ahead."

On the afternoon of their second day of travel, the lead wagon's wheel broke, and the whole caravan procession came to a halt while they made repairs. Colin took advantage of the pause and set off to hunt for their supper.

Miles ahead, he hobbled Una a short way off the road in a small thicket with moving water to graze. The stream was as fine a place to start as any. Walking alongside the burn, bow in hand, he studied the soft ground for tracks until he spotted one that gave him pause.

A wolf. The marks in the soft mud were still fresh, not even an hour old. He hadn't seen a wolf in many moons, as they were rare and hunted to small numbers. And along the same line, deer prints. Several. He was not the only hunter in these woods then.

Deeper into the woods, they led him; past boulders and boggy sections where the peat was thick and spongy. A light drizzle began falling from heavy grey clouds overhead as he crossed an open field with thick puffs of red heather. The tracks traversed an overgrown road and into another forest with deep ravines and hills so steep the earth seemed to have a hard time holding on. Large sections of water-logged soil broke away from the steeper hills, dragging saplings and boulders along with it. The ground he traveled upon was a blanket of bright green ferns and thick moss that crept high up the tree trunks. They gave the forest an eerie hue that muted all sounds but the high creaking branches and the scurrying of critters above.

And then he heard it, the high-pitched whine and yelp of a wounded beast. Crouching low, he moved among the low branches of evergreens and around thick, mighty oaks, allowing them to shield him from view as he moved silently around the bend of a steep, craggy hill. Following the pitiful sound, he paused next to the broad, knobby trunk of a wych elm.

There it was, the wolf, thirty feet away, and struggling on its side in the mud. Enormous paws clawed weakly at the disturbed soil, its thick grey and brown fur matted from the rain and muck. A buck lay close to it; a leg bent wrong, its neck strained at an unnatural angle.

Only dead things could be so still.

A glance up the hill revealed a rockslide had claimed the buck's life quickly but was unfortunately not fast enough for the wolf. Freshly churned soil and roots surrounded its two victims at the base of a young oak.

Colin leaned his bow against the elm and palmed the handle of his dirk. He would not allow the beast to suffer, and took a step forward, intending to kill it and take the deer back to camp.

The thud of quick human footsteps and the soft rasp of cloth against fern stalks made him pause. Abandoning his plan, he tucked closer to the lumpy trunk of the elm and waited for the newcomer to reveal himself.

A soft, melodic song exposed the newcomer as a woman, her voice smooth and deep as she neared ever closer. There were no words to her song, as it was more of a chant. It reminded him of the women that called their cows home from the hills, but these incantations raised the hair on his neck, and made his eyelids droop. Exhaustion muddled his mind, convincing him to take a wee rest. She was not there to harm; she was there to help. Eyes heavy, Colin watched the wolf stop its struggling and fall still, the only movement the steady rise and fall of its mighty chest... and the witch, Vanora, stepped into view.

Colin jerked himself out of his stupor at the shock of seeing her and kept to the shadows as she crept closer. Arms stretched out in front of her, she approached the wolf, humming gently, and lowered to her knees at its back.

"Prionnsa na coille, tha mi an seo gus an cuideachadh," she crooned, promising the prince of the forest she was there to help, and pulled a small dagger from beneath her faded black skirts.

From the cover of the elm, Colin relaxed, relieved that he would not be the one who killed it.

That relief quickly turned to alarm when she didn't kill the beast as he expected, but pierced her thumb and rubbed her blood on the wolf's black nose. Then she murmured a quick string of words he did not understand but *felt*. Her voice became stronger, louder. *Layered.* Both old and young, soft and rough, it was as captivating as it was terrifying.

The surrounding forest thrummed with energy. Birds took flight from their perches and red squirrels dashed from branch to branch in the canopy. Beneath Colin's bare feet, he felt the stirring of the countless tiny beings that lived under the surface of the earth, as though they searched for the source of power that swept through the forest. The tree he leaned against vibrated with energy, and all the leaves in the trees around him danced madly; their movements nothing to do with the light rain. The forest was awake. Like a sleeping giant, it opened a sleepy eye and focused wholly on the witch's song.

Colin's whole body erupted in gooseflesh as her melody altered. It was beautiful. He imagined angels sounded like this in heaven, and he felt his soul flooded with… was that *hope* he felt? It was overwhelming, wonderful, and warm, and he thought he could happily die right then and there if she would only continue those melodic words for a few moments more…

Captivated, his eyes brimming with unbidden tears, he watched the witch run her hands over the matted fur, gently examining its body while it lay still for her. Colin watched in awe when she wrapped her fingers around a thick sliver of wood a foot long and yanked it out of its belly. Curiously, the wolf didn't even flinch. Tossing it away, she continued to sing; her hand pressed to the wound.

Even with the distance separating his hiding spot from where she knelt behind the wolf, he could easily see the lifeblood pulsing from its belly. It coated the witch's hand with dark crimson while she reached out with the other to press flat on the bark of the oak tree behind her.

Stretched out, she tipped her head back and lifted her face to the sky and the light sprinkling of rain while she continued her chanting song. Colin couldn't take his eyes off her, so entranced that he failed to notice when the color began leaching out of the oak's leaves.

It was subtle at first, as though a cloud had passed over the sun and muted the green. But he had not seen the sun for hours, and the rest of the forest was bright—nearly glowing. Tearing his focus off her profile, he looked up to study the leaves of the oak and witnessed them turn brown and shrivel before turning to dust.

Colin could only blink, dumbfounded at the transformation, before the smallest twigs snapped off a moment later. The thicker branches followed; their splitting and cracking almost overpowered her resonant chanting. They rained down, landing everywhere but on the witch and the wolf. They hit the forest floor with heavy thuds, barely bouncing on the thick moss and churned soil.

When the tree could give no more, her voice fell thin and hoarse. No longer ethereal, the feeling of hope was banished, along with the preternatural beauty of the forest. The witch slumped over, her wavy hair wet and as limp as her body as she knelt there, sucking in great gulps of air.

Colin left the relative safety of the elm's shadow and crept forward on silent feet. He did not know what possessed him to advance. He knew he should be run in the opposite direction, but curiosity prevailed.

Catching him in her peripheral vision, she tilted her head towards him. Her strangely colored eyes were glassy and dazed with exhaustion, and her lips were wan and bloodless. Her once flawless complexion was now waxy and yellowed.

A slight spark of fear tightened her face.

"What are ye?" Colin whispered.

The wolf at her knees lay unmoving, it's breathing even and unlabored like it was before. The witch licked her dry lips and swallowed before she shrugged her slim shoulders and croaked out a response.

"I am what ye say I am, but I am no' the evil ye fear." She lightly ran her fingers over the wolf's thick coat. "Come see."

Watching her warily, he did as she asked and crouched on the other side of the beast to inspect the belly wound, only to find it fully healed. The only proof it was ever there was the bloody circle of smooth, hairless skin. Panic at the unknown crept up his back like some slithering thing, urging him to run and to run fast and far.

"Ye married a time-walker, and yet ye fear this?" she snorted, laughing sadly. "This wee magic?"

"That is no' *wee* magic," he said hoarsely and found himself looking past her, at the oak tree at her back.

It looked strange and unnatural, and a slight shimmering played down the ridges of the bark. Colin picked up one of the fallen branches and turned it over in his hand, surprised at its weight. Even more surprised to find it was now stone.

Standing, he stepped over the wolf, Gripped the oak's trunk that was no thicker than his forearm, and pushed it. A loud crack resounded in the forest when the stone trunk broke off at the base and fell rapidly to the ground. It fractured into several pieces on impact.

"I needed a life," she explained quietly. "To save a life, I must take life. Nothin' is ever free. It must come from somewhere."

Colin kept staring at the fallen stone-tree, desperately reordering his thoughts around this new truth, terrifying as it was. The witch was right, though. If he could accept that Meggie traveled through time, he could accept this.

"How is this possible?"

The witch looked up at him a moment before answering.

"My people hailed from Ireland; long ago. We're descended from the daughter of the druid, Mug Ruith. Our numbers are no' as many as they once were. Several of my sisters have died under the Rowan branches these last centuries. We are born with this gift and teach our daughters to master it. We use it for good." She heaved a heavy sigh when her voice returned to its normal strength. "Always good. Never evil."

Colin turned and gestured at the wolf that was still prone and sleeping.

"How long will it stay this way?" he asked, not particularly thrilled with the possibility of being around when it regained consciousness.

"Until I wake it," she said simply and rubbed the bloody pads of her thumb and pointer finger together.

Nodding, Colin marched over to the buck and, mindful of its two-point antlers, heaved its considerable weight over his shoulder.

"Do ye need the meat?" he asked.

She shook her head and studied the small knife in her hand. The wolf's blood that glazed her fingers was already drying and sticky. The sight reminded him of his own hands on a dark night, long, long ago.

"Go. It willnae follow ye," she said softly. Nodding once more, Colin turned to leave when she called to his back, "Should I worry? Do I have somethin' to fear from ye?"

He turned around, the cumbersome weight of the deer pulling at his center of gravity. Vanora held a guarded expression while she fiddled nervously with her blade. Her strange glacial eyes bored into him.

"Ye needn't fear anythin' from me," he promised and left her to wake the wolf alone.

It wasn't until he settled the deer over Una's back and led her back onto the road that he was able to take a deep breath.

He never wanted to see anything like that again as long as he lived.

CHAPTER 22

Meggie

As summer ended, autumn stretched its frosty fingers over the land, and morphed the green Scotland I had fallen in love with as a girl into a September treasure trove of colors. With the root cellars full of the summer harvest, farmers were busy planting the winter vegetables, and there was always the steady *chop, chop, chop* of firewood to get us through the frigid nights of deep winter.

I spent most of my time, if I wasn't off exploring the countryside with Colin, either in the kitchen with Iona or in the little garden Malcolm gifted me. A space to call my own, the little plot of land was located at the top of the hill that overlooked the loch. It was there that I spent most of July and August transplanting useful herbs, flowers, and berry bushes to ensure we wouldn't have to forage as far next year.

Thanks to my efforts and the knowledge my Nan had taught me on transplanting just about any plant or bush, I commanded a short hedge of blackberries and raspberries along the western wall; the direct heat of the afternoon sun the perfect place for them to thrive. I found a few blueberry bushes on one of mine and Colin's many afternoon excursions in the hills and begged him to help me bring them back with us. Those I planted close to the water's edge and ringed their bases with stones. Wild leeks, garlic, and the coriander and basil I grew from seeds thrived in the little beds I made and watered with a few trips down the hill to the loch. I even made a batch of British pesto before the first frost and saved seeds for next spring.

On one of my many investigations of the grounds around late July, I happened across a few pathetic rose bushes, leggy and miserable, within the swinging branches of a willow. After pilfering some honey and a few withered potatoes—a trick I learned from Nan—I successfully propagated six more from the original three. They all now flourished with fresh shoots and deep green leaves in a neat row along the path that cut down the grassy hill to the loch. I planned to do more of that come the spring and teased Malcolm that if I had it my way, I would rename the stronghold *An Ròs:* Gaelic for The Rose.

The enjoyable chore of weeding and watering filled the afternoons I didn't help with supper, allowing some time by myself. Save for the guard who walked along the lip of the curtain wall; I was mostly alone with my thoughts, free to sing modern songs I knew by heart and dreamt up ways I could make life better here without disrupting history.

With my sleeves rolled up as high as they could go, I pushed an errant lock of hair out of my face and resumed building my latest fairy house between the thorny shoots of blackberry bushes. I noticed the children playing in my garden the other day and decided to add a little magic to their lives.

While stabbing the ground with a sharp rock, my attention was torn between my creation and the conversation I had with Colin that morning.

He had woken me up early, in the way I had become accustomed. Lazily and full of passion.

"Are ye carryin' a bairn, sweet wife?" he asked, as he trailed light kisses along my jaw.

My toes curled when he closed his teeth lightly on the shell of my ear. I couldn't get enough of this man; the way he held me and touched me like I was his everything and more. He filled me with a joy I had never experienced before. Mornings were no longer unwelcome, but anticipated and yearned for.

I blinked at the ceiling rafters when his words sunk through my drowsy thoughts… something about… babies.

"What?" I sputtered and pushed on his shoulders so I could look up at him. I had never seen him look at me this way before. Full of wonder and… tenderness.

"Do ye carry my bairn, mo ghràidh?*" he asked again as he slid his palm over the flat spread of skin under my navel.*

Clearing my throat, I gently nudged his hand away and damned myself twice over for not having this conversation earlier. Sitting up, I hugged my knees against my chest.

"No, Colin. I'm not pregnant."

The perplexed look on his face had me searching for the right words. He wove his fingers through mine and raised his brows expectantly as he kissed my middle knuckle reverently.

"Ye've no' had yer moons since we married, Meggie. I ken that to be a sign. Surely ye do, too?"

Ah, shit. I could practically hear our first fight banging angrily on the door.

I cleared my throat again, and steeling my nerves, I guided his hand to the soft skin under my left bicep to run the pads of his fingers over the flexible rod just beneath the surface. He tilted his head with interest as he probed the odd shape.

"What is it? I've felt it many times."

"That's what gives me power over my body, Colin. It's called birth control, and I had it put in last year. It will work for another four years… or until I decide that I'm ready to be a mom."

"Birth con-trol." He rolled the words deliberately, foreign-sounding coming from his mouth as he dragged the vowels and consonants out. I knew the moment he realized what those words meant.

Brows lowered, his mouth tightened. Confusion. Denial. Disappointment. Anger. The emotions warped his face, and he yanked his hand out of my grasp as though I burned him.

"Colin… don't leave!" I hissed, reaching for him as he left our bed and stalked naked towards the side door that led to the adjoining room. Pissed off he was leaving without talking to me; I slapped the bed with a thump.

"Damnit! I told you before we married I was independent, that women are different where I'm from. You said you were okay with it."

He whirled around: his expression a mixture of disbelief and irritation.

"Aye, ye told me ye were different—ye told me a great many things—but ye didnae tell me this.*" He ran his hands roughly through his hair, and his brawny*

thighs carried him swiftly over the wood floor while he paced. "And when—when had ye planned to tell me, Meggie? A year? Two? When I voiced concerns I could no' give ye bairns?"

Numbly, I shook my head, unsure what to say, stunned at his reaction. At the betrayal in his eyes.

Bracing himself on the bed with a fist, he gently wrapped his fingers of his free hand around my arm. Holding my stare, his thumb lightly traced the faint outline of the rod.

"Or maybe when ye asked me to cut it out of ye," he growled.

Colin had left me then in the chilly bedroom, and I hadn't seen him the rest of the day. Una wasn't in her stall either when I stopped to bring her an apple on my way to my garden hours ago.

Focusing on my newest fairy house, I pushed smooth stones I gathered from the shoreline into the dirt to make a mini-pathway for the children to find later. The house I had crudely constructed with birch bark, sticks, and dry grasses.

Slipping my hands out of the leather gloves I used for gardening, I brushed off the dirt from the homespun dress I wore when I knew I would get dirty, and strolled down to the loch like I did most days to watch the sunset. With only a few wispy cirrus clouds above me glowing bright pink, the show of color on the horizon was a dazzling gold that melted into periwinkle and then deeper purples behind me. I shivered as Venus, Mercury, and Jupiter twinkled in a rough line above the horizon, and the last sliver of the sun dipped behind the hills. Like always, its abrupt absence invited a shocking drop in temperature.

I knew I needed to go in and clean up for dinner, but I would rather stand out here in the cold than see that look of disappointment on Colin's face again.

The fact was, I refuse to apologize for decisions I made well before I met him. Important, *responsible* decisions. I'd only had protected sex before, but I had also known that condoms aren't fool-proof, and I didn't want babies until I was ready.

The sky was in full dusk by the time I walked through the gatehouse and deposited my little bucket of gardening tools in the stable. Tired, both mentally and physically, I crossed the bailey with downcast eyes and nearly missed Colin waiting in the shadows against the trunk of the massive oak.

"I dinnae want ye out past dark alone, wife," he said as he shoved away from the trunk. I rolled my eyes, knowing the shadows were too thick for him to see.

"I've been watching the sunset for months now. We have one fight, and you're taking that away from me?" I snapped when I surged past him, my nose in the air. I could hear his heavy sigh as he followed at my heels.

"The sun set nearly a half-hour ago, lass. And ye huvnae ever tarried that long before."

"Then why didn't you just come and collect me?" I challenged.

We traversed the stairwells and hallways with me in the lead, stomping angrily at his order, even if it was in the name of safety.

"I ken ye were safe enough. Lorne was watchin' ye."

I pushed through the door to our room, past the two chairs facing the fireplace, and plunged my dusty fingers into the basin to wash my hands while he lit the candles from the coals in the hearth.

"If you knew I was safe, why are we having this conversation?" I snorted and cleaned the dirt from beneath my nails with a small brush.

"Because the watch has missed things before," he said wryly and sat down heavily on our bed, his forearms braced on his knees.

"Like the time you ran off into the woods and killed all those raiders?"

Colin jerked back as though he'd been struck. His eyes sliced warily to mine, and he stilled completely.

He didn't know I knew, then. Drying my hands off on a strip of white linen, I closed the space between us to stand between his knees. He looked haunted and sad.

"I don't hate you for what you did that day, Colin," I murmured gravely and lowered into a crouch.

"Ye ken it all, and ye dinnae fear me?" he asked in clear disbelief.

"I know it all, and I could never be afraid of you." Crawling onto his lap, I planted a kiss between his brows before touching our foreheads together. "Do you hate me for not wanting babies yet?"

Colin sighed.

"That was no' why I was angry, wife," he said with a shake of his dark blonde head. The waves of his hair caressed my face.

"Then why?" Pulling back, I waited for his answer. His hands tightened on my waist.

"I want no secrets between us. Ye should no' have kept that from me," he said, his voice soft. "I should no' have found out like that."

Oh. My relief mixed with regret, but I nodded in understanding. Taking a deep breath, I told him what I should have months ago.

"I'm not ready for babies. Not yet. But you're right; I should have told you," I admitted. "I just want to be married. I want us to have adventures, just you and me, for a little while. A year… but more than likely two or three." I added with a shrug of my shoulders.

The beginnings of a smile softened his face, and he pulled me close.

"Aye, I would like that verra much, Meggie."

On the morning of the Autumnal Equinox, I woke with an urgent need to put the past behind me and asked Colin to take me to the caves one last time.

"I need to do this," I implored. I dug through the trunks, shoving my jeans and tattered shirt into my leather rucksack, along with my broken phone, canteen, and hiking boots. "Trust me?"

He looked at me warily but nodded, and left our room to dress.

I felt giddy while Maeve helped me into one of my warmer riding habits, the color of deep rust, and wrapped a thin brown cloak around my shoulders.

My braid bounced on my shoulder as I hurried down to the kitchen. Snatching up few cheese danishes and a couple apples, I gave Iona a little wave and rushed off to meet Colin outside the stables where he had Jodee and Una ready and waiting. Their velvety nostrils flexed in the chilly morning air, sending out plumes of vapor as they huffed, impatient to get moving.

Astride, I led the way north along the paths I had learned over the last few months. The once green leaves that canopied the trails had morphed into vibrant yellows, burnt oranges, and fiery ruby reds mixed in with the dark green of pine boughs and ever-present emerald mosses.

Gripping Jodee's red-brown mane, I pulled my cloak tight around me and breathed deeply of the fresh air that nipped at my nose. It had taken me a while to become comfortable taking the lead without a bridle and stirrups. Until these last few weeks, I'd been content to let the rump of another horse lead old Jodee. Now, confident with riding nearly bareback, I led most of our outings and often took us to the farthest reaches of MacKinnon territory.

By far, my favorite spot had been a hidden pool surrounded by ferns and moss-capped boulders in the southwest corner of the territory. Colin brought me there for the first time a few days after we returned from the Gathering. The secluded pool, fed by a torpid waterfall that slid down a rock face at the foot of a steep hill, was private, and we were free to shed our clothing to cool off in the crystal-clear depths. I found myself already looking forward to next summer at the thought of idly spending a hot afternoon exploring one another in the shallows.

Scotland, I found, was made for romance.

I urged Jodee left at a waist-deep river and followed the shoreline up the hill to the fairy pools.

While Colin hobbled the horses, I left him to follow me with my pack and picked my way up the hill, careful where I put my feet so I wouldn't slide back down.

The caves looked the same as they did in June, and felt just as ominous as they did the day I fell through. The air, charged with a strange energy, instilled in me the dark feeling of foreboding. Creeping up to the largest opening, I reached out to touch the stone at its entrance when Colin snatched at my arm and yanked me back against his chest.

"What are you doing?" I asked, startled.

He was breathing heavily, his sapphire eyes wild and anxious as he looked fearfully at the cave entrance.

"Colin, I'm not going in. I just wanted to make sure this would work."

Slowly, I extended my arm to touch the stone and felt that dreadful vibration under the pads of my fingers. A low droning filled the air, the sound mixing with the rushing water on our right.

Vanora was right, after all. It opened on the equinoxes too.

Colin's arms banded tighter around me, and he dragged me another step back.

"I dinnae want ye anywhere near this place. I fear ye'll get sucked in, and I'll never see ye again."

My heart expanded, and I hugged him fiercely.

"Oh, Colin, that's not going to happen. We're here because we need to throw my pack in. None of that stuff belongs here."

I shoved the knowledge that *I* did not belong here either firmly away.

"Throw it in? Ye think that will work?"

"We won't know until we come back and check. I kept a couple of things, but there's no way my wallet can stay here, nor my boots."

I could only imagine what kind of uproar that would cause in the future. Or maybe I'm doing this all for nothing; I don't know.

"Just toss it in as far as you can," I said as I stepped back and looked at him expectantly. Colin ran his hand over the soft leather a few times and stared at the cave thoughtfully.

Saying a silent goodbye to Meghan Washington, I watched Colin whip the pack into the cave as hard as he could.

We did not hear it land.

I'm now fully and unequivocally Meggie MacKinnon, I thought.

It felt right.

It felt like destiny.

CHAPTER 23

Meggie

While standing beneath the canopy of bright-yellow ash trees, their leaves shedding from their branches in the breeze like fat, golden raindrops, Colin handed me the most beautiful dagger I'd ever seen. My fingers wrapped gently around the polished hilt, and I immediately recognized it as the finished stiletto Kerr had shown me in his workshop months ago.

"It's amazing."

I marveled at its flawless perfection and ran my finger over the stylized cross guard. The metal twisted like a unicorn's horn, just like the handle, each capped with a polished orb. To my delight, he embedded an emerald into one side of the pommel, and a sapphire on the other. The gems were the size of an acorn, roughly cut yet still enchanting despite their imperfections. The blade itself was triangular instead of flat, two of its edges barely sharp and the third smooth and gently peaked. Its tip made up in lethality what the rest of the blade lacked, as it was needle like and wickedly pointed.

A lady's blade indeed.

I shivered within my cloak, partly from the crisp chill of the late October morning, but mostly because I held something made to kill.

This was no *Wusthof* chef's knife.

"Yer first lesson—" Colin slid behind me and maneuvered my fingers into the correct grip, his breath tickling my ear when he pressed close. "Is to always ken yer range." He pulled our hands back and then thrust forward them, extending the tip of the stiletto to stab at the air in front of us. "But yer reach is the shortest when ye stand tall. Now, crouch down. Right foot behind ye."

I settled my weight down on my thighs and pulled the dagger back against my ribs.

"I feel silly," I admitted with a glance at him over my shoulder.

"Ye may, but ye will learn this regardless," he chided, and nodded forward. Letting go of my hand, he rested both of his on my shoulders. I faced the invisible target once again and listened to his instruction. "Ye have a far greater reach this way, lass. By makin' yer body seem smaller, ye can cover more distance in a surprise attack by pivoting yer body as ye stand."

Slowly, we lunged from our crouch. He pushed on my right shoulder and pulled the left one back, twisting my torso and extending the point out a much farther distance.

"Wow," I said, and we repeated the movement a few times. "What are the other things to remember?"

Circling me, he positioned my body to better my balance, his stare clinical and intense while I absorbed his expert direction.

"Dinnae stab yerself or me." He shrugged, the corner of his mouth quirking up when I gave him a droll stare. Motioning for the dagger, he sheathed it in its slim leather scabbard and secured it in his belt before swiping a stick off the ground about the same length and handed it to me.

"Ye want to focus on the belly," he directed, motioning to the area on the right and then the left of his navel. "If ye go in deep enough from the front, ye can pierce the kidney, and no man will be gettin' up from that."

He pointed over both lungs, lifting his shirt to show me where the largest spaces between the ribs were, and told me what I should expect it to feel like. My stomach rolled with the sickening thought of using enough force to power through rib cartilage, but I nodded and did my best to absorb Colin's how-to-kill-a-man-one-oh-one.

Before we left the ash grove, he fastened the sheathed blade at my hip with a thin leather belt embellished with silver buckles and then told me he expected me to wear it any time I was in the village or foraging with or without him. It thumped against my upper thigh on the ride home as though it didn't want me to forget it was there, its weight heavy in both mass and responsibility.

I said a small prayer that I would never need to unsheathe it.

I wasn't sure when it happened, but at some point, I had fallen deeply in love with my husband. Sitting across from him during the second Sunday supper of November, I watched Colin try to convince Malcolm to spar with him in the morning when a shadow fell over my plate. Turning in my chair, I found Kerr lowering his bulky body down to a crouch beside me and set something heavy wrapped in a simple burlap secured with blue yarn on the table.

"A wedding gift," he explained sheepishly. His cheeks flushed with embarrassment when the table fell quiet, and he shrugged his massive shoulders. "I finished it this morn."

"Thank you, Kerr." With a tug on the wool string, the rough fabric fell open to reveal a masterpiece within its folds, and I failed to suppress my gasp.

The carving was about eight inches high, ten wide, and six deep. He darkened the light golden wood in some places with ink and polished with oil.

Speechless, I reached forward and traced the fine back of the mountain lion that stood parallel to me, its shoulders hunched and its head lowered. The fearsome creature seemed to look straight into my soul with its black eyes, its body set in a rigid, defensive stance as it guarded the doe curled up below his belly.

With graceful, delicate legs tucked up under her body, her sweet face and large, gentle eyes were loving and kind as she looked at me, her ears alert but relaxed in the predator's presence behind her. They were both anchored and sculpted from one piece of wood, their pedestal chiseled to resemble long, flattened grass and flowers. The carving blurred, and I dashed my tears away before turning back to the blacksmith.

"This is the most beautiful gift I've ever received." I leaned over to kiss his prickly cheek before turning the carving toward Colin.

"I must agree with my wife, Kerr," he said hoarsely. Standing, he gripped Kerr's forearm over the table. We both spent long minutes staring at it after Kerr departed before I sent it upstairs, terrified it might get damaged.

Later that night, I had Colin place the carving in the center of the mantle, giving it prime real estate with the candlesticks pushed to either side. I would have slept with it if I could; I loved it that much.

"He must have spent a hundred hours on that, Colin," I marveled while I waited for him to join me in bed. He grunted in agreement as he slipped in between the covers behind me and enveloped me in the warm cage of his arms—a prison I never wanted to escape.

His lovemaking was different that night, slow and unhurried. He moved his body against mine, our fingers entwined as he paused each thrust inside me with a powerful curl of his hips. My emotions swelled like a cresting wave, threatening to spill forth my revelations of love and adoration. Barely keeping my thoughts contained, we fell asleep, wrapped in each other's arms, warm and satiated.

⌒⌄

I dug holes along the curtain wall in the chilly black soil to plant more dormant blackberry canes I found on our ride yesterday, eager to get them into the ground before the first snowfall that was due any day now. Tucking my cloak tightly around my body, my hands were warm enough in the wool gardening gloves I had ordered for the colder months.

The sun was still high in the sky, dinner hours away. It was a special dinner I had planned. It was Thanksgiving—or close to it—and I was determined to have a traditional meal. Or at least, as close to traditional as I could make it.

By luck, Bram brought in three wood grouse yesterday, and I practically snatched them from his hands when he entered the kitchen, laying claim to them. The large fowl, decorated with green, black, and brown plumage, were as close as I was going to get to turkey.

They were slow-roasting now, their skins stuffed with finely chopped and oiled rosemary, sage, thyme, and parsley. Their cavities I loaded with bread crumbs, onions, diced apples, and herbs for stuffing. The aroma filtering up from the kitchens permeated the great hall and made my mouth water when I slipped out the front door to spend some time in my garden.

With the canes planted and watered, I hurried back inside to warm my bones in the kitchen and help Iona with the last bit of my plan.

"Did they bring in the ice yet?" I asked when Iona pushed an apple pie into the oven.

"Aye, 'tis in the buttery; they just brought it down."

Pumping my fist with excitement, I rushed to retrieve it, and lugged the barrel half-filled with crushed ice into the kitchen before lowering a wax-sealed crock of sweetened cream into it. After adding a couple of handfuls of salt, I closed the lid to the barrel as tightly as I could and turned it onto its side. Bending over, I began rolling it around the room. Pushing it with one hand after the other, I made round after round, circling the long worktable.

"Are ye' plannin' to do that for the rest o' the day?" Iona yelled over the rumble of the barrel on the stone floor and the ice rolling inside it.

"Like an hour?" I laughed, giving her my best innocent smile when I passed her for the tenth time.

"Och!" Flinging her plump hands in the air, she marched up the stairs and returned a few minutes later with Banner and another sentry.

"Hie this barrel away from my sight and dinnae return for an hour!" she barked.

Banner gave me a look that said, *she can't be serious?*

"Just keep it moving, please. I promise to make it worth the effort," I said sweetly.

Banner half-heartedly rolled his eyes but motioned for his partner to help him carry the barrel up the steps without a word. I only hoped they wouldn't pop open my cleverly crafted seal and spill the cream.

Heading upstairs to change, I called over my shoulder, "If I'm not back by the time they bring it down, just take the cask out and put it outside to keep cold, please."

Maeve dressed me in dark blue wool with a petticoat for added warmth, white stockings, and fur-lined slippers. Catching my hair in the black beaded net, she dabbed some scented oil behind my ears and wrists and disappeared just as Colin appeared through the side door that always stayed open now.

"Why are poor Banner and Elliot rollin' a barrel back and forth, lass? They told me to ask ye because they didnae have the faintest idea." He chuckled while he washed his hands in the basin.

"You'll find out soon enough, and so will they. After tonight I won't hear complaining ever again when they're enlisted for help."

I grinned and ran my hands up his pectoral muscles and along the back of his neck. Curling my fingers into his hair, I tugged on the leather thong to let his hair fall around his face. I loved the look of those dark golden waves when they were loose and wild. It gave him that dangerous, barbaric look that I adored.

He lowered his head and playfully purred against my neck, bringing chill bumps to surface on that side of my body. Abruptly straightening, he rubbed his thumb over my pout.

"Let's go, before ye start somethin' that will take too long to finish."

With a devilish smirk, he folded my hand in his own and led me down to the great hall where we found Malcolm, Bram, Gavin, and Finlay already seated. Joining us was also Maeve, seated beside Finlay. Filling up the rest of the table were Banner, Elliot, Farlan, Gunn, and their wives. Gavin had his bright blue eyes firmly set on the kitchen corridor when I took my usual seat. His stomach growled violently.

"Aye, cousin, it does smell good," Finlay agreed from Gavin's left while he idly caressed Maeve's soft blonde curls. The way a blush colored Maeve's cheeks, I didn't think Finlay was talking about the meal.

"Just make sure you leave room for dessert, boys," I warned, and Bram grinned widely beside Colin, his hands rubbing together greedily.

Ever the good host, Malcolm filled my chalice with dark red wine, and the kitchen maids appeared with roasted grouse, stuffing, mashed garlic potatoes, stuffed mushrooms, and a carrot soufflé. Murmurs of appreciation rumbled along the table.

"I have news," Malcolm said after he filled his plate high. "We will visit Clan Chattan, departing the morn after Sunday's supper. During the Gathering, Laird Bothan requested my presence to talk further of an alliance... and I have accepted."

"An alliance in marriage? I didnae ken he had a daughter." Colin looked hopeful. Many nights he voiced his concern to me over the laird's bachelor status and worry that he may never find the love match he searched for.

"He does," Gavin said. "A lass of sixteen."

Eek. I tried to hide my judgment with a long sip of wine.

But sixteen was a marriageable age in the seventeenth century. Probably even as young as fourteen. From the look on Malcolm's face, I could see that he did not relish the near fifteen-year age gap.

His mouth drawn tight, he seemed to settle further on his bones when he said, "I want a guard of five ready to leave at dawn that day, yerself included, brother."

Colin nodded, flicking his eyes toward me before tucking into his meal.

"I would like the honor of standin' as your guard, my laird," Bram said, and his chest puffed with pride when Malcolm nodded in agreement.

"How far is Clan Chattan?" I asked, trying not to show my disappointment that I hadn't received an invitation to visit the neighboring territory. I idly wondered if I could convince Colin to take me to London in the spring, or at the very least, a major Scottish city like Edinburg.

"A full day's ride. Dinnae worry, I'll have yer husband back in yer bed within a week," Malcolm teased and grinned wickedly when my cheeks suffused with heat. He seemed to live to embarrass me lately, his playfulness coming out more and more since I married his brother.

While the maids cleared the remainder of dinner from the table, I hurried down to the kitchen to put together the apple pie a la mode with the vanilla ice cream Banner and Elliot had unknowingly churned. As soon as I spied a thick layer of ice on a water bucket the other day, I planned for this, and set out several shallow pans of water to freeze overnight. I knew I'd never be able to enjoy ice cream on a hot day again, but in the winter, served over hot pie? Just as enjoyable.

"A special thanks to Elliot and Banner for lending me an hour of their time today. Without them, this dessert wouldn't be possible," I gushed as I crossed the hall with a large serving tray. Two kitchen maids followed behind me.

Bram, no longer the skeptic when it came to any of my creations, was first to taste but the last to finish, always the one to take his time and voice the most praise.

"Sooner you all come back, the sooner you can have this again," I promised Malcolm as he sucked his spoon clean.

Later that evening, exhausted and more than a little drunk from Malcolm's ridiculous attention to my wine cup, I couldn't help but think of Nan, and wondered if she still had anything to be thankful for.

I fell asleep to a thick wave of guilt gnawing at my stomach.

The morning of their departure day, Colin slipped from our bed in the early hours when our room was still dark and the castle nearly silent.

"I'll see ye in a week, *mo ghràidh*," he promised. Kissing the tip of my nose, he smoothed my hair away from my face before pulling away. "Dinnae miss me too much."

I snatched at the lapels of his jacket and pulled him back down with enough force that he needed to brace his fists in the blankets on either side of me.

"This little bog monster misses you already," I whispered. It felt foolish to say since he was right there with me, but it was true.

A ghost of a smile graced his lips while he searched my face in the dim light. It was as though he was memorizing it and looked like he was on the verge of saying something. I was about to ask him what it was when he pressed a quick kiss to my brow and stalked from our room on nearly silent feet.

The door closed softly, but with finality.

I learned new things about my husband every day. Like how he had no qualms about leaving his weapons all over our room or how he lied when he said he wasn't good at chess (I had yet to win a match). He loves animals, big and small, often coming home from a hunt emotionally drained and melancholy for a time. I loved that he went above and beyond for those who needed help, sacrificing his own comfort for that of another. During several occasions on our outings in the village, he had stopped to help the occupants mend their roofs or wrangle loose livestock. I had never known a more selfless or benevolent person, and I was proud to stand by his side.

That early morning, I learned Colin hated goodbyes just as much as I did, and stared at our bedroom door long after he passed through it.

CHAPTER 24

Meggie

December in Scotland was cold and dreary. With daylight only lasting shy of eight hours and the sun setting around four in the afternoon, the frigid night air frequently chased me inside the thick walls of the keep hours before supper.

Colin had been gone for five days. Five lonely mornings. Five afternoons spent wandering the many corridors of the castle and exploring the relics in the towers. Five dinners eaten down in the kitchens with Iona.

And five breathtaking Scotland sunsets.

It was there on the jettying rock at the loch that I huddled within my heavy fur-lined cloak to watch the colors shift on the sparse, low-lying clouds. I had pinned my thistle brooch at my breast earlier today when I found myself a little homesick from Nan. The faceted amethysts of Scotland's flower caught the fading light, their shine trying their best to draw my eye and remind me not to forget where I came from.

The sun had just dipped below the horizon, painting the underbellies of the clouds above me in bright orange and coral. Huddled with my thighs tucked up against my chest, I rested my chin on my knees and wished for the first snowfall. We had seen a few flurries here and there, but the first real snow was late this year.

According to Maeve, the lack of an early snowfall was generally seen as a good omen, for not as many people would starve this year.

Shivering, I unfolded my legs and wobbled to a stand, curling and uncurling my chilled toes in my slippers before I started on the path up the hill to the keep. I could see Finlay on top of the wall, faithfully waiting for me to return after the sunset like he had the last two evenings he'd been on patrol. I had just passed the first of my dormant rose bushes half-way up the slope when my scalp prickled, and the fine hairs on the left side of my body lifted from my skin.

BOOM!

An explosion on the south side of the castle lit the stone silhouette with brilliant orange light, followed by black smoke that billowed up from the field near the barn. A mushroom cloud spread like an angry phantom, quickly surpassing the height of Ghlas Thùr's towers.

I froze when I felt the ground under my slippers vibrate a sharp beat and crouched down on instinct when I heard *fire, fire,* being yelled by men in the keep; their voices panicked as they bellowed orders for water. The darkening sky above the castle was hazy with black smoke.

Why is the ground still shaking? I wondered.

Then someone roared my name.

Racing along the wall, Finlay was pointing at me with his strung bow, screaming madly at me to *run, run, run,* before drawing an arrow from his quiver and aimed it straight at me.

Frozen where I stood on the crisp, dry grass, my veins turned to ice as I watched the arrow fly in what felt like slow motion. The ground thumped beneath my feet and in my ears, and I swore I felt the air displace around the arrow when it ripped past me. Missing my head by only an arms-length, I followed its path and watched in horror when it punched into the chest of a man who had been racing towards me from the tree line.

Two more men were close behind, their focus wholly on me. One jumped over Finlay's first victim, his scarred face set in determination.

Fear turned my bowels watery at the sight of them, and I turned to scramble up the hill. Finlay's arrows shrieked past me, one after the other, their fletching fluttering madly in the air as I lunged uphill. My legs felt like lead weights, and my pulse hammered in my throat. I heard a grunt when one arrow found its mark moments before someone jerked me backward by my cloak. The thick metal clasp at my neck cut off my scream, and my arms and legs flailed in the air. Landing hard on my back on the frozen ground, the wind knocked out of me, I struggled to get even the smallest sip of air back into my burning lungs.

Two pairs of punishing hands grasped my upper arms and began dragging me away, my attempts to free myself futile against their considerable strength and my complete lack of oxygen. Bucking my legs as hard as I could against the ground, I failed to make a sound come out of my mouth as my body fought against me, its pressing need for life-giving air overriding the need to call for help.

They dragged me into the forest, deeper and deeper, until I could no longer hear the panicked sounds at the castle. I must have started screaming hysterically at some point because one of them stuffed a wad of cloth into my mouth, cuffed me hard on the back of the head, and threatened me with death should I make another sound. The fabric tasted of sweat and dirt, and my stomach threatened to evict its contents. My dry heaving, their heavy breathing, and their pounding footfalls on the dry leaves were the only sounds in the forest as they half carried, half dragged me further into the darkness.

My petrified tears blinded me as I tried to pull away, to no avail. Their grasp tightened painfully, and they jerked my arms so hard I wondered how they stayed in their sockets. My weight didn't even seem to slow them down as I tried in vain to plant my feet and make myself heavier, my heels bruising quickly from roots and stones. They easily pulled me along, even when I tried my best to impede them, to delay them long enough for Finlay to catch up and rescue me. I could still hear the echo of him screaming my name, and I wondered how long ago the explosion had happened. It could have been a few minutes. Maybe even an hour.

Time blurred and condensed in the darkness: the forests with their thick shadows, the hazy cloud-cover muting the weak light of the crescent moon as we traversed the open, rocky fields. Through my terror, I vaguely realized that they made a half-loop, abandoning their westerly direction for a northern one.

When we approached a shallow stream, the men stopped, and I faced my captors for the first time. Their rough faces were grim and serious. The shorter man, who had long dark hair and the body of a wrestler, released my arm and stepped away to inspect his leg in the subtle light of the moon. The other was bald, tall, and broad in the shoulders. Now that I could properly take in their size, there was no wonder how they had moved me so swiftly away from the castle. I took a hesitant step back along the stream, and the bald giant turned toward me.

His meaty hand connected with my cheek so fast I didn't even have time to turn my face to lessen the blow. Stunned from the stinging pain of his unprovoked, open-palmed strike, I held my cheek and stubbornly blinked my tears away. I would not let myself fall apart and refused to show him how terrified I was.

His thick brows slashed angrily over his harsh features, now only inches away from mine. A nasty scar ran down from the corner of his eye to the top of his lip, the puckered skin distorting his mouth into a permanent leer.

He reached for my face, and a whimper escaped from my throat with the expectation of another strike, but his fingers only gripping the dirty cloth in my mouth instead.

"If ye scream, I willnae give ye another chance."

I tried not to let my surprise at his Irish accent show as I glared daggers at him. Hoping my face was enough to convey my hatred, I spat out the fabric.

Satisfied I didn't cry for help, he tucked the cloth into the pocket of his thick wool vest. Pushing me roughly by my shoulders, he spun me around until I was sitting on the sandy ground before aiding his companion's injury. Glancing behind me, I could see the seeping wound Finlay's arrow had made on the outside of the thigh muscle and was shocked that it failed to slow him down. I was even more disappointed that it missed an artery.

While they wrapped his leg and talked in hushed voices of splitting the trail up and taking me downstream, I panicked when I realized Finlay may not know which trail he should follow. Wrestling with my fear and ordering my thoughts, I casually slipped my shaking hands out of my cloak to pat the ground and began collecting pebbles and twigs. I needed to leave clues, and they had to be easy to read so that Finlay would know which way I went.

I knew it would be useless to fight off my kidnappers. I was completely unarmed, and they were warriors at least twice my weight with a wealth of skills I had no earthly idea how to defend against.

But I could outsmart them if I was careful.

Under the shelter of my skirts, I blindly arranged the pebbles I had found the best I could, and prayed Finlay would see them and know it was me. I wished I had worn my wedding band. Leaving that with the pebbles would leave no doubt, but I would have to improvise. Running my fingers along the hem of my dress, I searched for a loose thread to add to the pebbles, my pulse hammering in my throat. I tried to make myself appear small and meek in hopes that they wouldn't pay too close attention to me. They already thought me much weaker by not tying my hands together, and that was just fine with me. I would need my hands and feet unbound if I had any chance of escape.

Snapping a loose thread from the hem of my shift, I tucked it under a pebble to anchor it in place. As a second thought, I detached my brooch from my cloak and quickly tucked it up my sleeve just before one of the men swatted the side of my head.

"Let's go," the bald man said roughly, and waited for me to stand on my own. I made sure to hover over the pebbles and twigs, using the length of my dress to hide them.

They exchanged a quick string of words in Irish Gaelic before the shorter man turned to run upstream. Disrupting rocks and brush on purpose along the way, he left me alone with the scarred and scowling giant.

"I can either carry ye like a good lass... or I can toss ye in and then carry ye wet and freezin'. 'Tis yer choice," the man growled. He towered over me, waiting for my submission. I had no wish to be colder than I already was, and with his focus fully on me, I had no choice but to comply.

"Those aren't choices," I hissed through my teeth.

Rolling his eyes, he tossed my body over his shoulder like I was a sack of grain. Holding my thighs tight against his chest, he walked straight into the stream and followed it down the slight hill.

I felt disgust at the feeling of his hands on the backs of my legs and wished for his feet to freeze off in the frigid water. Holding myself away from his back, I searched the dark field to my left and willed Finlay to catch up. There was only one man to battle now.

But he was nowhere to be seen. There wasn't even a hint of movement on the southern hillcrest.

My captor carried me for nearly a mile, hopping from stone to stone or marching through the shallows until he stepped away from the riverbed and onto a soft spread of tall, dry grasses that were bowed down for the winter. He chose his path carefully. I could tell he did not want to leave a trail to follow and had selected this specific spot wisely. Bastard.

Tugging out my thistle brooch from my sleeve, I tossed it back towards the shore, where it landed with a barely audible thud on the pillowed grass. *Find me. I went this way;* I prayed as my eyes filled up to the brim with tears that raced freezing tracks down my cheeks.

"W-where are you taking me?" I croaked.

The man paused his stride but continued, silent and unnerved.

"P-please. My name's M-Meggie, I turn t-twenty-three next month—Ahh!" I yelped when his hand connected with a hard smack against the back of my thighs.

"Dinnae speak, lass. I already ken who ye are, and there's nothin' ye can say that would make me let ye go," he growled, and squashed any hope of humanizing myself.

I felt the gloom of the forest we entered before the first spindly branches came into my periphery, my captor carrying me toward a destination known only to him. My shoulders and lower back burned while I continued to hold myself away from his body, my braid swinging below my face. The white satin tie at the end of the plait sparked a thought, and I yanked it loose. After draping it over the first opportune branch, it fluttered in the slight winter breeze like a beacon in the dark before the woods swallowed us up completely.

The thick crescent moon was high in the sky when I chanced to speak again. My bladder was full to bursting, and his shoulder pressed into me painfully with each step he took. My arms and legs had gone cold long ago as my body conserved heat around my organs. A full bladder was only making me colder.

"I need to pee," I whispered.

My teeth chattered, and my back cramped from shivering. The man didn't slow, continuing his march ever northward.

Frustrated, I smacked his back as hard as I could and yelled, "If you don't let me down right now, I'm going to pee all over you!"

Without warning, he lowered me to the ground, where my knees buckled. I landed hard on my butt in the frozen grass, but my blunder gave me precious moments to peek at my surroundings from under the hood of my cloak. We were on the cusp of a large clearing surrounded by forest. My back to the trees, I looked past the legs of my captor. The thick smattering of stars in the heavens and the milky light of the moon illuminated the spread of a field... and a house on the other side.

My breath caught at the sight of the small hut and the thin wisp of smoke curling up from the chimney.

"Can I have some privacy?" I dared to ask, pointing to the tree line at my back, and the opposite direction of the house. His thick brow quirked up.

"Do ye think me daft?"

God, I hope so.

"Please? Maybe you can just face the trees, and I can go right here?" I begged, hoping with all hope that he hadn't seen the hut tucked on the far side of the field.

Glaring down with an irritated grunt, he moved past me and began rooting under his kilt.

"Ye have until I finish, lass, and then I willnae care if yer done or no'," he snapped , and then stared resolutely at the forest.

Mercifully, my body obeyed as I took care of business; my focus split between my captor's broad back and the hundred or so yards between me and possible rescue, a water well marking half the distance.

Adrenaline surged into my muscles as I readied myself to run and lunged from the ground, at the earliest opportunity, fear and trepidation fueling my legs as I ran. My skirts flew about my legs like floppy crow's wings, and my cloak billowed out behind me. I heard his curse a moment before he pounded after me and quickly closed in on my short lead.

"Help me!" I screamed, my throat raw from the freezing night air and the force of my cry. I barely felt the sharp rocks that ripped through the soft leather of my fur-lined slippers, my only goal being to escape, no matter what it took. I'd run barefoot over a field of glass if it meant my freedom. Bloody feet were nothing compared to being dead.

In seconds, I covered ten yards. Twenty. Thirty. I felt as though I was flying, not running, and I began to think I would make it, that I would get away.

Faster, faster, faster.

The wind tugged my hood from my head.

Forty yards. I was almost to the stone well.

"Help—"

A considerable force plowed into my back, and my kidnapper tackled me to the frozen ground. The soft skin of my palms scraped over the ground, and my right wrist barked in pain. The enormous weight of the Irishman pressed on my ribs, making it hard to take a full breath, and with his hand on my neck, he pushed my cheek firmly into the frosty grass.

"Dinna make another sound, or I'll slice yer throat and leave ye for dead," he said harshly, his scarred lip grazing my ear. A flash of his dirk in front of my face solidified his verbal threat, and I went limp beneath him.

Dragging me closer to the well, keeping it between us and the hut, he pressed his back against the mortared stones. With my body firmly caged between his legs, he covered my mouth and rested the tip of his blade on the soft skin under my ear.

My tears fell free to wet his fingers as I listened to the homeowner call out from his cottage. I could hear him calling out as he wandered the field and came ever closer to where I was hidden away. I must have made a sound because the man at my back pressed his hand harder against my lips, and the earthy smell of his skin filled my nose.

"I'll kill him, lass. Is that what ye want?" he breathed into my ear.

No, that's not what I wanted. I couldn't live with myself if that happened. Disheartened, I numbly shook my head.

It felt like hours until the door to the hut closed with a slam, and we were left alone, my only chance of escape thwarted by my reluctance to endanger another.

"Ye willnae try that again," my captor warned when he clamped his hand around my wrist in a bone-crunching grip and dragged me across the field.

I scowled at him when he glowered down at me angrily.

"Yer hair—" Halting at the threshold of the forest, he scanned the field. I knew he was wondering where I left the ribbon that held my braid, and I stared up at him defiantly, my bottom lip quivering.

He snorted his irritation.

"Yer no' a stupid lass, I'll give ye that. But yer waste yer effort. No one will catch up in time to save ye no matter how many clues ye leave."

Before I could respond, he hefted me back over his shoulder and resumed his pace. I had nothing else to drop for Finlay to follow, the brooch I left by the stream being the only jewelry I wore besides my tiny diamond earrings, and it was pointless to drop those. I tried pulling at the cuffs of my grey sleeves, but the stitching was too fine and the wool too thick to tear anything off to leave behind.

When the adrenaline of my foiled escape drained from my body, it left me exhausted, cold, and feeling strangely absent. At some point in the early hours before dawn, mentally and physically depleted, I fell asleep. Consciousness returned to me sporadically, jerking at the edges of my mind when my cheek bumped against my captor's back before I drifted back under again.

~

With the first rays of the sunrise, I smelled the familiar stink of a campfire and heard the low, droning of male voices. I opened my eyes and was surprised to find the Irishman carrying me along a well-beaten path.

"Ho!" the man holding me grunted. Past my kidnapper's hips, I could barely make out a group of men gathered around the fire. None of them seemed surprised or even bothered by the sight of a woman slung over a man's shoulder. Six horses stood waiting, hobbled on the outskirts of the rough campsite.

"Did ye have any issue?"

The hair on my arms raised in alarm, fighting with the fabric of my sleeves, and I stiffened. I knew that voice. Hanging upside down, I tried to peer around the thick torso of my captor and seek the origin of familiarity. The Irishman answered with a respectful difference.

"We lost one o' me men, Sean. Colm took an arrow in the leg, but he was hale and well enough to divert the trail west like ye requested."

With a grunt, the bald man dumped me onto the dirt, and I hastily pushed my wild hair out of my face, ignoring the sticks and grass that knotted in its length. The first men I saw were none I recognized, just regular soldiers in leather armor. Their features, set in grim boredom while they stared at me dispassionately, buried any hope I had in pleading with them to help me.

I would find no allies with them.

"A bigger cut for ye then. My thanks. Ye served my laird well," the familiar voice drawled behind me.

Whipping around from my seat in the dirt, I came face to face with a hateful set of black eyes I had hoped to never see again.

Baen Murray. His ink-dark hair was longer now, falling over his brow and collecting in the collar of his jacket. But that was the only difference. He still wore the same shrewd expression as the last time I saw him. The same dark aura surrounding him made me recoil from his presence.

"You…" I whispered, unable to believe my eyes. "*You* did this?"

"I did," he sneered cruelly and studied me from his crouch mere feet away. Glancing up to the Irishman, Baen tossed a small leather pouch over my head. The telltale clink of heavy coins snapped in the air.

"Always a pleasure to do business with Laird Murray."

Completely apathetic to my fate, the bald man—my trafficker— didn't even so much as glance my way before he turned on his heel and disappeared into the woods. I was just a transaction, acquired and sold.

Baen refocused on me, his shrewd eyes roaming over my face and down my body for a moment before he stood, his black leather pants creaking softly.

"Stand up," he barked, "Or must I carry ye the rest o' the way?" The dark look in his eyes told me he'd enjoy it if I put up a fight, and practically dared me to give him a reason to harm me.

Swallowing, I gathered my feet under my legs and stood. Swaying slightly, I wrapped my arms around myself under my cloak and glanced over my shoulder down the deserted path.

"I'd like to see ye try. But I warn ye, Meggie. Ye widnae get past the first bend in the road."

Biting down on my trembling lip, I wilted at the truth he spoke, and wanted to scream at my helplessness.

I despised myself at that moment and hated that I lacked the courage to fight harder. I cursed myself for failing to hiss and spit and claw my way back home when there was only one man to fight off and damn the repercussions. I loathed the fact that I wanted to live, and because I wanted to live, I had stupidly allowed the Irishman to bring me here, where I had absolutely no hope of escape.

And now what, what kind of life would I have?

Or worse: how long did I have left to live?

At the sight of my capitulation—or maybe it was a silent order given by Baen—the soldiers doused the fire and mounted their horses. Spiritless, I allowed Baen to lift me onto his mount. My skin crawled at the feel of his arm wrapped possessively around my waist, and I tried my best to keep my back from touching him when he spurred his black horse forward.

The warm rays of the morning sun did little to thaw my body while we rode hastily north and broke free of the forest. Beyond, I spotted a castle on a sloped, treeless hill. No, it wasn't a castle. It was a *fortress*. Only two stories besides the four fat turrets on its corners, the enormous structure stood proudly on the hill and dominated the landscape. Its dark stone walls were forbidding from where it loomed within a lighter curtain wall that stood halfway down the hill. Small windows and harsh lines gave the castle an ugly appearance, unhappy and forbidding. The dark stone seemed to soak in the morning light rather than reflect it.

I sat up straighter at the sight of the village in our path. Only a short field separated the last dwelling from the hill that sloped up to the curtain wall.

Hope fluttered in my chest the closer we rode to the village, and I searched for help only to deflate once more when all I found were people in hardship. It was a miserable place. I could not compare it to the bright, joyful village at Ghlas Thùr. No, this was a skeleton: empty and starving of any joy because the master of these lands did not care for his people.

As soon as we passed the first decrepit hut on the outskirts of the village, any people lingering in the street scampered away, ducked into their homes or, at the very least, averted their eyes when we rode past.

"Go ahead and cry out if ye like. They widnae dare help ye." Baen chuckled darkly at the same time he ran his hand possessively along the curve of my waist.

Anger blazed inside my belly at that touch, and fury at feeling so helpless forced my self-preservation to take a hiatus. Rearing back, I struck Baen's nose with the back of my hooded head. The slight feeling of satisfaction I felt with the wet crunch of impact was short-lived.

Recovering quickly, he wrapped his arm around my neck and cranked me back against his chest, cutting off my airway.

"English *ghalla*," he spat.

I clawed at his jacketed forearm and gasped for breath. Darkness closed in on my vision tighter and tighter, and I began to feel my consciousness flit away until he abruptly let me go. Coughing, I gulped down air and wrapped my hands protectively around my bruised throat when he spurred his horse into a quick trot.

Grabbing the back of my neck roughly, he pointed ahead with a bloody hand towards the castle as we neared the wall.

"Welcome to Bàs Dhubh. My home."

"And just what the fuck does that mean?" I wheezed. Fighting his hold, I turned around to glare at him. My Gaelic knowledge may be strongly centered around curses, but I knew *dhubh* meant black.

The sight of his bloody nose only made his almost-handsome features more chilling when he flashed his bloody teeth in a mocking smile.

"Black Death, o' course," he hissed darkly when we passed through the gatehouse and into the cage of the curtain wall.

I began to shake anew when he set me down roughly on my feet in the bailey, the dark stone walls of the offensive castle rising above me like a giant, blocky monster. Taking a few tentative steps back, I shook my head. I did not want to go in there. If I did, I would die.

"I hope ye enjoyed the sunshine today, lass, for ye willnae be seein' it again."

What?

Baen laughed from behind me just before something hard hit the back of my head, and everything went black.

CHAPTER 25

Colin

Five days he'd endured the stuffiness of the Chattan keep, their silly gossip, and their terrible food. Six days away from his wife and her saucy remarks, her infectious smile, and her slim legs wrapped around his hips. Tomorrow couldn't come soon enough, for he was more than ready to be on their way back.

They broke their morning bread in the great hall, eating overly salted porridge and sausage that was so fatty he imagined he'd choke if he attempted to take another bite. Pushing his plate away, he prayed they would be underway long before first-meal the next day. He'd favor hard bread or nothing at all over another meal of congealing meat.

Colin brooded from his seat on the far side of the high-table and watched his brother chat with Laird Bothan. They agreed upon a tentative betrothal for his daughters' hand, with the hard-won stipulation of her seventeenth birthday. Malcolm had insisted on that. Nearly seventeen, a few more months wasn't that unreasonable of a wait. It would be a spring wedding; carried out at Ghlas Thùr shortly after planting season.

Edeen Bothan was comely enough, raven-haired like Malcolm and of gentle disposition. Colin had been present as a second chaperone with the lady's handmaid on several occasions while the new couple toured the gardens outside the keep's walls or spent time after the evening meal playing cards. Judging by the conversations Colin overheard between the couple, it seemed as though someone had coached the lass on what to say. The subjects she spoke of were uninteresting and forced, and she became easily flustered when Malcolm tried to steer the conversation away to more exciting topics. She did not tease or play or even display more than a demure smile, and after the third day, Malcolm stopped trying to open her up.

"She's nervous and young," Malcolm had argued on her behalf when Colin broached the matter privately last night. "No' all women feel as free to share their opinions like yer wife does. Edeen will feel that freedom, eventually."

But Colin was not so sure. The Bothan lass was not who he would have chosen for his brother, but Malcolm had not asked his opinion. If he had, Colin would have told him to hie himself onto his horse, ride hard and fast for Ghlas Thùr, and never look back.

As it was, the betrothal agreement was being drafted and there would be a ceremonial signing that evening. Until then, Colin was destined to lord over this uncomfortable chair they directed him in for another day before they could depart. He'd never sat around so much in his life, and the thought of doing so, for even one more day, made him moody and irritable.

Bram caught his eye from across the table. Comically, his cousin's lip turned up in disgust at the greasy morning fare. He poked at the lumpy, boiled sausage with his knife as though he expected it to leap off the plate. Noticing Colin's amused stare, Bram chuffed a laugh.

"I miss your wife's cookin'," Bram muttered, his eyes shifting around the room to make sure no one heard him. "I swear I've lost half a stone since we arrived."

Colin snorted in agreement a moment before a commotion in the courtyard outside rose loud enough to penetrate the castle's thick doors. Everyone at the table turned toward the muffled voices. Colin and Bram stood quickly, weapons in hand, and placed themselves between the door and their laird.

A familiar disembodied voice bellowed outside, "Let me in, or so help me, I'll gut ye from yer bollocks to yer throat!"

"Is that Gavin?" Bram wondered out loud. He rushed to the door and flung it open, inviting the winter breeze to blast through the great hall. Colin stayed where he was but relaxed somewhat when he saw Bram sheathe his dirk and demand his cousin's passage.

"What is the meaning of this?" Laird Bothan sputtered as he heaved his rotund body out of his chair.

Edeen and Lady Bothan sat frozen in place, clutching each other's arms, their eyes wide with fear. It was so ridiculous, Colin expected them to either bolt from the room or swoon dead away in their chairs.

Malcolm surged up from his seat and strode over to take a position at Colin's back. Facing the door, Colin watched Gavin cross the threshold purposefully. His brown curly hair was windswept and knotted, his cheeks and nose painfully bright red, as though he had ridden hard and fast through the night. Bloodshot blue eyes found Colin's, and after a slight hesitation, his cousin quickly descended the three steps and came to a stop an arm's length away, his mouth set in grim lines.

"What is it, man?" Malcolm barked.

Gavin glanced over Colin's shoulder toward their laird before refocusing on Colin.

A deep sense of icy dread crawled up Colin's spine, and sunk its phantom talons in deep, piercing his soul. Without conscious thought, he reached forward and twisted the fabric of Gavin's vest in an iron grip.

"Meggie?" Colin knew there was only one reason his cousin hadn't addressed their laird.

Gavin's throat bobbed, and he nodded slightly, his mouth opening and closing twice before he finally spoke.

"Someone took her," he whispered. "Right out from under our noses."

Colin's grip tightened further, and the wool fabric in his grasp creaked with protest where he twisted it. His stomach mimicked the movement, and an ear-splitting roar echoed off the walls, drowning out all thought, all sound.

Warm, steady hands clasped either side of Colin's jaw, and Malcolm's face pressed in close. It was then he realized that the deafening noise was coming from *him*. Snapping his mouth shut, Colin released Gavin's vest and focused on his brother's warm brown eyes; on the one constant presence he had throughout his whole life. Steady. Calm. Certain.

"Continue," Malcolm ordered Gavin while he held Colin's stare. Malcolm's hands moved down to grasp his neck, then his shoulders. Their weight was grounding.

Gavin cleared his throat and took a tentative step around his laird.

"She was down at the loch watchin' the sunset like she has nearly every day. Finlay was atop the wall, standing guard over her... but they had planned this, cousin. We ken now that there were two groups. One set a powder keg aflame under a pile o' hay near the barn moments before the second revealed themselves. Finlay could do naught but fire his bow from the wall since we were already dousing the flames. He killed one o' the three that set upon her." Gavin shook his head, his eyes downcast with apology and self-reproach, "We did no' hear his cries for help until it was too late."

Voices rose from behind Colin, drawing Malcolm's indignant attention.

"Haud yer wheesht! Someone abducted my sister. We leave at once," Malcolm shouted.

Banner, Gunn, and Farlan dashed out of the keep to ready the horses and shouted orders to the rest of the men. Behind him, their host gasped and murmured condolences as though Meggie was not only taken—but killed.

"*She's no' dead,*" Colin snarled, rubbing at the ache that had built in his chest.

He hated—*hated* the cloud of helplessness he felt at being so far away. Of being gone when his wife needed him. This would not have happened if he'd been there—

"One more thing," Gavin said as he focused on Bram. "Finlay went after her."

⌒‿

This may be the longest day of my whole life, Colin thought miserably while he pushed Una as fast and as hard as he dared towards Ghlas Thùr.

The land seemed to crawl by; the minutes turning into hours; the hours bleeding into days. Every moment felt like a week. It was a never-ending road to hell, and Colin wanted to roar his frustration and helplessness at the world. Instead, he settled for feeding his anger quietly. He couldn't trust himself to speak, lest he shatter into a thousand pieces.

He would be no help to Meggie then.

Their group made the trek back in half the time, with a scant hour of light left in the day when they rode through the gates. White spume covered their horse's chests, and their great ribcages expanded and retracted almost violently to blow out clouds of mist into the chilly air.

The bailey, crowded with what seemed to be the whole MacKinnon clan, was silent of sound other than the nervous prancing of hooves until the MacKinnon laird vaulted off his great black stallion. Handing the reins off to a stable boy, he began barking orders, and Colin mutely stalked past his grave-faced kin towards the keep to gather his weapons.

Bram found Colin in the chamber that adjoined the one he shared with Meggie just as he bucked his short-sword to at his waist.

"We'll get her back, cousin," Bram said gravely.

Colin tested the blade edge of a dirk against the hairs on his forearm and was thankful that Magnus had taught him from a young age to keep his weapons sharp and ready. Taking a deep breath, he looked at Bram for the first time since breakfast. What he saw took him aback. Bram's normally bright eyes were dull, with dark smudges shadowing the thin skin underneath, his mouth a bitter, hard line. He looked as though he hadn't slept in a month.

I imagine I look no better, Colin thought grimly.

"Ye worry for yer twin," he murmured, and then narrowed his eyes at the quiver that peeked over Bram's shoulder and the extra weapons strapped to his belt. "Ye're no' goin' with me," Colin said sternly with a shake of his head. He stuffed black fletched arrows into his own quiver before slinging it onto his back.

Gone was his MacKinnon tartan, replaced with his black leather breeks, black shirt, a thick, dark grey vest, and a black woolen jacket. He'd already woven his war braids into the front of his hair on the long ride back. The tight plaits served to keep his locks from falling into his face, and as a warning to any that may cross his path.

Test me, and face my wrath, they promised.

"I am, cousin. He's out there alone. No one could follow the trail, although many tried. We cannae all track the way ye can," Bram argued.

Colin studied his younger cousin for a long moment. Bram was untested. Green, like his twin. Colin loathed shouldering the responsibility of a man's first bloodshed. And bloodshed there would be. Colin ground his teeth in frustration and crossed the room towards Bram. He knew he had no business in refusing the man's right to search for his brother.

"Ye willnae do anythin' reckless," he warned, and thumped Bram's on the chest with his forefinger as he listed off his conditions. "Ye will stay behind me at all times. Ye will do what I order ye to do— even if that means comin' back here. Ye willnae ask questions or speak unless I give ye leave. We travel silent and quick." Bram nodded sharply and opened his mouth to speak, but Colin continued while he inspected and tightened the straps of Bram's weapons. "No. Ye willnae thank me for this, cousin. No' yet."

They exited into the bailey ten minutes later to find several men waiting, similarly armed, as well as the Laird MacKinnon. Colin blinked in surprise at the sight of his brother and didn't think to hold his tongue when he said, "No, my laird, ye cannae come."

The warriors around them exchanged looks. No one told the laird what to do if they wanted to keep their position at the castle. Malcolm's brows hiked up in surprise before his face twisted in aggravated disbelief.

"Ye dare give yer laird an order?" he spat, his face red. "Meggie may be yer wife, but she was under *my* protection. In *my* goddamn keep!"

Colin cursed himself for speaking rashly, but there was nothing to be done about it but salvage his brother's pride and the precious little time he had left to track his Meggie down. The light was fading fast, and he'd already lost an entire day.

"No, my laird." Colin fell to one knee and lowered his head in submission. "I merely fear that my wife's disappearance is only just the beginning. I beg ye to keep yer warriors here to defend Ghlas Thùr, lest it's attacked whilst unmanned, and we lose more than just my wife."

Malcolm relaxed and stepped closer, turning that information over.

"Ye think they mean to draw us out to some other gain?"

"'Tis what I would do," Colin replied sadly. The warriors began talking softly amongst themselves while Colin looked beseechingly at his brother. "I have followed yer every order since our father died, brother. *Please*, I beg ye to reconsider," he whispered desperately.

Malcolm's lip pulled up in a snarl, but he nodded in agreement.

"Aye, go," he said gruffly, and clasped Colin's forearm to bring him to his feet. "Bring her home."

Colin nodded. "I will."

"Let me show ye where we lost the trail," Magnus offered, his ruddy features grim. He took off and led them down the hill and into the forest when the sun was less than a fingers-width from the horizon.

He was running out of time.

Colin read the tracks and the deep lines of disrupted leaves where Meggie's heels dragged and pounded the earth. She was fighting against her captors; he knew that much. The knowledge filled him with both awe and terror.

Magnus quickly led the way for close to two miles until twilight deepened into dusk and full-night blanketed the land.

"I'll leave ye here. We lost the trail up on that rise," he said as he pointed northwest. "I pulled the men once the trail went cold, so we widnae confuse ye."

Colin nodded, thankful for Magnus's foresight, and continued without another word, leaving Bram to follow in his wake.

He pushed himself as fast as he dared while he kept his eyes on the ground before him. Blessedly, it was a clear night, and the gibbous moon shone just enough light through the naked branches above for Colin's experienced eyes to catch the subtle shifts in the grasses, leaves, and moss. With that, they covered ground relatively quickly, despite the dark. They did not speak, but took comfort in their mission and one another's presence. As promised, Bram stayed ten paces behind, silently supporting Colin while he slowly read the trail in relative peace.

Sometime before midnight, thin wisps of clouds muted the moon's white light enough that they could not continue. Forced to bed down in the middle of a meadow, they tried their best to sleep until morning, when they could move much faster.

Nestled in the peat, Colin raged silently over the delay. Meggie had been gone a full day, headed for a destination unknown with unidentified men. The dead man that fell by Finlay's arrow had no identifying colors on him. Just a Celtic rune carved into a stone and tied with a thin strip of leather around his neck. He didn't understand. The MacKinnon's did not quarrel with the Celts. There would be no reason why they would abduct her. Furthermore, he could not fathom they would march north and not southwest to the sea and their island on the horizon.

Colin turned over question after question in the dark beneath the growing cloud cover before he finally fell into a restless slumber.

At the light touch on his shoulder, Colin's eyes snapped open, and found the grey light of predawn had lightened the sky. Bram stood above him, holding out a roll stuffed with chicken and cheese. Colin blinked a few times as yesterday's memories surged forth, and the dread he had felt renewed itself.

Over a day and a half now, she'd been missing.

Please. Let her be alive and unharmed, he prayed as he stood and shrugged on his quiver. Finding the trail again, he began to give chase when Bram snapped his fingers. The sharp sound was like a crack of lightning.

"Ye willnae be any help to her if ye're weak from lack of food," Bram said softly and pressed the roll into Colin's palm.

Knowing his cousin spoke the truth, he bit a chunk off and chewed. The herbed roll was tasteless and dry in his mouth and settled like river muck in his belly.

Over open fields and sparse forests, they moved swiftly while the sun rose over the far eastern hills and brightened the land. A mist rose from the grass, fogging up the air when they approached a stream at the bottom of a shallow hollow between two hills.

A strangled sound came from behind him, and Colin whirled around to see Bram's face blanch, his attention to their left.

Toward a man stumbling along the stream; his shirt saturated red with blood.

"Finlay," Bram breathed and bolted towards his twin like he was riding a swift wind.

At the sight of their approach, Finlay's knees buckled, and he sagged down to the sandy shore of the stream, breathing heavily and utterly drained.

"Where are ye hurt, brother?" Bram shouted as he fell to his knees beside his twin and began searching his body for wounds.

"'Tis no' mine," Finlay croaked, his voice raw and exhausted. He lifted ancient eyes to Colin's.

He is a different man now, Colin thought sadly. Crouching before his cousin, he palmed Finlay's blood-spotted neck and urged him to take a few breaths.

"Forgive me, Colin. I was no' fast enough and followed the wrong trail," Finlay said hoarsely, his bloodshot eyes haunted.

Colin shook his head, disheartened that his joyful, playful cousin would be forever changed.

"Whose blood is this?" Bram demanded, still not convinced that his twin was unhurt.

"I found him yesterday, miles and miles away. I dinnae ken in who's territory," Finlay began. He stared at the dried blood on his palms. "He was alone. I put five arrows in him when he tried to escape me… and I—I questioned him after. He widnae give up the information easily… but I ken where the other is taking her. Where she likely is already."

"Where?" Colin asked, impatient to move, to do *something*.

"Bàs Dhubh. Laird Struan Murray commissioned the kidnapping."

Heavy dread threatened to force Colin's breakfast up, and he wrenched himself away from the twins to hide his panic. Laird Murray was a calculating and hateful man, twice as awful as his heir. He ruled his territory with fear and malice.

The months he spent fostered there were the worst of his life.

"Ye will take yer brother back to the keep, Bram," he ordered. Bram opened his mouth to argue, but Colin spun around and pegged the twins with a hard stare. "Dinnae think to follow me. Finlay, ye did well, but yer part is done now. I continue alone."

Devastated, Colin turned away and followed the burn downstream until he picked up the trail where it looked as though Meggie and her captors had taken a brief rest. Eyes on the ground, his heart pounded when he spied an irregularity in the sand: the letter M; roughly molded out of pebbles, and next to it, an arrow made of small twigs that pointed downriver.

"Smart lass," he whispered and searched the area in wider circles for a print before concluding that his prey was clever enough to mask his tracks in the water.

Leaping the shallow stream, he looked over his shoulder one last time to make sure his cousins had indeed followed his orders and was relieved to find them walking slowly south; Bram's arm slung tightly around his twin's shoulders, and their heads pressed close together. Colin would be forever grateful for the lengths Finlay went to for him, even though he knew it cost his cousin part of his soul.

He only wished it did not cost so much that it ruined him forever.

Searching for prints on the ground, he grew frustrated when he came up short. Colin was sorely tempted to head straight for Murray land but refrained. He needed to find the second trail and follow their tracks on the chance Meggie had escaped. Following the stream for close to a mile, he feared he had missed their prints when a purple glinting caught his eye in the bowed grass and he nearly pounced on it. He remembered Meggie wearing it the day they met, and pride warmed his chest at his wife's bravery and forethought to leave clues.

Away from the burn, he tucked the piece of jewelry into his sporran, and where the grasses grew short, he found the trail. The bent and broken shoots tracked north in a direct route to Bàs Dhubh. Colin ran to make up the time he lost, easily following the trail, and when he stepped into the arms of a forest, he came face to face with a white ribbon. Draped over a naked branch, the ends were frayed and fluttered softly in the breeze. Snatching it up, he wrapped it around his knuckles, squeezing tight, and kissed it.

When the sun touched its zenith, Colin arrived at a large clearing where the tracks took him on a sharp left through the middle of the field, heading straight for a small hut. Jogging past grazing sheep, he called out to an old man chopping firewood.

Just before the well, the tracks changed and hinted at signs of a struggle. The grass flattened against the eastern face of the well. Crouching down, he searched for signs of blood, but found none. The old man came closer.

"Have ye seen a man and a woman about? Perhaps midnight or the wee hours this morn?" Colin asked hopefully. The regretful look on the sheep farmer's face had Colin gripping a handful of grass to keep himself grounded.

"I didnae see them, milord. I did hear a cry late last night but didnae see anythin' when I came out," he said apologetically.

Colin nodded his thanks before turning away and followed the tracks that continued north. His lips thinned, and he gnashed his teeth. So, she tried to escape. The lack of blood on the grass was reassuring, but he knew that even the most terrible injuries were bloodless. Refusing to let himself dwell on that possibility, he headed towards yet another forest. The single set of prints revealed she was being carried again, which meant her captor was a strong one if he could heft her weight for miles without stopping to rest. But it mattered naught if he was a giant. Colin would gleefully strangle him with his bare hands if he ever caught up to him, and he would enjoy watching the life fade from his eyes.

He continued his march over the land, stopping only to drink from the many burns. Sheer determination fueled his body. Deep in Murray territory, he found himself on a beaten path that snaked through a pine forest where the evergreen boughs kept the ground in a year-long shadow.

By late afternoon, he came upon a camp and a cold firepit in the middle of a small clearing littered with orange pine needles. The boot prints he had been tracking shot abruptly west into the woods, and small, feminine handprints smudged the dirt near the sharp departure. Slippered feet shuffled toward hoof prints and then disappeared again. He frowned at the signs in front of him.

The sharp sound of a snapping branch had him spinning toward the sound. Crouching low in a defensive stance, Colin held a deadly honed dagger within each palm and faced a familiar-looking dark-haired man wearing the Murray colors of black and dark blue.

"I kenned ye would come. Been waitin' for ye all day," the man said as he stepped further into the clearing. His dark brown eyes were wide, and he held up his hands in surrender. "They have her, Colin."

"Ye will come no further," Colin warned, raising his weapons slightly. "Who are ye? I ken yer face."

"I am Toran. I was the Murray champion this year at the Gathering, but we had met a time or two when ye fostered."

"Why do ye come here?" Colin asked, confused as to why this man would defect and help his laird's enemy.

"Ye are an honorable man, Colin. And my laird is far from it. He's a devil... and I've been a coward before now."

"How so?" Colin gripped the leather wrappings of his daggers, a movement not lost on Toran. His throat bobbed.

"She is no' the first he's kept in that dark pit," he said, his voice laced with nervousness.

Colin's blood heated with rage. The look on his face was surely the reason for Toran's growing panic.

"Wait—I want to help ye." Slowly, Toran reached into his sporran and pulled out an iron key, tossing it to the ground at Colin's feet. "That opens the western grate that leads into the tunnels below. I'm on sentry duty tomorrow on the wall above. Ye can get in through there when we change watch at dawn."

Colin blinked at him.

"There are no tunnels under the keep," he spat. "I would have found them when I fostered."

"There are, I swear to ye. From within the keep, one can only access them through the laird's apartments. I doubt ye had ventured in there unless ye had a death wish. So, unless ye plan to walk through the front gate and battle his entire garrison of men, this is the only way."

Colin ground his teeth in frustration.

"I cannae wait another day. She's been there too long as it is." Fighting to calm his breathing, he pointed at Toran with the tip of his blade. "How do I ken I can trust ye?"

"I have no reason, other than that ye must. Ye cannae get in otherwise." He jerked his chin toward the key on the ground. "Enter at dawn, exit just before sunset."

Colin turned over the half-cocked plan. It could work, but—

"They'll ken it was ye that helped me. Why do ye risk it?"

Toran shook his head, and his shoulders seemed to grow heavy with the weight of the world.

"My wife died in childbed last month... I overheard Struan laughin' about it. My beautiful Les would haunt me from her grave if I left yer wife in that pit to die in her condition. She told the laird she was carrying yer bairn, ye see. I heard her." His face turned red, and he looked away with shame.

Colin schooled his features to hide his confusion. His Meggie was *not* in that condition. Not with that blasted rod still residing beneath her skin. The rod he had harbored a hidden hatred for until that very moment. Now, he was only grateful for its presence. But if the guilt of Meggie's imagined bairn spurred on Toran's risk to help them, then Colin would surely use that vulnerability to his advantage.

Toran shifted on his feet, his hands pressed together as though in prayer.

"Ye must trust me. She willnae survive if ye cannae get inside the keep… and ye cannae get inside those walls without me. I willnae live with her death on my conscience. May God strike me down where I stand if I speak false."

Colin ran through his options; remembered all those months he'd spent as a boy in that fortress. He knew how well defended it was. There were no weaknesses he could exploit… save the guilty one standing before him.

With his resolve solidified, Colin dipped his chin, just once, toward his unlikely ally.

"Dawn then."

CHAPTER 26

Meggie

Black and red flames danced over my closed eyelids when I woke, and I slowly cracked them open to find myself lying on my side in a stone-walled room. The walls were dark and wet as though I were in a basement, and the only light source was an oil lamp hanging on a hook next to a lone door. Pain sliced through my head when I tried to lift it, and a low groan escaped my mouth.

No sudden movements then. Okay.

Fucking bastard, Baen, I seethed and wished I had broken more than his nose.

Lifting my hands to inspect the back of my head, I jumped at the clink of metal scraping over stone and gasped in horror to find manacles clasped around my wrists. Oh God, I felt sick at the sight of them. The oiled bands of iron circled my bones, leaving no room to pull my hand free. Connected by only five links, my bonds were weighed down by a thick rusty chain that snaked over a trapdoor in the middle of the cold stone floor and attached to an iron bolt on the far wall.

No, no, no! I clawed at the manacles, my nails ripping to the quick, but found no weaknesses in the thick metal.

This can't be happening to me! I wasn't sure if I was screaming out loud, or just in my head, but my sobbing became so hysterical that I slapped my hands over my mouth and looked fearfully at the door.

I breathed heavily through my nose as all my life experiences raced through my mind. Like a Rolodex of useless information, my brain scrambled to find a way out of this situation... and came up with jack shit. Absolutely nothing in my life had prepared me for this.

Gingerly, I stood on my sore feet, and when the room stopped spinning, I looked down at myself. Nausea roiled like a tempest in my gut to find that someone had undressed me and left me in only my sleeveless linen shift and the stockings that were riddled with holes and runs. I still wore my slippers, although they were nearly in tatters, and did little to keep me warm from the chill that crept up from the stone floor. Blessedly, my fur-lined cloak was in a heap by the door, and as I limped across the floor to retrieve it, I could feel every bruise and cut I had received from when I fought and ran from my abductor.

Snatching the cloak off the floor, I quickly wrapped it around my shoulders. Not only to warm myself... but to hide.

Stumbling to the thick, solid wooden door, I heaved my weight against it as hard as I could, barely rattling it on its hinges. My gut was queasy from both my situation and the throbbing pain in the back of my head. Vertical was not so good for me right now.

Sinking to my hands and knees, I crawled around on the floor. Dragging the heavy chain around with me, I searched for a wire or a sliver of wood I could use to open my bonds and found nothing but dust and crumbled mortar that flaked off the walls. I even peeked under the heavy trap door to find only the blackest of darkness so thick, the warm, flickering light from the oil lamp failed to penetrate it. The only bit of furniture in the room was a rancid bucket that stood in a corner next to a pile of moldy hay. Just the sight of it reminded me I hadn't eaten or drank anything for far too long.

I licked my parched lips, my tongue thick and coated with sandpaper. I wondered how long it had been since I sat in the warm, dry kitchen with Iona and laughed with her while we ate chicken soup. Judging by the way I felt, my best guess was twenty-four hours ago.

I glanced up at the low, roughly chiseled ceiling, blackened by years and years of oily soot, and at the damp stone walls that lacked windows. I had to be underground. Most likely a dungeon. Staring helplessly at my surroundings, I came to terms with the truth of my circumstances.

There was no escaping this room.

~

Eventually, I settled on the only part of the floor that wasn't freezing. The smooth wood of the trapdoor was warmer than the stone, but only fractionally. With my knees hugged to my chest and my cloak tucked tightly around my body, I stared at the lone door and waited. I would have preferred to press my back against the wall, but the need to keep my body heat outweighed the feeling of being exposed.

To pass the time, I listened to a steady drip, drip, drip of water I could not see, the sound of it driving me mad with thirst. Hours I must have sat there. Or maybe it was less? The lack of sunlight was disorienting, and I wondered if it wasn't the sun that was in the sky, but the moon, when I heard the faint rasp of footsteps beyond the door. My shoulders hiked up around my ears, and my breath froze in my lungs as they became louder and louder.

At the first tumbling click and snap of a key turning in the lock, I scrambled back. The manacles bit sharply into the skin of my wrists, and my knees barked in pain as I crawled away. Tucking myself into a far corner, I trembled as the door slowly opened and revealed a face I never expected to see again.

"Ye remember me," the man—the one who had been watching me at the Gathering—said with smug satisfaction.

His voice was not particularly deep, but it was hard and rough. The sound of it made me wish I could melt through the stones that bit into my shoulder blades. He looked much the same as he did when I found him staring at me after Colin's tournament. Dressed from head to toe in black, I recognized those dead, ebony eyes now—the familiar twist of his lips as he sneered at me. He had the same features as Baen, just aged. It was as though I was looking twenty years in the future. Black hair shifted to silver; harsh, cruel lines at the corners of his eyes. The only major difference was the greying beard.

"Laird Murray," I said, the breathy words barely audible.

The weak smile that flitted over his mouth vanished a moment later, as though it was incapable of holding anything other than a scowl.

"Aye." He pushed the thick door closed behind him before setting a hunk of bread and a cup of what I hoped was water on the floor. At the sight of it, I licked my lips and swallowed. It took every ounce of will to wrench my gaze away from that cup and focus on my visitor.

"Why am I here?"

He stepped farther into the room, and I pressed myself deeper into the corner. A rough stone poked my shoulder painfully, but I would endure the pain over being closer to him than I needed to be.

Laird Murray tilted his head slightly. "Vengeance, o' course."

I blinked at him, surprised at his answer.

"Against whom? I've done *nothing* to you."

He narrowed his eyes at me and took another menacing step closer, his hands clenched at his side and said, "Elsbeth MacKinnon escaped me nearly thirty years ago. I have no' forgotten it. And while ye have no' committed a personal slight against me, her betrayal has still become yer burden."

I stared at him blankly, confused by his explanation, and nearly asked him to elaborate when his pupils dilated, and his gaze hungrily traced the outline of my legs beneath my cloak.

"Come here." He pointed to the space in front of his feet, and I shook my head under the hood of my cloak. No way was I moving even an inch closer to him.

"I own ye now, and ye will do as I say, one way or another. Although I'll admit that there will be more enjoyment in it for me if I need to break ye." His hands flexed open and closed as he said, "Ye'll find I'm a patient man when it comes to discipline. I never tire of it."

We stared at one another for so long I wanted to scream, but I would not give him the satisfaction of looking away first, even though my nerves screamed at me to submit. After long, agonizing minutes, he turned around to open the door, and I rested my head against the wall in relief that I had won this small round of wills.

With his attention on something else other than me, my focus went straight to the cup filled with the unknown liquid. I imagined it filling my mouth and slaking my burning thirst. He just needed to leave, and I would be free to abandon my corner. Free to roll that cool liquid over my dry tongue. Let its moisture slide down my parched throat. I could almost feel it pass between my lips and settle in my belly—

"Put her in the pit," Laird Murray snapped.

Fixated on the contents of the cup, I didn't quite comprehend his orders until two soldiers entered the room and I looked up at their emotionless faces. A scream ripped up my throat when one of them reached down and wrapped his hand hard around my upper arm, hauling me up. With my hands bound, I could do nothing but kick and scream, trying my best to connect with the soft tissue between his legs and failing. I bucked and twisted as I cried out for help, pleading for anyone to come to my rescue.

"No one can hear ye," Laird Murray called out over my cries. There was a manic glint in his eye while he watched me try to fight off the guard. "No one is comin' for ye, and no one will save ye. Maybe a day in the depths will have ye more readily obeyin' my orders."

The second guard opened the trapdoor in the middle of the room before grasping the chain that secured me to the wall. He reeled in the slack while the other carried me ever closer to the black pit in the floor.

Terror like I'd never felt before flooded my veins, and I screamed anew. I begged and lied, trying desperately to coax even a shred of sympathy out of my tormentors. I told them I was pregnant, that I would die if they put me in there. Surely there wasn't enough air, and I would suffocate within minutes. Besides the slightly looser grip on my arms when I mentioned pregnancy, my pleading went unanswered.

Closer and closer. The guard propelled me towards the opening on the floor, and every inch of the way, I slammed my bruised heels against the leather armor of his protected shins. My torn slippers did as much damage to him as a downy pillow would against the side of a building. Laird Murray watched the scene with indifference the whole time, his hands clasped behind his back.

Lowering me through the square opening, the guard let go of my arms, and I dropped into the darkness before the chain snapped tight, my bodyweight caught by the manacles. Hanging by my wrists, I grasped the links connecting my bonds. My legs swung madly in the air until my toes connected with a hard surface, and I could stand. It was only then that the second guard released the chain. Pushing my hair out of my face, I looked beyond the lip of the opening that was just out of my reach and found Laird Murray peering down at me.

The gross satisfaction on his face was the last thing I saw before he let the slab of wood fall closed with a deafening thump, my chain fitting perfectly in the hole cut out of the corner.

I stood there, my ears straining while I listened to retreating footsteps, and focused on the light of the oil lamp that barely illuminated the outline of the square door above me. So long as I had that line of light, I would survive this.

All I needed was that tiny bit.

I would be okay.

I would be fine—

"We shall see how you receive me after some time in the hole," the laird called out, and to my terror a moment later, he snuffed out the oil lamp, slammed the cell door, and left me alone in the ominous black.

Darkness like nothing I have never experienced pushed down on me from all angles, the weight of it thick and unkind. I stood there with my eyelids peeled back as wide as they could go, but I could not see even the tiniest flicker of light. Could not see my hands when I waved them in front of my face.

This was what it was like to be blind.

My throat closed with panic, and I began to sob anew, the sounds I made loud as thunderclaps in my sensitive ears. It was as though my other senses had instantly compensated for my loss of sight. Even after only a few moments of blindness, everything amplified. I could hear the blood whooshing in my veins, feel the pumping of my heart, tasted molecules of air that raced down my throat and into my lungs. There was even a slight click I had never heard before each time I blinked.

The air was pungent with an underlying hint of rot and old urine. I envisioned the walls down here lined with thick pads of mold that reached grimy, invisible fingers towards me; could almost feel them brush against my hair.

Against my will, my heart rate ratcheted in tune with my imagination. Fighting the urge to scream, I toed the stone I stood on and felt a bit of vertigo when the edge dropped sharply off. I was standing on a slab, roughly three feet around. Who knew how far the darkness plummeted past my little perch? Lowering carefully down, I tucked my knees against my chest and rocked myself. I kept my eyes open, staring sightlessly into the infinite black on the off-chance that they may catch a little light.

There was no way of knowing how long I sat there. With only my thoughts for company, each one of them centered on Colin. Somehow, I became comfortable enough to curl on my side and pillow my head on my hands.

Blinking in the lightless gloom, I reminded myself that I was a rational adult. There were no boogeymen down here with me. No monsters that lurked in the darkness, waiting to eat my bones.

I was alone. And after what seemed like forever, I finally relaxed enough to drift to sleep.

⌒⌣

Something woke me.

My eyelids popped open, and every nerve in my body screamed that something was near. I looked up through the darkness and listened for footsteps, fully expecting the trap door above me to open. So intent on what was above; I did not expect the gentle tug on my cloak that came from below.

A gasp clawed up my parched throat, and I snatched at the fabric, the hem heavier than it should have been. Something was crawling up my leg, its sharp nails scratching through my stockings. Panicked, I rained my manacled fists down wildly on the furry beast that tried its best to crawl up my body.

Rats. There were *rats* down here with me in the darkness. My skin crawled as I grasped a tail and flung it away. The scampering sound of several sets of little pink feet skittering over stone gave me a full-body shiver. I could hear them jumping, trying to find purchase on the slab I now stood on.

For what felt like an eternity, I raged war with the creatures in the dark, kicking madly as they converged relentlessly upon me. Only adrenaline and fear fueled my fight, for God knew I had nothing left otherwise. My lips cracked and bled in the corners, and my tongue had the texture of cotton from dehydration. And all the while, I screamed in terror and frustration; the lack of sight making the rat's assault even worse. There could have been five or five thousand, it didn't matter. They never let up.

When the trapdoor creaked open, I didn't care who reached down for me; I grasped their hand like a lifeline and wept with relief to see again. Once out of the pit, I sagged down to the floor, gulped in a great lungful of clean air, and looked fearfully at the now-closed trapdoor that led to what I fully believed was a tenth circle of hell.

"Ye didnae like that, I imagine," Laird Murray drawled. He leaned against the door after the guard who had pulled me out of the pit exited the room.

"Not particularly," I rasped and drew myself up on weak legs.

He chuffed a laugh at my response, if you could call it a laugh. It was more like an escape of air.

"They never do."

Refusing to dwell on who *they* could be, I ignored him completely and eyed the cup that sat beside his boot. The bread was still there as well, but less appealing. Licking my cracked lips uselessly with my bone-dry tongue, I briefly weighed my chances of success that I could get to it, and flinched when he spoke again.

"Thirsty?" he asked politely.

I nodded right away and took a step closer.

"Yes, please." I fisted my hands in the fabric of my cloak. Trembling with the need for whatever was in that goddamn cup, I cried out when he kicked it over with his heel, and the life-giving liquid spilled to the stone floor.

Disregarding all self-preservation, I crossed the floor and fall to my knees beside him. My bloodied fingers grasped at the water as though I could pick up the droplets, only to watch in agony when it seeped through the cracks. I nearly bent down to lick the floor, but madly whirled on my captor instead. Jumping to my feet, I tried to claw at his face. My attack, full of rage towards him and at my suffering, was unplanned and sloppy.

One moment I was intent on prying his hateful eyes out of their sockets, and the next, I found my cheek pushed firmly against the door. With his forearm pressed on my neck and his thigh crammed between my legs, he stole my ability to kick by using my clothing to trap me. I raged ineffectively as my bound hands pressed into my belly, the cuff of the manacles digging painfully into my wrists.

"Ye forget yerself, woman. Yer *mine* now. To do with as *I* please," he barked, ground what was unmistakably his arousal against the base of my spine. Bile threatened to rise, choking off any reply I may have made as he continued.

"Anything ye receive, ye receive because of *my* good graces. No one else." He hummed his approval when he lightly ran his hand along the curve of my waist, over my shoulder, and then tucked my hair behind my ear. "My bastard may have enjoyed a bit o' a fight, but I dinnae. No' anymore."

"I don't know what the hell you're talking about." Refusing to look at him, I closed my eyes tight.

Laird Murray pressed closer, petting me, one hand soft, the other like a vice on the back of my neck when he said, "My bastard. I let him loose on the land a year ago when I grew tired of his madness. My son told me he made his way farther south than was wise... but that was his mistake." I felt him shrug, dismissing the subject. "I will let ye go now.

Ye willnae attack me again, or ye'll be goin' right back into the pit, and I'll leave ye to rot for a week."

As soon as the pressure lightened from my neck, I fled from him and squeezed myself into the far corner. Unfortunately, he didn't leave like I expected him to.

Adjusting himself in his leather pants, he rolled his shoulders and said, "Let's try one last time. Kneel."

With trembling lips, I shook my head. There was no way in hell.

A ghost of a smile passed over his lips, and his eyes raked over my body from head to toe and back again.

"I thought ye may still resist, though I'm no' worried. Yer a headstrong woman, and I suspect it may take years to fully break ye. I promise ye, I'll enjoy every minute. Now, *kneel,* and ye'll have somethin' for yer thirst. I can only imagine the pain ye must be in..."

My knees wobbled when he spoke of my thirst, and my body yearned to surrender to his request even while my mind jerked frantically at the reins.

"W-what happens after that?"

I was not naïve enough to wonder what he had planned, but I needed to hear him say it and fully prepare myself. The promise of water had successfully broken my spirit, flayed my pride wide open, and set fire to my honor. The backs of my eyes pricked with heat, but no tears fell. They had nothing to give. Even my fear failed to conjure sweat.

Laird Murray only shrugged a shoulder and raised an arrogant brow, patiently waiting for me to capitulate. He knew he won, and I hated him all the more for it. He was a monster parading as a human, for there was nothing human about this man.

When I read magazine articles about women who had been abducted and later rescued, I never understood why they didn't fight harder. I said to myself, *I'd never let anyone treat me that way. I'd shred them with my bare hands. I'd tear out their eyes and their throats before I bent to anyone's will or allowed them to defile me.*

I never understood why they didn't fight to their last breath... but I understood now. They wanted to *live*. They wanted to *drink*, and to *eat* and to have a moment of goddamn *peace*... so they paid whatever price they could to get it.

Like the price I was about to pay.

On shaky legs, I lowered myself to the floor, my stomach twisting with disgust. Disgust in myself, disgust at how one human could do this to another. Shame reddened my cheeks, and I settled back on my heels, staring at the space between me and the floor.

I could feel his satisfaction cloud the air as he calmly closed the distance between us, relishing in my submission.

"If ye attack me, ye willnae receive a drop," he reminded me as he came to a stop only inches away, the toes of his boot nearly touching my knees.

I gripped the thin, cream fabric in my lap tightly while his calloused fingers traced my jaw and forced me to face him with his thumb and forefinger tight on my chin. I lifted my eyes to glare at him, my lips tight and jaw clenched.

"I think I will prefer ye in my possession much more than I would have enjoyed being married to Elsbeth." With a nod, he turned my face right and left while he studied my features. Confusion must have shown in my face because he said, "Ye didnae ken Elsbeth was promised to me before Angus MacKinnon stole her away?"

I vaguely remembered the story Colin told me months ago about how his parents met. He told me Elsbeth's father had promised her to another... and that she had been against the match. But Colin hadn't even hinted that he knew who the mystery man was, and I wondered if his mother had known either, because if she had, surely she wouldn't have sent Colin here to foster when he was a boy?

"No one ever told me." I needed to keep him talking. Talking was better than what could happen to me in my compromised position.

The laird sneered down at me and pinched my chin hard before rubbing his thumb over my bottom lip.

"Aye. She slipped away the day before her father would have given me his answer, and by then, she was forever out o' my reach." Stepping away from me, he paced the room, his anger palpable as he clenched and unclenched his hands. "If she had married *me*, Colin would have been *mine*. The most undefeated warrior in all of Scotia would have been *my* son if she had no' run off to play the MacKinnon's whore," he raged; his dark brows pulled down tight. "Unfortunately, I could no' rightfully start a war in a time o' peace over her, a common woman, and no signed contract, so I waited... and watched. For decades I have bided my time. And then I saw ye—"

"—But they're dead. It doesn't matter anymore!" I cried out when he grabbed a fistful of my hair faster than a snake strike.

"But *I'm* no' dead yet, and I *will* have my vengeance. Elsbeth stole a warrior son from me." He looked meaningfully at my flat stomach. "And now I've stolen his."

A thin thread of hope wormed its way into my chest. The laird believed me when I told him I was pregnant. I wasn't sure if that was a good or a bad thing, but I was pretty positive that meant he wouldn't kill me or do any mortal damage to my body. At least, not until he realized I had lied. I bit my lip to keep my mouth shut. Right now, my only goal was the water he promised me if I knelt.

"Heed me, and I will reward ye," he promised, his voice deceptively soft. "Remember that."

Thrusting my head away, he turned on his heel and stalked out of the room. A guard appeared a moment later to set a bucket full of water just inside the door before he left me alone. He hadn't even finished turning the lock before I crossed the floor and lowered my lips to the surface. Guzzling the cold water as fast as I could, I swished it along the insides of my cheeks, over my teeth, and nearly mewled like a nursing kitten with each gulp, ignoring the metallic taste of blood from when the water passed over my ruined lips. I was just relieved that it was fresh, and not scooped out of a nearby pond, as I expected.

Fatigue, heavy and insistent, pulled me under once my belly was full of water and the stale bread. Tucked firmly in the corner farthest from the door, I wrapped my body around the water bucket, just in case someone came for it while I slept.

Nightmares plagued my dreams. Visions of rats the size of horses hunted me down, their mouths spewing fire as they herded me into a forest of dead trees. The rats then morphed into vagrants wearing the faces of the two men that had chased me through the woods six months ago. They neared closer and closer, no matter how fast I ran, and my soundless cries for help got stuck in my throat while I fled. And then they caught me. Their filthy, rat-like hands pawed at my body, gripping my arms and legs, and then dragged me toward the darkness of a cave—

I shrieked as I came awake; the nightmare chasing me into reality, and found Laird Murray watching me from where he leaned against the door. I hadn't heard him enter and idly wondered how long I had slept. I thought I had just closed my eyes. They felt scratchy, like a pound of sand had taken residence under the lids that were still heavy with exhaustion.

Disturbing the half-empty bucket of water when I sat up, I quickly brought it to my lips and chugged the contents, afraid he would take it from me unless I obeyed another order. When my belly was full to bursting, I set the bucket down, the last two inches sloshing on the bottom.

"Thank you for the water," I said softly, relieved he hadn't moved from his vigil against the door while I had my face in the bucket.

I decided before I fell asleep to lure him into a false sense of attained dominance while I searched for a way to escape. I may value my life, but I wanted to get the hell out of here just as much.

His eyes glittered darkly while he surveyed me from across the cold room, and the silence between us became as uncomfortable as our conversations.

"How long have I been here?"

"It doesnae matter," he replied.

I nearly rolled my eyes at his patronizing tone and settled against the wall instead. Wrapping my cloak tightly around my body, I regarded him warily from the shadows of my hood. He stared down at me, unmoving for a time, before he left me again.

As soon as I heard the turn of the lock, I rushed for the filthy bucket in the corner to take care of my body's demands—the first in an alarmingly long time—before retreating to my chosen corner.

⌒

"Wake up," someone barked, and nudged my shin.

My eyes snapped open in confusion, and I looked up to find Baen leering at me. He was lowered into a crouch, his midnight hair falling forward around his cruel face to frame the bruised skin on either side of his nose. Painful-looking purple and blue wings spread under his eyes.

Anger sparked like wildfire in my veins at the sight of his smug face, and without thinking my actions through, I kicked my foot out as fast as I could. Thanks more to surprise than skill, my wild aim connected with his cheek, and he toppled over with a curse.

If I hadn't been so damn petrified, I would have laughed, but all I could think about was that I had fucked up. Spinning on the floor, I clumsily crawled away, my shackled wrists making my retreat awkward and painful. I had nowhere to hide as Baen found his feet and rushed me.

"Ye'll pay for that, ye stupid cunt." He spat on me, his lips thin with murderous intent.

Helpless, I crawled along the wall until his foot connected sharply and repeatedly with my thigh, ankle, and hip. Crying out in misery, I pressed my back against the wall and protected my head with my arms, pulling my legs up tight to shelter my belly. The chain rattled against the stone floor as he struck my forearms.

Angry male voices erupted in the room, halting Baen's assault. From where I cowered on the floor, I chanced a peek through the gap between my arms to see father and son arguing.

"Ye willnae come down here again! Ye have yer whores; *she* is no' one of them," Laird Murray snapped. "Take him away, Athol, and dinnae let him in here again if ye value yer life."

Shoving his son out the door and into the arms of a guard, he pulled it shut with a resounding slam and closed himself in with me. Breathing heavily, he turned his calculating focus on me and bent down to grab the long length of the chain.

"Come here."

Whimpering, I hesitated long enough for him to yank on the metal links, tearing my hands away from my face.

"Ye can either come on yer own, or I'll drag ye. Yer choice."

Those are not choices! I wanted to scream at him. *You've taken all my choices away from me!*

Wiping my face free of my tears, I rolled gingerly onto the balls of my feet and stood. Testing my weight on my legs, I was grateful that Baen wore soft-soled boots and not harder ones. Because of that small-luck, I had no broken bones but could feel the beginnings of a contusion on the inside of my right shin and my left elbow. Feigning severe pain, I limped my way across the floor, my arms tucked in close to my chest, and stopped a few feet away from him.

The back of his hand connected with my cheek so fast I didn't have time to react, and my head whipped violently to the left. Stumbling to catch my balance, I held my throbbing cheek with both of my shackled hands and looked back at him in shock. The taste of pennies welled in my mouth from an interior cut, and I probed my bottom lip with my tongue to find it had split as well. Blood trickled from my nose and landed with a splat on the stone floor.

Staring at the way the dark red spread over the grey stone, I started shaking. I knew what was coming and was powerless to stop it. I wanted to be gone from my body, and yearned to be free of this room, and the cruel stare of the man in front of me when he said the one word I now hated above all others.

"Kneel."

Hot tears blurred my vision as I slowly sunk to the floor.

Gripping the fabric of my hood, he didn't even bother with the clasp that held my cloak together at my throat, and roughly tugged it over my head. With only my thin shift to hide my body from his evil gaze, the look on his face was disturbingly excited while he stared down into the gapped bodice of my shift.

I watched with dread when he reached for his belt with one hand and bent at the waist to grip my chin with the other. His black eyes bore into mine, filled with the promise of pain.

"Ye willnae fight me, lass, or I'll take a cane to yer naked back and throw ye back in the pit as punishment." Rooting in his pants, he freed himself, and the sight of him made me dry heave. Wrenching out of his grip, I turned my face away, desperate for any amount of space between us, and clenched my teeth so hard I felt as though they may crack.

He took a bold step closer to me, and that's when I heard a faint jingle that was unlike the sound of my bonds.

The jingle of *keys*.

My senses sharpened at the sound, and I searched from under my lowered brows for the source.

There. Hooked to the loosened belt near his hip and partially hidden by his jacket. I would bet anything that the keys to my manacles were on that loop. Energy thrummed in my veins at the opportunity to fight for my freedom. If I was unsuccessful, I was certain Laird Murray would make it so that I never had the chance again, but I had to try.

I would die trying for that chance.

Pushing aside the threat of what would surely be an agonizing and terrifying punishment if I failed, I looked up at the monster that stood above me. Blinking away my tears, I marshaled what little courage I had left to execute my insane plan and willed my face to show the subservience I did not feel.

"P-please, d-don't hurt me," I pleaded. "I'll do anything, just d-don't hurt me anymore." I reached out for him as though I would give him what he wanted and grew bolder when his face morphed from lecherous to triumphant.

He believed he had won: that he had cowed me with enough pain and mental manipulation that I would choose to allow him to do unspeakable things to my body than endure any more.

Not today, fucker.

Driving forward on my knees, I wrapped hands that turned into claws deep into the soft flesh of his testicles and squeezed with all my strength. Twisting them, I wrenched violently down with the weight of my body.

Caught off-guard, his garbled shout of pain cut off abruptly, and he dropped like a stone. He landed on his back, passed out cold from the agony of almost having his nuts pulled off his body, and the back of his head made a dull pop when it hit the floor.

I retched from the feel of him on my skin and struggled to keep myself from vomiting while I pulled off his belt, the little bundle of keys coming free. I dropped them five times before I could marshal my shaking fingers enough to fit one in the lock of my manacles. The first one didn't work. The second or third one didn't either. A sob escaped my mouth when the fourth key opened them with a snap, the most beautiful sound I'd ever heard. One cuff off, then the other. I let them fall to the floor and leaped over Laird Murray's unconscious body.

Slamming into the door, I heaved my weight against it and swallowed a sob when it opened without resistance to reveal the glowing of oil lamps hanging from hooks down the hallway to my right and left.

Despite the relief I felt when I found the guard who had escorted Baen away still absent from his post, it took me two tries until I found the correct key that fit in the lock of my cell. With the laird trapped within, I dashed to the left and sprinted as fast as I could, past door after door. Slipping on the damp stones underfoot, I searched the gloom for a staircase to take me to the surface.

This place was an underground labyrinth of windowless hallways and countless dark rooms that mocked me with each turn and dead-end while I searched for a way out. I ran for so long I was beginning to think the tunnels must spread beyond the curtain wall; it was so vast.

The sound of footsteps ahead brought me to a halt. Shadows played on the walls ahead: the moving silhouette warning me of an approaching guard from a hallway to the right. Panicking, I lunged into the open area to my left before I could be spotted and continued my escape.

My wet slippers slapped loudly on the stone floor, and the ghostly cream of my linen shift showed in stark contrast in the gloom. The stubby candles were few and far between, and I stretched my arms out before me, moving as fast as I dared, and prayed the floor was free of holes or debris.

"Who goes there?" someone yelled when I careened past another hallway.

My heart skipped into my throat as I ran faster and lurched around corner after corner. This place was enormous; it seemed to have no end, and I felt hopelessly lost. The tunnels just looped around. It was disorienting, and I wondered if I would lose my sanity long before I saw the sun again.

I could hear the heavy footfalls of the man who chased after me, their echo bouncing off the walls, and glanced back to check my lead on him when a darker, denser shadow moved to my right.

No!

A hand clamped firmly over my mouth, weakening my startled cry, and before I could dart away, an arm snaked around my belly to drag me deeper into the darkness of an unlit hallway.

Unable to breathe past my bloody nose, I fought against the firm hold on my body like a wildcat even though my legs barked in pain from their many injuries. Grunting when my elbow connected with his ribs, my assailant subdued me further by pressing me securely against a wall. With no space left for me to fight, he grazed his lips against the shell of my ear.

"*Be still, wife.*"

I froze.

Colin.

He had come for me.

With a whimper, I fell limp against him and gripped the arm that now banded across my chest tighter against me. Removing his hand from my mouth, I took a deep breath and felt a new trickle of blood run over my lips.

Heavy footsteps still approached, slower now, just around the corner. The light of a torch brightened the hallway I just ran down.

"Close yer eyes, lass, and dinnae make a sound, no matter what ye may hear," he breathed, his lips fluttering against my sweat-slick skin.

I jerked a nod and watched his dark form move, wraith-like and wrapped in shadow, toward the advancing guard. Even though his broad shoulders blocked my view, I squeezed my eyes closed, pressed my forehead against the rough stone, and willed my ragged breaths to even out. I did not want to see what he was about to do, knowing the sound alone would be enough to haunt my dreams if we ever got out of this terrible place.

Standing alone in the darkness, I counted every second he was away from me.

One. Two. Three. Four. Five—a scuffle against the wet floor. Six—a sharp inhale of breath was severed prematurely. Seven—the sound of a body collapsing. Eight. Nine. Ten—the scrape of heels dragging over the floor shifted behind and past me. Eleven. Twelve— the halting sound moved farther and farther away. Thirteen. Fourteen. Fifteen. Sixteen. Seventeen. Eighteen. Nineteen. Twenty. Twenty-one. Twenty—

Gentle, calloused fingers lightly brushed my hand, and I gripped them tightly. Turning around, I beheld the man that stood within the soft glow of the fallen torch.

The MacKinnon Eidolon.

CHAPTER 27

Meggie

He was a specter of black shadows that clung to his clothing, his face, his hair. Slowly, as though he expected me to shy away from him, he raised his hand towards my face: a hand that was dark and insubstantial in the faint light. Gentle pressure grazed my cheek when his thumb traced the line of my tears.

"You found me," I breathed and reached for him as we stared at one another.

Wiping a tentative finger down the column of his neck, I could barely make out where his skin ended and the fabric of his shirt began. It came away black, and when I rubbed my fingers together, the pads felt slightly gritty and powder-like.

He coated his skin with charcoal, I realized. His hands, his neck, his face. Every inch not covered by black fabric. He rubbed it into the bristles of his beard; even his golden locks fell dull and lank around his shoulders, his war braids muddy-looking in the warm orange glow of the torch. He had made himself undetectable in the darkness of the oubliette, only revealing himself to his enemies when it was too late for them to escape.

He became the Eidolon once again. For me.

"I'll always find ye," he murmured.

Smoothing my long, knotted hair away from my face, he inspected my nose with a gentle touch. From his pocket, he pulled a white square of cloth and gingerly wiped away the blood from my chin and neck, then pressed it under my nose. Any pain I felt seemed to melt into the background of my solace at seeing him again.

"This pace is a maze. I've been searchin' for ye for hours. Where were they keepin' ye? How did ye get away?" he asked in hushed whispers.

Pulling me closer, he pressed his lips firmly against my brow as he ran his hands down my back, over my arms, probing softly for more injuries. Swallowing thickly, I frowned at the bloody square of fabric and tucked it in my shift just between my breasts in case my nose bled again.

"He kept me in a room... a cell. I don't know where it is. The laird... he... he hurt me, and he was planning to—" my voice broke, and I shuttered at the memory of the rats and my burning thirst and the sight of him undoing his belt. "—But I fought back, Colin. I fought back and left him locked in that room. He's been plotting this sick revenge on your family for *years*... he said he was supposed to marry your mother, and he was going to use me..."

Colin wrapped me in his arms and pulled me tightly against his chest. Anger radiated from his body like the heat from a forge.

"I don't think I'm the first woman he's held down here."

Shadow-wrapped hands cradled my cheeks, and I looked up to find his expression enraged as his white teeth flashed.

"Ye will be the last," he vowed to me.

I believed him.

Colin took the keys I still clutched and led me from one deserted hallway to the next until the deep booming of a heavy fist on thick wood drew us to the corridor where they held me captive. Hidden in the shadows of a dark corner, we watched a guard trying frantically to open the locked door of my cell, Laird Murray angrily thumping all the while.

"I dinnae have the key, my laird," the guard yelled at the wooden door. The reply came back muffled, but harsh enough to cause the guard to step back as though it had struck him.

"I—I'll go fetch the spare s-straight away," he stammered and hurried away.

Colin firmly pressed me against the wall, a silent command to stay put, and pursued the retreating guard with silent footsteps.

A muffled yelp echoed in the hall a few moments later, and I cringed, knowing the guard wouldn't make it any farther. I pushed away all thoughts and feeling about Colin's actions. Later. Much, much later, I would sift through my emotions and catalog them. Right now, I focused on surviving and felt nothing but numb indifference to his death.

Peering down the hallway, I stepped out of the shadows and crept closer to Colin. He was staring at the door to my cell, the man captive behind it now quiet and awaiting rescue.

"I dinnae want ye to witness this, Meggie, but I cannae leave him alive," he admitted, his head bowed. He gripped the ring of keys in one hand and a bloody dirk in the other.

I opened my mouth, unsure how to answer him. I've never wished another human dead before. At least not until now, and I wasn't sure what kind of person that made me. Colin looked at me as though seeking some unspoken permission, and Lord help me, but I covered my ears and turned my back to him.

My breath was loud in my head when I pressed my hands hard over my ears and swayed on my feet. Rolling my weight back and forth, I softly sang a lullaby and tried my best to drown out the sound of a man accustomed to having his way come face to face with my wrathful husband.

My singing became more of a hum the longer I stood there and stared down the gloomy corridor until Colin stepped in front of me. His features were grim and cold, but he settled my cloak around my shoulders and deftly clasped it at my throat.

"Let's get out o' here," he said with a squeeze of my shoulders.

I followed Colin as quietly as I could past the closed door of my cell. Maybe one day I would ask what happened to Laird Murray, but right now, my imagination of his gruesome death was enough, and I took comfort knowing he wouldn't be keeping any more women captive down here.

"Wait, Colin." My thought stopped me in my tracks. "What if there are more?"

He turned around to face me before gazing back down the hallway; at the doors that looked much like the one that kept me locked away.

One by one, we opened the cell doors, and with each revelation, I expected to find a woman beaten half to death or near starving. By the time we got to the last one, I released the breath I wasn't aware of holding back and broke down in tears.

They were all empty.

"We cannae stay here, Meggie," Colin murmured urgently as he kissed the top of my head and rubbed my back.

With a shaky nod, I fisted one hand tightly in the folds of his black shirt and gave him a little nudge to lead on.

We navigated the dark hallways for so long I was convinced we had gotten lost again before I spotted a rotting door. Fresh, chilly air shoved its way through the gaps in the wood, and Colin pushed through to reveal a narrow tunnel carved through the rock and the faint light of day beyond. I whimpered at that beautiful sight. *Daylight.* It had been days since I saw it, but it felt like weeks. Years.

I squinted when we stopped at a metal gate set into the stone, my eyes unaccustomed to anything brighter than a candle flame.

"It willnae be long 'till sunset, which is good. We'll need to run soon."

I nodded and stared at him in awe as I took in the visual of his fierce presence. He had bladed weapons of all sizes strapped to his body. His boots each held two, and an assortment of daggers and dirks buckled at his waist. He sheathed a wicked hunting knife handle-down on a leather strap that crossed over his chest, and I blinked up at him, speechless.

334

He prepared for a war to get me back.

"We'll run as fast as ye can for the tree line. I dinnae care what ye see or hear, ye willnae stop runnin', ye hear me? Once under the cover o' the forest, we head south." He cupped both of my cheeks and touched his brow to mine, his brilliant sapphire eyes boring into me. "No matter what happens, I need ye to promise me that ye willnae stop... that ye'll continue south to MacKinnon land."

"Nothing's going to happen," I said defiantly, my voice strong and belying the unease I felt inside.

He released my face and handed me a small dagger. "Ye remember how to use this?"

"Don't stab me or you," I said lamely, and tucked it into the deep pocket of my cloak.

He didn't smile like I had hoped he would. If anything, the slash of his mouth grew grimmer, and the soot-black skin around his eyes tightened. Pulling the hood of my cloak up over my hair, I gaped at him when he unlocked the gate.

"How in the hell did you get a key?" I squeaked when he tucked the key back into his sporran and looked over his shoulder at me.

"An unlikely twist o' fate," he said cryptically, and scanned the gently sloped field before us, the village perimeter to our left, and the pine forest in the near distance. "It willnae be long now. Be ready, and dinnae let go o' my hand."

We stood there together: my body tight with anxiety and his loose in the way only warriors can be, patient and waiting for some unknown sign. The light faded and faded, the cloud-covered sky turning the periwinkle-grey of twilight while I stood silently in the cage of his arms.

It was subtle, and at first, I wasn't quite sure if what I heard was natural: the sound of a skittering of stone crumbling down a rock face... or perhaps a curtain wall. A moment later, a rock the size of my fist landed with a thump in the over-grown winter grass that grew wild outside of the gate. It was the signal Colin had been waiting for. I was about to ask him who had helped in my rescue when Colin pressed a finger to his lips and grasped my hand. Tugging me along with him, he pushed open the freshly oiled gate and started us on a punishing run as soon as our feet hit the grass.

His long legs pounded the ground while I tried my best to keep up. My legs twisted over the uneven terrain, the pace he demanded of me absolute hell on my exhausted legs and bruised feet. Colin kept me propelled forward, pulling me along and stretching my strides out as far as they could go. If it wasn't for his hand firmly gripping my arm, I surely would have fallen a dozen times.

I kept expecting the cry of a sentry or the bite of an arrow to pierce my back while we ran swiftly toward the forest's growing shadows. My lungs screamed in my chest even as the fear of capture pumped my legs, and Colin half-dragged me by the time we neared the tree line. Tears of relief and from the biting cold streamed into my hair when we crossed the threshold of the forest and continued until we could no longer see the castle before veering south.

I tired much sooner than Colin did, to which he allowed us to slow, but only fractionally while he murmured reassuring words to keep me going. The cold winter air was like razor blades in my throat. It leached warmth from my torn slippers and from beneath my cloak as I ran. Gasping for air, I fell to my knees on a blanket of pine needles when he stopped us next to a hollow log, and watched in amazement when he pulled out a vest, jacket, a small pack, and a bow with a full quiver. He had planned our escape well. Hauling me wordlessly back up to my feet, he kept a constant hold on me as my weakened, malnourished state slowed us down.

"Just over this hill, Meggie and ye can have a wee rest, I promise," he muttered as he tugged me along.

I tried to keep up, I really did, but my general lack of nutrition became apparent and hard to ignore, and I soon struggled to simply place one foot in front of the other. My feet felt as though they were cased in cement and weighed a thousand pounds. Then the cramping started to seize up my calves and I felt the beginnings of the mother-of-all-charley horses creep into my muscles when they accordioned together. Halfway up the hill, I collapsed entirely, my legs refusing to hold my weight up any further.

"I can't," I cried.

Frustrated with my body, I began to crawl, and clawed at the prickly amber needles. Without complaint, Colin scooped me up and continued his brutal pace as though I weighed nothing.

I gripped his shoulders tightly, and when we crested the hill, I openly sobbed at the sight of a grey draft horse hobbled in a clearing and munching happily on a pile of hay. Colin settled me on its back and vaulted behind me. Draping a thick wool blanket over the opening of my cloak, he anchored me to his chest tightly and squeezed the enormous beast with his legs.

As we trotted swiftly between trees, a smile began to play at the corners of my mouth at our successful escape when I heard the baying of hounds in the distance. A horn then trumpeted angrily in the evening air, and gooseflesh blossomed up my back and into my scalp.

Alarmed, I twisted around in time to see Colin's soot-stained expression harden with grim determination.

"Yer absence has been noticed."

And so, it was then that the hunter became the hunted.

∼

I devoured the strips of cold rabbit meat Colin thrust into my hands, the smoky taste of them better than anything I'd ever eaten at a five-star restaurant. When my belly no longer cramped with ravenous hunger, I sagged against Colin's chest while he guided our mount south. We left the pine forest behind long ago and wound through thickets and over plowed fields. Our mount carried us miles away by the time true-night descended, and with its arrival, the temperature plummeted. The clouds above were low and soft; muting the light of the nearly full moon, they washed the land in monotone colors of silver, pearl, and slate.

Unaccustomed to traveling great distances, our horse considerably slowed when we neared closer to the Mackinnon border. The incessant droning of hounds became louder and louder as they drew their hunt ever closer, their ululation echoing off the hills. Constant anxiety frayed my nerves, and with each direful howl I imagined how their teeth would tear into my skin before they dragged me back to that cell.

"We're goin' to make it," Colin whispered in my ear.

We traversed through a large meadow, our horse picking her way around the boulders that rose from the ground. She had stumbled a few times already, nearly tossing me over her neck.

And then Colin pointed to the rise a half-mile ahead of us.

"That's the border, lass. We're close."

I knew from our forays through MacKinnon territory that we were still two hours away from Ghlas Thùr, and I slumped at the distance. We could hear the shouting of men now woven in with the baying of the hounds. Too close. They were too close, and we were all alone out here.

The first snowflakes started falling an hour ago, and the small flurries that danced on the slight breeze doubled and tripled in size until they were fat clumps that landed on the grass and bushes of the meadow with a hiss. Colin cursed when he twisted to look behind us as we plunged into the shelter of another thicket, and I turned to see our trail clear as day through the white.

Our pursuers wouldn't need their beasts to follow us any longer.

"What are we going to do, Colin?"

He only shook his head, urged our horse a little faster between the trees, and kept looking over his shoulder. Suppressing a shiver, I cuddled deeper against his chest for both comfort and warmth. If Colin's steadfast confidence was wavering...

My lower lip trembled at what that meant, and I bit down on it hard to keep myself from falling apart, reopening the barely mended skin in the process. I refused to believe that we would overcome all the odds escaping those tunnels beneath the black castle, only to be run down like a pair of foxes in the night.

Miles later, on the crest of a hill in MacKinnon territory, I was beginning to think we had lost them when Colin grunted and jerked against my back. His arms wrapped tightly around me and bowed over my shoulder, sheltering my body from the snowfall.

"What—" I cried out just as an arrow fluttered angrily over our heads and disappeared into the night. Two more bolts pierced the snow-covered ground to our left and one to our right.

With a curse, Colin kicked our mount harshly to get out of range, and we held on for dear life while she stumbled down the hill toward a river. It wasn't very wide, but the bank was rocky, and there was nowhere for our horse to cross without breaking a leg.

Pulling me to the ground with him, Colin smacked her rump hard, sending her down along the edge of the river in a spray of mud and snow with our supplies still strapped to her back. Dragging me by the hand towards the rushing current, he threw me over his shoulder when we reached the water's edge. Without pausing, he boldly waded in, the frigid water swirling around his hips, then up to his ribs. It must have been agonizing, but he barely made a sound except for the few sharp pulls of breath between his teeth while he powered through the swift current.

Behind us, I could see the glow of a lantern on the other side of the hill, could hear hoofbeats and the growling of beasts that knew they were close to their prey. As Colin climbed out of the water on the other side, the white fletching of an arrow caught my eye, and I gasped when I realized it was protruding from his side, just under his ribs.

"You're hit!" I shrieked, but he only lowered me down to my feet and began hauling me upstream.

I couldn't take my eyes off the arrow as I held the blanket taut around my shoulders with one hand and kept my grip tight within his with the other. The freezing temperatures dug icicle claws through my holey stockings, and with the absence of our horse's body heat on my legs and Colin's warmth at my back, the cold wracked my body with shivers within minutes.

Struggling to keep up, I refused to show my discomfort, knowing he was in worse shape than I was.

We had only run a hundred yards when he looked behind us.

"We've run out of time," he panted. "I thought we could make it... I'm sorry, Meggie."

Downstream and at the top of the hill, seven men appeared on horseback with two enormous wolfhounds tethered to long leads. They began barking wildly at the sight of us. The snow that now blanketed the ground made us visible to all, even in the darkness of full-night.

"Don't say that," I hissed through my chattering teeth. "We'll make it. We have to." I knew I failed to sound convincing. I knew we had too far to travel, and our hunters were too close on our heels. But we had to *try*.

Colin pressed his lips together and pushed on.

The snow came down harder, and behind us, I could barely make out the impressions of the men descending the hill when a curtain of white swallowed us up.

The snow packed into the small rips and tears in my slippers and biting cold stabbed into the soles of my feet. Soon, my whole foot would feel like my toes, which had turned numb long ago. I barely felt more than a slight twinge of pain when they grazed against the stones hidden beneath the snow anymore.

We must have run a half-mile when we came to a chokepoint between the river and a steep hill littered with large boulders. The sight of them looked eerily familiar, but I assumed it was the way everything looked familiar when covered in a blanket of white and black. Halting abruptly, Colin grasped my shoulders and pulled me against his chest, his embrace nearly violent as he shuttered.

"Why are we stopping?" I demanded.

I could keep going. I would run with him until whatever end, as long as we met that end together. We both glanced down at the bloody tip of the arrow protruding from his side. Brow tight with pain, he looked down on me in anguish and regret.

"I ken why ye were sad for the Morag all those months ago, *mo ghràidh*," he breathed and pushed my hair away from my face.

I stared up at him dumbly while snow swirled around us. His thumb traced my cheek reverently.

"I understand—I've understood—for a long time now."

"What are you talking about? Let's go. We can still make it!" I grasped his forearm with both hands and pleaded for him to follow, but he didn't budge. His shadowed face held a mixture of sorrow and resignation, and he shook his head.

"We willnae make it to the keep," he sighed, and spread his palm along my jaw. But the next thing he said stopped me cold. "'Tis the winter solstice, Meggie, and midnight is upon us… ye can get away."

I blinked once. Twice. He couldn't mean what he was saying.

"No—"

A bone-chilling snarl came from below us, and a beast full of snapping teeth and wiry grey fur sliced through the falling snow at full speed.

"Run!" Colin bellowed.

Pushing me behind him roughly, he unsheathed his hunting knife from across his chest and buried it into the belly of the wolfhound as it leaped upon him. The whimpering of the wounded and dying animal blended with my own, and when Colin turned to face me once again, his panicked features were pleading.

"*Please, Meggie.* I'll shield ye for as long as I can, but I need ye to go. *I need ye safe.* Follow the river; it will lead ye straight to the caves."

I stood rooted in place and gaped in horror when he snapped off the head of the arrow. Ripping the shaft from his side, he tossed it into the river. Even in the faint light of the snow clouds, I caught sight of the unmistakable sticky dampness of his blood coating his jacket when he turned his back on me.

Unsheathing another wickedly honed blade from his belt, he spread his legs wide in a defensive stance and barred the way.

"Ye're the best part o' my life. Now live the rest of yers for me," he said over his shoulder.

"Colin," I moaned. My heart was dying, the pain like a constricting vice.

"Go now!" he snapped, and tensed, ready for the second hound that galloped through the snowfall.

A strangled whine stalled in my throat, and I cringed when the wolfhound's powerful jaws snapped onto Colin's forearm. But it died much like its companion and dropped like a stone. The snow around his feet was awash in a spray of blood that looked black.

"Please, wife. I need ye to go."

It was the worry in his eyes and the anguish in his voice that made me turn on my heel and run up the hill. I felt like a coward, and my tears raced icy tracks down my cheeks and the column of my throat.

But with the first sharp sound of metal parrying against metal, I halted.

I can't abandon him. What if he kills them all? I asked myself. If he killed them, we would be free to stop long enough to bandage him up. Their horses were still on the ridgeline, and we wouldn't have to walk the rest of the way to Ghlas Thùr. Surely, they have supplies we could use to bandage him up, and I was so cold, I wasn't above stealing the less bloody clothes from the dead to stay warm.

We could make it.

Hope surged within me, and I crept back downriver, squinting through the curtain of snowflakes. Snow now coated the ground in nearly two inches of fluffy white, muting all sound but the rushing of the river to my left, the sword fighting down the hill, and the strange crunch of my footsteps. When they came into view, I crouched behind a small evergreen bush.

Two men already lay dead on the ground, and another crawled away, the dark trail he left behind assuring his imminent death.

I nearly cheered when two more went down in a flurry of movement, their tandem attack unsuccessful. They fell, one on top of the other, to bleed out in the snow.

I gripped the thin branches in front of me and watched the remaining two men advance, slow and calculating, towards Colin. From the relative safety of my hiding place, I only saw them as faint silhouettes; but I would recognize Baen's stature and cocky swagger anywhere. My lip turned up in distaste, and I found myself wishing him a gruesome death.

Baen's accomplice sliced down and then up with his sword, hacking savagely and with murderous purpose. Colin parried with his shorter blades, his movements sinuous and powerful. The clash and trill of honed metal edges connecting and sliding against one another set my teeth on edge and my broken fingernails biting into the palms of my hands. Under my grip, small needles of the evergreen bit sharply into my palm; the sting of them helping me stay silent.

Just as Colin's dagger sliced open the sixth man's throat with a savage slash, I watched in shock when Baen fired three arrows in rapid succession into Colin's body. Two in the leg, the third in his belly, Colin staggered back to clutch at his wounds. Clapping my hands over my mouth, I screamed, horrified and wholly unprepared, when my world tilted on its axis.

Taking advantage of Colin's shock, Baen rushed the few yards that separated them. Whipping the end of his bow against Colin's cheek, he kicked Colin into the surge of frigid water where the black current seemed to part, welcoming him with open arms, and swallowed him up without a trace.

He did not resurface.

Baen paid the river only a moment of his attention before he rested his bow and quiver against the side of a boulder and focused intently on the area where I huddled behind the bush. The snowfall had let up just enough that I could make out his vile grin, and with nothing and no one else to stand in his way, Baen began his ascent.

Terrified of what would happen if he caught up to me, I abandoned the blanket and clawed at the ground with frozen fingers as I half-crawled, half-ran up the hill. Nothing looked familiar around me, but I nearly sobbed in relief when the earth blessedly leveled out. I lurched past mounds of snow-covered heather and leaped over a fallen log, my cloak flapping behind me. The freezing air took advantage of my exposed limbs and snatched mercilessly at my skin.

The vision of Colin falling in the river played in my mind like a broken record and smashed my heart into tiny pieces over and over. I railed against my guilt. He'd still be alive if I had never fallen through time. I did this to him. *Me*. My beautiful, strong, kindhearted warrior, who had his whole life ahead of him, snuffed out because I felt the need to have an adventure. Regret and shame ate at me so hard I nearly careened into a half-frozen fairy pool and threw myself to the left a moment before I would have plunged into its icy depths.

"Ye cannae escape me," Baen called out calmly as he halted thirty feet away. His breath puffed out in plumes of fog, his hair wet and hanging in ropes around his face from the snow.

Shaking on the ground, I pulled out the small dagger Colin had given me from the pocket of my cloak. Flinging its sheath wildly towards his head, I held the short blade in front of me in warning and rose to my feet. Keeping him in my line of sight, I moved backward and felt the hidden terrain with my toes so I wouldn't find myself up to my neck in freezing water.

"Leave me alone!" I screamed, waving the dagger between us. "I won't let you take me back!" With my fingers numb and my shivering nearly uncontrollable, I gripped the leather wrapping hard to keep from accidentally dropping it.

Baen cocked his head like the wolf I had likened him to all those months ago. Drawing his sword, his mouth twisted in a sneer, and he took a few steps closer. Every bit of space I put between us, he ate up, and then some.

"No, lass, I dinnae think ye have a choice. I *will* take ye back… and I plan to start where dear auld Da left off," he hissed, his eyes locked on mine while I carefully climbed the steep hillside at my back.

It was hard, and several times I stepped on the hem of my cloak. Baen caught the fumbles, and the corner of his mouth lifted with satisfaction.

"Colin did me a favor by killin' him, ye ken. I've been wantin' that bastard dead for a long time. And now that I've made ye a widow, maybe I'll take ye to wife."

He charged at me then, startling me so much that I dropped the dagger and whirled around to scramble up the hill on my hands and feet. I only made it a few yards before a sharp compression on my neck cut off my airway. With no hope of withstanding the force, the clasp at my neck snapped, and he ripped my cloak from my shoulders.

With its loss, the winter air immediately wrapped around my bare arms, shoulders, and back, the steady caress of falling snow a strange combination of a featherlight kiss and the quick prick of a nettle. I chanced a glance behind me just in time to see Baen fling the heavy fabric to the ground and stalk after me.

Hauling my weakened body up the hill, I could see where the incline leveled off ahead when Baen's gloved hand closed around my ankle and wrenched me backward, causing me to fall face-first into the snow. My lip reopened at the impact, painting the white with a splash of deep red. Sputtering and kicking, I dislodged his hand, and my tattered slippers flew off my feet as I clambered higher and higher.

I nearly wept at the sight of the caves and rallied my flagging energy for one more burst of speed. They were close. So close—

A rough push connected with my back, and I cried out for my balance when Baen pushed me bodily into the snow. Hands slipping on the slick, snow-covered moss, my brow connected with a barely hidden rock nestled in the blanket of white.

Stars and shadows gathered in my periphery, and I tried to shake my vision clear of the blood that ran into my eyes. *Get up!* I did not want to go back to that hole in the earth.

I would die first.

Gathering my legs under my body, I turned to face Baen in a crouch and pressed my frozen fingers into the snow. I was searching for a rock to throw when they closed around a thin branch, smooth and free of bark. Feeling along the length of it, my thumb brushed against the sharp end, and I grasped it, keeping it hidden behind the fabric of my shift.

"Enough, Meggie. I grow weary of this game. Ye'll be comin' back with me. *Now*," he barked, and sheathed his sword at his side.

He took a threatening step towards me, certain he had me cornered and helpless, before he stopped and peered at the caves at my back. A low, droning rumble, eerie and menacing, raised the hairs on my arms and drowned out the hiss of the snow.

Apprehension passed over his features, and I readjusted my grip on the stick. There wasn't much time left. I only needed to maim him enough to get to the cave, and he wouldn't be able to follow me. And if he did, according to the witch, he would wind up somewhere completely different. I took comfort in that knowledge and wiped the blood from my face so that I could see clearly.

"Let's go," Baen snapped. His hand outstretched, he made to reach down and grab me, his focus torn between me and the caves.

Adrenaline and clarity sharpened my mind, and I imagined I felt Colin's warm, heavy hands rest on the dip of my waist to guide me when I lunged from my crouch in the snow.

Just like he had taught me in the clearing among falling yellow leaves, I gripped the stick tightly as though it were my dagger and thrust my arm out with unbridled force. A primal roar of rage, savage and desperate, tore from my lips, and I plunged the sharp end of my natural weapon deep into the soft tissue on the right side of Baen's neck.

Oh, no.

I had aimed for his eye in the hopes that it would give me the time to get away and cursed myself when I missed entirely. Before I had the chance to turn and run, Baen's hand wrapped around my already bruised wrist in a bone-crunching grip and held on mercilessly while I struggled against it.

His black eyes narrowed with malice, and he touched the pale wooden shaft that I left in his flesh. Thin lips peeled back from his teeth, and he hissed at me.

"Ye'll regret that. I'll spend the next *weeks* making sure ye never dare to lift a hand to me again." With a quick tug, he pulled the stick out of the wound. "I'll—"

Neither of us was prepared for the first thick pulse of blood that shot out of his neck. Or the second or third. They landed in a thick, grotesque spray on the trampled snow between us. A few drops landed on the tops of my feet. Using his surprise to my advantage, I wrenched free of his grip and stepped back.

"What's happening?" Baen clutched his neck, but it was hopeless and futile. With his elevated heart rate and the adrenaline of his chase, his blood pulsed out from between the seams of his gloved fingers, fast and relentless.

An artery. Whether it had torn from my attack or when Baen yanked the stick out of his own neck, I'd never know. I wasn't even sure if I wanted to claim his death, even after all he and his father put me through. I wasn't sure what that would make me if I did... because I was not sorry. And even though I had not intended for him to die, I couldn't bring myself to wish for his life.

With his life's blood pouring from his neck, Baen fell to his knees, pale and weak from blood loss. I couldn't tear my stare from his even if I had wanted to, helpless but to watch the life fade in front of me.

With a deathly sigh, he fell to his side, one hand reaching towards where I stood, the other palm up. The snow, indifferent to Baen's evil nature, wasted no time and began to cover him up with its purity before the flutter of his pulse had completely stopped—as though he were a stain to erase and could wait no longer.

Blood from my lip and brow continued to slide down my chin to drip chilled droplets on my chest, distracting me from my shock. Numbly, I fished Colin's handkerchief out from my bodice and wiped off my face until the once cream-colored fabric soaked up the red and could hold no more, forever stained and altered forever.

Just like me.

I felt dead inside, knowing that Colin's body was now miles away. There was no way I would survive long enough to find him.

Shivering from shock and the deep cold, I became aware once again of the deep thrum coming from the caves: the promise of the survival that Colin wanted for me and sacrificed his life for.

Turning my back on Baen's still twitching body, the snow beneath my ripped stockings crunched and compacted as I shuffled up to the largest cave mouth. Rubbing the bloody square of fabric between my fingers, I took a deep breath and ducked inside. Within, the roar was deafening.

Detached, I let the handkerchief fall to the dry, sandy ground, closed my eyes, and let the darkness swallow me up.

CHAPTER 28

Meggie

I shouldn't be this warm, I thought, and then groaned deep in my throat when I tried to move my body.

Pain rippled up my fingers and toes like lightning. Cracking my heavy eyelids, I was shocked to find myself in a modern room with florescent lights and wallpaper, not the soft candlelight and stone I had grown accustomed to. I could taste astringent in the air as I looked around.

Sunbeams streamed through open slatted blinds onto a green recliner that stood underneath a black screened TV mounted on the wall. Flower arrangements of all sizes dominated a small table near the window to my right, their slight fragrance mingling oddly with the strong hospital smell. Reaching out to touch a pink petal, I choked on a painful cry when I moved my fingers, and the steady *beep, beep, beep* to my left started to go crazy when I found both of my hands wrapped in white gauze. Patting my face gently with my palms, I realized my nose was splinted.

Help me. I peered down my body to discover both of my feet similarly wrapped, and a scratchy white sheet covered the rest of my body from my bare ankles to my chest. Wires flowed out from the neck opening of my hospital gown, connecting to the screaming machine.

"Help," I croaked. I did not want to be alone. What year was it? What month? Anxiety cleaved through me, and I choked on a sob.

"Help me!"

A nurse in light blue scrubs rushed in through the open door of my room; her face pinched with concern. Standing over me, she rested her hands on my shoulders and held me down firmly against the mattress while I struggled to get up.

"Ye cannae get up yet, my dear," she said patiently.

I focused on her blue eyes. They weren't quite the color of Colin's, but they were close enough to hurt, and a wave of grief tightened my chest.

I'll never see those sapphire eyes again.

"Why? Where am I?" I asked as I looked around for some clue as to *when* I was. The caves could have spit me out at any time. I may have lost months, years.

Decades?

"Yer in the Southern General in Glasgow. Been here for two days," she explained, and tucked my sheet back firmly before motioning to my bandaged hands. "Ye came in with hypothermia, though how that could happen to ye in the dead o' summer is beyond me. Yer fingers and toes are frostbitten."

"Did... did I lose—"

"—No, my dear," she said quickly and pressed a button on my bed to raise me into a slight incline. "Ye still have ten o' each, but the skin is badly blistered and will need a few weeks to heal."

The sharp staccato of sandals slapping on tile came from down the hallway, drawing my attention to the door as they approached.

"Meggie!"

Nan flew through the door in a rush, her short white hair nearly standing on end, her eyes puffy and rimmed with red. She looked as though she hadn't slept in weeks. My jaw dropped open at the desolation that lined her mouth and the dark smudges under her eyes. She nearly shoved the nurse out of her way in her hurry to reach me and placed her cool hands on my cheeks. She smelled of apples and pepper.

Her touch was light as she smoothed my brows and asked me how I felt, if I needed anything, if I was in pain. Each question rolled into the next before I had a chance to answer. Speechless, I closed my eyes and let the voice I never expected to hear again wash over me.

"I was on my way back from the cafeteria when the station nurse told me ye were awake. What can I do for ye, sweeting?" she asked again.

"I—I'd really like a hug, Nan," I managed to whisper, my voice breaking when my emotional floodgates opened and my eyes filled with tears.

She climbed onto the bed with me and wrapped her slim arms around my shoulders. Burying my face in her neck, I breathed in her scent and soaked up her strength while she rocked me gently.

"I was so worried for ye," she whispered when my tears subsided.

I hiccupped and wiped my face, only to hiss in pain.

"Let me." Her tapered fingers stroked my face dry, and she gave me a small, sad smile.

"How long have I been gone?" I asked.

Nan looked at me oddly as her brows pinched together.

"I called for help when ye didnae come home Sunday night, and by mornin' the verra next day, a search party o' nearly a hundred started combing the MacKinnon land." My brows raised at the number of people who had looked for me as she continued. "Night and day there were search parties, checkin' acre by acre until Saturday mornin'. One o' the MacKinnon's found ye in the caves in the hills. They said ye seemed to have fallen through a sinkhole caused by all the rain."

A week, then. I nodded absently, grateful that it hadn't been the six months I had experienced, for Nan's sake. She looked terrible from experiencing a small fraction of that. I doubted her heart would have survived if she had never found me.

I am a wretched person; I thought as shame reddened my cheeks.

It had been only months ago that I chose to stay in the seventeenth century knowing Nan would be looking for me. Guilt over her worry, and heartbreak over who I lost, battled for dominion over my heart, and I felt as though I was at war with myself.

Looking out the slatted window, I reminded myself of where I had been, who I had been with, and what I had seen.

Unaware of my internal struggle, Nan kissed the top of my head and cleared her throat delicately to draw my attention.

"I dinnae ken how ye came to be frostbitten, but the doctor said yer injuries are consistent with a concussion from the fall and severe dehydration. That and the days ye were missin' makes sense as to why ye lost so much weight…" She reached down to trace the very prominent line of purple bruising on my wrist, her touch feather-light. "But for the life of me, Meggie, I cannae understand how a fall would make a mark like this… or why ye were found wearin' a sundress and stockings."

She let her words hang in the air, her eyebrows raised in question while she waited for an explanation. I turned back to the window, unwilling to meet her gaze.

I didn't want to lie to her, but I couldn't tell her the truth either. A large part of me wanted to, but it was so very unbelievable. Biting my lower lip, I shook my head slightly, willing her to drop the subject.

I had no such luck.

"Meghan Washington. If someone did somethin' to ye out in those woods—"

I flinched, the sound of my maiden name a stab in the gut. *I'm a MacKinnon!* I screamed on the inside, but all Nan saw was the hardening of my jaw.

"I fell. That's all."

"Then why will ye no' look at me?"

She said it so kindly, so apathetic, that my eyes filled to the brim with tears, and my throat swelled to a hard, unyielding lump. I wanted so badly to confide in her. To tell her I had fallen in love with a wonderful man. That I lost him horribly and tragically and then fought for my life. That he gave his life so that I might have the chance to continue living mine. The words practically railed on my tongue in their haste to escape, but I choked them down and told her I was tired instead.

I knew she didn't believe me even for a second, but she nodded and covered me with a knitted blanket, mindful of my bandaged toes, and then took a seat in the pleather recliner. I could feel the weight of her worried gaze on me as I closed my eyes and let myself drift into a restless sleep, where churning black water and thick spurts of blood on lily-white snow haunted my dreams.

⌒

"Remember, dinnae pick the scabs. Let them fall off on their own to limit scarring and use the ointment three times a day," the nurse reminded me for the fifth time on how to care for my fingers and toes while she wheeled me through the lobby and out the automatic doors to Nan's waiting car.

After three long days of countless visits from therapists and detectives trying their damnedest to open me up like a mental can opener and confide in them the origin of my mysterious bruises and wounds, they released me into my grandmother's care. My blisters had hardened over, turning the tips of my fingers and the skin around my nails and knuckles a deep brown. My hands looked as though I had spent the day gardening and neglected to scrub off the soil.

Leaving the nurse and her wheelchair behind, I shuffled my way into the front seat of the car, the soft slippers Nan had bought for me cushioning my toes. Settled and buckled, I watched through the side-view mirror while Nan and an orderly arranged my flowers and belongings in the trunk for transport home.

I did not know who had sent the flowers. Nan had urged me to read the cards, but I declined every time. I didn't want to read notes from strangers, even ones who meant well. I felt bad for feeling that way, but I couldn't help it. I couldn't bear to read *get well soon*, when there was no quick return from where I came from or how I felt.

I felt removed. A ghost. A thin shell of the girl I once was. I figured I left my soul back in the seventeenth century, and that was why I felt so hollow. But since that was where Colin is—was—I figured that was exactly where it belonged.

Resting my forehead against the window, I watched the city race past as Nan sped home. I was looking forward to being back in the relative quiet of Nan's little farm and away from the stink of the city and the noise that kept me up night after night in my room on the second floor of the hospital. I thought I would go mad with longing for the peace of the blue room at Ghlas Thùr.

When I finally did sleep, a fierce, golden creature stalked me from the depths of a lake. Haunting me, it always swam just out of my reach. I wanted desperately to join it and would call out mutely as I thrashed in the water, my voice nothing more than a thin breath of air. It was always at that moment that I would come awake drenched in sweat, a strangled cry in my throat, and Nan's face hovering above me. She promised me I was okay, that it was only a dream.

But I *wasn't* okay. Not in the slightest. And I *wanted* that dream.

I never told Colin I loved him. For months I flitted away from the subject, too scared and shy to say it first. Content to show him with my body in the nightly hours what I felt for him.

I hated myself for never telling him.

That night in the snow, when he mentioned the Morag, I didn't understand—too terrified in the moment to remember the fairytale the minstrel had sung in the great hall during my very first Sunday supper. The song of the Morag and the maiden he stole. How he kept her in a world not her own, fallen in love... and then set her free.

Colin told me he loved me, that terrible night in the snow. Loved me so much he gave his life to buy me time to escape back to where I belonged.

The creature in my dreams was Colin, taunting me from under the surface of the water. Forever out of my reach.

~

"Enough is enough!" Nan barked. Standing abruptly from her chair, she threw her napkin onto her plate.

I stopped pushing around the Coq Au Vin I made for our supper and blinked up at her. Since I made the meal to perfection, I couldn't imagine why she was so upset.

"Dinnae ye look at me that way. Ye ken what I'm talkin' about," she fumed, and plunked her fists on her hips. The motion reminded me so much of Iona that I lowered my eyes to hide my emotions.

Iona's dead, I reminded myself. *Just like everyone else.*

Three weeks ago, Nan had woken me from an afternoon nap and told me I had to either tell her *"what the feck was wrong,"* or I had to participate in life. I chose the latter, however begrudgingly.

"I'm cooking again as you told me to, Nan. I've been going to the store and helping with the chores..." I set down my fork and eyed the hallway that led to my room. My shoulders slumped. I knew better than to try to escape her. She'd only follow me. It was her least redeeming quality.

"Aye, yer doin' all that, but yer still a ghost! Ye barely eat, ye cannae sleep without a light on, and ye call out in the middle o' the night. There's no life in yer eyes anymore. I've tried to take ye to a therapist and ye sat there for an hour without speakin' a single word. I dinnae ken what to do for ye, Meggie."

"I'm sorry, Nan," I muttered.

I was sorry. She didn't deserve to have me there, haunting her home. She probably thought I was some pod person, but I couldn't seem to find any happiness.

Because my happiness died in a frozen river.

Some of the fury deflated out of my grandmother's sails, and she turned away to light the stove and fill her kettle. Apparently, it was time for tea. Sighing inwardly, I helped her clear the dishes, storing the leftovers in containers for another day. Maybe I would have an appetite tomorrow.

Back at the table, I studied my fingertips while Nan busied with the tea. Six weeks had done them good. The scabs fell off long ago and revealed new, pink skin. Soft and silky. My knuckles would suffer a few scars, but for the most part, they healed quite well. The mirror reflected a normal girl again, not the haunted victim—survivor—that escaped Bàs Dhubh by the skin of her teeth.

No, all *those* scars were on the inside where only I could see them. And I saw them every day.

A couple weeks ago, I learned that the Bàs Dhubh had fallen within a few years after I escaped. A vague blip on the internet told me that internal struggles within the clan had been the downfall of the fortress shortly after someone mysteriously murdered their laird. Scholars presumed his only legitimate son had killed him before disappearing. Without firm leadership, the castle was open for attack and then passed from one conqueror to the next until it fell into disrepair and eventually succumbed to the elements.

A few Google images showed me the castle's skeleton: its dark stone reaching out of the grassy hill in random rises and falls. The curtain wall was gone completely, and the tunnels beneath filled with centuries of sediment. I wondered if Laird Murray's ghost haunted those tunnels, doomed to wander with perpetual thirst and hunger. I hoped so. I hoped he never found peace.

Nan settled the teapot between us and filled two filigree teacups. After adding a generous pour of whiskey in each, she sat down and turned the full weight of her focus on me.

Damn, she meant business tonight.

Taking a deep breath, I chewed on my lip and cradled my cup between my hands. The pads of my fingers absorbed its heat while I traced the lacework on the rim with my thumb. The silence was nerve-wracking as we sipped our tea and she watched every move I made while I did my best to look anywhere else.

With nothing else to do but wait for her to begin her inquisition, I quickly finished three cups of tea and began to feel warm for the first time in what felt like forever.

"What happened between Sunday mornin' and Saturday the week ye were missin'? And dinnae tell me '*nothing*,' because I willnae believe ye this time," Nan said fervently but calmly while she filled my cup up again. Her whiskey pour was heavy, just like the last three cups she served me.

I watched, mesmerized, as the two liquids swirled within the white porcelain until they blended together, and opened my mouth to speak. I nearly spilled the whole story all over the kitchen table when I caught myself. Nan's fingers tightened around her cup, her back ramrod straight, her stare like a brand. Waiting. Hopeful.

I snapped my mouth shut.

She thought she could loosen my lips with her tried-and-true *special tea*. I nearly smiled at her effort. It almost worked. I hadn't had any alcohol since I got back. I declined it at every turn because I was unwilling to numb any part of what I felt about Colin's death. I wanted to feel it all. Every raw, heart-rending moment.

That pain was how I knew it was *real*. That it happened.

That *we* happened.

"I know what you're doing," I whispered.

Nan rolled her eyes and downed her tea in two swallows before dashing her hand across her mouth. Chopping the blade of her hand down on the table, she spoke, "I need to understand, Meggie. Ye were gone for six days. Six. *Somethin'* happened to ye, and ye willnae tell anyone what it is. No' the therapist, no' *me*—"

"—I told you what happened. I fell into the cave and hit my head."

I pushed away from the table, and she did the same. Her fingers brushed my shoulder when I passed by.

"Then why do ye look so damn brokenhearted?" she yelled at my back.

I froze in the doorway and looked back at her, stricken.

Because I am, I wanted to say. *I'm hurting because I wanted years and decades, and no one knows he was stolen from me!*

At my silence, she shook her head in bewilderment and let her hand fall to her side with a soft slap.

"Ye look like I did when yer granddad passed. *Why*, Meggie? Can ye no' confide in me? I'm yer Nan, sweeting. Ye should be able to tell me anythin'. There is nothin' ye could say to me that would make me love ye any less."

Her words tore at my guts and flayed me wide open.

Biting down on my trembling lip, I hustled down the hall, through the living room, and out the front door. Shoving my feet in some garden clogs, I ran as fast as my legs could carry me into the woods and to the two people who knew all my secrets.

The angel in the clearing greeted me with sad eyes and welcomed me to lie at her feet so I could pretend once more that my parents could hear me.

On my back, I watched the shafts of sunlight filter through the high branches. Butterflies flapped a drunken dance above me, and birds flitted from one bough to the next, their happy song carrying on the slight breeze. Out here, if I closed my eyes and concentrated hard enough, I could almost believe I was under the willow next to my garden at Ghlas Thùr, at least until the sound of a diesel engine roared down the highway. But for a few moments, it was a comfort.

Nan's soft footsteps preceded her, and she sat down beside me, patting her lap in invitation. Scooting over, I rested my head on her thigh, and she began pulling debris from my too-long hair.

"I'm sorry," I whispered.

Her eyes flicked to mine before she shrugged and bopped me on the nose.

"Yer so much like yer mother, Meggie. She widnae talk about her troubles 'till she was good and ready." She sighed. "A closed book, that one. She always felt so strongly. Every emotion amplified. When she loved, ye could feel it in yer soul, and when she was angry... och, some days I would swear I saw steam shoot out o' her ears. When she was happy, she would sing, and the sun would shine brighter in the sky. She had the loveliest voice I ever heard." Her voice caught, and her eyes grew distant. "But when she closed up, no one had a chance at breakin' through. Until yer father came along, that is. God bless that man."

"I'll try harder," I promised, and tasted the ghost of vanilla on my tongue.

When the yellow and orange blush of sunset morphed into twilight, she helped me to my feet and led me home with her arm wrapped tightly around my shoulders.

Later that night, while I lay on my bed in the dark, I stretched my hand into the cool, empty space beside me. Hot tears collected on the bridge of my nose and fell with an audible plop on the pillowcase.

There was a burning stone weighted deep in my belly, a raging fire that I could not douse. The pain stayed with me through every moment of the day. I had been living, and barely surviving, with its dreadful presence since that night in the snow. Since the moment I became a widow.

This pain. It's reality, I realized. A reality I refused to accept. I couldn't bring myself to acknowledge it, afraid of what it would mean if I did. So, I ignored it the best I could... and let it beat, unanswered, on the interior walls of my soul.

I'm not ready for you yet, I thought. Reality could wait a little while longer.

I closed my eyes and imagined Colin spread out beside me, his blue eyes boring into mine and his lips curled into that devastating, lazy smile I loved so much.

"I miss you," I whispered into the empty room.

The next day, while Nan went to her Sunday service, I drove to the church that Colin and I had married in. Located two miles away from the MacKinnon estate entrance, it was still in excellent condition. Sadly, the town that once surrounded its short walls was long gone except for a few outbuildings with historical plaques posted on their crumbling walls.

But for all I meant to, I couldn't bring myself to enter it. I stood on the stoop for nearly an hour in the drizzling rain, listening to the worshipers sing hymns, and fled when service released.

I did not go back again.

───

Two weeks after my failed church visit, I found Nan in my room after my morning shower, my hair blown dry for once, and a towel cinched tightly under my armpits.

"I told ye to throw these out last week, lass. It's bad luck to keep dead flowers in here and they've been dead for over a month," she tsked.

Shaking her head in annoyance, she plucked off all the unread notes from the little plastic tritons and set them on my nightstand before stuffing the wilted and dried flowers into a garbage bag.

To be honest, I hadn't looked at them much. I hadn't noticed when their scent disappeared or when they lost their color. I frowned at the now-empty glass vases, the water inside them either all dried up or cloudy and moldy from decaying stems.

"I'll clean them, Nan," I said as she hauled the bag of flowers out of my room.

Sitting on the edge of my bed, I snatched up the cards and ripped open the first little pink envelope. It was from the ladies at Nan's church wishing me a quick and safe recovery. The second was from Nan, telling me she loved me. The third was a notecard, generic and plain, with typeset print.

Welcome Back! We're Glad You Made It
M. MacKinnon.

My skin pebbled and spread from my neck down my arms, and I stood up; the remaining unopened cards slid from my lap onto the floor. I was still staring at the slip of paper in my hands when Nan breezed back into my room.

"What is it?" She stopped short, concern on her face as she peeked at the note in my hand. "Oh, aye, the MacKinnons called to check on ye nearly every day while ye were recovering in the hospital. It was nice o' them to send ye those flowers, though the message is odd, and I thought it rather strange they sent ye *thistles*." She snorted as she gathered up all the vases, despite my assurance to clean them myself moments ago.

M. MacKinnon. *Malcolm* MacKinnon. Welcome *back*.

The coincidence was too much for me to ignore. Letting my towel drop to the floor, I yanked open my drawers and quickly donned a bra and panty set before yanking a navy sundress over my head. With my heart hammering madly in my chest, I shoved my feet in a pair of black flats and sprinted for the kitchen.

"Where do ye think yer goin'?" Nan asked as she arranged the vases in the dishwasher.

"Um, to the MacKinnon estate," I said quickly and grabbed the spare truck keys out of the drawer. I never did recover the pack that Colin threw into the caves. "I want to thank them personally. For the flowers and for helping, you know... to look for me."

"Alright. But do be home for supper... and *no* hiking," she said when I kissed her cheek and rushed out the door.

~

I bounced slightly in the old Ford's seat as I turned off the highway and navigated through the open iron gates and the winding private drive lined with oaks before I caught sight of Ghlas Thùr and slammed on the brake.

It was so different. The curtain wall was gone, replaced by short iron fencing and red blooming roses.

Tightening my fingers on the steering wheel, I steeled my nerves and finally took my foot off the brake. The gates were open and welcoming as I drove past them, leaving the pavement for a wide pebbled circular driveway that looped around an odd stone sculpture. Parking the truck, I got out and looked around.

Modern additions like the updated windows and iron-studded front door complemented the historic stronghold. The stone, free of cracks in the mortar, was scrubbed clean, and there were new shakes on the roof. Topiary drew my eye to the right, where bright green grass sloped downhill towards the loch.

Gone was the stable, replaced by a detached garage with barn-style doors. The gatehouse barracks were also missing, and a pair of willow trees, already in their old age, dominated the space it once occupied. I spied a pair of weathered marble benches under their canopy and smiled sadly at the sight of them. Malcolm would have loved reading under those trees.

At the crunch of footsteps behind me, I spun around and came face to face with a young man of about eighteen. He stopped short and looked at me strangely before grinning and ran full speed back the way he came, disappearing around the corner.

Well, that was weird, I thought. Dismissing him, I looked up at the castle, my home. It still felt that way, even with all its changes. Sucking in a deep breath for courage, I climbed the front stoop and reached for the heavy copper knocker when the door opened, and the sight of the man that opened it filled with a crushing sense of déja vu.

It was Malcolm's face on the stranger that greeted me. Though his hair was a light golden brown instead of raven black, he had the same brown eyes and straight nose. The similarities were strong enough that I felt an overwhelming need to throw my arms around him.

But the Malcolm I knew was dead too, as well as everyone else I had grown to love and made friendships. Clenching my teeth, I drew my shoulders back and stood up straight. I could do this. I could thank him and hightail it back to the truck where I could breakdown in a puddle of misery.

Blinking away my tears, I wiped at the one tear that tried to escape before I introduced myself.

"Mr. MacKinnon, I'm Meggie… Washington. I came to thank you for assisting in my rescue." The words felt stiff and awkward, but the man smiled kindly and reached for my hand, enveloping it in his larger ones. Malcolm had definitely passed on his breadth and staggering height to his descendant.

"Meggie," his voice, filled with something akin to awe, rumbled down my spine. "I'm Morrison… I've been waitin' to meet ye all my life."

What an odd thing to say. I frowned and tugged my hand from his.

"I don't understand."

Morrison just smiled warmly and shoved his hands in the pockets of his jeans as he nudged the door open wide.

"Would ye like to come in?" he asked.

From where I stood, I could hear small children playing somewhere inside as well as quick-speaking, excited disembodied voices. Nodding slowly, I stepped over the threshold, and the feeling of nostalgia rose within me as I beheld the great hall.

So many changes, but I would have recognized the tapestries hanging on the walls anywhere. The great hearth, swept clean and empty for the summer, still dominated the wall to the left, and the original candelabras stood proudly on the massive mantle above. An inviting sitting area with a live-edge coffee table replaced the original dining table. The dining table itself, further aged and dented from the passing centuries, they had pushed against the wall to my right. Displayed proudly upon it were old books under glass and other relics of the past. Drawn to it, I didn't think to ask for permission when I crossed the room. There was an old tartan of the MacKinnon colors, some pottery, a two-pronged fork... and a familiar jeweled stiletto. I ran my fingertips lightly over the glass case that contained it, and the memory of the day Colin gifted it to me raced through my mind. Of us standing in the ash grove, their golden leaves falling all around us while he taught me the very lesson that ended up saving my life.

"It's a beautiful piece, isn't it?" Morrison asked from behind me, his voice soft in a tone I couldn't discern.

"Yes, it is," I whispered, and cleared my throat.

Moving past the table, I focused on some display cases against the wall. They were all lit from within with soft, white light.

Kitchen utensils, an embroidery kit, more books. Some artifacts were familiar, and some were from the eighteenth and early nineteenth centuries. Little plaques identified the objects with the year of their origin. Some even had an original owner's name with their birth and death dates. Morrison waited patiently, and I took my time looking at each case until I came to one that stood alone near the stairs. What was in it took my breath away.

It was Kerr's wedding gift to me. The lovely carving of the doe and the mountain lion took dominion on the top shelf. My gardening gloves, hair combs, brush, and the necklace I wore on my wedding day were all displayed together. Underneath the carving was my name. My real name, *Meggie MacKinnon,* etched on a little bronze plaque with the year 1658 underneath it. No birth or death date. Where were Colin's things? I found the urge to hold something of his overwhelming, and I nearly asked when Morrison rapped lightly on the wooden railing above me.

"Would ye like a tour?" he asked as he looked down at me from halfway up the steps. I hesitated.

"I thought the keep was private beyond the great hall."

One side of his mouth twitched up in a very familiar grin.

"For ye, I'll make the exception."

I followed him up and to the right, down the south wing. Electric sconces lit our way through the hallways, and he showed me how the old blended in with the new. Radiators were in each room he opened, negating the need for the massive amount of firewood required to heat the place in the winter. They had converted some rooms into bathrooms with Victorian clawfoot tubs and porcelain sinks from the late nineteenth century.

No more garderobe for the modern man.

The library looked nearly the same but for the plush cream seating, the modern books on new shelving, and the lack of animal hides. Any of Malcolm's books that had survived the test of time were safe behind glass in the great hall. The chess set I had spent so many evenings playing with Colin sat on a low table beneath the wall of mullioned windows.

"Thank you for showing me all this," I said when we left the library.

I felt raw, and I wrapped my arms around myself, eager to leave so I could finally crash and burn.

"There's one more room I want to show ye," he said as he guided me towards the staircase leading up to the third story. Following numbly behind, I expected him to show me the laird's old apartments above the library when instead, he took a left at the top of the spiral stair.

"This way."

I slowed the moment I realized where he was going, and my breath froze in my lungs. I did not want to see how my room had changed. I did not want to see a modern bed or find the tapestries I loved so much replaced with unfamiliar art.

Morrison came to a stop before the door, the door that had an added scene carved into the wood. Curiosity getting the better of me, I demanded my shaking my legs to carry me forward.

The flowers and grasses still ringed the edges, but it was the detailed thistle plant in the very center that was new, its three blossoms in full bloom. It looked strangely familiar.

"No one but the direct decedents o' the Laird Malcolm MacKinnon have had access to this room," Morrison said softly. He slid his palm over the carving and stared at me intensely before he grasped the chain of his necklace and lifted it. A large amulet made an appearance from beneath the collar of his shirt.

With a closer look, I realized it wasn't an amulet at all—it was my thistle brooch: the one I tossed onto the grass the night of my abduction. But someone had altered it. The shaft of an iron key now dropped from the flower's silver stem.

"How did you get that?" The words escaped before I could stop them.

Morrison smiled again and shook his head.

"I told ye. I've been waitin' my whole life to meet ye, Meggie. Ye see, my ancestors passed down a story for the last three hundred and sixty-one years. The story o' the lass with mismatched eyes, one the color of moss, and the other of the morning sky."

I stopped breathing and dented my palms with half-moons. Morrison noticed, but continued speaking.

"Legend foretold that she would get lost in the wood and reappear at an undetermined time later. To be honest," he said as he ran his hand through his thick hair, "we didnae expect ye to arrive back until the winter solstice, but ye shocked my brother-in-law when he found ye only a week later. He told me he heard a clap of the loudest thunder in the wee hours of the mornin' even though there wasnae a cloud in the sky. He set off straight away with nothin' but a flashlight and his nightclothes to check the caves. And there ye were, soaked to the bone and cold as ice."

"How?" I breathed, stunned that someone knew—that someone *believed*—I had traveled through time. "How did you know? I didn't tell anyone but Colin—m-my husband—and he died the night I came back. No one else knew. How did the story not get lost? How could you possibly believe it?"

Morrison's deep brown eyes became glassy with emotion as he held the key between his thumb and the knuckle of his pointer finger. Shaking it softly at me before inserting it into the lock, he turned it with a snap and said, "The MacKinnon clan has never found it a hardship to believe in the impossible, Meggie. To believe in *magic*. And I think—*I'm positive*—that all yer questions can be answered inside this room."

And then he pushed the door open.

CHAPTER 29

Colin
December 1658

He burned as though someone had set him aflame, and he'd been longing for death, when he felt someone grasp him under the arms.

"Hold on, I've got ye," a gruff, familiar male voice grunted in his ear as he hoisted Colin bodily from the river and dragged him through the snow.

"This is goin' to hurt, but I canne see any other way…" The voice trailed off before agony ripped through Colin's stomach followed by two sharp waves of pain in his leg.

"Blunt tips. That's good. Now for the rest."

Colin's limbs barked in pain when the man roughly tugged his sodden jacket from his body, followed by his vest and shirt. He vaguely noted the sound of his belt and weapons landing on the ground. Blinded by the layer of ice on his lashes, Colin was at the man's mercy and tried to form words. He wanted to tell the stranger to leave him to die and find his Meggie. He failed to kill them all, and she was still in danger. But only a low moan crawled up his throat, and he failed to work his tongue.

"Dinnae try to speak," the man grunted as he stuffed Colin's arms into something warm and dry. He cut the wet leather from Colin's legs next and awkwardly crammed them into large, homespun breeks.

"We're no' far. Come on now, help me out a bit. That's a good lad."

With his head reeling and his skin feeling like it was being flayed from his bones, Colin helped the familiar stranger as best he could, and with a low groan, bent his body over a broad shoulder like a sack of grain. His wet hair hung off his scalp in frozen ropes, and he tried once again to pry his heavy eyelids open.

The sight that greeted him would have been comical if Colin wasn't a step away from death's door.

As it was, he was more concerned that the stranger had given up his own clothes and now hauled Colin's weight through the snow nearly stark naked; practically running while he bellowed into the silent night for help.

Colin's last thought before he lost consciousness was that he hoped his wife made it to the caves in time.

⁓

"Wake up! Wake up, ye big bastard!"

A slap on his cheek had Colin's head rolling, and he became aware of the flames that licked at his feet, at his hands. The pain was near unbearable as his spine curled off the mattress with violent shivering. Hairy legs rasped against his own, and capable arms pulled him against a masculine chest.

What manner of hell was this that death would put him in bed with a man and not the heaven between his Meggie's thighs?

"Wake up, brother!"

Malcolm. That was Malcolm's voice. Why was he in bed with his brother? His thoughts were so slow to form and muddled. All he could focus on was the pain in his limbs. The flames that bubbled his skin slowly changed from fiery inferno to a warm smolder as rough palms chafed his naked back. With a low groan, Colin shoved his frozen fingers into his brother's armpits and ran his toes awkwardly against his shins and blankets as he sought more warmth.

"M-m-m-m—" He couldn't form the words, the shivering still in full control of his body. His teeth were clacking together so hard he thought they would shatter if he didn't keep his jaw tightly clenched.

"I'm here, brother," Malcolm crooned and continued to rub Colin's chilled body.

"Build that fire up higher," he snapped at someone in the room.

He'd never heard his brother sound so scared, so uncertain.

Scuffling thumped across the room as the person rushed to do his bidding, and hushed whispers drifted around the room. Colin didn't bother trying to figure out who else was with them. The only thing he cared about was willing his body to soak up Malcolm's body heat faster.

His Meggie needed him.

~

Consciousness returned to him slowly. He focused first on the sound of heavy footsteps shuffling on a wood floor. A door opened, then abruptly shut, cutting off a gust of chill air. He recognized the comforting pop and fizz of pine in a hearth.

Colin cracked open his eyes and found everything to be blurry at first. Squinting hard, the wooden underbelly of a bird frozen in flight came into focus, and he realized he was in Kerr's home. In Kerr's bed. A glance to his left provided him a close-up of Malcolm's sleeping face. Lines of exhaustion and worry marred his features, making him look anything but restful.

Clearing his throat to speak, he nudged Malcolm awake. Brown eyes flew open, alert and sharp, and his brother heaved a relieved breath before resting a heavy palm on Colin's cheek.

"I thought I was goin' to lose ye," Malcolm whispered, and Colin blinked at him in confusion before his memories resurfaced.

"Meggie," Colin rasped, his vocal cords raw as though he had feasted on broken glass and struggled in the heavy sea of blankets and furs. "Let me out, damn ye!"

"Dinnae move," Malcolm hissed as he slipped from the bed and pushed on Colin's shoulders firmly. "Ye had three arrows in ye and evidence o' another when Kerr found ye face up in the river outside the village. Now tell me what happened. I'll send men to look for her."

"Let me up, ye cannae keep me here," he growled as he fought his brother's hold, his limbs and abdomen barking in pain.

Colin hated the helplessness he felt. He couldn't just lay here, injured or not. Did Malcolm not understand? His wife needed him! Throwing his shoulder against his brother's weight, he freed his arm from under the blankets and threw it out to shove Malcolm away, when he froze in horror.

Oh, God. No' my hands, he thought.

Angry blisters tipped his fingers and pale, sickly skin warped the rest of his hand. He'd seen men with afflictions like this. It was never good.

Malcolm looked down on him with pity and tried to coax his arms back under the furs. Ignoring his brother, Colin yanked the rest of the blankets off with a painful hiss. Just the simple act of gripping them brought tears to his eyes as agony shot up his arm.

"Och, no... no!" Colin moaned as he stared at his blackened feet. Fresh blood bloomed through the white wrappings around his torso and leg. Further evidence that he would be no help to his wife.

Satisfied Colin wouldn't try to get up again, Malcolm bent to retrieve his leathers and shirt, flashing him with a second eyeful of male buttocks since his escape from death.

"Send someone," he rasped. "Send someone to the caves. She could be hurt. Baen could have gotten her."

Colin sank further into the blankets. His quarrel with them sapped his remaining strength and left him humming with pain that rivaled his worry.

Malcolm strode barefoot to the door and yanked it open to reveal Finlay standing watch, his expression grave while he listened to his laird's orders: to gather five men with all haste to look for Meggie at the caves. When Finlay left to fulfill his orders, Malcolm then called out for a wagon to be readied.

"Tell me what happened," Malcolm said as he sat down on the bed. "I dinnea ken anythin' that happened after ye sent the twins back."

Colin told him as succinctly as he could. The clues Meggie had left him and the fated meeting with Toran in the pine wood. How he spent the entire day before he entered the oubliette planning their escape on the slim chance they got out of the castle alive. He told of the countless hours wandering in the tunnels under the black castle and how eventually Meggie had unknowingly found him in the darkness.

He was just about to round a corner when he heard footsteps fast approaching and found the warm, flickering light of a bobbing torch illuminating the long hallway. Pressed against the wall, he peered around the corner and was shocked to see the silhouette of a woman, her long hair streaming behind her as she ran. He could hear the terror in her labored breath, and when she turned to look behind her, he was able to make out his beloved wife's profile.

Emerging from the shadows when she careened past his hiding place, Colin wrapped his arm around her and captured her cry with his palm. Her elbows pummeled his ribs, fighting against him wildly as he dragged her into the darkened hallway and pushed her against the wall.

"Be still, wife," he said, as he kept his focus on the approaching guard. The scent of Meggie's terror was thick in his nose, enraging him to a level he had never experienced.

Dispatching that guard did little to calm his temper as he dragged the body further down the hall and left it in a small room out of sight. After, he found her still huddled against the stone in the torchlight, her shoulders shaking with fear, and again when he turned her around to face him. All he wanted to do was kiss her, but the sight of her swollen lip and the trail of blood that ran down her chin and her neck made his ears ring, and his blood boil with rage.

Leading her down darkened hallway after hallway, he focused on her wee fingers gripping the fabric of his shirt at his back. Her presence beat back the terrible possibility that they may not make it, that they would miss their sunset deadline to escape.

It was a pounding that drew them towards a hall lined with thick doors that he had not yet discovered, and the guard that hurried to retrieve the spare key and free his laird from the cell died quickly.

He never even glimpsed who had wielded the dagger that sliced his throat open. Colin did not care. He barely registered that the man's blood still pulsed when he shoved his dying body into an empty cell. Stalking back down the hall, he directed all his focus on the locked cell. He knew who awaited him inside, what monster he would find when he opened that door.

Meggie found him then, staring at the thick iron-banded door as he tried to calm his ire. He did not wish for her to see, but he could not leave Struan Murray alive. Understanding passed over her features a moment before she turned her back to him and pressed her hands tightly over her ears.

Meggie sang of bluebirds and rainbows, her hoarse voice catching off key on the unfamiliar lullaby. The space behind Colin's sternum tightened while he watched her rock from side to side, her fingers digging into her hair. She pressed her palms harder against her ears.

Clenching his teeth hard, he turned the key, slipped into the room, and closed the door softly behind him.

"About feckin' time!" Laird Murray snapped from where he relieved himself into a bucket in the corner. His back faced Colin while he leaned against the sooty wall.

Colin's fingers tightened around the leather-wrapped hilt of his dirk, grounding himself. Settling his weight, he absorbed the details of the room. Meggie's cloak lay in a heap next to a trapdoor, and the manacles that chained her open between them.

Laird Murray continued speaking, "Did ye catch her yet? I want her feet shackled and her mouth gagged—"

If he had been more beast than man, Colin would have snarled low in his throat and bared his teeth at The Laird of Bàs Dhubh when he turned around.

Snapping his mouth shut, Struan blanched white as cream when he beheld the wrath of the vengeful husband before him. Colin took satisfaction in knowing he looked like a reaper come to collect an errant soul.

"Ye held my wife in here," Colin said smoothly and with a cadence that belied the inferno that burned his gut. "Stole her away for some vengeance that had naught to do with her."

Struan Murray had an air of authority that Colin had cowered from and avoided at all costs when he fostered at the black castle. That presence was now watered down. Colin watched the older man look fearfully between him and the door to freedom, and wondered how he had ever feared him.

"Nothin' to say, auld man?" Colin sneered, and then realized he had no interest in the man's reasoning. He took a step closer.

Laird Murray's focus was so fixated on Colin's bloody blade that he wasn't prepared when Colin's free hand wrapped around his neck. Lunging forward, Colin slammed the older man into the stone at his back. The hollow pop of his skull bouncing off stone was music to Colin's ears, and he let the man fall. Slumping to the floor and upturning the bucket of piss, the laird held his hands up. He was weaponless, so sure of his dominance in this awful room, preying on those weaker than him.

"If ye kill me, ye'll start a war," Struan warned. "Do ye want that on yer conscience? Over a woman?"

Sheathing his blade, Colin picked up the manacles from the ground and turned the metal over in his hands. He visualized Meggie's slight wrists bound within them and his gaze snagged on the trapdoor.

'She's no' the first he's kept in that dark pit."

Toran's words, said moments before he tossed the key at Colin's feet, echoed in his mind like a roar over mountains. Rage hammered in his veins when he realized what the warrior meant.

Colin flung open the heavy slab of wood open to reveal a black abyss. The musky stench of fear rose to tickle his nose. So strong. So recent.

His Meggie had been down in that darkness.

Not the first... but she would be the last.

"Do I want to start a war over a woman? No." Colin's vision sharpened when he turned back to Struan and found the older man rising unsteadily to his feet. The metal of the chain was cold in his hands, and he thought deeper on the question put to him.

"But, would I start a war over my wife*... who ye stole from her home and had dragged across the country in the dead o' night... who ye tortured, and*

terrorized—" Baring his teeth, Colin whipped the heavy chain straight into Struan Murray's face.

He felt no satisfaction in the crunch of bone or the flood of blood. He felt no justice when he wrapped the cold length of rusted metal around the laird's neck and trapped the air from his lungs. Wrenching the chain, Colin hauled him back against his chest and whispered his answer through clenched teeth.

"Absolutely."

It was at the sight of the laird's fingers scrabbling uselessly at the links around his neck and the sound of his strangled groan when Colin plunged his dirk deep into the soft belly of his enemy that he finally felt atonement.

Colin pressed his mouth close to Struan's ear.

"Find comfort in the fact that I dinnae have the time to slice off yer skin layer by layer and relish in yer screams o' pain while I kept at it for hours, as ye deserve. And I will find solace because ye will die in this pit, surrounded by whatever hell awaits ye in its depths."

Tightening the chain once more, he shoved the man who had abused his wife and so many others into the darkness and noted the frenzied squeak of rats that greeted their meal when he slammed the trapdoor shut. Seething, Colin calmed himself as much as he could before he snuffed out the light from the oil lamp and left the muffled moans of the dying man behind him.

Colin shrugged off the memory and locked eyes with his brother.

"We rode into the night, the sound o' their hounds growin' ever closer. I thought we had a large enough lead, but our horse was too slow, and we could no' ride fast enough... they caught up at the river, and I sent Meggie to the caves." Colin stared up at the wooden birds, seeing but not seeing while the images of the previous night played in his mind. "It was only natural that she didnae listen to me. I heard her scream before the river swallowed me up, so I ken she stayed behind."

"O' course Baen would need the help o' four arrows and exhaustion to best ye," Malcolm snorted. "But why send Meggie to the caves? She would have been trapped there."

"To send her back to her own time," Colin said, and huffed a humorless laugh. "It was the only way to keep her safe."

Malcolm's brows drew low over his face, and he laid a hand on Colin's brow.

"'Tis no' a fever talking! 'Tis the truth!" Colin yelled. Batting his brother's hand away, he hissed when the pain reminded him of his injuries. Malcolm's lips tightened.

"Let us get ye to the keep, brother. Ye will feel better in yer own bed."

"No, I willnae. My body may be dyin', but my mind is still as sharp as yers," Colin snapped and glared up at his brother. "Do ye no' remember the day I brought Meggie here? Do ye no' recall her strange speech and garb?" Satisfied with Malcolm's slow nod, he continued, "'Tis because she's no' from here. She's from a place and time far in the future, and I need to ken that she made it and wasnae dragged back to Bàs Dhubh where she will have no hope of another rescue."

Blinking back tears of frustration, he couldn't look at his brother's pitying stare any longer. Pushing his head deeper into the pillow, he thought of Meggie's anguished cry when Baen kicked him into the river.

"She already thinks me dead. She widnae survive that dungeon again."

Mrs. Cook fussed over him while he lay in the bed he shared with Meggie for hours. Normally, he wouldn't have allowed Mrs. Cook to play nursemaid, but she was nearly as frantic as he was for news of his wife, and he didn't have the heart or the energy to send her away. Surprisingly, she played the role quite well, her touch light and confident while she spread a salve on his fingers and toes. She was changing the bandage on his leg when Finlay entered his room.

"What did ye find?" he demanded, unable to read his cousin's face.

"It was hard with the new snowfall, but we found six bodies and two hounds close together. The carrion birds made them easy to find." Finlay's eyes snapped to Mrs. Cook's a moment before he continued, "We found Baen dead outside the caves. I assume he died from the small hole at his throat, but I dinnae ken or understand how such a wound could have felled him."

"What of Meggie?" Colin asked, although he already knew.

She had made it.

A fierce pride swelled in his chest as he imagined his lovely doe striking out at her hunter. Pride that a moment later mingled with the sorrow over never seeing her again.

"This is all we found," Finlay said. He tugged a red square of fabric out of his jacket pocket and extended it to Colin. "Her tracks led into the caves, but they disappeared... ye dinnae look verra concerned, cousin."

Colin accepted the handkerchief and held it over his heart. "I'm no' anymore. Thank ye."

Mrs. Cook's eyes filled with tears as she watched Finlay depart and then turned on Colin angrily.

"I dinnae understand. How are ye happy she's lost in those caves?"

"I'm no' happy. I'm far from it." He sighed and told her in hushed whispers of the cave's ability to bridge time.

Mrs. Cook's features were grave while she listened without interruption, her hand pressed to her bosom and her lips drawn tight.

"So ye see, 'tis better that she's back where she belongs." Colin lifted his blackening hand and waved it at his useless feet. "What good am I to her like this, anyway? She should no' be tied down to a man who cannae walk to the garderobe unassisted... or who willnae be able to touch her as a husband should." His voice cracked at the thought of never touching his wife again, with or without his decaying fingers.

"Meggie would no' have cared, lad. She loves ye too much." She rested a gentle hand on his shoulder.

"Well, I'll never ken now, will I?" Colin said bitterly as he patted the bloody fabric that rested over his heart.

～

"*Iosa Crìosd*, send for the healer!"

Colin barely registered his brother's presence from where he shivered and thrashed in his bed. Too focused on the ghost that stood silently in the corner, he tried his best to keep his hooded gaze on Meggie's comforting apparition. She had watched him all night, keeping silent vigil while his body burned with fever.

"*Mo ghràidh*," he moaned when his brother heaped yet another blanket on top of him before rushing to feed the fire.

The hours blended from one to the next, and the village herbalist came and went after bathing his body and cleaning his wounds. She already voiced several concerns that the damage was beyond her ability.

Send for Vanora.

Meggie's voice, muted and insubstantial, drifted into his ear.

Colin's bleary, red-rimmed eyes snapped toward the specter wearing Meggie's form in the corner.

Send for Vanora, she said again, her lips unmoving. Her lovely face frozen in the same grave expression.

"Vanora…" he murmured.

"The midwife?" the healer asked, looking up from her ministrations to his belly.

"The witch… the good witch. Bring her here."

"I dinnae ken what a midwife could do that I cannae, but I will send for her," the healer grumbled as she slipped through the door and left him alone with his wife's ghost.

What he wouldn't give to see her smile. But no, she only stood there, watching him. Waiting for something.

Maybe she waits for me to die, he thought.

Surely she would not have to wait much longer.

"She's here, Brother," Malcolm announced from his surveillance out the open, east-facing window days later.

Colin cared more about the breeze that caressed his flushed, sweaty face. It was a welcomed reprieve from the heat that licked at his body while his fever broke for the third time that day.

Minutes later, Gunn pushed through the door with the witch in tow, her long, unbound hair wild and tangled and her nose red from the cold. Colin watched her cross the room from under lowered, heavy lids. It was taking more and more effort of late to keep them open, and he wondered if he should just stop trying, that he would finally die and thus end his suffering.

"How long has he been in this condition?" the witch snapped when she touched her hand over his forehead.

Grimacing, she peeled the blankets from his body. The stench of rot and infection permeated the room from his wounds, curling Malcolm's lip in disgust from his station by the window. Colin didn't take it personally; it offended him as well.

"Six days," Malcolm answered as he waved Gunn out of the room.

"His hands and feet... I have never seen such damage from the cold," she murmured in her low, honeyed voice.

Colin knew she was touching his flesh only because he was watching her. The blisters turned black days ago, the death of his skin spreading down past his second knuckles like grotesque ink, greying the rest of his fingers and most of his palm. He stopped feeling sensation with them the previous day.

"He spent an untold time in the water after a battle. Our blacksmith keeps odd hours and found him in near to the village."

Malcolm had told him that Kerr sacrificed his own body's warmth to save Colin, carrying him for nearly a half-mile with naught on but his shirt and his boots in the dead of winter's night. His call for help woke most of the village by the time he arrived.

"Ye're a very lucky man," Vanora said.

Peeling back a corner of a bandage on his belly, she hissed before yanking it off entirely and threw the putrid mess into the fire. She did the same with the rest.

"Where is yer lovely wife, warrior? Surely she would be here attendin' ye."

Malcolm cleared his throat; his face strained as he faced the window.

"I sent her home. But somehow, she's still here." Colin groaned when she manipulated his belly, and his wounds wept anew.

Her strange, icy eyes snapped to his before she followed his stare to the corner of the room where Meggie's ghost stood vigil.

"Ah. She must be a great comfort to ye."

With a nod of understanding, she perched on the edge of the bed and stared at the bloody square of fabric and the jeweled thistle brooch that rested under his hand over his heart. Kerr delivered it with his sporran the other day, along with the weapons he had stripped him of when he pulled him out of the icy water.

"'Tis all I have left o' her," he said in answer to her unspoken question. When he tried to clutch the objects closer, a tear escaped past his temple when he remembered for the thousandth time that he would never hold anything again. With the black decay that nearly covered his entire hand, his command over them failed.

Her pale, grey-rimmed eyes brightened when they focused on the rusty-red linen square under his hand.

"That's her blood?"

"Aye. I used it to clean the wounds on her face."

"No other's blood is upon it?" she asked. Her gaze settled on Malcolm, her eyes sweeping from his head to his feet as though appraising him.

"I cannae see why there would be," Colin sighed.

God, he was so tired; he just wanted to sleep. He could feel the exhaustion pulling him further into the stuffed mattress at his back. Vanora licked her lips and leaned back on her hand.

"Did yer wife tell ye anything o' the future, Colin? Did she tell ye if this castle still stands in her time?"

What an odd question to ask, Colin thought.

"Aye, she did. Our descendants will continue to hold it," he murmured as he fought against sleep's pull.

Vanora's lips spread into a ruthless smile.

"And what would ye say if I told ye that ye could see yer wife again? In the flesh, no' that fever-ghost in the corner ye cannae tear yer eyes away from."

Colin shook his head weakly. "'Tis no' possible. Ye said the caves would take me to another time entirely."

"Aye, they would." Her gaze flicked to Malcolm once more and then returned to weigh on Colin heavily.

"And just *how* would he see Meggie again?" Malcolm demanded as he crossed the room to stand near Colin's head, his arms intertwined over his chest.

Ignoring the pointed question, Vanora leaned closer to Colin.

"Do ye remember what ye saw in the wood, warrior?" At his weak nod, she continued, "And do ye remember what I said when ye asked me how long the wolf would sleep?"

A thrill shivered up his spine as she smiled ferally down at him, her arresting eyes bright and piercing.

"Ye said, it would no' wake 'till ye wanted it to."

Vanora nodded her head slowly. "What would ye say if I offered this to ye? A second chance with yer wife, in the future?"

Hope bloomed in his chest at the possibility.

Malcolm rolled his weight from side to side and looked down on the witch with anticipation and a little fear.

"Can ye truly weave such magic?"

"I can, Laird MacKinnon. But there is always a price." She added, "A life for a life, o' course."

"I've seen her do it with my own eyes, brother," Colin said, and then told him how she pulled the life force from the tree to heal the dying wolf.

"Aye, a life for a life... but to fuel yer body over the centuries *as well as heal it*, I would need *two* lives."

Vanora glanced meaningfully at his brother once more. Horror pounded heavily in Colin's chest at the thought of his brother dying for him, the very suggestion repulsive and abhorred. He shook his head weakly; the motion making him queasy.

"*No.* That is too high a price," Colin growled, and glared up at the witch. "How could ye ask that of anyone? I'd rather rot as I am and die honorably. The answer is *no* and always will be."

Vanora threw her head back and laughed, deep and throaty.

"I didnae say he had to *die*—I want his *whole* life, lived fully for many, many years." Her face fell serious as she smoothed her homespun skirt and took a deep breath. "My people are being killed. Tried and sentenced to death by priests and witch hunters alike. They hang and drown us along with the innocent, all because they fear the unexplainable. Guilty until proven innocent—and we all ken there is *never* an innocent among those accused o' witchcraft. No' in the eyes o' priests who fear anything no' o' their god."

"Witch trials," Malcolm murmured, and Vanora nodded cautiously.

"I have a daughter, Coira. My only want in life is to keep her safe. That is why I offer yer brother this chance. Coira would be forever free from the fires if she were the Lady of Ghlas Thùr."

The very air in the room stilled while Colin processed her words and then rebelled against them.

"*No.* My brother is betrothed to another," Colin spat. He craned his neck on the pillow to pierce Malcolm with a hard stare. "Ye willnae marry a witch for me; *I forbid it.* Ye'll marry Edeen, like ye swore to do, and have a chance at love. Ye deserve that."

Malcolm looked like someone had struck him and opened his mouth to argue, but Colin grunted through his frustration.

"Dinnae ye bloody argue this with me!"

Malcolm ground his teeth and turned towards the window next to the bed. He glared out on the loch and the wilds beyond the wall, his mouth set in a grim line.

"'Tis his choice," Malcolm said, his voice low. "Will ye still heal him?"

Vanora shrugged her shoulders and stood, clasping her hands.

"Aye, but I need yer word that my… *magic* needs to stay secret if I do this for ye. I am under enough danger as it is, so I must wait until all are asleep."

"Ye have my word," Malcolm promised, and escorted the witch out so that Colin could rest.

"I'm sorry, *mo ghràidh*," Colin confided to the apparition in the corner. "Her price was too high."

~

Colin stirred from his restless dreams when his brother slipped through the door, his chamber awash in golden light from the setting sun. Wagging his thick, dark brows, he held up two healthy measures of whiskey in ornate glass tumblers triumphantly and then dragged Meggie's favored chair away from the fire to settle it beside the bed.

"We still have hours yet until yer witch makes ye whole again." He pressed a glass loosely into Colin's blackened hand. "And I thought, what better way to pass the time?"

Colin snorted weakly and cocked an eyebrow at the cup resting on his chest. "Ye'll have to bring it to my lips, brother. I willnae be able to hold anythin' until I'm healed."

"Aye, well, 'tis best that ye dinnae get used to this," Malcolm teased, and lifted the glass to Colin's lips. "I am yer laird after all."

The cool liquid raced over his tongue and burned a trail of fire down his throat. Shaking his head, Colin sputtered at the bitter aftertaste and coughed, glaring at his brother's fiendish grin.

"A wee bit different taste, aye? Was Da's. I found it years ago and kept it for a rainy day," Malcolm explained, and held the glass to Colin's lips once more. "Why did ye no' ye accept her offer, brother?" he asked as he urged a sip down Colin's throat, followed by another and another, until the cup was nearly empty.

"Och, that has a proper bite to it. No more, have mercy. There's a reason Da didnae drink that one," Colin complained before he sighed heavily and thought on his answer for a moment.

"I… I didnae have Meggie for verra long… but the months that I did… och, they were heaven, Malcolm. She is everything good, and soft, and lovely... even when we quarreled—*especially* when we quarreled. She made me want to be a better man... and then she *made me* a better man. I want ye to have that. I want ye to ken what it feels like to find the other half of yer soul in another." Colin paused to swallow and fought against the pull of sleep. "I ken I spoke against the match to Edeen, but she's yer choice. Ye *chose* her, and ye'll grow to love her. Ye willnae find love with a witch."

Colin's throat became tight, and his insides twisted at the unavoidable certainty of never seeing his wife again. Never touch her or hear her boisterous laugh. Staring past Malcolm's shoulder at Meggie's ghost, he panicked when her vision started to blur. Her image faded, faster and faster, until she closed her eyes and dissipated into the shadows like fine grains of sand slipping through his fingers.

"She's gone," he breathed, the words faint and slow to form around his numb lips. His tongue had become thick and senseless in his mouth.

Confused, Colin swallowed and found Malcolm staring at him intensely. His head sunk further into the pillows when the room began to spin, and his eyelids became heavier than anvils. His skin felt heavy as well, as though it stretched too tight over his bones.

Malcolm leaned over the bed, a sad smile upon his blurry face. His warm palm pressed affectionately against Colin's whiskered cheek.

"She's gone because she's waitin' for ye," he said roughly and then smoothed away the tear that trailed down Colin's cheek with a firm swipe of his thumb.

"Forgive me, little brother."

Alarm raced through Colin's sluggish body and fading lucidity a moment before he understood: Malcolm had never been the kind of man that let anyone tell him what to do.

When he lost consciousness, Colin had never been more grateful for his brother's stubbornness.

CHAPTER 30

Malcolm

T he MacKinnon laird almost felt bad for his deceit as he peered into the nearly empty cup he had forced upon Colin and tossed the rest of the watered-whiskey into the fireplace. The liquid splashed over the red-hot coals with a quick hiss.

Rubbing a hand down his face roughly, he thought of his earlier conversation with Vanora, the witch.

After leading her down to the library where he knew they'd have privacy, he closed the doors firmly and leaned back against the wall, his arms folded across his chest.

"I need to ken how ye would do it," he demanded.

"How would I do what?" she inquired coyly over her shoulder while she toured the bookshelves, her graceful fingers sliding over the leather spines.

Malcolm clenched his teeth as he fought for the slim hold on his temper. He needed this woman's acquiescence, and he had a feeling that if he was anything but cordial, she'd march straight back to where she'd been found and not help them at all.

"Make it so Colin can be with Meggie again," he said with feigned patience.

"Ye would go against yer brother's wishes?" She did not seem the slightest bit surprised that he would. If anything, there was a note of satisfaction in her voice.

"Ye ken I will. I would do anythin' for him. Even if he was hale and whole, he'd still be half a man without her. And now that I ken there's a chance for them... does yer offer still stand?"

She stared out the windows at the snow-covered hills in the distance before replying.

"This is no' my first visit to Ghlas Thùr, ye ken."

"No?" He bit the inside of his cheek, aggravated that she would make him wait for a straight answer. He did not expect the one she gave him.

"I was invited here to tend yer mother for yer birthing."

Malcolm stared at her in surprise when she turned around to face him. Of all the things she could have said, he did not expect her to bring up his birth and was stunned to silence as she continued.

"For two weeks I stayed down in the maid's quarters as she neared her time. Ye were a late babe, and her belly stretched to bursting. Hers was a hard labor, and neigh on three days she strained until ye finally came unto the world."

Her eyes became unfocused, and she stared at the space between them, held captive by the memory. She held her graceful hands out slightly as though she was pulling a child from the womb.

"But ye had taken too long. Yer life faded with every beat of yer little heart, and yer mother... she was bleedin'. Badly. I was unable to stop it. Both of ye were dyin' right before my eyes."

Malcolm swallowed the thick lump in his throat.

"She begged me to save ye, said she'd pay any price I demanded. So, I told her: 'Tis the same price we all pay when it comes to the matters o' death." The witch's pale, grey-rimmed irises bore into his own, the streak of white hair framing her face stark and practically glowing in the faint candlelight. "What is the price, Laird MacKinnon?"

"A life for a life," he breathed, and his guts tightened with unease. "Ye killed my mother?"

Vanora shook her head resolutely, her mouth tight.

"No. She was dyin'. She just had yet to draw her last breath. I need ye to ken—to understand—it was yer mother's love *that spared ye from death that day. Yer mother allowed me to take what life she had remaining from her body to ensure yer survival. She would be happy to ken ye grew into the man ye are. A fair and just laird ye have become." She studied the open palms of her hands as though she'd*

never seen them before. "Ye were the first o' many lives I have saved. 'Tis only fitting that yer brother will be my last."

Malcolm frowned at her words even as he reeled from the story of his birth. He had always wondered if his mother had died before seeing him. Now that he knew, he was unsure if the information was a comfort or a curse.

"Will ye pay my price?" Vanora asked. "Marry my daughter, keep her safe, and in return I will make it so yer brother survives the passing o' the centuries in sleep."

"Aye," he croaked.

Without warning, the witch crossed the room, and Malcolm pushed away from the wall in alarm. In one fluid motion, she brandished a short-bladed dagger from a fold in her skirts and made a quick slice in the meat of her palm. Dark red blood welled out of the wound, and she held her hand out impatiently for his opposite hand. After making a twin-cut deep into his palm, she grasped his hand with surprising strength, her skin unnaturally hot against his. Their united blood squeezed between their joined palms to drip onto the wood floor below.

Malcolm watched in fearful fascination as their linked hands took on a glow, as though illuminated from within, their bones mere shadows through their skin. Then the witch began to speak, her voice strong and sadly musical. His hand throbbed, his heart hammered within his ribcage, and the hairs on his head lifted off his scalp.

"Laird MacKinnon. As payment for yer brother's life and future happiness, do ye so swear to collect my blooded daughter, Coira, before the marsh violet blooms? Do ye swear to join yer life with hers and keep her safe from all and sundry as long as ye draw breath upon this earth?"

Dear God, what have I brought within these walls? *he thought.*

"I do so swear."

Energy pulsed from between their palms; there was a quick burn… and he felt the spell settle in the bones of his hand. It weaved its way up his arm, into the core of his soul, and settled like a sleepy beast within his chest. He could feel it, the oath he made, a living thing of phantom claws and muscle and sinew. Struggling to calm his ragged breathing, Malcolm realized he would never be able to break the pact he just promised.

He would have a witch for a bride or forfeit his life.

Withdrawing his hand, he inspected his palm and found the cut already healed over, the scar smooth and white under all the blood. Vanora rubbed her hand against the hip of her black dress and cleared her throat.

"As soon as possible, bring yer brother to the center bailey along with that bloody cloth he's been clutchin'. It willnae matter now who witnesses."

And with that, she slipped past him and through the doors, leaving him alone with his unsettled thoughts.

Slumping down in the chair beside Colin's sleeping form, Malcolm stared down into the empty glass. It had taken almost all of Mrs. Cook's valerian root to knock him out. When he had asked it of her, she'd put up such a fuss he shared with her his plans, lest she refuse altogether.

Her puffy eyes had filled anew with tears, and a mix of hope and heartache pinched her face while she steeped the ground leaves and poured a concentrated concoction into the cup he provided.

Leaning over Colin's sleeping form, Malcolm pressed a kiss to his fevered forehead.

"Ye never did learn, brother. Ye cannae tell yer laird what to do."

⁓

Malcolm stood in front of Vanora in the center bailey after he ordered Farlan, Bram, and Finlay to carry his brother's considerable weight down from his chamber. She knelt beside the thick trunk of the great oak in the center bailey between its roots. With the setting of the sun, the deeper shadows of winter's night converged, beaten back only by the flames of torches and oil lamps.

"Do ye ken how old this tree is?" she inquired when she rested her graceful hand against the rough, gnarled bark.

Malcolm handed her the cloth with Meggie's dried blood on it before shoving his hands deep into the pockets of his jacket and shrugged.

"It was already old when they laid the foundation o' the keep three hundred and twenty-six years ago. The first Laird of Ghlas Thùr chose to build around this particular tree after he married his wife under its branches. Apparently, he was a sentimental man. Why?"

The witch turned her ethereal eyes upon him and smiled, the whites of her teeth flashing in the flickering light from the torches and lamps set into the surrounding walls.

"Because its vitality will help fuel yer brother's body until his wife wakes him." She stroked the bark like one would the wiry pelt of a wolfhound. "He will need no food, no water. He will pass through time in sleep until he is either woken… or the energy I transfer unto him runs dry. In which case, he will die."

"Ye didnae tell me that!" Malcolm seethed as his cousins and guard appeared from the keep, Colin's sleeping form snug in the sling of the litter between them.

"The tree is old enough that it should no' happen, but ye need to listen to me, Laird MacKinnon, and listen well. Ye *must* burn this blood once I am done. 'Tis how the spell is broken. It cannae touch him again," she hissed, shaking the handkerchief between them. "*Only* her blood has the power wake him, no other, and I can only complete this spell once. Dinnae waste it by failing at this one specific task."

She patted the damp space next to her when the men neared, and the trio lay Colin down gently before backing away. Malcolm could see that his brother's face was pale and waxy even in the dim light, as though he was courting death's door.

"I will do it. What else?" he barked, anxious with the feeling that they were running out of time. Why couldn't she tell him these things after she saved him? She was wasting time!

"Be sure to tell yer heirs of what happened this night. Keep it secret from all others but yer direct line. They *must* pass down the knowledge of how to wake him—and to look for her. She willnae ken he is waitin' for her."

At Malcolm's promise, Vanora's lips tightened into a hard line, and dipped the bloody cloth into a bowl with a small amount of water. The liquid wicked up the rough fabric to make it soft and pliable once more.

"I will begin now as he grows weak. Dinnae touch us, or ye will fall under the spell as well, and if that happens, may the gods help ye."

Malcolm ordered everyone to move back and for Bram to shut the keep doors when he saw the kitchen maids gathering at the threshold.

"Ye willnae be shuttin' me inside," Mrs. Cook snapped as she barreled past, her eyes blazing with challenge. Hands up in surrender, Bram allowed her to bustle past him before he shut the door.

Nearly the entire garrison populace milled either around the courtyard's outer edges or along the curtain wall high above. The ghostly faces of the castle's residents peered down from the windows of the keep, intrigued by what might happen under the branches of the oak with the peculiar stranger in black. Vanora breathed in deep of the night air, the light from the torches playing ethereal shadows on her smooth complexion.

At the first lyrical note of her voice, Malcolm felt his heart skip a beat in his chest, and he swayed on his feet. It was very well the most alluring and terrifying sound he had ever heard. Layered like an echo in a cave, deep and profound, he watched as the witch carefully folded the wet cloth saturated with Meggie's blood.

Continuing her song that was not a song, for he could not discern the words that came out of her mouth, she twisted the fabric and wrung out the moisture. Red-stained droplets fell upon Colin's bare chest and ran in rivulets to collect at the base of his throat before cascading off his neck. Setting the cloth back into the bowl of water, Vanora rested her right hand upon Colin's sternum. And when her fingers splayed out on his pale skin, she tilted her face to the sky, and began to sing. Both old and young, and deep and resonating, her song drifted and spread throughout the courtyard like smoke.

Every inch of Malcolm's flesh pebbled, and he felt the earth move slightly under his feet when the tune changed. Glancing down, he saw the shallow puddles from the snowmelt stir in the light of the torches in time with the witch's voice.

Gasps and quiet prayers whispered throughout the bailey. A few guards leaned against the curtain wall, their faces blanched and fearful, but they were unable to retreat, incapable of tearing their eyes away from the witch while she sang her haunting song.

When her voice hit a crescendo, Vanora closed her eyes and rested her left hand upon the trunk of the oak. With a groan, the oak shivered, and the thin tips of its enormous branches clacked together as though it were caught in a phantom wind that came from all angles.

Against the deep blue-black of the night sky, Malcolm wasn't aware that what he was seeing were the tips of the barren branches disintegrating until they dirtied the snow in a soft fall of dust. Listening to the witch's song, he barely noticed when the thicker branches broke off and landed with a splash in puddles and mud. He was only just aware of men tackled to the ground by their comrades when they were drawn to the spell—until the strength of another yanked him back and locked their hands over his chest.

When the largest limbs snapped off the thick trunk, they speared into the earth where they fell to make a crude lean-to around the base of the tree. Hidden from his sight, the witch continued to sing, her song becoming weaker and weaker, and when the last of the cracking echoes faded into the night, her voice wasted away to a whisper and then fell silent.

All at once, Malcolm's mind was again his own, like a fog lifted with the morning sun. Shrugging out of the arms of the man who had been holding him back, he sprinted forward and wiped away the tears he had no memory of shedding.

"Help me move these limbs," Malcolm ordered, and when he peered through the thick limbs, a thin branch snapped off in his hands with a sharp crack.

"Stone," Bram said in awe, and broke off another piece to inspect. Rotating it in the torchlight, it shimmered as though it were brushed with a pearly luster.

On the other side of the mighty trunk, men wielding hammers pulverized an entrance in quick order. Barely any light shone through spaces between the stone limbs, and he called for a lantern to be brought closer. Pushing his way through, Malcolm crawled over the roots on his knees and blew out a breath of relief when he found his brother's sleeping form free of debris and his chest rising and falling with an even rhythm. Even in the shadows, Malcolm could plainly see the smooth scarring on Colin's belly instead of the angry, infected wounds that had been there minutes ago. Snatching up his brother's hand, he pressed Colin's fingers to his lips when he found them no longer black and decayed.

"Thank ye. He's whole again." Malcolm's voice caught, and he broke his scrutiny of his Colin's healthy body to look upon the witch. "Let us get ye out o' here—"

Her stillness alarmed him as much as the chalky pallor of her face and hands. Eyes closed, she leaned against the trunk of the now-dead tree, her body lax with the stillness of death.

"Is she… dead?" Bram asked in surprise and held a lantern closer to her face. "Why would she do that?"

Unable to answer, Malcolm's heart filled with sorrow for the woman who helped deliver him into the world. With a heavy sigh, he tossed the bowl of water, and, keeping it well away from his brother lest it touch him, tucked the bloody square of fabric in his pocket.

Indeed, as Vanora said, her spell needed *two* lives… but he never fathomed it would be her own. And all for the price of securing her daughter's life, health, and safety with a near stranger.

Under the light of the moon and lanterns, Malcolm watched his men carry the witch's limp body out from under the stone and wondered how he was going to explain Vanora's actions to her daughter come the spring.

CHAPTER 31

Meggie

"Go in, Meggie," Morrison urged as he held the door open for me. "He's been waitin' a verra long time."

I peered into the darkened room to find the shutters closed tight. Only a few thin shafts of sunlight sliced through the gloom from the western-facing windows. I could make out the shapes of mine and Colin's chairs in front of the fireplace, of the chests against the far wall, just as they had been the last time I saw them. It smelled of lemons and soap, as though someone oiled and polished the furniture recently.

Morrison's words finally penetrated my mind when my eyes settled on the prone figure on the bed.

He's been waiting...

A garbled cry that could not have possibly come from me pierced the silence, and I rushed into the darkened room—and placed my shaking hands on a face I never expected to see again. A face that had been lovingly haunting my dreams for months.

Colin's broad frame stretched motionless atop the bed; a simple tartan wrapped around his hips, his feet and chest bare. The normal golden-hue of his skin was dull, and his breathing even but shallow, but it was still the most beautiful sight I had ever seen.

"How? How is this possible?" I cried, torn between laughing and bawling my bloody eyes out.

"I dinnae ken." Crossing the room, Morrison opened the shuttered window to the right of the bed. "Unfortunately, we lost that particular ability over the centuries."

We?

Sunlight flooded the room and illuminated new scars on the cool skin of Colin's belly. I traced them both, remembering all too well the violent way he received them.

"Why won't he wake up?" Leaning over his chest, I smoothed his dark blond locks behind his ear and traced a finger over his bottom lip. "Do I have to kiss him?" I pressed my lips to his. Once, twice. "It's not working. Why isn't it working?" I looked up found Morrison grinning widely beside me.

"No, Meggie. This kind o' magic requires somethin' a bit more than a kiss to break." He dug a small knife out of his pocket, and after he flicked the blade open with a sharp click, extended it to me, handle first.

Shaking my head, I shied away from the knife.

"I can't hurt him."

"Och, it's no' for him, sweet lass," Morrison chuckled. "It's for *ye*. Ye need to shed some blood on him if ye want him to wake. Only yer blood will work. I dinnae ken the how or why, only that ye must."

"How much?" I accepted the knife with trembling hands and tested the sharpness against my thumb. Morrison shrugged and took a few backward steps toward the door.

"Why dinnae ye start with a wee bit and work from there?"

Okay, Meggie. You traveled through time, escaped a dungeon, fought for your life, and survived... you can prick your damn finger, I told myself.

Sucking in a quick breath, I touched the tip of the knife to the pad of my thumb and gritted my teeth against the sharp pain. Blood welled from the shallow cut and slid down the digit to gather in my palm. With a prayer, I turned my hand over and placed it on the center of Colin's chest.

Electricity snapped between us at the contact, and I gasped when my thumb burned at the same time Colin's chest expanded with a full breath. Before my eyes, the sallow color of his skin blushed with life, and the golden color of health radiated from where my palm rested upon him.

I barely noticed the gentle closing of the door behind me when I dropped the knife on the floor and ran my palms over Colin's shoulders and down his arms. Marveling at the feel of his skin warming under my touch, I leaned over him, his beautiful face blurry through my happy tears.

"Colin," I whispered, and kissed his brow and the tip of his nose before resting my cheek over his heart. I listened to the pump of muscle within his chest grow stronger and stronger, the steady *bu-bum, bu-bum* music to my ears.

I closed my eyes. Contented to wait.

And wait.

And wait.

Gentle fingers wove into my hair, and I popped my head up to find Colin's sapphire eyes fixated on my lips and his eyelids heavy from his sleep through the centuries.

"Hi..." I breathed a moment before my eyes spilled forth those fat, happy tears once again.

I climbed on top of him, his hips cradled between my thighs, and reveled in the feel of his arms across my back.

"Ye found me..." he sighed, his voice weak from misuse.

Laughing into his neck, I nodded and kissed the comforting pulse on his neck. His rough hands roamed over my back, the bare skin of my arms, and the smooth skin of my calf.

Happiness and relief so enormous seemed to burn me from the inside out, and I almost believed I would shatter into a million pieces from the magnitude of my emotions. I wanted to laugh. I wanted to cry. I nearly squeezed the breath from his chest before I peppered him with kisses, my silken hair falling like a veil around us. Sheltering us.

He would never escape me again.

"I thought you died... how are you here?" Looking down on him, I grinned like a maniac and soaked up the sight of that lazy morning smile I knew so well and suffered without for two months.

His smile faltered, and his throat bobbed.

"My brother is a stubborn man."

"Malcolm did this?" I asked in surprise.

"In a way. I'm sure he'd likely take full responsibility for it, but no. It was the witch, Vanora. Ye ken, the one ye met at the Gathering."

"Holy shit," I whispered as I sat up. Resting my weight on his hips, I inspected the tiny scar on my thumb in wonder. "Witches truly are real."

"Aye. A fact I will forever be beholden to." He frowned at the drying, sticky blood on my hand and the smear on his chest. "I was so scared he had gotten ye."

I did not have to ask who the *he* was that Colin was referring to and flinched inwardly at the memory of Baen's face. At the thick spray of his blood in the snow.

"He almost did." Swallowing, I shook my head to banish those awful moments that threatened to cloud this happy reunion. "I wish I had known; I would have come sooner. I've been walking around like a zombie in Nan's house. She thinks I've lost my mind."

Colin waved his hand between us, silencing any regret I had.

"We're together now. That's all that matters. But I am curious... how did ye ken how to wake me?"

"Morrison told me. He's Malcolm's ancestor. A great-great-great-grandson or something. He knew who I was when I showed up and brought me to you. Apparently, we've been a part of every generation for over three hundred years."

"Malcolm's descendant... I would verra much like to meet him." Wincing slightly, he squirmed beneath me. "But first, I will need the garderobe."

I barked a laugh and scrambled to the floor to help him to his feet. With my fingers knotted with his, I led him toward the hall, my smile nearly splitting my face in half as I said, "Allow me to introduce you to the modern invention of the toilet."

~~

Observing Colin marveling the changes to his home was bittersweet and very much like following a toddler around while he explored his new world. After flushing the toilet fourteen times and numerous flicks of every light switch he came across, I finally dragged him downstairs, where Morrison and his lovely wife and children waited to meet him. Also downstairs was Morrison's brother-in-law; the young man who ran off at the sight of me when I first arrived.

Still wearing his kilt and one of his amazingly preserved white shirts, Colin strolled around bare-footed in the great hall. His features shifted with a myriad of emotions. Watching him, I fiddled with my wedding band. I found the ring tucked in with the rest of the jewelry in the blue room, the etched gold band a familiar hug, and now snug and comforting around my fourth finger.

"'Tis a shock to find myself surrounded by my kin, yet they are no' here," he murmured and leaned over a glass case where Malcolm's sword, passed down through generations, was displayed. "This is my home... but so much has changed."

"We kept a detailed account o' yer money and yer assets," Morrison explained. "Ye'll find that ye willnae be left wantin' for much in yer new life here. I'd be happy to show ye when yer ready."

"Assets?" Colin pushed away from the relics and reached for me as though I was his anchor to this time, and if he went too long without me he'd float away. Wrapping my arms around his waist, I rested my cheek against his muscled chest and gave him a reassuring squeeze.

"Aye, all yer weapons are still in yer room. Meggie, yer jewelry and most o' yer gowns are still in the trunks. We air them out periodically, so they're in good working order to sell to museums if ye so choose.

And ye have a sizable bank account, too. We passed it down through the generations for ye."

My eyes must have bugged out of my head as I wondered what three centuries of compounded interest would be because Morrison's wife laughed musically. Her dark, textured hair bounced in soft curls around her face.

"Whatever sum you have in mind, Meggie, triple it, and you may be close." She giggled, her American accent odd to hear after living so long in Scotland.

We spent lunch and most of the afternoon at the castle. Colin followed Morrison from room to room and kept his hold tightly on my hand, his fingers constantly dancing with mine while he asked question after question. When were the outer walls taken down? The barracks? When did they erect the greenhouse off the south wing?

"Do ye ken what became of my brother?" he finally asked when we strolled down the stairs down to the great hall at the end of the tour.

"That, I'm afraid, we dinnae ken verra much about. We lost much o' the history to time and decay. Books back then didnae keep as well as one would hope. All I ken is that he had seven children and died asleep in his bed."

I caught the subtle clenching of Colin's jaw and his thick swallow as his throat bobbed. My heart ached for him. I already had two months to absorb the fact that everyone I befriended and loved in the seventeenth century were dead and gone. Iona, the twins, Maeve... Colin had *hours*. His brother, his cousins, his friends—his beloved Una—all gone. Clearing my throat, I tugged him toward the front door.

"I'd like to take Colin home with me now. We can come back tomorrow or the next day?"

"This is yer home. Ye can come and go as ye please. I hope ye do. And often. We're yer family, Colin." Morrison rested his hands lightly on both of our shoulders and gave a little squeeze. "Ye still have a family." And with a nod, he turned away and called out to his five-year-old daughter, who was playing with her toy horses near the great hearth.

Out in the sunny courtyard, Colin paused and dropped my hand, only to jog over the gravel towards the ugly sculpture in the circular drive.

"I preferred the oak," I griped when I sidled up beside him and studied the tall, grey-brown mass with its irregular crown of oddly rounded spikes. Smooth etchings of whorls and waves decorated its surface, along with runes carved deeply into the base.

Colin ran his fingers down the smooth stone and turned towards me. "This *is* the oak."

There, in the sun-drenched courtyard, Colin told me of the day he saw Vanora heal the wolf in the forest. Of Kerr pulling him out of the river, his frostbitten hands, and how close he was to death. I traced his slightly scarred fingers with the tips of my own. And then he told me of Malcolm's bargain and how he ultimately bound himself to a witch for the rest of his life to ensure Colin reunited with me again.

Months and months ago (or maybe it would be centuries and centuries) I told Malcolm to settle for nothing less than requited love on my wedding day. Now, when Colin came to the end of his story, tears of gratitude spilled down my cheeks, and I hoped with all hope that Malcolm found just that with his witch bride.

"Well," I said, and pulled him down for a quick kiss. "I'm pretty sure Malcolm would insist that you live your best life with me... so how about we start it off with a ride in my truck?" Dangling the keys in the air, I jerked my thumb towards the old vehicle behind me with a grin. "It doesn't go very fast, but I'm pretty sure we could get it up to sixty on the highway."

After showing Colin how to buckle himself in, I bit my bottom lip when his eyes peeled wide at the start of the engine, and then ambled down the long drive at a snail's pace. He seemed to hover between a state of horror and fascination, his lips pulled down as though he was unsure of whether he should smile or scream for mercy.

At the end of the long driveway, I passed the gates of the property and patted his thigh. "Are you ready?"

"For what, lass? There cannae be more than this."

My fearless warrior.

Checking for oncoming traffic, I pulled out on the highway. Rolling my window open to allow the wind to roar through the cab, I urged the pedal down and built up speed while we traversed the lazy roads. We were nearly at the speed limit of fifty when I glanced over to find Colin nearly white as a sheet. With a white-knuckle grip on the 'oh shit' handle and the edge of the bench between us, the tendons of his neck stood out in stark relief as he tried and failed miserably to relax.

Taking pity on him, I eased down to thirty and flicked the radio on. The melodic voice of London Grammar filled the cab. Pointing out the building in the small towns, I told him I couldn't wait to bring him into a grocery store and the movie theater. Twenty minutes later, I turned onto my grandmother's driveway with an hour left until suppertime.

"So… this is home," I said as I parked and hopped out, suddenly emotional. "My Nan's inside."

Colin tore his gaze away from the cottage to give me a knowing smile. "Then lead the way, wife."

Inside the cottage, the smell of freshly baked bread and savory chicken soup greeted us, as well as the soft piano music Nan enjoyed playing in the evening.

"Hello, Meggie!" she called out from the kitchen and then cursed like a sailor in Gaelic when she dropped what I assumed was a pan in the sink.

Colin's brows popped up high, and he bent down to whisper, "I like her already, *mo ghràidh*. She's just like ye."

Following me down the hall, he stooped slightly under the door jams. He looked enormous in this small house, his broad shoulders nearly filling the hallway while he followed silently behind me.

Nan had her back to us, elbows deep in soapy water while she hummed to herself.

"Did ye have a good time? What was it like over there?"

"It was everything I could have hoped for," I replied honestly, and cleared my throat when Colin rested his hand on the small of my back and his thumb gently traced the line of my spine.

"Nan? There's someone you need to meet... and I have something I've been dying to tell you."

Nan's slim shoulders stilled a moment before she pivoted on her heel and pushed her white hair out of her eyes with a soapy forearm. Stone-faced, she regarded Colin from head to toe and back again.

"Well, yer a big one, aren't ye?" she murmured before she turned her focus on me. "I thought ye went to the MacKinnon keep, lass, no' a historical reenactment."

I opened my mouth to speak but ended up barking a laugh before I could compose myself.

"You're not entirely wrong there, Nan."

⌒⌣

Hours later, after dinner and two pots of Nan's *special tea*, she stared at us both when I finished the whole tale.

I told her everything. From the moment when I first crawled out of the caves, to the night I walked back into them. Colin even interjected a few key points of the story I hadn't been aware of. Her face unreadable, she listened intently and didn't speak a word besides to ask few questions here and there.

"Are you going to say anything?" I squeaked, and rethought my decision to tell her the truth—not that I could go back in time to change it. *Har, har.*

Nan stared at the gold band on my finger, then at the way Colin's arm draped across the back of my chair before she reached across the table and took my hands within her slim, cool ones. The pads of her fingers felt smooth as glass as her thumbs glided over my knuckles.

"I've experienced magic in these hills... but I never imagined anythin' like this would be possible." Her voice was faint, barely above the softest whisper, but what she said next wore heavy in my heart. "Och, Meggie. The way ye were in the hospital, and every moment after... I had a feelin' that it was heartache that haunted ye, but I just didnae understand how that could be. I should no' have pushed ye... please forgive me."

I shook my head and abandoned my chair to crouch at her feet.

"There is nothing to forgive. I wanted to tell you every day. I nearly began a hundred different times." Kissing our clasped fingers, I looked up at her with relief. "But now you know, and I couldn't be happier."

Nan's arms wrapped around me tightly and she hugged me so fiercely that I felt in the depths of my soul.

"So, since yer a MacKinnon now..." she broke away and tucked my hair behind my ear, "can ye bring me to Ghlas Thùr? I've always wanted to see inside of it."

Laughter bubbled out of my mouth, and I nodded eagerly.

"I think we can arrange that."

~

"I love yer grandmother," Colin confessed hours later when we lay under the stars long after the sun set.

After I told to her the truth, Nan had ceremoniously kicked us out of the house so that she could better prepare her home for her new grandson-in-law. But I thought maybe she wanted us to have some time alone together.

Sprawled out on a thickly woven blanket, I let my bare toes hang off the hem and enjoyed the way the short summer grass tickled my feet. Far off from the pasture where we lay, the cottage windows were a faint glow of warm light, welcoming and kind. Few clouds hid the bright stars above us, the night air cool and comforting. We lay wrapped in each other's arms, my chin resting on Colin's pectoral, and his fingers gliding down my spine to draw lazy circles above my tailbone.

"And she already loves you... because I love you." I confessed, and Colin's eyes sliced to mine, his hand splayed on my lower back. "I never told you that... and it's been my biggest regret. I wish I had told you a long time ago."

Colin's mouth opened and shut before he grinned widely and blurted, "*Mo ghràdh* doesnae mean bog monster."

I blinked at him in confusion—and if I was honest with myself, disappointment—at his reaction to my revelation.

"Um, okay. What does it mean, then?"

What he said next brought tears to my eyes.

"My love," he said, his deep voice raspy as he traced a finger down my cheek. "It means, my love."

My heart swelled to ten times its size and threatened to tear my body into a million pieces from sheer joy. He'd said it for the first time on our wedding night and countless times thereafter. For months I'd been thinking it was just a silly term of endearment.

As it turned out, it was the ultimate term of endearment.

I clutched my hands into the fabric of his shirt and blinked away my tears until he was no longer blurry.

"I love you, Colin. I'm going to love you for the rest of my life."

He pulled me higher upon his chest, and his lips pressed over my pulse, my jaw, the shell of my ear. My toes curled, and my body practically glowed from his attentions.

"Say it again, wife, for I will never tire of hearin' it."

So, I did.

Epilogue

Malcolm climbed the same steep path that he had nearly every week since the witch enchanted his brother to sleep. He didn't know what he was hoping to find, if he would find anything at all, but hope brought him back again and again. It was a private thing he did and refused guard or comrade to accompany him, only to return to the keep heavy of heart.

Autumn was fully upon the wilds of Scotland, and he pushed past rust-colored bushes and crushed brown and golden leaves under his boots. Cresting the hill, the caves came into view. He knew how they worked; Colin told him while he lay dying in his bed before the witch saved him.

Malcolm shuddered at the memory of Vanora's song, how it had wormed its way into his blood and promised him things he never knew he wanted while the great oak cracked around them, and she funneled the life force of the ancient tree into his brother.

Striding up to the largest cave entry, he ducked inside, and his labored breathing echoed strangely in the cavern. Once his eyes adjusted to the gloom, he moved deeper. The equinox was two days prior; he was always careful to avoid the caves when they were awake and hungry. Malcolm had no desire to be taken away, either by accident or with purpose.

Studying the wet sand under his feet, he found nothing but the small tracks of woodland animals and no sign of another human having passed through since his last visit.

Chewing on his cheek, Malcolm glowered in the darkness, irritated with himself that he had come all this way yet again, only to leave frustrated. Huffing a breath, he turned to leave when his eye caught something that seemed to glow in the shadows. In a few long strides, Malcolm retrieved what was a white envelope wrapped in a clear, flexible vellum of some sort. With shaking hands, he hurried back out into the late afternoon sun and cracked open the clear, smooth pouch.

Inside was an impossibly crisp envelope—the paper, the cleanest and most pure white he had ever seen. His name was written neatly in Colin's handwriting next to a smear of dried blood, dark and rusty. After tearing the seal, a handwritten letter waited within.

Collapsing heavily on the trunk of a fallen tree next to the burbling water, he smoothed the creases and hungrily absorbed his brother's words.

My Laird, My Brother,

We hope Meggie's blood will bring you this letter and finds you in good health. Words cannot express how grateful I am for having such a stubborn bastard for a brother, for I am the most blessed of men to be reunited with my Meggie.

Life is different here, loud and fast. I spend time with your descendant, Morrison, who reminds me of you in more ways than one. His friendship eases some of the aches in my heart, but I fear I will always mourn your absence even though I am grateful for it.

I am happy, fulfilled beyond measure, and only wish for you to find some semblance of the same happiness with your witch.

With love,

Colin, Meggie, and Malcolm

Confused by the signature, Malcolm folded the letter to slip it back into the envelope only to find resistance. The paper caught on something. With a frown, he reached in with two fingers and pulled out a thin painting on glossy paper.

The painting, done so masterfully, Malcolm could make out every strand of hair and eyelash. Sitting on the front steps of an unfamiliar house, Colin and Meggie sat close together, their smiles radiant while they looked down on a young boy sitting in Meggie's lap. Brown hair the color of Meggie's flopped over his forehead while eyes of piercing sapphire-blue looked directly at the artist.

Their son—his nephew—maybe two years of age. All plump cheeks and bare feet. The sight of him made Malcolm's heart swell painfully while he soaked up their happiness and memorized every inch of their perfect likenesses.

Relief so profound washed over him, and he felt like he could finally take a whole breath for the first time since that fateful winter night. *This* was what he had been hoping for, a sign that he had made the right choice. Tucking the letter and painting into the breast of his vest, Malcolm gazed south, towards Ghlas Thùr and his witch-bride within.

When he picked his way down the hill for the last time, a small, confident smile tugged on the corner of his mouth, and by the time he reached the bottom, the MacKinnon laird decided he didn't want to be married to a stranger any longer.

The End

Thank you for reading The Shield and the Thistle

The Oath will be the next book in The Grey Tower Chronicles

Please consider leaving a review to help this story's success.
A review doesn't need to be long to make a difference, and they mean the world to an author.
Especially this one.

Please take a few minutes to read through this potentially lifesaving information.

1-888-373-7888
National Human Trafficking Hotline

Call the National Human Trafficking Hotline, a national 24-hour, toll-free, multilingual anti-trafficking hotline. Call 1-888-373-7888 to report a tip; connect with anti-trafficking services in your area; or request training and technical assistance, general information, or specific anti-trafficking resources. The Hotline is equipped to handle calls from all regions of the United States from a wide range of callers including, but not limited to: potential trafficking victims, community members, law enforcement, medical professionals, legal professionals, service providers, researchers, students, and policymakers.

For urgent situations, notify local law enforcement immediately by calling **911**. You may also want to alert the National Human Trafficking Hotline described below so that they can ensure response by law enforcement officials knowledgeable about human trafficking.

Source: www.state.gov/identify-and-assist-a-trafficking-victim/

Human Trafficking Indicators

While not an exhaustive list, these are some key red flags that could alert you to a potential trafficking situation that should be reported:

- Living with employer
- Poor living conditions
- Multiple people in cramped space
- Inability to speak to individual alone
- Answers appear to be scripted and rehearsed
- Employer is holding identity documents
- Signs of physical abuse
- Submissive or fearful
- Unpaid or paid very little
- Under 18 and in prostitution

Assuming you have the opportunity to speak with a potential victim privately and without jeopardizing the victim's safety because the trafficker is watching, here are some sample questions to ask to follow up on the red flags you became alert to:

- Can you leave your job if you want to?
- Can you come and go as you please?
- Have you been hurt or threatened if you tried to leave?
- Has your family been threatened?
- Do you live with your employer?
- Where do you sleep and eat?
- Are you in debt to your employer?
- Do you have your passport/identification? Who has it?

Source: www.state.gov/identify-and-assist-a-trafficking-victim/

Signs of Scouting for Human Trafficking

- The abductor approaches you while you're alone
- They say they are from another city or country
- Their self-description or story is inconsistent
- They pay only in cash and say things like they *don't have a credit card* and ask to use yours to avoid being tracked
- Forces you to take drugs or consume alcohol
- Lures you in with friendly conversation
- Shows signs of aggressive behavior
- Verbal or sexual abuse
- They talk about having you come visit their country in the near future
- They deny being married or having a family of their own (this is typically a man who is seeking out a younger woman)
- They make sexual moves on you without your consent
- When they find out you're not in need of money, a daddy figure, or job their interest shifts
- They seem put off when you mention your family lives nearby
- When you Google their name, and the city of residence, all you find is the exact description, but the photo is someone else entirely. (They use this identity on the move and they will use it on the next innocent person they interact with while on this mission of recruiting those for human trafficking.)
- 80% in the clear: They say they are leaving town the next day and will be away on business for at least a week (if the city they are visiting is one listed above, beware)—If this happens they have had a change of mind and don't plan on abducting you.
- 90% sure you're in the clear: They disappear, don't reply phone calls or texts when you reach out–they have moved on to scouting out someone else

Source: www.lifeofpolly.com/human-trafficking-resources/

How to Protect Yourself from Abduction

- Be aware of your surroundings
- Carry pepper spray with you on your key-chain
- If you sense you are being chased down, or about to be kidnapped call 911 immediately
- Stay in tune with your intuition, it will not lead you astray
- Mentally prepare yourself to fight off the abductor
- Never reveal private information to a stranger
- Get to a safe spot as soon as possible.
- If you do talk to a stranger, let me know you have friends and family in the area
- Let them know you're a supporter of guns and the second amendment
- If you're on a date, never leave the table until dinner is finished to avoid the other person slipping anything into your food or drink
- If you begin to be attacked, make a scene, yell for help, and fight back like your life depends on it (because it probably does)
- Be observant and use your brain (knowledge is power)
- Allow 3 of your closest friends or family members to track your phone via GPS so they know your whereabouts at all times—you can do with on most cell phones and allow a select few to have access to your location for 1 hour, 1 day, or indefinitely
- Don't let anyone know where you live until you get to know them—so for a date, meet them at a public place for the first few times until you get to know them and feel comfortable
- Stay in contact with friends and family if you're out and about alone or with someone you don't know very well
- Always keep your doors locked
- Before walking out of a store or restaurant, have your keys out so you don't have to try finding them as your walking to the car (abductors love a distracted person)
- Remember what you've seen in the movies. That stuff can actually happen, and you can use some of the same methods to escape from a bad situation
- If you suffer from trauma or psychological damage post the incident, seek professional help and don't be ashamed of it. Getting help is a courageous act.

Source: www.lifeofpolly.com/human-trafficking-resources

ACKNOWLEDGEMENTS

To my husband, Josh, your certainty in my ability to write this story meant the world to me. Thank you for letting me hide from the kids for countless hours so I could get these words on paper. For always listening to me ramble while I worked through scenarios, and for the wonderful idea of tossing Colin in the frozen river. I love you. You know.

To my work-wife and bestie, Jessica, thank you for your friendship, 'moral support', and memes.

To my sister, Chelsea, I'm always grateful to have you in my corner.

To my parents, thank you for the first Goosebumps book that started my obsession with reading.

To Brooke, I know I can always count on you to boost my confidence.

To Emily, who read this novel *twice* to check for typos. You are my hero.

To Jennilynn Wyer, I don't know how I'll ever repay you for taking time out of your busy writing schedule to fine-comb my work. I hope we meet soon.

To my clients and friends who have been listening to me talk about this story for the last year and a half… I never once spoiled the ending for you!! Let me say, it was HARD!

And lastly, to my readers. I am grateful that you allowed me to provide you with an escape into my mind. I hope you liked it there.

ABOUT THE AUTHOR

Jillian Bondarchuk lives in Charlotte, North Carolina, where she is living her own happily ever after with her husband and two small children. When she is not writing, you can find her elbow-deep in hair color, murdering succulents, or with her nose in a book.

Jillian loves to hear from her readers and makes the time to respond to each message.
Follow her on Instagram
@jillianbondarchuk
for information on her latest work.

Lightning Source UK Ltd.
Milton Keynes UK
UKHW022215130921
390533UK00010B/419/J